Black & Orange

BENJAMIN KANE ETHRIDGE

Black & Orange

ANAHEIM - CALIFORNIA

FIRST EDITION

Cover Design, Interior Design & Typesetting
by César Puch

Copy Editing
by Jamie La Chance, Leigh Haig, David Marty and Steve Souza

Bad Moon Books Logo Created by Matthew JLD Rice

ISBN-10: 0-9844601-9-5
ISBN-13: 978-0-9844601-9-9

BAD MOON BOOKS
1854 W. Chateau Ave.
Anaheim CA 92804
USA

www.badmoonbooks.com

To my Family and Friends, those with me and those on the other side of here and there.

Acknowledgments

Many good souls helped me bring this book to life, but no other as passionately as Mr. Michael Louis Calvillo. I thank him dearly for going to bat for me and my Halloween fantasy. Likewise I'd like to thank Roy and Liz at Bad Moon for a genuinely exhilarating experience. And for reading the novel in its various stages, I lay heaps of thanks upon John R. Little, Nick Mamatas, Greg Lamberson, Jonathan Mayberry, Gene O'Neill, Nate Kenyon, and Rio Youers. Also gratitude goes to—the HWA and its dedicated members, Zach McCain, World Horror 2010 Brighton, my lovely wife Irma and daughter Rachel, my wonderful and supportive parents, Fantasy & Horror in their many forms, and of course the work of Sam Cooke, the man who gave the Nomads their song.

Prologue

October 31st of Last Year

W*HERE WAS* T*ONY* N*GUYEN*? W*HERE WAS THE* H*EART OF the Harvest?*

Martin couldn't answer that. He'd lost his gun, his mind could not conjure another mantle—he was powerless. The answers he desperately needed escaped him. He just ran. Teresa wove through a field of tall grass and he followed. The brittle blades swept across his face, snapping and hissing as they went. The children flooded into the field, their dark orange jaws snapping in concert with the disruption in the grass. Martin could hear Teresa wheezing. Her pace slowed. He had to match it; she wouldn't be left behind, not like—

Where was Tony?

Thousands of little fiends chomped hollowly, hungry to fill that hollowness—instinctively Martin attempted to throw a mantle and dissect the crowd, but his brain had gone completely dry; he'd overdone it. There was no mental power left. He'd failed Tony. They both had. Now the Church of Midnight would have their sacrifice. The same realization flooded into Teresa's cold face as she sprinted through the darkness ahead. He'd wasted his power, she was ill and the Church was too damned powerful now.

Chaplain Cloth was too damned powerful. And he took Tony. Somewhere along the line Martin and Teresa had lost the Heart of the Harvest, Tony Nguyen, that single soul that was theirs to protect from sacrifice.

The nightscape sloped. One of the children clamped onto Teresa's leg with its serrated teeth and twisted its head to rip at the tendons there. Martin brought down a boot on its pumpkin shaped skull. The head trauma forced the jaws open. Martin jumped forward to crush it. The thing growled and jumped to meet him. Teresa swung around and stopped the creature mid-flight with the butt of her handgun. Her frayed jeans grew dark with blood, but she ran on. The other children gained. Colorless trees flooded past, the open field turning into dense forest.

Maybe Tony had gotten away somehow. They couldn't lose another Heart of the Harvest. The gateway grew too wide already—another sacrifice would bring the other world too close to theirs. Goddamnit, where was Tony Nguyen? Did he trip and fall somewhere? Martin's foot hit a root. He tumbled sideways, landed on his elbow in a wet bed of leaves. Teresa took his hand and ripped him to his feet. But it wasn't Teresa. This person wore a new face and new eyes.

Martin twisted away from the old monster. The shark-belly skin, the night black suit and orange tie. Trees exploded behind Martin in a rush of splintery debris. He found his strength, forced on a path of adrenaline, and brought up a mantle that moment. The invisible shield wrapped around his body and deflected the attack. Martin's heel caught mud and he slid fast into a black ravine. He lost hold of the mantle when he splashed down. His protection vanished. *Where was Teresa? Where was Tony?* Martin was alone.

His legs slopped through a waist-high stream. Chaplain Cloth hadn't come down after him and as much as that might have been a relief, it meant his direction had turned elsewhere. Martin couldn't let that happen, not to Tony, not to Teresa. He charged hard through the cold stream and broke out of the arresting water onto a steep embankment. The memory of Cloth's face burned in his mind: needles of pitchy hair swinging over one black eye, and the orange eye engulfed in hate. His teeth were raw pink like flayed muscle, colored from past harvests, colored with those Hearts that never saw another November.

Screams echoed from a bubble of light somewhere north. Martin's legs burned red-hot. *Can't stop.* He focused to build another mantle. The cold spot in his brain, where mantles were drawn, bloomed with power. The light in the forest intensified. Shadows became more distinct. A voice yelled for him.

"Martin! Here!" Teresa peered out between some stunted trees. Her face was streaked in dirt and dried blood. "Get over here."

He dove into the hiding place and sidled up next to her. Her words came out between gulps of air. Her wheeze sounded dry, but he knew it'd get worse soon in this dampness. "We have to get back to the van. We've lost him Martin. They have Tony. Tony's gone! Let's go."

"How do you know? Did—?"

She guided his face over, leaving dank mud on his chin. In his confusion he'd overlooked a nearby ledge over a washout. Pine trees wreathed the area in a nighttime vertigo. At the other side of the washout stood an old brick structure, a primary school left to ruin. A gaping mouth opened through the bricks. The gateway leading to the Old Domain stretched forth impatiently, power starved. At the other side of the bilious corridor, human arms pushed and pulled and wrenched to open a fist-sized hole separating the worlds. The arms withdrew a moment and a woman's face filled the hole. Smiling. It was a lovely face with corpse cold eyes.

They shrunk back as Chaplain Cloth strode from the gathering of trees adjoining the school. Tony Nguyen's furrowed body hung limp in Cloth's arms. He was alive, but Martin knew that wouldn't last long.

"We have to do something," he whispered.

"You know there's nothing we can do now," said Teresa. "We can only hope the gateway will shut again. This was bound to happen again."

"We can try—"

"No," she said, firmly, "I'm calling this one."

Tony wasn't scared, although the abrasions from Cloth's children had almost bled him out. So very brave—thought Martin. How had they let this happen? They were too slow.

Without warning, the boy's torso twisted back; the spine snapped in three places. The Chaplain rested his hand on the damp white shirt and it jumped apart at the poisonous touch. Through Tony's abdomen, the ribcage surfaced through the skin like the hull of a sunken ship. Once each bone was exposed, they shattered in succession. Cloth blinked back at the chalky discharges. Strands of muscle and skin ignited and burst into tiny organic filaments. Cloth worked a pale finger around the dense muscle in the cavity. Pulled the heart free from Tony's chest.

The Heart of the Harvest didn't glow, or shimmer, or change colors. It looked like a human heart, like any mammal heart, a tough piece of bloody flesh. But then Martin saw—everything for miles around had been deprived of color. Teresa's face looked gray beside him. Even Cloth's black and orange

eyes were two smoky discs. Yet the heart had a burgundy hue so ferocious it looked like something from a surreal dream, an apple galvanized with cinnamon steel.

Tony's jaw clicked as his body met the forest's carpet of twigs and leaves. He was carrion now because of them. This kid, this great kid that once explained in detail how he planned to code videogames after college, and once he mastered that, wanted a large family—he wasn't one of those guys who hated the idea. Becoming a good father someday was his ultimate goal, because his own father left so much to be desired. Tony had wanted to have a life after this Halloween. And now he would be fertilizer for the forest. Dust.

The heart was placed outside the gateway. The arms inside thrashed frantically as the brilliant red lump boiled. A swarm of children attacked the organ, taking measured bites of the fruit. Their bulbous bodies fled inside, charged with radiant power. Hundreds detonated. Through the eclipses of darkness and light, layers of the hole collapsed into soot. The opening widened and a slender arm, the woman's arm, came through with her head. She moved quickly through, for the gateway would repair and soon.

"They're coming through." Teresa swallowed the words.

"I don't think it will stay open forever," Martin told her. They'd lost Hearts before, but he still wasn't sure.

Laughter scaled the peaks of the hovering pines. More church members clamored through the forest toward the new arrivals.

Teresa tugged at him, but Martin couldn't move. All he could do was think about the end. His body came off the ground with a surge of strength. "This is done, Martin. We have to go!"

Thousands of demented orange faces exploded around them. Teresa flung a mantle and it powered through the children like a cannon ball. Martin followed her through the maze of twisting trees, trusting her to lead them to the van.

Chaplain Cloth's laughter followed them all the way back.

October 26th - This Year

One

MARTIN SPENT THE LAST OF THEIR CASH ON A PACKage of cookies and drinks. The Messenger usually left them enough money for the year, but in the past few months they'd resorted to selling off some equipment and arms to eBay thugs and pawnshops. That had only lasted so long; the road was expensive, and their cash flow thinned to a trickle. Maybe this was a punishment for losing Tony last year.

Martin could only afford a cheap, diet raspberry ice tea. He ran the gamut of other drink options: beverages in Styrofoam cups (so, *benzene* poisoning), aluminum cans (so, *aluminum salts* and Alzheimer's to follow) and plastic bottles (so, *bisphenol-A* to disrupt your hormones). Some drinks were sugared or chemicaled. Too many were caramel colored, caffeinated, and energized with herbal supplements the FDA still hadn't bothered investigating. But raspberry tea always gave him butterflies. He never remembered if he liked it or hated it. It sounded good; so he let go his inhibitions. *Enjoyed the lingering question.* It thrilled him like the early-morning charge of heading out on an unknown road in their '79 Ford Quadravan, windows down, cold air deep in his lungs and the whole day before him.

Teresa slept with her cheek smooshed against her shoulder. Only a Nomad could sleep so comfortably in that position. The sun winked over the distant hills behind her, the day still buried in piles of shadow beyond another prehistoric gas station tipping over the edge of American stupor.

He gagged suddenly on the drink. "Ick—too sweet."

Teresa stirred.

He dropped the bottle in the cup holder. "I thought you were the one that didn't like raspberry."

"Peach," she answered.

"Are you feeling better?"

"Chest still hurts. I think I fractured a rib coughing yesterday."

"Exaggerator." He tickled just under her tricep.

Her eyes opened, that dangerous blue of open water. "Don't screw around Martin. I'm not playing." She shut her eyes again and softened her tone. "Where are we, anyway?"

"Nowhere."

"There again?"

He spent a moment admiring her. She had hit fifty in August but looked younger—even with the cancer. His thirty-eight year old body had taken as much mental and physical abuse as hers, and yet, glancing in the rearview mirror, he could see the old man gimping to the surface. Sometimes he wondered if this was genetic, if his parents had prematurely aged. He wished he could remember them better. All of his photos were either destroyed or left behind somewhere in the sprawling galaxy of roadside motels.

Eighteen years without seeing another person diminished everything to dry details. He remembered his parents held him at a distance because he was different, then because he reminded them of the *other place*, and then because they knew he'd leave someday anyway, to do the Messenger's work. Birthdays were spent in solitude with heaps of unwrapped presents: butterfly knives, smoke grenades, m80s, and pellet guns. They knew his destiny. His mother would be off Windexing windows and his father would be on duty doing good-guy police stuff, and Martin would always be left alone to think on his future, with no idea what kind of man he'd become, a man worried about the saccharin content of this horrible raspberry swill.

Teresa stared at him now. "Are we going to leave or what?"

"Or what what?"

"The last letter said the Heart of the Harvest would be in San Bernardino County this year, so I think we should head that way before we run things too close."

"Like last October?"

Teresa said nothing and rested her head again. She'd looked a deal worse than this before. Right after the diagnosis, after the pneumonia, he'd wondered if she would even make it to another autumn.

She had.

She wiggled in her seat and glanced unhappily at the bottle of water he'd brought her. "Did you waste our last three bucks on that? I told you to pick up my Djarums."

His morning rush vanished and Martin turned the ignition. "They only had regular cigarettes."

Two

PAUL'S BEST FRIEND WAS STILL.

Pieces of Justin's skull stuck into the Joshua tree like shards of cinnamon glass. The ugly desert tree slowly dripped in ruby streams, thin and thick, dark and light. Its bayonet leaves (drip) trembled from the impact of Justin's body falling back—*drip, drip.*

Paul felt his eyes water. The ugly bastard of a palm and cactus had given him allergies. The sneeze wouldn't come though. *Come on, sneeze!* His mother, who Paul affectionately referred to as the Whore to End all Other Whores, once said all you needed to do was stare up at the sun a bit to catch a sneeze.

The sun wasn't far off. Rose shadows gradually colored the toasted landscape. Paul holstered his piece in his coat and knelt. The gun's discharge had sent several kangaroo rats scurrying out from the coarse bushes nearby. A few of the stunted rodents inquired around Justin's spattered pant leg with twinkling black eyes. Paul half-considered shooting one, just to see what design a fifty caliber would leave behind in the dirt. It was a trifle cruel though, not to mention *loud.*

A bit of human meat—one nostril in its bloodless center—swung from a reluctant branch of watery flesh. Paul could still see Justin's open eye in the mess. The lonesome eye wasn't posing a question. It wasn't demanding a cause. Causes were out of the game now. But the eye persisted, *We were friends, cocksucker.*

"That's right Justin," Paul told the corpse. "But that's love, isn't it? Some kind of fucked up shit."

Unseen bugs chirped nearby, or maybe his ears still rang from the bullet. Paul smoothed a hand over his head and gripped a wad of his blond hair at the back. Sweaty, oily. He would need another shower something fierce after shuffling around in all this dirt, before people started offering him pocket change.

The eyeball stared listlessly.

"It's the only way, Justin. You know me and women. I don't jerk off; *I get off.* You should have let the job go to the right guy. I warned you."

The right side of the speckled face wasn't sympathetic. Paul shifted onto his other knee and put a hand in his inner pocket. He brought out the suicide letter that had been folded in a neat square, as he knew Justin would have done in his hyper-obsessive way. "I want you to know that this is no small thing. It's beyond pussy, pal. This is on a different scale. *She* is on a different scale. I don't expect your naïve ass to understand." He tucked the square inside Justin's pants and patted his hip.

He could just imagine Justin's rebuttal and in reply said, "You think I'm being unfair calling you naïve? You're the damned nature boy. When have I—in all the time you've known me—ever asked to drive out and see a desert sunrise? I was afraid you'd think I was coming on to you. Ever since bishophood you've been a big ol' pile of fucked up, Justin. You just slipped man, you slipped. It's a fine resting place out here though." Paul stood at a gradual, respectful speed. More and more, blowing Justin's head off was making him feel giddy, and worthy. The friendship had meant something to him, and so it was a just sacrifice. For the Priestess.

And Paul Quintana would keep sacrificing. His place in line was next and he would be named a Bishop now. There could be no sidestepping him this time. Hell, there would be a string of "suicides" if it came down any other way. He'd see to it. Things were full circle, finally. The eighteen-year-old whelp who'd left home and never said goodbye, that boy had known this day would come; he would have the ideal woman, even if it killed him.

Paul's heart jumped and his body followed. Through great, rolling plumes of dust, a limousine sped around the foothill and accelerated at him like an out-of-control coffin. His comrades had found him. The Church of Midnight had come. Dust clouds wrapped around him and he let out a fierce sneeze into his shoulder. He couldn't enjoy the sneeze though.

The limo shuddered to a halt. Paul heard a door open but couldn't see anything at first. The dust cleared and Cole Szerszen stepped out, a leaning fortress in a faded Giorgio Armani. The suit might have been scrubbed over river rock for all its wrinkles. Had it ever been black? Cole's thick unruly hair matched the suit, as did his ashen eyes. For a Bishop of Midnight, he took little pride in grooming.

Two others fell out of the stretched deal. Raymond Traven and Melissa Patterson. Ray unsheathed his road bottle of Wild Turkey. The burst capillary hue of his cabbage nose took on a sudden happy glow. Melissa sidled close to Cole and yanked tight her well-ironed pants suit. She kept her eyes down. Her mortification made her look overcautious, like an old lady trying to avoid breaking her pelvis. No way was she going to look Paul in the eyes. Not with Cole standing so close nearby.

The Bishop's cool expression bore into Paul. His drafty voice often sounded to be nearing discovery. "You know what the Tomes say about days like this?"

Paul shrugged. He gave his best-natured grin, despite the corpse. Regardless of what they thought, he had to stick to his story.

"You should remember the passage, Quintana. I have it you've been hitting the Tomes hard lately, like a college kid cramming for finals."

"I'm trying to remember Bishop, but I've got a shitty memory. I only look at the pictures in the Tomes."

"In *Ramifications* it states that 'indescribable beauty in the world can foretell a transformation in the beholder. Beware the lures of beauty'."

"That doesn't sound familiar, Bishop Szerszen. You're not ad-libbing, I trust."

"Still have that Magnum?" Cole's gunmetal gaze drifted to the red disarrangement before the tree. "I see you do. Take off your coat. Slowly."

A spray of dirt blasted up and Paul shielded his eyes. "Wait goddamnit! Don't shoot! I'm taking it off. I'm taking it off."

The dust layered the air still. The three had their weapons drawn, but only one shot had fired. Melissa's Beretta, still trained on Paul, seemed comical in her small hands, but he didn't doubt her intent. Her expression told the story. Melissa still had his taste rolling around her mouth and she didn't like it much. She didn't like it at all.

Paul unbuttoned his coat and sucked in his disgust as he dropped his black Joseph Abboud on the ground.

"Now your holster," Cole instructed.

"What?"

The Beretta shifted.

"Whatever," he answered. "Can I check the safety?"

"No."

Next, his holster and weapon clunked below. "Now can I explain?"

Cole jerked an order with his head and Ray Traven obediently moved forward, his drunken gait directing him to his goal on a strange, slithering route. Cole caught Ray's shoulder before he could get too far and put out a palm. Ray's lips pressed together like a forlorn toddler. He handed over the Wild Turkey.

Paul's spine stiffened. Ray tripped over a kangaroo rat hole on the way over to the tree. He stared back accusingly before stopping at the dead man. Leaning over the Justin mess, Ray inspected the scene in drop-mouthed awe.

"Is it Margrave?" Melissa asked behind the Beretta.

"Not the best parts of him."

"Leave him for nature," said Cole.

"No rites?"

"Leave him," Cole said in his *last time* voice.

Paul's heart pounded in his ears. Were they even going to let him tell his story?

"You've killed a Bishop of Midnight." Cole swiped up the whiskey from the hood and regarded it like something he'd never seen before.

"Can I tell you what happened?"

"With your sudden interest in the Tomes, and with October 31st approaching, I find it fairly obvious. You might have gone after me, but since Justin and you were sewn at the hip, this was a simple transaction. I get it."

"You're implying—"

"Wasn't implying, was *stating*. You scored perfectly in the gauntlet and Margrave over there scored half as well. You had the highest score, yet he became a Bishop. The Church nearly had to force you to take the test last year. I could cry jealousy, but I don't think you care about bishophood, Quintana."

Paul took a deep swallow before he proceeded. "So killing Justin for ascension would make no sense, but you still don't believe me?"

"Killing Margrave for status only wouldn't make sense, right, but something else certainly does. *She* will be at this year's conclave again."

Christ, thought Paul. Was he so transparent? He had to redirect this quickly. "Look, Justin wasn't doing so well. He wanted to clear his mind, so we came out here. We were talking about responsibility and duty and then he suddenly clammed up. I didn't even see it coming. His gun came out before I knew it—"

Cole widened his eyes in feigned shock. "And what? He couldn't take living anymore? Shit Quintana, that's weak, though I suppose it'd work for most Inner Circle dimwits." The big man tilted his head, amused, "Hey Traven, was his firearm drawn?"

Ray reviewed the corpse. "Nope."

Paul cringed.

"Putting a gun in his hand would have been a trifle more realistic, don't you think?" Cole lifted the Wild Turkey. He flinched at the flavor and set the bottle back down with sidelong disgust at Ray.

"Hey, there's a note." Ray sorted through a few credit cards and the folded note from Justin's pocket. He took the note by a corner to unfold it.

"Leave it," Cole ordered. His face brightened with an intense thought as he studied Paul. "Forgery will not be enough. You realize that the Archbishop will see right through that, just as I have. Margrave had Colombian contacts. What could you offer the Church, Quintana? A list of your favorite poontang?"

"I don't understand—"

"Stop lying to me or the vultures will have two bodies for dinner."

"What do you want then?" asked Paul.

"In order for Margrave to go unmissed, you need my support, and you need to follow my every order to the syllable, word, sentence and exclamation point."

"Of course Bishop Szerszen. You have my word."

Cole took three heavy steps toward him, got right in front of Paul. His breath burned of whiskey. "You're an asshole Quintana, but you also happen to be an asshole that scored the gauntlet perfectly—even Archbishop Pager can't say the same for himself. I *want* you to be named Bishop. I need you, and as awful as that might sound to me, it's the truth."

"Okay, I'm confused."

"I have my plans, no different than anybody else." Cole stepped half a pace back and appraised him. "So tell me, should I let you pick that Magnum up? Can we go on our merry way and leave the truth to rot out here?"

Before he could answer, Cole said, "Traven, you'll be driving Quintana's car back to the chapel."

Ray winced in the spreading sunshine. "Paul, is that Corvette a stick? I can't drive a stick for shit."

Cole's eyes settled gravely on Paul again. "Are the keys in the ignition?"

This was insane. Paul shook his head to gain back reality. It didn't work. "Just what are you trying to accomplish here, Bishop?"

Cole's caveman hand dropped on his shoulder and squeezed. From the raw strength Paul felt a roadblock of blood in a neck artery. There was something bizarre in the grip too, a hint of power that only a Bishop could know. "I want what's best for the Church of Midnight. Through you Paul and through Chaplain Cloth, I can bring our new era."

Paul's body felt stickier than before, sticky and cold. "You're going after the Archbishop, aren't you? You want to ascend."

Cole's scarred lips hooked into a smile.

Three

MARTIN WAS STIR-CRAZY. TRAVELING FOR MOST OF your life required overcoming restlessness at every stage. Being a Nomad meant ignoring your shaking leg, your tapping fingers, your racing mind. He and Teresa used meditation, exercise, and pleasure reading to battle the anxiousness between Halloweens. Today, Martin forgot to read his books this morning, didn't have a chance to go for a run before they headed out, and couldn't think of any meditation effective enough to numb his overactive mind. He felt a slow insanity creeping out of the endless white dashes in the road.

Teresa was wheezing again. The wheezes soon led to soft, rolling snores, which usually indicated serious snoozing. That was good, he thought, good for her, get some rest honey. But the snoring and the incessant hum of tires had brought on road dementia and Martin ached for the radio, even the condescending barking of commercials. *No radio though.* He wouldn't try that unless he wanted to arouse a sleeping nicotine fit waiting to happen.

But still—maybe just turn on the radio real low—his fingers fondled the volume knob for a moment. He checked his passenger; Teresa had an aura around her, as though a kinetic challenge floated above her. *Go ahead, try me.*

To hell with that. Martin withdrew his fingers and his intent.

There was a suicidal lull to the desert's grays, browns and yellows he hadn't noticed at first touch, but he was deep inside the odd part of his mind now, tapping that glacial pinprick in his cortex. A shiver raced from the cold shiv and surged to his eyes. They felt frozen from behind and burning on the surface. He took a healthy fistful of ghost-matter from the place of his ancestors, the Old Domain.

Mantles were a reflection of matter from the other world. Here they could be made to interact like physical matter but couldn't be seen with the naked eye. With a lifetime of practice he and Teresa had learned to use them as shields, knives, crude explosive devices, and sometimes as tools for espionage. Mantles formed in that cerebral zone where epiphanies lived. No matter how many times he'd conjured one now, summoning a mantle always sustained a moment of revelation.

Martin concentrated left of the road, just inches above the flying carpet of dirt and piss-weed, and found himself gripping the steering wheel harder. The cold point in his brain churned and wrapped over itself again, and then it was a here and a there and a slip and a stand and a glimmer and a dying black hole—a salty metal taste spread in his mouth and this signaled his mind was at the ready.

Building mantles took several minutes, but once he had hold he could go for hours. Teresa had a different proficiency. She could build one at a moment's notice, no waiting required, but creating complex shapes had always been difficult for her. For years Martin worked on speeding up creation to match hers and she'd struggled to create less elementary structures, but they'd finally come to terms with the fact that some people had it, some didn't, and some who tried hard to have it, never would.

But Martin felt he'd conquered other mental mountains. Creating mantles inside structures had also once been a problem and now he could see *through* things using them. He could fold one into a lockpick and insert it into a keyhole and see the tumblers turning inside the lock. Duration was another challenge he'd almost mastered. He was fairly certain he could create a permanent mantle, one that would never vanish from this world. Doing something like that would probably kick the everlasting shit out of him, probably put him into death throes, but he knew it could be done with the right amount of energy and time.

A cautious look at Teresa, Martin sucked in a breath and drove out the mantle like an axe blade. Cacti along the road began to slice in half. *Thomp, Thomp, Thhhuwump.* The succulents leaned in every direction and dust clouds coughed up. A rapid-fire succession of new *thomps* sent green flesh spinning. With a hollow sounding punch, a fist of cactus struck the hood and buggered off the side.

Teresa bolted up. "—the shit?"

"I think a bird hit the van."

At once she slumped back over, closing her eyes. "Poor birdie."

Quick as light, Martin brought the mantle back, only three inches away from his window. He couldn't see it but felt it just outside. The transparent guillotine pulsed with activated heat. Even through the window he could feel the friction burn on its sharp edges. With an exhale, he launched it as far as his mind could track it, and then reeled it back—it was the flexing of a muscle. The more he did it, the better. Even if Teresa said building one drew unwanted attention, he had to practice for the 31st. These mantles weren't just used for barriers, after all. And he wasn't going to lose another Heart of the Harvest. Not this year.

Something roared beneath them. The steering wheel violently jammed to the left—Martin hardly heard the tire explode when his shoulder momentarily popped from the socket and bucked at the counterforce. The blowout had sent the van sideways. The tires shrieked and the desert shrugged to one side. Somewhere to his left, the mantle thinned into the atmosphere. A big rig's horn blared another time. Martin's hands sought power uselessly—the creation had thrown mud over his reflexes. He cried out, still spent from bringing the mantle. A thought trickled down his mind and into his heart. *I can't believe I did this to—*

—Teresa's hand caught the steering wheel. The van jumped off the road, the truck rushed past, and the world jackknifed around in a sepia screech. Martin threw up his hands to block his head. He heard Teresa's knuckles strike the van's ceiling and she shouted so loud his ears rang. The radio had turned on and unintelligible music cut through the buzz of surprise.

And as soon as it all happened, it stopped.

The big rig had come to a stop a quarter mile up the road. The driver was probably emptying his pants out right about now, but nobody was hurt, no damage was done. Martin didn't look over, but his heart lightened when he heard Teresa's voice. It was sweet to hear the forgiveness in it, despite the ragged quality of her tone.

"Goddamn tires were only a month old."

Four

THEY BOTH FELL ASLEEP WAITING FOR THE TOW TRUCK. Martin had fought against dozing off, but with no spare tire, no radio reception, no outside world, there wasn't anything left to do. It was strange how his dream took him to somewhere completely different and yet he never thought to question the absurdity. Sense no longer mattered. He drifted in a hot air balloon over eighteenth century London. Should he feel this was absurd? In the real world he possessed an ability few knew possible, so anything could happen; it was perfectly reasonable to suddenly be in a royal purple balloon, swinging over baroque architecture. Forget rationalization—he was above everything; this was heaven.

He curled into a tight ball in the corner of the balloon's basket. The wind burned his face. There was a jet of fire overhead—it nosily blew upward. After brief inspection, Martin's body stiffened. There were supposed to be sandbags in the basket. Weren't there? Where were the sandbags? Didn't he need those? How would he get down? This was a dream, so he shouldn't care. But he did. He peered over the side. Buildings swam beneath. Above, a ripping sound went from east to west.

His heart lashed out, caught in its cage. *This balloon was deflating.* Why had he chartered something so asinine?

But there was a trapdoor in the bottom of the balloon.

Of course there was.

He tugged the handle, and rather eagerly, maybe grasping this was a dream again. This was the only intelligent way to escape the sky—to fall out of it. If he lost Teresa to cancer, this life didn't have much more in store for the likes of him anyhow.

He dropped through the trap door. It felt like he left someone behind. Falling was sluggish, as though he'd been dropped into an atmosphere of transparent worms. His chin and fingers raked across something slimy. There was too much pressure, too much terror for him to open his eyes, so there was nothing, there was black, but the black came apart in hot colored shapes that rained upward and stabbed sideways.

And that was it. He was sobbing and balling and grunting and he lost energy weeping—he was spitting out slime. He was, once again, losing composure, many times after vowing never to take so seriously the tangled dream logic forged from Chaplain Cloth's taunting.

He shouldn't have brought Cloth into this. He shouldn't have thought of him.

Evil had its eyes on Martin now. The slime had coated the wall of an alley. He hadn't been falling really, just standing in the alley, clawing at the bricks and freaking out. It was daytime. Steam lifted from rain puddles and dragged heavy through the air. The sunlight sawed away at the plumes of dark factory smoke. Martin blinked into the alley to see something, anything that would make a shape he could understand. He shielded his eyes, but his arms had stuck in the slime. Tears came from the light's attack and he tried to kick...something had closed over his legs too. Animal sounds of panic rumbled in his throat as he tried to conceive something different, something happy and from a different place. *But there were things filling the alley.* He knew what they were too. He'd seen Cloth's children too many times not to recognize how they moved and breathed, even if he couldn't distinguish their little bodies in the rapiers of unfriendly light. He tried to create a mantle but in his dreams he was a normal man: feeble. The children fell around him, swiping away tufts of skin with spread green claws. Their bloody fangs drank the light. He squirmed, locked to the wall, ready for more abuse, their bare-bone abandon, their clandestine abattoir, their delightful abdication from all mercy. Hair and flakes of skin and red streamed into the air in celebration. There were footsteps in the back of the alley. Cloth came. He walked the cobblestones, laughing like a sick jester, his expression hinting at the black things he would do with Martin's body. The sun cut through and between two tresses of light he saw Cloth's eyes, one black and one orange. His heart valves slammed closed. Evil had its eyes on him.

Martin shot up in his seat.

Teresa and the tow truck man wheeled around. They stood a few paces up the road. Martin sank a little in the seat, his back dream-sweaty and face hot with embarrassment. Before they looked away he searched around for the real crazy man who'd yelled out. There was only desert though.

Luckily the drive to the next stretch of civilization was short on distance and conversation. The little town wasn't much to speak of, but there was an automotive repair shop located right off the highway, even if it was closed today. The tow truck driver had almost an opalescent sheen to his slick black hair and his pocky skin looked like charred cherry wood. "Sorry there. It's bad timing, I know."

Martin used what Teresa called his Buddha voice. "We would have to wait until tomorrow. Isn't there something else around here?"

"You could find someone to give you a lift to Kingman, but it's another sixty miles. Sorry I can't."

Martin laughed. "It's a lovely town, but I don't even see a Mickey-Ds."

"There's a bar, *Jarrie's Place*. They serve sandwiches sometimes." The man shifted at the blaring reality of the statement and quickly returned to the subject of the auto shop. "So they work four-tens every other week to fit the trucking schedule better. It's their rules. I can't do nothin' about that. They open early tomorrow, around sixish— "

Martin smiled. "Come on. It's only one tire. Our roadside is covered, right? We're good. If someone rolls one out, I'll put it on all by myself."

The man shrugged. "Not happenin' guy. It's the shits."

Martin sighed through his teeth, and with two fingers scratched his head. He hoped if he stared at the guy long enough it would change something.

Didn't.

"Thanks for your help," he said.

"Hey, no problem. Stay outta the sun."

Martin walked back to the van, opened the door, and draped his body over the seat. After a manic moment he rolled his eyes back. "For fuck sake."

"What's going on with the tire?" asked Teresa.

"Oh that." He leaned back. "Well, I guess we're going to have to camp out here until tomorrow."

"We're already running behind. Let's just try filling the spare. It's a slow leak."

"And maybe be stranded where nobody lives at all? We don't have any money left for even a truck stop sandwich. If you hadn't noticed, the Messenger hasn't left anything yet."

"Maybe he won't. Maybe he found new people to be his Nomads."

"That's rich. Don't fool yourself. Nobody would waste such able-bodied slaves. We'll be used up, like batteries."

"Now you're seeing."

Martin gave Teresa a once over. In the last few months it was clear she'd given up on herself, just as he had. She never wanted to try his herbal remedies, never attempted to do the healing yoga routines, and hadn't quit smoking cloves above all else. He'd begun to gradually turn the concern-dial down to zero. She just didn't understand. To her it was nonsense; a bunch of rainforest sticks and leaves wouldn't take away the tumor in her lung. Why quit smoking then? She would succumb with or without his intervention. And she was overdue. Tony Nguyen probably could have attested to that, had he not been devoured last year.

Martin scrubbed his face.

"Stop being that way," she said.

"Which way?"

"Disparaged. I don't want to deal with the disparaging Martin today. Not so close to the 31st. Okay?"

"Whatever you say darling."

"I do have some good news."

"Oh please, tell me, quick."

She held up a deformed twenty dollar bill. "Found this at the bottom of my duffel. In my humble opinion, it's not too early for a drink. That is, if you let me drink and don't give me any shit. We can try and see if that bar's open. This should be enough money for a beer, right?"

"For domestic, I'd say it's plenty."

Martin remembered saying that before. *Déjà vu*. But there was something oddly misplaced in the feeling, different than experiencing a recurring sound or setting. The sensation frightened him, but he couldn't say why, not offhand. It did seem though that this *déjà vu* belonged to someone else.

Five

JARRIE'S *PLACE* HAD ONLY ONE CUSTOMER. MARTIN COULD sense Teresa's disapproval and he made it his goal to head straight for the bar, his eyes never veering. But he had seen. A young woman in a low cut tangerine dress sat alone near the video golf game that all sporting alcoholics seemed to thrive on. The dress was expensive and overflowing with this woman's endowments, and a shrill warning inside suggested that Martin ignore everything about her.

He hadn't addressed the honey blonde. So far so good. He brought his elbows up on the scuffed bar and hoped for the best. He and Teresa weren't married or anything. And could a common law marriage even exist on the road? He was his own person; he wasn't bound but knew the real answer. A sign over the bar elaborated: *You can ask for the man in charge. Or you can ask the woman who has all the answers.*

He'd read that sign somewhere before. *No, someone else had*—the bizarre feeling of displaced *déjà vu* continued.

A wall of black and red flannel moved toward them from behind the bar. The Paul Bunyan looking bartender limped a little from going too fast, at first not noticing them coming in.

He put his thick hands down on the counter and tried on a weak smile. "So what can I—?"

"Djarums?" asked Teresa.

Martin tried to contain his scowl.

The brown beard vibrated. "*Crackles.*"

"How about something with extra tar?" Martin suggested.

"I have a few packs of cloves." The man opened a large cabinet full of cigarette varieties. Teresa eagerly took the black box from him. He slid over a matchbook.

"Yes, I'm buying them, so don't ask, Martin." Teresa tore off the plastic. "Are you going to get on me if I have one?" she asked the bartender.

"No, ma'am. It's not a problem. Is it a problem for you Mabel?" His eyes pointed over their shoulders to the vixen.

Martin turned around. Not turning would make the whole avoidance seem as fake as it really was. He hadn't been with another woman for more than ten years. Many romantic bonds had been forged before his and Teresa's and some *during* as well, but he didn't like to think about those days anymore. Teresa, on the other hand, must have remembered all of Martin's other women, from their names down to the shoes they wore. She probably wanted to forget but couldn't put it out of her mind. Martin just hoped she realized he wasn't that man anymore.

"Do you want one hon?" Teresa lifted a clove. "They're quite crackly."

"No thank you, ma'am," the woman named Mabel answered. She had a strange cadence to her voice. It wasn't a neutral sounding Californian accent but more of an attempt at it.

"What are you two drinking?" The bartender folded up his rag.

"Nothing for me." Teresa blew out a dragon billow of smoke. She suddenly looked more at ease and more alive. Times like these made Martin think those doctors were full of shit.

"Dark Heineken?" Martin asked.

"We have Newcastle."

"Sure then."

Teresa's dark cigarette crackled like a sparkler. Shadows moved over the bar like restless ghosts. It didn't feel right. The bartender pushed over a cold, wet bottle of Newcastle with one hand and an ashtray with the other.

"You got sandwiches or something to eat?"

"Only bags of chips," said the bartender. He halted on the last word, as though chips had been a word he'd had difficulty with at one time, perhaps with a speech impediment.

Martin wiped a bit of beer off his lip. "We'll take what you have."

Red-gray ash sprinkled into the pewter tray as Teresa gave her clove cigarette three solemn taps. She stared into the rows of bottles. Martin watched her closely. "You going to Mars again?" he asked.

"Remember the shooting range last week?"

He finished the beer. Softly burped. "Okay."

"When you were filling out the forms the TV was on. There was a commercial."

The bartender spotted the empty bottle, pointed at it and Martin hummed an affirmative.

"I thought it was a commercial for a tampon at first."

"I hate those," Martin admitted, "so much."

"But this wasn't about tampons. There was this woman, actually about your age, who went about her daily routine: she played with her dog, went to the movies with her friends, took in an art gallery, went tanning, laughed at something a handsome guy said to her at a coffee shop—then the commercial narrator reveals the woman has cancer. See, that wasn't really a tanning bed I saw her in, she was getting radiation therapy."

"Teresa—"

"Hold on. Whatever insurance company or drug company it was—they made it seem like this woman had penciled in her radiation appointment like another entry in her planner, put there between the coffee shop and buying groceries—like going to do something like that is just another check on the to-do list, because *you don't want to get too gloomy.* Oh hell no. Don't let a tumor get in the way of all your fun."

"I want to see your point." Martin cranked back his new beer.

She took a deep, trembling breath. "I can't even have the dignity to die like a normal, self-absorbed American. I'm too damned worried we'll have another bad October 31st."

"They're all bad."

"You know what I mean. Tony—"

He sighed. "Teresa, I was enjoying myself just a second ago."

"I saw—got a whole eyeful back there."

The beer tasted sour now. "Don't start. Come on. Look, you have to take care of yourself. For a change. I can't help a woman who refuses to be helped."

She slid out another clove. "You're fooling yourself, kid. I can't help her either."

He grasped her clove hand. "Just stop," he whispered.

Carefully, she wiggled her hand free.

"The gateway might open forever this year, so let's knock off the foolishness and talk strategy," he said. "Last year we set mantles on a perimeter that the Church never even crossed. It was a wasted effort. We could have saved our energy."

"Your idea."

Martin cleared his head for a moment and nodded. "Yeah, I got Tony killed."

The bartender glanced over, but they ignored him. Teresa lit the end of the new clove with a splintered match. After several generous draws, she went sideways on her stool. He almost grabbed her arm to yank her back but didn't get the chance. Mabel, the woman in the orange dress, stood a foot away now, completely changing the subject.

"Are you taking Route 66 all the way through Arizona?" Mabel asked.

Teresa and Martin, knocked off guard, shook their heads in synchronization.

"A lot of people try to go as far as they can." Mabel presented all her perfect teeth. *She is something else*, thought Martin. Had he seen her before? What had brought them here? A flat tire, or something unseen?

"Good luck on your trip. Don't forget our little bar next time you travel through this township." Mabel stuck out a hand. Martin took it and consumed it in his own. She brought her other hand over and pressed her thumbs into his wrist, gently rubbing circles there. Her eyes caught his for a moment before she released. Mabel shook Teresa's hand in the same fashion. When their eyes unlocked Teresa's gaze looked degaussed.

Mabel gave the bartender a peck on the bearded cheek. "I'm going back to study, Daddy."

It was only too apparent. The bartender loved being called daddy. His eyes never left Mabel's slight sashay until she was out of the miserable little bar. With her going Martin had a sick feeling that he'd never see this woman again. But Mabel was a stranger, after all, so why was that disturbing?

Two beats passed and the bartender said, "Another Newcastle?"

Martin indulged another beat and then nodded.

"Give me one too," Teresa added.

Six

I am what they call the Messenger in some places, the Interloper in others. That's a title that some have come to revere, though I can't explain why. They've put me on a higher plane of existence, but I'm not a god. I watch the worlds and read minds. I attempt, in the only way I know, to help my Nomads lessen their burden. I must protect them every day and especially guide them into every October. Martin and Teresa have blood ties to the Old Domain, but being from this world, they know nothing of its nature.

While they drank at the tavern, the Church of Morning prepared for the new season on the other side of the gateway in the Old Domain. The church balanced on the thin garnet steps of Azinraith temple. Their devotional number's hands clasped together, minds locked as one, giving thanks to the new harvest to come. Warm red threads plunked from one temple step to the next, searching for even ground. The flow would eventually reach the base of the steps and fan out. The shared thought of the church members pronounced this as good. They would be thankful for the offer and pay tribute. They would bring temple butchers to make gifts for the Archbishop: bone necklaces and pendants, leather bracers, baskets woven from hair and sinew, water bladders, and there would be a new display of unprecedented fecal runes on temple walls, lacquered over for new generations to praise and draw power from.

The Church of Morning estimated the great channel had opened ten spans since the Day of Closing thousands of autumns ago, but the potential foreseen this autumn could widen the channel twenty spans more. That was enough space to set the pillars in place and lock the channel open. *Bloodthanks* would be carried out in both worlds, the two churches would unite again, and new, glorious Tomes would be scribed.

Chaplain Cloth would bring them victory again.

The Heart of the Harvest, the blessed fruit, comes into the world every autumn for a single day. This year it has come again, with a potency that rivals even those early sacrifices at the circle of stones. *Something was special about this year's Heart,* thought the Church of Morning with great study, *something intrinsically powerful that the Interloper wouldn't allow them to see.*

They would find out. The plan had been set and the worlds would move under their clawing fingers.

The blood pooled at the temple's base and a collective sigh hollowed the air as they rocked back and forth on the temple steps, hands clasped together with smiles alike, minds locked as one, giving thanks.

It was enough to make me turn my eyes back to the other world.

Seven

PAUL HAD BEEN TO SOME CHAPELS THAT WERE ABSOLUTE dives. Lingering drug addicts thumped their veins in spiderwebbed halls, hookers petted your arm as you walked past—inner city gangs frequently had a presence over those small time operations and it often felt like it.

Walking the halls of the Mojave Chapel, however, Paul prayed he'd never visit one of those sorry places again. Here, the expansive halls and richly furnished chambers were built through dedication and focus, and the layout contained a sense of history that some museums even failed to possess. Two decades and millions of laundered dollars had transformed a dead silver mine into an underground palace. The glazed orange-brown walls secured every boulder in its place with mortar and chicken wire, and load bearing beams and support struts weren't composed of rotting timber but gold flaked black marble. There were even air conditioning ducts in the ceiling.

Paul noticed none of the scenery impressed Ray Traven. Tongue firmly caught in his teeth, possibly to concentrate through his overboozed mind, Ray swiped at the freight elevator's leather strap to pull it down. The elevator's door horizontally opened and shuddered nosily above and below. Ray went to about-face but instead staggered inside the elevator and struck the opposing wall. The impact looked to be momentarily sobering.

A knot of Inner Circle church members en route for the refectory stopped at the sharp clang. Paul didn't recognize them and waved them on. Judging from their fresh new suits and blouses, he suspected they'd flown down for this year's Harvest from some overseas chapel. "He's fine. Keep moving brothers and sisters," he said. They might not have understood English that well, but his tone garnered a few sour looks.

While his drunken tour guide handled the descent, Paul digested the situation. What was he going to say to Archbishop Pager? This was bound to work with Cole's backing anyway, but that didn't mean he couldn't still blow things. Paul knew his weaknesses and strengths, and thinking on his toes wasn't a strength. It was just bizarre that things had gone this way. How easy would it have been for him to be out in the desert, rotting beside Justin's body? Probably shot with his own gun too.

Paul didn't want to think about it and yet he couldn't be certain he was completely safe. He'd definitely have to keep an ear to the ground for Cole Szerszen's rumblings. The big guy could have any number of surprises planned for Paul's "psychic acumen," many of which could end in death and dismemberment, maybe not in that order. But, he thought with some emerging happiness, he was going to be a bishop in the Church of Midnight. That was something else.

If only his mother could see him now.

Raymond, pale and past enjoying himself, crouched against the elevator cage. He smacked his lips and grimaced at the flavor of his words. "You're smiling, Paul"

"Guess it's being in the chapel. I've never been."

Darkness roared outside the cage, an endless brown scream.

"Might move Val out here," said Raymond. "New life. New change."

"Val your wife?"

Raymond nodded. "Money though. Money, money, fuckin' money."

The elevator stopped and the swiftness and displacement of motion made Paul's stomach twist. Raymond, on the other hand, merely puked on his shoe. The air filled with a strange scent, like tuna in apple cider vinegar. "Kipper snaps," Ray mumbled in disgust.

Paul yanked the elevator strap quick and opened the freight doors, then took *big* steps outside. The lower level had to be the most impressive so far. The passing hallways were carved through the rock and worked as smooth as Mother Nature might have intended through slower methodology. A black and orange checkerboard carpet planed over the floor. On the rock walls hung oil paintings featuring Archbishops from Stonehenge to present. An unsaid desire rang in the painted eyes, accentuated above fans of warm orange recess lighting.

Ray struggled from the elevator, kicking vomit off his loafer. Over the last two years Paul had witnessed the poor fool sinking deeper into the bottle, ever since a Federal Express truck took a blind turn too fast and hit his kid. Not that Raymond wasn't a drunk before, but losing his son dried up all the excuses for cutting back. It was a pitiful story, but Paul didn't feel too sorry for people like Ray. Bottom line, as far as Paul Quintana was concerned—thirteen years ago the guy should have pulled out of his wife and saved himself all the heartache.

"One moment," Ray burped.

"I got antacids." Paul smacked his breast pocket. "Oh, I loaned them to Justin this morning. Son of a bitch didn't give them back." He was going to laugh but let it go. Being a bishop would require more reserve; he had to start practicing.

"No more Wild Turn-Keys. For me. I hate those birds. In a bottle." A ragged chuckle exploded from Ray's lips and then he went silent. His body straightened, electrified with the need to be more sober, and he padded to the end of the hall. Ray plunked his knuckles against the shiny black surface of a door there. They waited. He plunked again, slightly louder.

Footfalls echoed unnaturally. Ray adjusted his oversized suit coat and tie. He didn't look shitfaced anymore. Actually, he looked how Paul supposed he himself did: afraid on a level that had snapped him back to infancy. Paul already felt cold when the air conditioning cycled on overhead.

The deadbolts turned. The door opened, a block of obsidian slipping into a ravenous nothing. Two green eyes stared back, pupils dilated. There was no light beyond the eyes; emptiness soaked around the face. The voice sounded harsh, diminished chords in a mal-tuned pipe organ. "None other, save Bishop Margrave and Szerszen, may tread in the residence without written consent."

Ray attempted words. "Bizup Mar-gave killed in the morning..."

Paul moved to hush him, but Ray waved a cautionary finger back and forth, indicating control. Unconvinced, Paul spoke up, "I'm seeking audience with the Archbishop. Bishop Margrave passed away this morning. I was with him when he took his own life. Brother Traven here is my escort to the Archbishop's presence."

The placid eye rolled to both men and needled them. Paul's throat dried from tip of tongue to the root of his stomach—breathing wasn't even a question.

"Yes, Brother Quintana, the Archbishop was informed of your meeting."

"Then why'd ya ask?" Ray threw up his hands.

Paul just stood there, frozen, heart thundering. The door swung open. He flinched, unable to question the tradition he was taking part in. He hoped it was a tradition. From the darkness a noose dropped around his neck. His guide, Ray Traven, a noose now around his own neck, shot a grimace before the ropes tightened.

With a single yank Paul hit the floor with Ray. He could hear Ray's teeth click. His body slid forward and the door closed swiftly behind. He tried to speak, to scream, but the invisible force just hauled him along. Rolling across a dank corridor, he kicked out, swung his body over to save his lip from being torn off. Air deprivation made the darkness crackle with fireflies. He clutched at his burning neck. Just to let a thread of air inside, he tried to wiggle his fingers under but the hempen rope sunk deeper into his skin.

Screams came lofty and low. Laughter and hell-play ricocheted off the unseen rocks. Subterranean breathing; burning chest; burning throat; wheezing; working just for one lousy gasp. This was it. Paul knew his struggle would be the ghastly punctuation of his life—

It ended quickly.

In a dream the noose was removed by church sentinels. No, not a dream. They had removed the noose and set Paul in a chair. How long had he been sitting here? Had he lost consciousness? The lingering burn remained so intense he touched the tender flesh to be sure. Paul even *saw* the red length of rope coiled around the sentinel's fist and this wasn't reassurance. Ray's body slumped over an old monastery table. A sentinel stood fast behind the red velvet chair, probably to catch the drunk when he eventually toppled sideways. Paul had never seen interior guards before and in the scarce torchlight he only distinguished banded muscle and black armor—barbarian warriors with assault rifles and ammo belts.

From the end of the long table, a door squeaked like a rodent. The sentinels shuffled noisily to attention. A man walked in, but in the shadows Paul only saw a mouth gliding into the room. Like the guards, the mouth didn't appear to have the capacity for expression; it was an axe wound turned clammy in the grave. On the far wall, something rattled happily at his approach.

The Archbishop took a seat and his soft, girlish face became a nest of torchlight and painted runic design. Shaped eyebrows were delicate over a barbarous nose and mirrored sunglasses. Sandeus Pager folded his gloved fingers. The smell of women's perfume, *Chanel* maybe, drifted across the long table.

"I apologize for any injuries, brother Quintana, but the trial of ropes has been performed since the rule of Kublai Khan."

Paul tried to clear his throat. "Archbishop, I—"

"Tell me Quintana, do you really think you can kill your way to the top? There are other ways to sit at *my* side."

"Justin, he was depressed—"

"Better yet, don't speak just now." Pager took off his sunglasses, folded their stems neatly and set them down. "I've already heard the suicide story from the sentinels. I laughed then. Don't make me laugh now. Humor turns my reasoning very quickly, and I want to remain fair."

The Archbishop took out what looked like a bronze cigarette case and set it on the table. "You're resourceful and young, and have a natural acumen with powers of the mind. Justin Margrave was several rungs closer to complete naïveté, but there are plenty of other strong individuals in the Church of Midnight—even some acolytes better suited for my flank." Sandeus made a face like he'd just heard glass shattering. "Yet, there was the Gauntlet. I really wish we could get rid of the fucking thing, but there it is, just like the trial of ropes—a tradition.

"Since you scored the highest in the Gauntlet and are in good standing, I can't very well dismiss your ascension. My authority would be questioned by the European contingency. They wanted to restructure and I had them fat, happy and *quiet* with Margrave's trade deal. But the Columbians don't trust me to continue. They trusted the man you killed. And now that's over.

"So it stands at this: I don't want anybody questioning my policy, Quintana. Cole Szerszen finds you worthy of bishophood and though Cole might sometimes be a little too dreamy and farsighted about the Church of Midnight, I tend to trust him. *Tend to.*"

"What—" Paul began, but the Archbishop raised a glove. He opened his cigarette case and took out one thinly rolled cigarette. Paul knew he wouldn't win this, so he waded through those muddy eyes. "What now?"

"What now indeed!" Sandeus slapped the table and Paul jumped. Raymond stirred and a pained expression crossed his sweating, sleeping face. The cigarette came zigzagging over the table. A book of matches hissed over after them.

"I have asthma," said Paul.

"You want the title, don't you?"

Pursing his lips, Paul took the cigarette.

The Archbishop continued, "When smoked the *marrow seeds* rolled into the tobacco will spread evenly through your lungs. I pray your garden will blossom with balance."

"Seeds?"

"Collected in the Old Domain and brought to us through the gateway last year, their effect is similar to peyote and gypsum weed, but a more aggressive hallucinogen. And, of course, more special. Think of this as dropping a foot into the Old Domain. You'll never be the same after. It's an honor to imbibe these seeds, Quintana."

"I don't understand."

Sandeus impatiently rubbed his chin. "Only Bishops who sit at the left and right of the Archbishop may reap the seeds' power. But why sit here and explain when the answer's in your hand. *Smoke.*"

Paul took his eyes away from the savage male-female glare and stuck the cigarette in his mouth—he tore off a match, snapped it against the book and lit the end, took a deep draw. The sharp heat made him cough like a circus seal. It took him a while to recover. The Archbishop said nothing. Soon Paul realized there wasn't any substance to the peppery smoke, certainly not a tobacco flavor, and he realized that his tongue had stopped perceiving flavor altogether and once he realized that, he also realized his body exploded with realizations—realizing the reality of realizing—was he instantly insane? He became a mash of disturbed parts, which throbbed between numbness and pleasure, strobe lights in his nerve centers.

"How much do I—?"

"All of it." Sandeus's voice crawled through Paul's episodic fits. "Until you hit the cotton filter. Don't you dare stop."

Paul's smile went rubbery and refused to quit his face. He took another drag. One of the sentinels stepped forward and put a stone ashtray on the table. "So kind," he told the big man in black armor, who sank back into the darkness. Not long ago this man had almost choked him to death with a hemp rope, but now, brotherhood.

Eyes bugging, Paul took another strong, cartoonish pull on the cigarette. This was a profound experience. Enjoyable too.

Something rattled in the wall again.

Paul's nose dripped snot, but when he touched the skin he found it dry as coal. As he tapped off wreaths of ash into the ashtray, he made a promise to get a hold of himself, if possible.

"So pretty boy, do you still want to know what's next?"

Reality crashed. Real things had been at stake, career things, life and death things, and Paul'd completely forgotten. He was panting, "What Archbishop...what is next?"

A long fillet knife with an ebony grip slid across the table. The knife circuited for a moment before stopping. The Archbishop's eyes settled on Ray. "Cut this man's throat."

Paul jolted and a hand pushed him down in his seat. He glanced at Raymond Traven, who still slept soundly. "Why would you ask that of me?"

"Difficult? Every murder has a purpose and price, brother Quintana."

"I don't want— "

"We're past what you want! We were actually never there. Understand?" The Archbishop leaned back in his seat, anger fading to irritation.

Paul waited a few seconds and sucked in the last of the cigarette in a burst of red light that smelled similar to how it felt. He crushed the scorched paper and cotton into the tray.

The effect of the seeds had come on strong. The walls twisted and a mummy spoke to him from the ceiling. The words came out of the mummy's mouth in black and silver ribbons with an aroma of shit braising in onion broth. Embryos with wagging wet tongues fell out of the walls and bounced rhythmically with Sandeus's voice—

"Here are your choices: cut his throat, or retrieve Alexander. The Tomes of Eternal Harvest call for a Bishop to know his time and place even in the face of distortion. Prove yourself."

"I'll retrieve Alexander," Paul mumbled, unsure what the hell that meant. Was it some nonsense his mind had popped into the Archbishop's mouth? He wasn't sure.

Sandeus grinned through the fogginess like a shark through sparkling silt. "You've chosen the easier path."

The fillet knife was taken up so fast it seemed to lift into the air on its own—

Paul shielded his face as something red jettisoned from Ray Traven's throat. Pinpoints of warmth seethed on Paul's shaking hands.

The sentinel dropped the fillet knife on the table and backed off, stroking blood off his heavily muscled arm. The marrow seeds had juggled Paul's senses and there was no fooling himself out of the wild synaesthesia. The red smelling drops that came from Ray's throat had a different personality, not the liquid-soft feeling one would expect. Paul was screaming at the life slaloming down Ray's hairy arms. Ray thrashed for a minute before entering a series of twitches, then passing out; the barbarian's cut had gone too deep for him to live long.

"Are you ready?" Sandeus glided over without giving the dead man a glance. He hopped on the table, sitting in the blood as he would a wading pool. Paul noticed now that the

Archbishop's salmon undershirt had white lace frills peeking out at the neckline. Covert lingerie. His perfume curled like the lace and traveled outward to pet Paul's face—he violently shook away the notion.

The Archbishop of Midnight laughed through his nose. Then, casually he looked at one of the sentinels, who understood the silent question and hurried off, rifle clacking on plate armor. After the guard vanished down the room, Sandeus slipped two fingers into Ray's wound and pulled the flesh apart. "Per compliance with the Tomes, if you survive the initial onset of the seeds, the Archbishop of Morning must bless your new status."

The Priestess's church, from the other world…"Church of Morning? But how would we—"

"Contact someone in the Old Domain?" asked the Archbishop.

The sentinel came back with a machine resembling some type of robot scorpion. A wicked nest of insulated wires ran along the perimeter of a phonograph plate, which was affixed with a bronze arm and jeweled needle. The machine was placed carefully on the table near the body.

"Listen to music?" Paul mumbled. *Fine, fine, fine, and fine. Just be done. Get me out of here,* he thought.

"Oh, but your task is to bring Alexander. I need venom to loosen the blood cells. Hurry up now."

"Excuse me. Did you say venom?"

Sandeus Pager sighed and rolled his eyes. It looked terrifying. "Alexander is a snake, Quintana, a Western Diamondback. Didn't you notice the tank back there?"

Paul's brain walked in place...*a snake?* He peered into the shadows and started. There was a glass tank against the wall. His eyes had not picked up on it in the gloom.

In the meantime Ray's blood spilled from its vessels in loud glug-glugs—the sentinels behind Paul muttered with helicopter lips—the Diamondback rattled its tail now or the memory of the sound had returned—the lacy fringe beneath Sandeus Pager's suit groped around Paul's face like ivy and slipped down into a shocking mask and—

—brought Paul to his feet, sweating, head pounding. He said something formed as a question, though the meaning remained elusive. It must have been gibberish because the Archbishop only sat there calmly fingering Ray's wound.

Paul slipped around the monastery table. It stretched into infinity, yet the tank loomed over him and widened. He could *smell* the tank widening. Two large steps brought him closer, still conscious of finishing this and leaving here, getting the hell away from this place. Quickly. Paul flooded with adrenaline. The tank leered and snickered. Paul turned at a sound and he threw his hands to his throat to search for a knife wound. There was no wound that he felt, but his tears were so real they actually felt terrified for him.

"I'm too high for this!" he shouted back at the Archbishop. "I can't pick up any damned snake!"

"Just grab Alexander behind the neck." Sandeus tittered, looking to the guards, who chuckled from the dark smears at the back of the room.

Gears turned inside and Paul went into a different mode. It wasn't fight or flight. No, this was something bent and sharp and altogether usual for him, even high. This was kamikaze. This was suicide-bomber stock. This was *I know what happens next, but I'll do this and then it will be finished for good.* He treaded over and pulled off the tank's plastic lid. Silence chimed around him. His invincibility deactivated when he looked inside the tank. He wasn't hallucinating any longer and that was even more awful than the loop of black and orange scales below.

"Not a Western Diamondback. Alexander was brought from the Old Domain as well," said a starchy voice behind Paul. "I didn't want to scare you before."

The kindling of more laughter burned Paul's ears.

The snake moved. Its two black jelly eyes opened. Paul lifted a hand. The tail rattled alien chatter. He sucked in a breath and hoped for luck. Quickly, his hand moved into the tank. It grazed the side and his trajectory went off target. He took a slimy handful, mid-body, but he didn't wait (fuck no) and jerked the snake out like a whip. Alexander lashed out and Paul could see black fangs bare as it rounded. He dropped the snake on the floor and it shot for his ankle—sidestepping, he then lunged, caught the snake again, this time at the rattle. His shoulder turned involuntarily and he flung it onto the table. Its bright orange designs gleamed like blood and honey as it slithered away in a tight S-shape. Archbishop Pager fell forward and pinned the snake behind the neck.

Paul's heart felt punctured. Every beat hurt. "Now you're going to tell me the snake's venom isn't even fatal, aren't you?"

"No," replied the Archbishop, "I'm not going to say that at all."

Paul watched as Sandeus wrangled the snake and the sentinels hooked wires from the phonograph to Ray's exposed vocal cords. Paul hallucinated that it was he, himself that sat there with his throat opened and wires clamped to the fleshy strands inside him. Paul started to cry and his tears began to scream.

Eight

Melissa Patterson had to tread lightly now. If Paul passed the trials and ascended to Bishop, her past would follow her around, ad infinitum. Things could get tricky with all her dishonesty to Cole. Lying wasn't something that came easy for her, but she'd had good reason to make herself a twenty-five-year-old virgin; it wasn't a good idea to test the jealousy waters with Cole Szerszen. Once she saw him slap the teeth out of some young guy who'd made the mistake of asking her the time. It wasn't that he'd merely spoken to Melissa; he'd remarked how lovely her watch was and actually touched the band. Never mind that the man's flamboyant demeanor suggested he may have been gay; Cole didn't balk at any threat. At the time Melissa hadn't said much about past relationships, although he'd pressed her on the issue to the point of driving her crazy. After this blow up, it made sense to erase any old entanglements and become an innocent, awkward person—like Cole was. She especially had to keep her brief involvement with Paul Quintana close to the vest. Even if Paul fit into his plans, Cole couldn't even say his name without sneering.

With most of the Inner Circle packing belongings for this year's hunt, the archive stacks felt like a dusty leather-bound tomb: every sound heightened the chance of discovery. She and Cole silently had focused, unrelenting intercourse. He trembled and she gripped his arm tightly to show him how powerful he was. He liked that, bought into it. The chair thumped the shelves, making too-loud *thwacks* and unsettling dust in gray dervishes. She tried to close her stance, make him retreat, and then—he spilled inside her.

"Sorry," he panted, "didn't have the chance."

"That's fine," she lied. But she wasn't going to tell him she liked how it felt. She'd done enough for his ego. Pretending he hurt her the first time, that he'd broken her hymen, that there'd been blood, which she'd known would be a safe lie because his disinterest in afterglow became immediately apparent as soon as he came.

Cole pulled out a hanky from his colorless suit. The warm comfort she felt was replaced with disappointment. Weird scarring and creases flexed through the broad, toady face. Hard years of unloading church supply trucks and scuffles with other acolytes had made those creases. The scarring, however, was anyone's guess. He never spoke of it. Not to her at least. The impressions sunk into the flesh like third degree burns made by a red-hot pickax. Around his temples, around his throat, around his ears, the scars always looked fresh; she easily imagined smoke rising off them, and the spicy odor of gristle.

Cole cleaned off. When he was finished he folded the soiled linen and returned it to his pocket, not offering it to her. Melissa frowned and wiped herself with the already damp bridge of her underwear. A moment later, they were dressed and the chair pushed back against the rock wall.

"Traven should be back by now," he said.

"You know he's passed out somewhere."

"Never again." Cole shook his head. "Not trusting that lush ever again."

"How long do you think Quintana will be down there with the Archbishop?"

Cole's gray eyes glowed. "Interested in *Paul* now?"

"Don't start that, Bishop."

He pulled her close to his bank vault of a chest. "The thought of you and him—"

Her regret in that drunken event with Paul was so deep that no acting was required. Her desire for it to be untrue was mightier. Cole gently released her; he'd never be satisfied with her performance, no matter how convincing.

Cautiously, Melissa pressed on, "So, again—how long will the trials last? We've got a lot of work to do before Chaplain Cloth returns."

Cole folded his arms and his suit lifted, too small on him. He needed a new one, badly. "It took me a day before the effect of the seeds wore off. Then my garden grew. Balance of the blossoms could take most men their entire life—like with that poor dead son of a bitch Margrave, it may never happen." Cole leaned his gigantic shoulder against the wall. His face was tragically tired, and clearly not from sex. "Justin Margrave was a waste—we won't have to worry about that with Quintana. He can achieve balance in time for the Heralding."

"Will Chaplain Cloth accept someone so new?"

"If Quintana fails then he'll make me take his place. I can't go through another Heralding and still put my plans into motion though. The act pulls too much vigor from my body—it almost killed me last October."

"I remember." She hadn't known Cole that well at the time, but she recalled him being in the infirmary for several weeks. The scars might have been forged on that occasion for all she knew. The Heralding was supposed to be a brutal ritual, and Cole had done it more than many bishops before him. "It makes me wonder if all this is necessary. We're doing well enough, aren't we?"

"Sandeus Pager isn't worthy," Cole snapped and then caught the volume level of his voice. "He hasn't been out on the Hunt in more than a decade, and I don't think he's ever been to a Heralding. He's imbibing more marrow seeds every year, when the Tomes prohibit overindulgence in more than twenty sections. *Twenty*, Melissa. Sandeus Pager's an atrocity. I will be the Archbishop the Church needs."

She did have a xerox of that inventory count for the marrow seeds. Now, Melissa wished she hadn't given it to Cole. Even though it had pushed his plans forward, it also made her vulnerable. Besides which, she wouldn't have been surprised if the Archbishop hadn't really taken the seeds but merely misplaced them—the man was more absentminded than anyone she'd ever known.

"But I'm not stupid though," Cole said, "Chaplain Cloth isn't a man. He has his own ideas about the world of human beings."

She froze inside his thunderhead eyes. "What then?"

"I won't take anything for granted, not with Cloth," he replied. "I don't have that luxury this 31st with the gateway so close to opening indefinitely. Last year I felt it was closer, and had that Heart been just slightly more potent the Old Domain would have spilled into our world. That could happen this year. When the time is right I will, of course, tell Chaplain Cloth my plan and ask for his blessing."

"What if he doesn't give it? Cole, what if he tells the Archbishop?"

"I don't think he cares about church politics, just as long as he obtains the Heart of the Harvest."

"Are you sure he doesn't care though…about Sandeus, I mean?"

Cole walked out of the archives and she followed him. She waited for an answer, but he never gave one.

Nine

THE SONG OF THE MARROW SEEDS STILL RANG OPERATIC through the colonnades of Paul's mind, just a hint of pipe organ blitz and impish balladeers in both ears exchanging lyrics. *The pinkest smells like cat heaven! Heaven, like pink, smells so pink. Pink. Pink. Pink. Slippery hot pink kitty cats. Paulo, Paulo, Paulo, my Paulo.* After some consideration he discovered these voices were not conjured from psychedelic influence—the imps had been performing in his mind for a long time and only now were they free to sing openly. The singing went from tinny to soft, and he understood. They sang the same song his mother sang him at bath time.

Paul just let it be. So much time had passed watching the sentinels hook up the phonograph that he'd forgotten the context and let his mother's voice rule the hour. Far, too far, back, cowering behind a survival instinct, was the notion Paul might be in some danger. However, hallucination did not remove the corpse sitting next to him. Ray Traven sat like a gruesome doll, his skin a delicate white, a brilliant explosion under his jaw. Twenty or more wires fed into that explosion. Their little brass clamps bit onto the meaty strands as though to jumpstart him.

The setup of the phonograph might have taken five minutes or five hours. It felt like both. A great deal of time had been spent staring into Ray's phlegmy scarlet eyes and pondering not a thing at all. Sandeus could have spoken sometime during this epic journey, but Paul wouldn't have known.

Paul wagered that Alexander the snake, after being venom-robbed, had been returned to the tank. This was a lost event though—he just knew positively that it wasn't *him* who took the scaly motherfucker away. It couldn't be. He wasn't able; he could hardly sit; his body urged to reconsider his position and just slide out of his chair onto the stone floor, perhaps *into* the stone floor, and there he could sleep amongst the stars.

Archbishop Pager took out several thin stone discs from a battered blue suitcase. He reviewed the grooves of each disc with a painted fingernail. His eyes flitted over to Paul once. Those eyes—the wrongness in them—made Paul imagine Sandeus would laugh out in sadness or rip off his own skin from his nearly bald head, just to prove his love.

The stone disc dropped with less weight than its appearance suggested. The needle came down on the perimeter and a hollow note struck from an unseen alto ghost. Pink foam frothed up in Ray's ragged tracheotomy.

"Quintana! Must I ask again?"

Paul's eyebrows jacked to the limit. He'd pissed Pager off somehow but hadn't a clue how or why.

"Hand over Alexander!"

The snake? But hadn't it been put back in the tank? Where the fuck—?

Then a cold swamp smell filled his nose. He brought his head down, carefully. The weight of the moist, fat thing around his neck became heavier and he knew that four black fangs would latch into his jaw if he made a sudden movement. Paul raised a hand and the snake's arrowhead shaped skull turned. Its pitchy eyes glittered. He dropped his hand. "Who put this on me?"

Sandeus adjusted several switchboxes on the side of the phonograph. The process didn't seem to be going as smoothly as he liked because he was scowling. "You put him there, Quintana."

"But I'm high as a kite— " The room faded to sky blue now and swabs of cottony clouds streaked past with a million lavender kites hanging in the horizon like purple paper spirits. Paul didn't let this distract him; he hadn't forgotten Alexander and when he looked down the hallucination sky disintegrated in moldy blue threads.

Paul gasped as he felt the snake writhe around his neck. He couldn't touch this damned thing. The thought of touching it again made his balls tighten to little fists. "What's the point of terrifying the shit out of me?" he demanded.

The Archbishop, solemn and sincere and overflowing with intolerance at the same time, "Do you actually think I enjoy watching you suffer?"

"No, I guess not."

"Well you couldn't be more wrong. In this case however, there happens to be a practical purpose also."

Paul tried reaching for Alexander again and the black and orange head snapped and he drew his fingers away.

"If you're going to be seated as Bishop, there are things you cannot sidestep. The marrow seeds unfold with an individual's own personal blossoming. We cannot afford flinching. We need strength. You have the talent for balance but not the will yet."

"Yes but—"

"You need to understand the challenge before us, Quintana. Their names are Martin and Teresa. The same two Nomads have done the Interloper's work for nearly twenty years—keeping alive that long is unheard of. Yes, the Church of Midnight has had its successes, harvested many Hearts and weakened the gateway. But with handling the Nomads, we've failed. I have failed. Therefore, you must be tested beyond a single snake if you're to survive through the holiday. If you cannot, you will not be seated. And without my counseling or Bishop Szerszen's, the marrow seeds will drive you mad."

Paul was not far from that now. But the Priestess was everything to him. She was worth this torment. Thoughts of her drove his mother's lavender scent away—he slid his hand across his chest, carefully, toward the snake.

Paul saw the Priestess of Morning last October at the celebration.

He edged his fingers down and touched the snake's back.

Justin Margrave had said through sips of his blackberry wine, "She came through the gateway, my man. Belongs to the Church of Morning. The sacrifice opened the gateway wide enough for her to slip through from the Old Domain. Lucky for us."

Paul's fingers glided to the head—the tail rattled, the snake moved.

Gazing at the Priestess's soft body under her semitransparent gown, he'd understood why a woman that perfect had to be from another world.

He caught the neck and Alexander sunk into a ropy mass. Sandeus took the snake and pinched its jaws over the foaming blood. The foam receded with little carbonated pops. A sentinel with a burlap sack stuck Alexander inside. *Good riddance,* thought Paul.

Sandeus poised his lips over the amplifier cone. "Archbishop of Morning, do you hear me? Kennen, are you there, brother?"

The needle treaded a few minutes. Paul shifted in his seat. His mouth tasted ashy, he was hungry, he was horny, and he was soaked to the bone with fatigue. Waiting made him nervous. He didn't want to see this man go crazy, frilled at the neck and perfumed to the gills. Most of all because Paul's mind hungered to see something exactly like that happen. But the needle treaded against the tablet. Static. Nothing.

Then Raymond Traven's mouth contorted around a string of unhealthy sounds. Ray's words did not belong to a person from this world.

Ten

MARTIN STRETCHED HIS EYES TO THE SAND SHADOWS flowing over the town, a crumbling relic on old, broken Route 66. Crawling over the cactus, dominating the mounds of thirsty grasses, thrusting out from behind the foothills, something approached...what? He wanted to get out of the van and soak up the ambience to better understand it. Too bad they didn't have some trout or chicken fillets. He could take out the Coleman and grill outside, listen, wait, understand, pretend it was summer and clean blue waves were crashing at his heels.

He and Teresa had spent an involved hour practicing mantles. The game was an old one for the Nomads. She'd taught it to Martin twenty years ago. He still remembered her then, a much younger and frightened Teresa, still morose from losing her last partner, David Wessing. The game's concept was a simple distraction for them both. *Mental push-ups*. Each person formed a mantle and set it against the other, pushing it toward the opposition until someone grew too weary. They had quite a rally going, but Martin's mind wandered and he took apart his ghost-matter, reshaped it. He imagined the form of a rubber ducky. Even though mantles were invisible, Teresa sensed the reshaping and frowned as her rigid block pressed into his duckbill.

Her eyes were shut with complete seriousness. "You're going to tire yourself out. That isn't part—"

"Just because you can't shape them—" He immediately corrected his tone, knowing she'd take it as a challenge. "Look, I'm just getting bored is all."

"You haven't pushed my mantle out yet," she reminded. It was a prod at his competitive side, something she knew he did not possess but always felt determined to unearth.

"Can I wave the white flag now?"

"No."

He let go anyway. "You need your rest."

He felt her mantle slip into divisions and extinguish from this world. Teresa opened her eyes and went right to her pocket for a clove. All Martin could do was sit there, back sweating against the driver's seat, stomach gurgling for anything solid, just watching her, listening to the crackling fiberglass, smelling the cinnamon-sweet burn. How could he hate her so much and love her so much at the same time? He'd treated her so poorly these last few months. There'd been no other way to deal with her self-immolation. *But come on,* he thought, *pushing someone away because it's easier than losing them?* Martin had to admit it was childish distancing, at best. He had no delusions about his tactics. Clove after clove though, Teresa didn't care about breaking his heart, so why should he tend to hers? The thought was sour in his mind—*Because she's dying, you asshole.*

But should he apologize for her mistake?

Not like this and not now; Teresa understood his thinking probably better than he did himself and it would do him no good. He always got snippy closer to the Day of Opening. Morale had definitely slipped since meeting that buxom girl and the lumberjack bartender. Even though he couldn't explain it, Martin got the impression they weren't supposed to meet those two, at least not on that day. Their flat tire might not have even been part of destiny. It wouldn't have surprised him. On the unpredictable nomadic path, Martin had learned that anything and everything went. But if in the bar there'd been some kind of interference, who was responsible? Around the 31st things could go wonky, and time and space could be jimmied—not changed, just toyed with. Spotting trouble had become a sixth sense for Martin, and those two in the bar got the sirens blaring for sure.

There was another thing wrong though. Something, or some person, had perished somewhere close. Not like death wasn't constantly happening everywhere anyway, but what Martin sensed wasn't flesh and bone and wasn't literally dying. This death, unraveling over the hills and afar, was not earthbound; he got this feeling every October. His kidneys twisted like a doorknob that would open the way to the answer.

Never had though.

"The Messenger's close," Teresa told him quietly, bands of sweet smoke lifting around her face.

Until now.

Sam Cooke's voice was joyful through the sketchy speakers. Another Saturday night, and Sam ain't got *nobody*. It was actually Friday night, but the song still had forlorn poignancy. Even in the company of another, loneliness happened on the road sometimes, a sucker punch to the aorta. He and Teresa had never really had any private space of their own and so they learned to tune out each other's existence.

Then there were times when each other's presence was too well known. Like today. That whole day Martin spent sitting in the van with Teresa, eating chip shrapnel from a greasy bag, taking walks out in a desert as empty as his mind, or listening to the radio until it got too annoying. Road-weary madness seeped into his brain and suddenly his voice became hers and hers his. His loathing of her sickness turned into self-loathing, which spawned new resentment when he thought about their last trip to the doctor.

Teresa brushed her nails clean and went to filing the other hand. Martin didn't think it had hit her until the hospital. She probably wouldn't be around this time next year. She might die in a motel room, surrounded by bloody paper tissues, maybe some wilted get-well flowers from Martin. He could already envision himself softly crying over her, and feel the tears burn hot in his eyes. The lump in her lung would be a melon-sized bomb by then. Maybe a lung rupture would kill her or maybe something messier and less dignified would. How would Martin deal? Would the Messenger give him another partner, like what happened with Teresa when David was killed?

The silent scratching of the nail file pissed him off and she sensed his anxiety right away. "We haven't organized the weapon cache for a while," she suggested.

"You go right ahead. It's already an anal compulsive's wet dream."

She glanced over. "Some of the labels are peeling off."

"I'll just read the name on the box of ammo, thank you very much. And I know the difference between an M-1000 and a smoke grenade."

"You're just going to get hemorrhoids sitting there. Get up and do something, Martin."

"Don't order me around."

Teresa slapped her file on the dash and burst out laughing. "I'm sorry," she managed. He glared. "I don't mean to laugh. You're just hypersensitive."

It was a puzzle for him sometimes, which was more difficult: having only one partner to protect the Heart of the Harvest, or to be bound to that one person rather than taking on the Church on his own. It was completely a no win deal.

"I've had nothing but potato chips and beer. I'm about to shish kabob a kangaroo rat with some cactus chunks."

"We've eaten worse."

He thought about this and added, "And you've had nothing but cloves. I haven't even seen you drink a glass of water."

"I'm not thirsty."

"Teresa— "

"Drop it, Martin."

"Teresa— "

"*Drop it.*"

He fell back against his seat and stared at the hanging fabric on the roof of the van. It looked like the overhead of a circus canopy—one lousy circus at that. "It's just— " he began, appearing uncertain as to why he even bothered. "Can't you ever let me help?"

"I told you to check the weapon cache."

He sat up straight. "I may be twelve years younger, but I know enough to know what's good for you. I ain't a spring duck—or chicken, whatever."

"If this is about eating that seaweed shit again, I don't know how many times I need to tell you that I don't believe in that Eastern stuff."

"Fine, but can't you give me some credit? Can't you trust

me and try new things? For me?"

He could tell she wanted another clove right then and was thinking hard about lighting one up. She was wise enough to know it would only make things worse.

"Let me tell you something," he said, trying to soften his tone, "I remember one morning my father went to kiss my mother goodbye before going to the station. Shit, it's been so long the memory seems to belong to someone else—but he bends down, puts his lips on hers and accidentally steps on her foot. She screams. *Loud.* So you know what my father does?"

Teresa shook her head.

"He went to his patrol car all red faced and nostrils flaring. He was pissed off like he was the one who had his metatarsals crushed."

"Why though?"

"It was like he had suddenly confirmed something about my mother. That was *his* kiss and it didn't blow her away like it should have, maybe like it did when she was younger. She should have still enjoyed the kiss, even through the pain. She didn't though. She decided to scream in his face."

"But he stepped on her toes."

"He didn't speak to her for three days—he never said sorry either."

"What a jerk."

"But she's the one who really messed up. Even hopping around with a taped-up foot and crutches, she couldn't see something extremely obvious. She refused to believe my father had done anything wrong—she even told me he apologized when I knew damn well he didn't. My mother didn't want anybody to think she was unhappy. Because being wrong would mean the pain was a truly real thing. And that's what you're doing too Teresa. You're pretending nothing's wrong when it suits you, and you despair the rest of the time."

"Nice psychoanalysis."

He closed his eyes. "Do whatever then, smoke yourself silly," he whispered. "With everything else we go through every year, I'm so through with this shit."

"Let's concentrate on the matter at hand," Teresa said, straightening in her seat. "Somewhere out there a new Heart waits for us. We have to do it right this year. Cloth can't take another one—if he does, that gateway is getting a whole lot larger. I think that's a bigger deal than one person's bad habit. Don't you think?"

Martin didn't answer, just kept his eyes closed, practiced breathing at first, and then pretended to be dead.

Teresa didn't deserve Martin sometimes. She hadn't deserved David either, for that matter. So many years passed where she couldn't bring herself to even think about David. Lately it felt like he was standing before her with his cool bright smile, smelling like spicy incense with a scandalous electric look in his eyes. David Wessing had taught her everything she knew about being a Nomad, made her who she was. There was no blaming him for her faults though. How could she? David's last word had been a screaming plea that went unanswered. It echoed in her heart still.

She knew how to push the horrible memory away—it was simple. Just think about the job ahead. It had actually been easier right after David died. She focused only on Martin; they went to see the Messenger's small, special operations group: Ramson CuVek, Bill Masters, Li Chu, and Robin Escal. They worked Martin down to the core and some of the mentors, self defense mentor CuVek especially, hadn't taken it much easier on her. The mentors knew what was at stake and what they were up against. They had all once lived in the Old Domain, after all. The only way to help was to train them well.

A year had passed before she could get close to Martin. Under a strict time constraint, Bill Masters had tasked them to set eleven mantles and something like sixteen C4 charges around an abandoned metal finishing plant. With Martin backing her, they passed the test, even with a time limit of twenty-three minutes. They even found time to have a first kiss in the slanting shadows beneath some rusty scaffolding.

The first encounter had been intense and welcome, but she hadn't known then if she could love Martin the same way she'd loved David. Martin had kept her hope alive through difficult times. Then one day she'd gone to pick up road supplies but got halfway before remembering her wallet—back at the motel she found Martin with some woman. A waitress, she wagered, from the Denny's uniform spilling over a chair.

That was a long time ago. Now Martin wouldn't seek anyone else—that brand of carelessness wasn't in him any longer. She wasn't sure if that was a good thing. Breaking some emotional ties might make this failing thing between them easier to watch disintegrate. That was what her heart told her, despite the endless miles stacked against the notion.

She had slept on and off all day and now that it was pitch-black her body bounded with energy. She considered building a modest mantle tent around the van. Something freezing dripped over her neural receptors and she shook away the idea. She was happy not being exhausted for a change.

She ducked into the back of the van and took up a *Black*

Belt magazine Martin had bought her a few months ago as a joke. Lying down on the full size mattress, she could still see his shape lounging in the front. Boredom had gotten the best of them. Reading, she tittered at a side panel featuring a man in a camouflage gi, hammer-kicking a wood board. The first few paragraphs were actually intriguing, if technically flawed, but then any true content fell away as the writer began to recount a past tournament in New York. Teresa's chest cinched with pain anyway and her stomach bubbled with hunger. Having nothing else to keep her mind occupied, she'd be coughing soon and probably wake Martin up.

She needed to write a will for him. It would be the first step in accepting this with a modicum of dignity. Dying was easy for Teresa. Leaving the pain behind for someone else wasn't. David had done it to her and now she'd do it to Martin—and just like with David, there'd be nothing left behind, no money, no property, no assets of any kind. Just a body, and the indelicate task of disposal.

A Sam Cooke song flowered in her ears, a gospel ditty, "Hem Of His Garment."

If I touch it, I'll be healed...

Something moved outside the van.

Her body shifted. She pulled Martin's M1911 from under the mattress. It felt good and heavy with singular purpose. Flicking off the safety, she glanced back. Martin still slept. *Take it slow,* she thought. *Calm. It could be a coyote.*

Or black suits.

She edged sideways. Her legs trembled as she hunkered down, gun clasped in both hands. She stopped. The cold desert night seeped in through the sides of the doors. There was another long, scraping sound—a claw over glass.

Now came a tapping. The world rocked. Teresa wanted control back, just to tell herself this was her nerves, but there seemed to be no end in sight. She brought her gaze over the back window, through the pane. A tumbleweed edged along the bumper, scraping it with a sound like steel on steel.

Martin came awake and twisted out of his seat. She felt him summon a mantle, but she shook her head and signaled all clear. With a slow unfolding of her arm, she dropped the gun down on her hip and moved the safety into place with her thumb.

Martin blew some air out and released his mantle. He slumped against the threshold. "You okay?"

"I'm so hungry I think I'm getting the jitters."

He nodded groggily. "We don't know when the next letter will arrive."

"Or if there will be money," she added.

"He gives us some every year."

"Maybe this time's different. Did you feel the displacement at the bar?"

He slowly nodded, although it seemed he didn't want to admit this for the sake of it being true. "It probably has nothing to do with the Messenger."

It started to rain outside.

"We can't go on this way. What if the letter doesn't come until the 30th? Do we starve until then?"

Martin closed his eyes, trying to fall back to sleep. "We've used the mantles to steal before. It's all right. Nobody's going to hell."

"Too much exposure, I think we need to make a stop in Flagstaff."

His eyes opened and his face colored now. "That's not on the way."

"I haven't seen Mom and Dad in *thirty* years, Martin. They'll give us money when they see how badly off we are. Besides, they need to know about what's happening to me. You said I should own up. Well, here you are."

"What the hell are you talking about? There's no time Teresa. Your parents might not even be alive anymore. And the Messenger said we couldn't go back— "

She hit the lever and the back doors popped open. The tumbleweed hopped into the dark brown emptiness. Rain snapped loudly against the pavement. She lit a clove anyway and sucked in. In the rain, the smoke struggled for shape. Her lungs suddenly burned with relish.

"The Messenger has never missed a letter yet," said Martin, following.

A mouthful of smoke fell out and stung her eyes.

"Is this really about telling them the truth?" he persisted. "Be honest with me, goddamn it. We don't have the time to piss away."

The smoke started to hurt. She smashed the half-smoked clove under her tennis shoe. He watched her a long time, seeming unsure how to proceed. The rain stopped as suddenly as it had begun. Moonlight bent over the glistening road and made everything look bathed in tar. Martin finally dropped outside and took her waist, pulled her close. His heart thumped quickly underneath his T-shirt. She laced her fingers around his puka shell necklace and toyed with one shell for a few moments, then rested her face on his warm chest.

"We'll go," he told her.

Eleven

PAUL QUINTANA REFLECTED ON THE RECENT PAST, AND not fondly. It was a change from dwelling on the nightmare of his distant past: the smell of his mother, her bright eyes when he flipped the lamp on, the sound of her startled cry, the heat in her skin from the pleasure she thought her boyfriend Freddy had given her—that whole sequence of events was a hateful ambrosia Paul drank daily. But today he couldn't taste it; things had been reconfigured and he couldn't decide if that was good or not.

He thought perhaps it wasn't black and white. Or orange.

The rectory sentinels had draped him over a granite coffin. Paul wagered it belonged to some old witch who wrote a Tome or two in her day. The catacombs beneath Mojave chapel had the distinction of housing thousands of Church members, all in hand sculpted tombs. The brisk winds from lower corridors blew through them in wild trajectories, sounding like wraiths maiming each other.

Paul's eyes flicked to turning, bleeding shapes that wound around helixes of darkness. The smell of liquefying meat, a death-reminder smell, hovered around him. If the power of the marrow seeds did not wear thin soon, his heart would not last against the intensity.

You know why we're here? sang a dissident chorus. *Don't you?*

The black feast.

"Hello?" he cried into empty space.

The song crept back into his ears, *Everyone knows why we're here. Thanksgiving to the black feast.*

A fetid thing leaned over him now and extended what looked like a set of dangling keys. As they poked through the darkness, closer to the soft surface of his eyes, he distinguished bladed fingernails atop dark orange fingers. Paul turned away. His jaw chilled against the stone coffin. The claw tips grazed his scalp and down his neck before lifting. Instinctively, he pulled his knees up to his chest and clutched them there.

Thanksgiving to the black feast.

The food. The salt of old times.

Thanksgiving to the bleeding feast.

He tried to disregard the chorus. In the morning he would be alive and well, maybe resting among cadavers but still breathing air and living and needing. This torment was no longer for the mother he'd fooled in the soft, wet darkness. This torment was a purer kind. He didn't have to pretend he was someone else with the Priestess of Morning. She could change him. He knew she could.

Paul's mind ripped him backwards, back to the meeting with the Archbishop. Both Archbishops…

Raymond Traven's dead lips were syncing with a man's from the Old Domain.

"We have a new Bishop, brother," the Archbishop of Midnight said into the cone.

The Archbishop from the other world gasped with delight. "Another Bishop, already brother? Slippery business, so, so slippery there. I smell red."

"His name is Paul Quintana."

Raymond's lips bubbled with each syllable and his dead eyes moved to Paul. "Welcome Bishop. The Church of Morning recognizes you." The eyes went back to Sandeus Pager. "Have you dispersed the seeds amongst any others?"

Sandeus took a moment and then said, "The other contingencies haven't any members worthy of accepting their wisdom, brother."

Raymond's eyes went gray. A string of bloody snot coursed from his nose and swung into the crook of his mouth. "You must prepare, brother. Chaplain Cloth is already on his way."

Sandeus's posture changed. "But...it's not yet the 31st."

"The world has changed. The seasons have little power to hold him any longer. The gateway is ready to burst wide and the pillars are at the ready. Give thanksgiving to the blood! Drink it from the brain carafe. Drink and drink, brother. The Tomes are read as such. This is our time. The Time of Opening. The Time of Arrival. The time of Tomes with wet script. Thanksgiving to it all."

Paul shot up as the memory left him. The snorts and grizzly chuckles slid down his mind in oily black clots.

A door opened then and a shimmering red glow of torchlight wiggled into the grooves of the distant coffins, illuminating the runes scrawled into stone. Paul's eyelashes fluttered. The symbols began to make sense, not that he ever learned their complexities, but there were thousands of other little brains growing in his lungs, and *they* understood the runes—they understood much about the Churches of Midnight and Morning—and the Church Eternal, the house of Chaplain Cloth.

The marrow seeds grew inside his lungs (slippery black blossoms sprung forth among others boiling orange in color). Paul became sidetracked with the horrible growth, which amplified in a frenzy. He remembered a door in the catacomb opening. Footsteps echoed off the cavernous planes. He thrashed like a snared rabbit and his bladder quivered uneasily.

Black feast: let us taste the night.

Orange feast: let us taste the dawn.

Everlasting: let us taste it all!

A real voice floated into him and he clenched the sides of the coffin. He wasn't bound, and though he had full knowledge of this, his other brains would not allow him to slip off the side, gain his feet and run like hell. He was staying. The marrow blossoms said to remain and he would.

Paul, we'll set your soul out to rot and slip apart. Paul, when it's gone she will be the only thing.

"Who are you?" The bustling wind through the tomb stopped. Silence drove a spike of doubt through him. Was the damage from the seeds permanent? Would this never end? "This is bullshit! *Who are you?*"

A hand caught his sweaty, cold, ruined suit. Snaps of light danced across his vision. His head must have struck the stone.

"You know who I am."

"Cole?" Paul sighed with relief. The ugly visage bobbed above him.

"How are things, Paul?"

Two thick fingers pressed down on Paul's lips before he could yell something caustic. After a moment Cole slid his fingers off and leaned against an adjacent coffin.

"They killed Traven," said Paul.

"Pricks, I'll have someone call Val." Cole sniffed, as though idle conversation had already worn on him.

"What the hell are those seeds?"

"The blossoms are now a part of you, like a thousand new organs. You've been blessed."

"How long do they last?" Paul's muscles were still confused by general numbness and the retardation of nerve impulses. "Do the blossoms make us...like the Nomads?"

The Bishop scratched his scarred jaw. "The Nomads have the blood of the Old Domain in their veins. Marrow seeds open doors for us the Nomads already had open at birth. Theirs is a power wasted and unappreciated—the Nomads cannot do what we do, nor can we possess their ability. We are converse to them. Only the Chaplain has full control of the Old Domain's power. I thought you read the Tomes of Eternal Harvest, Quintana."

"Don't chastise me! I've got *voices* singing in my mind!"

Cole's eyes ignited. It startled Paul because there was no light to make them well up with gold, and they managed not only to conjure the sparkling hue but to hold it. "*The children have already called to you?*"

"Who?"

"You have a natural connection. This is better than I could have hoped for." Cole tasted something in the air and savored it for several moments. The flavor almost put him into a trance. "Have you any idea what happens every 31st?"

"The Heralding, the Hunt and the Harvest."

"Yes, you know the simple version, the child's story. You know that Chaplain Cloth comes to visit once a year with his children, to hunt and kill someone *special*, but you have no clue as to the significance of the act itself. Every time the Nomads fail to protect the Heart, like last year, things move more quickly—that gateway to the Old Domain may be large enough now to open permanently. Finding this year's Heart is essential to our future. And I'm not just talking about the Church of Midnight. I'm talking about you and me, Paul. Our futures. So you need to listen."

"Whatever you say, Bishop."

Paul's throat constricted under Cole's forearm and everything lapsed into pain and suffocation. "I have no time for flippancy."

Paul gulped for air.

"Will you backtalk to the future Archbishop of Midnight. Will you?"

He couldn't shake his head, but Paul did so with his eyes. Cole released him and he gagged as his Adam's apple righted itself.

"Just keep listening to the children's call and we will be fine at the Heralding. Take this obligation seriously and you'll get your Priestess."

Paul's voice was burning and hoarse. "I don't know what you mean."

Cole drifted back and the darkness ate his hulking form. "After the Heralding, everything will make sense. Just keep listening to Cloth's children."

Paul waited in the dark, with the cold and with the ghosts, hoping for morning. Everything drained from his old life and spilled into his new life. When things had finally been righted he opened himself up again. Listened for the call.

October 27th

Twelve

SUNSHINE AND MORNING, TWO OF MARTIN'S FAVORITES. All he needed was some fair-trade coffee and he'd despair through this big mistake just fine. After Teresa went to sleep last night he tossed and turned a little. She went right to sleep, probably since her demons had poured out and the burden of containing them had left. Martin, on the other hand, had to fight the urge to wake her up every minute and throttle some sense into her about this Flagstaff visit.

This morning he woke and felt no better. He pulled out a medical book to delve into the mysteries of the lungs' pleural cavity. He'd been reading these same two books for a few months now, but Teresa couldn't have named them if you asked her. She rarely took notice of his books; she read magazines and romance novels and he read an occasional DC comic book chased by surgical manuals and acupressure guides. *The Merck Manual of Diagnosis and Therapy* and *Cancer Treatment: Complimentary and Alternative Medicine*, a nice mingling of Western and Eastern. If he actually got Teresa to a hospital, no glassy-eyed doctor was letting his Teresa die, not out of indifference. Not on Martin's watch.

After they haggled with the tire shop to take a bad check, they got back on the road. His stomach was past the point of needy, angry, snarling, twisting ache. Now the organ was cold-silent like an ocean mine ready to detonate. He released his eyes from the road for a minute. Teresa sat beside him with little indication of the same painful hunger, even if the truth surfaced in her fading skin and crabby circles around her eyes.

"We could try that credit card again."

Her women's magazine had her fixated. She swept a page to the side and smoothed it down. "The canceled one?"

"I thought that identity was still clean."

"The card-holder is in collections. We broke our ties with that one back in Duluth, remember?"

"Are you positive the card no longer works?" he asked.

"You'd have to swipe all four pieces."

"You cut it up? Do you still have the pieces?"

"Hold down your desperation, kid. Do you really want the law on us again?"

"Do you really want me to answer a rhetorical question?" asked Martin, almost to himself.

Teresa took out a fresh box of cloves from her shirt pocket.

He persisted. "We don't even have money for another tank of gas—this is cutting it close."

She shook free a black stick and regarded it with dreary impatience. The expression made her look well beyond fifty.

Martin laughed in dismissal. "We're losing our touch. We should have talked Señor Swindle into a better deal—no way was that tire eighty bucks. It hardly looks better than the one that blew out."

"He took the check, you could give him that. We're lucky they had a tire for this hunk of crap."

"This hunk of burning nostalgia, is what you mean."

"You're going to miss the exit."

She was right. Martin cranked the steering wheel right and cut off a fluorescent lime jeep that promptly barked with its horn. The van hitched at the sudden redirection and Martin prayed the new tire would prove worthy, just like this detour.

A few years ago they'd gotten adventurous and drove through Teresa's parents' neighborhood in Flagstaff. It wasn't the first time they had made a drive-by visit and Martin figured it was enough for Teresa to see whether her father's Cadillac was still parked sideways in the driveway or that her mother's rose bushes remained trimmed. He'd spent enough time with Teresa to realize that visits here were never easy for her; even though she could stare something daunting directly in the eye on Halloween, Martin often sensed the silent aftershocks of her missed youth on trips to this neighborhood. She'd wanted to knock on their door for some time now.

This time, as Martin wheeled the van around every suburban turn, the weight of that last visit must have stymied her courage. Teresa looked absolutely pale with the prospect of meeting her parents again. He couldn't imagine their roles reversed. He was scared to death for her. If you told him his family was just ten feet away, he'd have probably run in the opposite direction and kept running until his legs gave out. Not that he hated them or anything, just that he wasn't *supposed* to see them ever again.

And that must have been the feeling in the air this morning. Something heavy pushed down on the Santa Fe tiled roofs and crisp greens lawns. The homes slowly resembled terracotta monsters with wide-hinged jaws. Maybe the rosebushes would be dead. Or the Cadillac would be under a greasy tarp. How would Teresa react to seeing something like that? They were breaking the Messenger's fundamental ground rules: *"No permanent contacts. No family. No friends. You must keep moving. Always moving."*

He noticed Teresa sat straighter. Her fulsome almond hair had become slightly oily without showering, but for the most part she scrubbed up nicely in the auto shop bathroom. She saw him looking and said, "My mother was always anal about appearances. How do I look?"

"No makeup?"

She poked his shoulder sharply with two fingers. "Ass."

"You look awesome," he said.

"You should think about seeing your parents too, while we're on this coast," she said.

"They'll be the same, which means they won't appreciate the visit."

He could tell Teresa was prepared to argue, but they pulled alongside the humble mission-styled home, which was older than the others on the block. The house had finer tiling and stucco, and the lawn looked freshly mown. Sunrays bent off the blue shell of a Cadillac sitting in the driveway and the rosebushes had reached full bloom. Martin glanced over. His partner's face had become stricken at the sight of them.

Teresa waited before the old cedar door, a step from a straw welcome mat with pumpkins and ghosts. With Martin standing close behind, she glanced to a sun faded cardboard witch peering through the leaded-glass window. These tired decorations were things for other people, for acquaintances, for trick o' treaters, not for the people who lived in this house. Her parents would have skipped this holiday completely if they had the choice, and Teresa could scarcely blame them.

"Are you going to knock?" Martin asked her.

She rapped the door so softly she doubted her knuckles had made contact.

"For crying out loud." Martin slammed the knocker three times against its bronze plate. A door shut somewhere inside and Teresa took a step back.

"It's going to be fine." He took her by the arm.

She said, "Maybe this was stupid. We could go begging for change— "

The door opened.

Teresa couldn't deny this woman was her mother. This woman was an older Teresa with flowing gunmetal hair, eyes set sharper and owl-like, no possibility for humor. Had her mother been born to this world, her features may have been described as Hispanic, but no, the soft nose and subtle cheekbones were in an exotic class of their own.

"Here to serve the papers?" Her voice was in need of oiling though.

"Are you Mrs. Abigail Celeste?" Teresa asked.

The door closed an inch. "Should be."

Teresa tried a smile. "I'm your daughter, Teresa."

"My daughter was kidnapped when she was a teenager."

"There's no reason to put on an act. You knew where I was going that day, Mom. We were all together when I left. Why not let us in for a minute, so we can talk?"

Teresa waited a moment, but the old woman looked frozen. "Abigail," said Teresa, "I'd like to come in awhile. We had nowhere else to turn. There are a few things we need to discuss before we get back on the road."

Abigail's resolve drained from her face. "You weren't supposed to come back. *Ever.*"

"Things have changed, you see— "

"So I see. You're sheet white. You look bad, not just older." The woman appraised her with eyes that could blanch the skin off an apple. Then she turned on Martin. "And who is this? He's not the black one you left with before."

"David passed away about eighteen years back," she said softly.

Abigail's cruel eyes boiled, but Teresa bulldozed her way inside. The old lady shuffled away, astonished, as Martin followed with an apologetic grin.

"I should call the cops," Abigail pointed out, slamming the door.

"You won't call anyone," answered Teresa. She changed the subject. "I see the Caddy still gets waxed every week."

"I have an immigrant kid do that."

"Dad's not—?"

She sniggered. "He's not dead. Just gone."

"Is he coming back soon?"

"To hell with him. Just tell me what you need so you can be on your way."

Teresa brought up two hard coughs into her fist and swallowed down the pain. "He's my father—this was my only chance to see him again."

"Oh fine and dandy, you just want me to open up my business to a complete stranger, is that it?"

"I'm *not* a stranger," Teresa shot back. Martin stiffened at her side.

"Do you want to know how he left me? It's a good story. I tell everybody. It just amazes the hell out of me for some reason." An angry light flickered behind her eyes. Abigail took two steps closer to them and they both went rigid. "I was at the table with a mouthful of pancakes. I couldn't even answer the son of a bitch. Like he planned it that way! Serves me right I guess, my blood sugar and all. I hadn't even finished swallowing before the front door shut. Talk about a quick getaway."

"Why did he go?"

Abigail didn't have any interest in the question. "The wetback kid also takes a Polaroid of the car to send to your father. I write threats at the bottom about rubbing bird shit into the paint with some brillo pads, but it doesn't faze him like it might once have. Maybe one of these days I'll get the nerve to just set the thing on fire. That'll be a nice shot. I think I'll do it landscape." She crossed her arms over her sheep pajamas. Something hit Teresa then. "You didn't recognize me. You thought we were here serving divorce papers?"

"Yeah," her mother replied blithely. "Bastard's in Texas, went to some redheaded whore who could stomach his bullshit, not to mention his retirement check and real estate."

"Dad's into real estate?"

"Interested are you? Did you come here to learn about him? Why don't I send you to the source? I can give you his address. Then you can leave me to my crossword puzzles."

"We're actually here for money," Martin cut in. "I'd like to say we'd pay you back, but it would be a lie."

"Oh, the truth! How wonderful it is to hear," the old woman sang.

Teresa shook her head. "Aren't you happy to see me? It's nice to see you."

Martin smirked but said nothing.

Abigail hitched over to a small kitchen area and sat at a round table where a bottle of butterscotch syrup and a half-eaten breakfast rested. The bacon looked cold and deformed. Teresa and Martin grabbed a pair of uncomfortable wrought iron stools at the bar. Abigail lifted a coffee mug with a smiling duck painted on the side.

"Martin likes coffee," Teresa hinted.

"That so?"

Martin shrugged.

"Well, there's a Starbucks down the street. Have at it."

Teresa's eyes narrowed. "What are you mad at? That Dad left? Or that I did? I came here to tell you that I'm sick. I don't have much time left—this might be our last chance for words."

"I thought you were here for money."

"We are," Martin assured. "We don't have a penny. We haven't eaten, and there are important matters headed our way."

Teresa's throat went dry. "I just wanted to say that over these years I thought about you and Dad all the time. I missed you. I've been here a few times before, but I was too afraid to come inside. I wondered—I sometimes wondered what my life would have been if the Messenger hadn't chosen me."

"Well I never wanted to remember you, Teresa." The woman winced, obviously not prepared to say something so acerbic. "What would be the reason? The letter told me I would never see you again. The Messenger doesn't lie. And here you are, after all this time, back to beg for dollars."

"The letter said you *shouldn't* ever see me again. Do you remember that you told me to come back if I needed help?"

"Did I say that? Well if I did, I was wrong. It's best not

to finagle different meanings from the Messenger's letters. His word's usually plain."

"You think the Messenger's a man?" asked Martin. He was always interested in this subject.

"Of course he is," Abigail replied. "He's obviously got a heart the size of a cherry pit. I don't need any other proof."

Tears waded in Abigail's bloodshot eyes while the old woman sipped some more coffee. Teresa looked away. Her voice sounded dry, but her words felt stronger than intended. "What does life mean without family?"

Abigail raised her thin eyebrows. "Family? *Family* did you say? Families go away. Our situation is not as unique as you want to believe. When you were a little girl I never told you anything about my life because I didn't want to scare you. See, I lived in the Old Domain until I was seventeen, with six brothers and eight sisters, a mother and father. I would have *died* to protect every last one of them. Now I can barely remember their names, but I remember feeling my loyalty.

"So the Messenger sent word about temporary gateways, kept secret from the Church. The letter arrived a day after my womanhood trials. I was to be a concubine to the Church of Morning if I didn't leave as soon as possible. My oldest brother had to invoke the gateway and I believe it twisted his body in such a way that he probably died shortly after I came here.

"But something had to be done. Hearts were dying every year. The harvests were sickeningly effective back then. Hell, back then the Nomads were born earthbound without your power. The Nomads of my time had only their wits to survive on and it wasn't enough to avoid Chaplain Cloth and his children. My destiny and those of many others were sealed. Do you think it was easy? Hardly. But I said goodbye to my family at almost the same age you did. Because I had to, Teresa."

Abigail picked up a remote control and a flipped on a small TV on the kitchen counter to a game show. She tapped the volume down a little before dropping the remote next to her plate.

"Your father had already lived in Arizona for eleven years when I crossed over. He remembers less of our birthplace, which has caused him to be foolishly idealistic. He remembers only good things about that place, none of which were actually *good,* but he recalls them that way. I realize I escaped something terrible. I'm happy here, and yet, here I'm indentured to seclusion."

"Would you ever go back?" asked Martin, not hiding his curiosity.

"I've tasted nightfire and one taste is enough. This world has its own insanities, but you can avoid them more easily." Her gray gaze wandered. "I miss certain things though. The quiet of the Onyx wilderness, the splendor of the Castle of Trees, the Olathu Ocean stretching off into the night. Every day of my youth it seemed I peered into the silver wells to pick jellyroot from the sides, sometimes until my fingers bled. I won't see such things ever again…although I will dream. And then one day it won't matter; I'll lay face-first in a pancake, or trip over a brick in my rose garden—I'll die doing the same things I've done for the past fifty years."

"You have an interesting way of—"

"Putting things?" Abigail finished and nodded. "Of course I do. What else do I have, other than levity? Now, if you don't mind, I'd like to get on with my puzzles and there's a show on."

Teresa slowly stood from her stool. Martin rose to join her. "We won't bother you any further," she said, and meant every word.

Abigail slid a wallet off the counter and with two fingers forked a collection of twenties from inside, then a yellow business card. Her withered hand held out the offering. Teresa didn't budge, but Martin cheerfully took what they'd come for and nodded his thanks.

"Look your father up when you get the chance. I'm sure he would enjoy seeing you."

Teresa glanced away and concentrated on keeping her eyes bone dry. "I would…but this was my last chance to say goodbye."

"That's what you think." Abigail huffed. "I thought we already had our last goodbye."

"I didn't have cancer then."

Martin stiffened at the word, but Abigail's frostiness did not thaw. "Try to see him. I think your father will do a sight better at showing how much he's missed you. I'm fairly sure of that."

Teresa had once imagined a long awaited embrace, but she only said, "Maybe we'll meet again on the other side of here and there."

"I wonder what that would be like?" Abigail turned her face down for a deep sip of coffee.

They were gone when she came back up.

Thirteen

Everything was stone to Cole. With Paul Quintana softly snoring in the back of the limousine and Melissa driving in her early morning fugue state, Cole had time to meditate on the liquor stores whipping past, followed by the check cashing convenience stores, the carnicería meat markets, the dollar stores. There were only abandoned buildings where they were going. Abandoned buildings with abandoned people and abandoned pride—abandoned spirit. Cole knew his job would be to find a core and blow life into it, make it grow. The new Church of Midnight would make this world vital again. He was worthy of this challenge. It was his vision. In the end, foremost, he would have Melissa at his side.

He looked over at her. She drove with two fingers on the wheel and her elbow poised on the driver's door. In the morning Cole avoided trying to get a word out of her until eleven o'clock and even then she could be bitter as all hell if she wasn't caffeinated. Cole had only been with acolytes before her, all of them begging to be given their suits and secured in the Inner Circle. He'd always planned to cut those women loose eventually. There hadn't been anything there. Melissa was different, but he still wondered what her intentions were. If she didn't love him, if she was like the others, she was the best actress of the lot. Melissa claimed to be a virgin, and made love like a virgin their first time. It wasn't impossible. But there'd been rumors about her and Paul Quintana.

Cole ripped that thought out of his head. He glanced over his shoulder to the man in the back seat who slept with his mouth wide open. Cole could sympathize with him a little. He'd rather stomp a baby to death than endure another series of marrow seed hallucinations—from ten years ago Cole still remembered his own trial too clearly, and although he'd since trained his mind, the nightmares rang true from time to time.

Paul recovered quicker than Cole had and he immediately learned the mental exercises. The exertion had put Paul to sleep and there were lessons yet to be administered, but for Cole, things were looking up. Quintana would perform the Heralding. The children already called to him—he was a sure thing. Justin Margrave couldn't do half as much after months of practicing. Still, the Heralding could kill Paul. Live or die, both outcomes would accomplish what Cole had to get done. With Paul's fortitude, it would *work*. This morning he had to prove himself, of course.

Melissa stopped along the curb. There was something in her bookish face, a manner shadowed in her mousy hair, a light reflecting off her horn-rimmed spectacles. "This is the place? Sure you don't want me to call some people in? It's easy enough to get a few acolytes down here."

"I don't need acolytes," he said, turning in his seat. "I have sleeping beauty here. Hey, Quintana! Wake up!"

Paul opened a blood shot eye and pushed up with one arm. "Time is it?"

"Time to get a move on," said Cole. He stripped off his seatbelt. "You're going to follow my lead. Remember what I showed you earlier."

Paul rubbed his eyes. "Why are we here, again?"

Cole got out of the limo and ducked down a moment to wink at Melissa. She mustered a smile and he closed the door. Paul slid out of the back. His designer suit was mangled. Cole walked down an alley between a chain link fence and a thrashed tenement. Paul followed in step with him.

"This chapel reported a member gone missing," Cole told him. "They believe the man is this year's vessel for Chaplain Cloth."

"Does Cloth surface this early?"

"Not usually, but we're not taking their word on it either. This chapel in particular has sold information to the Nomads in the past. Nobody could prove it or they'd all be put out, but I have my suspicions about whether this latest news is a lure for more handouts. It's their style and things could get heated."

"Well it's an honor to be at your side, Bishop."

Cole couldn't tell if Paul was being a smartass. He stopped at a decaying door and knocked two times. "You don't have to call me Bishop anymore."

"Splendid." Paul pinched between his eyes and opened them wider, looking to wake himself up. He patted his jacket and his face went ashen. "Where's—?"

"I left our pieces with Melissa."

"What in the hell?"

Cole glared at him. "If we are worthy to the Church, we can stand on our own."

"Are you kidding me? How stupid is that? Half of these chapels aren't even legitimate."

"Quintana," Cole sighed. "We never stop testing ourselves. Always strong—"

The door cracked open and a Glock nuzzled its way through. "You Inner Circle?"

"And then some," Paul spoke confidently. "Bishop Szerszen and Bishop Quintana."

"Here for the *word*?"

Cole nodded and the door opened wider. The man shoved his gun into the back of his baggy jeans and offered a hand. "Brother Hector. Nice to meet you two."

They both shook hands. Dry red spiders of marijuana cooked in Hector's eyes. Several dark blue teardrops tattooed his cheek and there was old English calligraphy on his neck and chest.

"Who has information on the vessel?"

Hector controlled his laughter with a fist to his mouth and then waved for them to follow. "I'm sorry Bishops. I'm not feeling myself today. Come in, please."

They walked down a hallway stripped of paint, carpet and character. The walls were a spray-paint mural, but only some of the designs and names had relation to the Church of Midnight. Cole saw that the rest was rubbish. Through doorless doorways, he watched more miscreants sitting against walls, some behind sheets of cottony smoke and others gripping bongs or pipes. A skeletal white couple fucked at the end of an empty hallway, her bony legs in a V and his shadowy ass dunking, their breathing quickening as they reached where they needed to be. Paul studied them with some amusement before Cole bumped him to move on. These scenes made Cole too angry to think straight. He'd show them the way home. Why would Sandeus Pager allow this? It was so easy to send an Inner Circle down here to give the Church a face. It was laziness. That's what it was. As Archbishop, Cole would restore direction in these little chapels, or die trying.

"Where do you keep your Tomes?" he asked Hector. Paul simpered at the question.

"Somewhere around," Hector answered quickly.

The Tomes were probably holding up a table with three legs somewhere, thought Cole. Not a surprise. By the looks of things, the Tomes of Eternal Harvest would be lost on this lot anyway—and Cole had to change that too.

Hector sat at a picnic table on a folding chair. There was an intricate hookah on top of several stacks of pizza boxes. He shoved the mess to the side and pointed to a pair of folding chairs against the wall. Cole shook off the offer. "We'll stand. You said you had information. Chaplain Cloth hasn't contacted us yet. What makes you believe he took the body of one of your own?"

"Ramon freaked out! Thought he was on acid or something. Turning pale, screaming strange shit. Goofy fuckin' guy," said Hector. Cole noted Hector's wild hair and eyes made him look part rodent. Hector picked up a withered joint from a naked lady ashtray, lit the end and nursed at it. Cole had to fight the impulse to snatch it out of his mouth.

"Did this Ramon say where he was going?" Paul asked.

A pungent cloud flowed toward them. Cole had always favored the earthy smell but otherwise never touched the stuff.

Hector leaned on two chair legs and touched his head to the wall. "You said on the phone you'd discuss funding. You can see our chapel here, well, she could use some upgrading. Don't you think?"

"This isn't a negotiation. We came to visit fellow brothers

and sisters in the name of the Archbishop. You'll be paid an extra contribution for your assistance." Cole pulled out an envelope from his inner pocket and tossed it across the table. Hector tore through the top of the envelope. He reached inside and frowned. "Hey, there's like only five hundred dollars here."

"There's the two-fifty for your monthly and two-fifty for the information. I didn't have to give you anything except your monthly, but I doubled it," said Cole.

Hector slapped down the envelope. "Five hundred ain't shit for Inner Circle, and you, I heard you're one of the bigshits that goes out on the Hunt every Halloween—"

At least Hector knew about the Hunt. *That shouldn't be so impressive*, thought Cole.

Paul stepped forward, taking the lead. "What does that have to do with your compensation?"

Hector narrowed his eyes. The tip of his tongue ran the length of his bruised lower lip. He didn't seem to enjoy Quintana's presence all that much. Cole could have smiled for that. "Your monthly dividend isn't meant to support your chapel. You better start selling shit, not smoking it all."

"Hey, I'm not for disrespect. I don't give a fuck how big you think you are. This shit, *here*, is my chapel. It may not be all that, but I got more than twenty jonesing for a place. I deserve my share. I quit the LP-12." He flashed a gang sign. Cole couldn't understand its symbolic logic.

"You're free to disband. We don't need leeches," said Cole faintly.

Hector shook his head angrily. "Fuckin' almost got my ass capped for leavin LP-12, homie. I gave up some real shit, lost one of my boys and now they're sending some *pendejos* to deliver junk-drawer change. Fuck that shit. That ain't fair. I had a feeling this would happen."

"And I had a feeling you'd want more. But you're not getting more, so tell us about Ramon."

Paul glanced back. Cole had sensed it too. Someone filled the doorway behind them. It was a girl, about nineteen years old, pretty except for the pencil-line eyebrows and overcoat of facial powder. She pointed a Glock at them at a bizarre sideways angle. He'd love to see her try and fire it that way and dislocate a shoulder.

"This is the Inner Circle to pay for Ramon?" she asked. In a way Cole was relieved. Her voice was sober and sounded a few leagues deeper with intelligence.

"Don't say shit," Hector ordered as he stood.

The Bishops of Midnight watched carefully and neither made a move. "We are part of something bigger," Cole said. "You need to calm down, put those guns away and tell me where Ramon went. You want more money for your chapel, fine—we can send some tasks your way. But you have to deliver on them."

Some eager faces bobbed in the hallway, some white, some black, some brown, all smiling for blood.

"Last chance, fellows." Hector lifted a gun out of the back of his pants.

"We can help you clean this place up. It doesn't just take money. It takes courage. You don't want to kill us, Hector. Reducing our number doesn't help anything."

"Fuck that shit," a bubble of spit popped on Hector's lower lip.

Paul sighed and shook his head. He glanced accusingly at Cole before he bolted away with his head down. Cole's leg flew out behind him and his foot planted in the girl's ribcage. She pulled the trigger and the gun discharged into the ceiling. Plaster fell and a cloud mushroomed up from the floor. She grasped her side and charged him. Paul grabbed her from behind, hauling her up. Hector tried to aim through the mess of struggling bodies.

"What I taught you!" Cole yelled back.

It was already happening. Paul's fingers sizzled against the girl's porcelain neck. Hector fired a shot as Paul fell to the ground with the girl in his hold. The bullet caromed off an exposed plumbing fixture in the hallway and plugged a reedy guy in a wife beater. Another shot fired as Cole spun around and clutched Hector's wrist. At the pressure the gun popped out of Hector's hand.

"Back me up!" Hector wailed. The hallway ambled with confusion around the two quickly dead bodies and broiling flesh. Hector's eyes widened. "Back me up!"

With a desperate scream the girl twisted around and snapped Paul's head back with an elbow. He let her go reflexively and put his hand to his jaw. Curdled skin fell from her neck as she scrambled into the hallway. "What did he do to me?" she pled out to everybody and nobody. "What the fuck did he do?"

Cole felt his own gun slide out of his hip holster. He flung Hector around for a shield. A young man, high school aged, had Cole's gun drawn. The gun was too heavy for the teen to steady, so it wobbled right to left. Thick beads of sweat pushed out of the teen's forehead and at the prickly base of a premature mustache.

Paul tried to stand. The wagging barrel pointed his way. Cole shook his head. "Stay there."

"You asshole, you said you didn't bring a piece," Paul complained.

The gun returned to Cole and the kid spoke firmly, "Let my brother go now."

"Shoot him, Chuy! Shoot his ugly ass!" shouted Hector.

"Put the gun down and step into the hall with the others," Cole ordered. "We didn't come here for this, brothers."

Chuy blinked at the sweat in his eyes.

"Do as I say!"

"Fuck that Chuy! Dome this motherfucker! *Acábalo! Acábalo!*"

Cole had no choice. Some people wanted fear. Only fear. It was the truest language they spoke. He put his hand at the back of Hector's neck and gripped. The marrow blossoms in Cole's chest filled with life from the Old Domain. His bones chilled with their power and he immediately felt every atom in Hector's neck.

From the ground Paul Quintana watched, sharing an understanding of the wonder.

"You shouldn't have traded guns with the Nomads," whispered Cole.

"Fuck you. That's eBay shit—" Hector's tongue stopped and dropped to the side of his mouth as his nerves went limp. Bubbling pockets undulated from the interior of his skull to the surface until Hector's head was crawling in its own juices. Hair sizzled away like ignited fiber optics. His eyeballs twisted in their housings and evaporated and all bone structure lost integrity before tucking inward. The flesh, spinal cord and esophagus tore away from the vanishing head with a sucking sound. The head was gone.

The hallway thundered with the sounds of retreating shoes and echoing shouts. Chuy dropped Cole's gun and backed away, mouth overflowing with shock. Paul took the gun quickly and trained it on the hallway.

Several blisters popped in Cole's face, leaving behind bleeding coin shapes, currency exchanged for such power, not the first he'd spent in his long tenure as a Bishop. He dropped Hector's body with a twinge of regret. The headless form hit the folding table and sent it screeching sideways. Chuy stared at his brother and whispered something in Spanish, and repeated it several times.

The unnamed forest outside Strath had always been famed for its monstrous scarlet trees that reached skyward. I've never been there myself, but on my travels I have read that in the springtime the Church of Morning have orgies beneath the canopies of parasol flowers and sacrifice jackrabbits in the russet shadows from the translucent red leaves. Things are supposedly lovely in that forest. Once again, this is from my limited knowledge of that region.

Even with that limitation in mind, it must have come as quite a shock when a pilgrim spotted a human head lying sideways in the dirt, mouth unhinged and eyes still glowing white. Particles of foreign red flesh dotted the face like hives.

Hector Gonzalez had put eyes upon the Old Domain. Cole Szerszen had granted him this privilege, if only for a few seconds.

Cole put away his gun. He dabbed at the wounds on his jaw, which bled freely, as head wounds liked to do. A cold feeling pulsed in their center, indicative of transfer. Hector's head had taken a trip, but not completely alone. A little smidgeon of Cole Szerszen had gone with it, as well as some pieces of the pretty girl Paul had sent.

Cole was better now at controlling his personal loss but still had a long way to go. From what he'd seen, Paul was capable of preventing the wounds altogether. Perhaps Cole could stand to learn a thing or two from him. Unfortunately.

Fighting through fatigue, Cole centered himself. He'd overdone it. Paul turned to Chuy, who still stood there like a posed action figure. "Where did Ramon go?" asked Paul.

His brother's corpse appeared to be the only thing of importance.

Paul's voice firmed. "Hey, tell me where that guy Ramon went."

Chuy glanced at Cole. "You...melted him. Hector…"

"Kid, Ramon? Where is he?" Cole staggered over.

The boy's eyes still couldn't unlock. "Ramon changed all of a sudden. Where's Hector's head at?"

"Where is *Ramon* at?"

"Going to California—Reche Canyon, Hector said. How did you—? Why did you do that?"

Cole almost felt like laughing through his adrenaline, but he bit his lip. "The Church didn't need Hector. That's why." He paused and then added, "The envelope on the floor has money in it. Use it on something worthwhile. It's yours."

Paul silently followed Cole outside, pointing Hector's gun into every hall along the way. Cole felt his heart drop south faster with every step. He was close to passing out and didn't expect Paul to try and catch him if he fell. He needed water, he needed food, he needed more air. The walls of the world were shattering and everything was coming down. Only when they got back to the limo and he saw Melissa's face again, did Cole feel any better.

Fourteen

STILL NO LETTER. THIS WAS GETTING SERIOUS. EVEN though they had some spending money now, Martin wasn't at ease. The Messenger was never this late. What if they missed a letter? That happened one time before, four or five years back. They arrived in the target city too late and the Church set a trap. Martin blew out his knee and took a bullet to the deltoid. Teresa almost got mauled to death by Cloth's children. They essentially had to push in all their chips to break even. By a narrow margin, they won their lives. Martin couldn't say the same for the Heart of the Harvest, a sixty-year-old investment banker named Morton Elisa; after taking the sacrifice from the old man's chest, Cloth didn't even leave remains that appeared human.

Martin thought of that year as a big fluke though. Usually the Messenger delivered no matter when or where. Despite his optimistic delusions, Martin expected they'd find a letter sooner or later. He prayed, however, they found one before the thirtieth. A day to prepare wasn't realistic, especially given Teresa's condition.

The blue toilet water had magically cycled green a moment earlier. Inside the rippling surface Martin's face begged for a shave—soon he'd have a full-blown beard. The father he no longer knew looked back at him with kind, sad eyes. *You know I love you, right?* Those parting words from his dad had been enough for the rest of Martin's life. He didn't have to go see his father to be at peace. As a kid his parents had always been ghosts. So let them stay that way. Poor Teresa should have known better than to dabble in the past.

Martin flushed the green water and went to wash his hands. Gazing beyond the chalky lime deposits and fingerprint signatures, another mirror-Martin met him eye to eye. The toilet water version had looked so much better, not this exhausted man plagued with worry. He pulled down his lower eyelids with his pointer fingers. Even the red hidden beneath had a tired, influenza color. *Quit feeling sorry for yourself,* he thought. *Think about what Teresa's going through and suck it up buddy.* He snatched a hanging paper towel. Just one. Conserve. After the brown towel came apart in damp shreds he relented and took a second one to finish.

As Martin returned to their table, restaurant life rattled deep in his head: the clicking plates, the scraping forks, the blithe chatting—it all sounded like the digestive system of an enormous, annoying organism. And probably smelled like one too. He'd seen too many good diners and too many bad diners to know the difference. Dead ahead a skinny kid let a whole mouthful of hash browns tumble onto his plate in a steamy white pile. His mother silently reprimanded him by stabbing his fork back into the lump to force feed him. *Okay, so this was a bad diner.*

Since their visit to her mother, Teresa's coughing and retching had worsened. She waited for him in the red booth, a serene lady bathed in crosses of sunlight, and even though her fist went to her lips for a silent fit, Teresa's eyes were so alive they looked clairvoyant. The burden was lifted. It'd been a long time, but he'd waited for this moment patiently, waited for a glimpse of a healthy Teresa again.

The leather seat blew out underneath Martin. He shoveled down a pair of sunny-side eggs, short stack of buttermilk pancakes with banana syrup, and crispy hash browns (which scalded his tongue). He conceded that even though the place didn't have cage-free eggs and fair-trade coffee, he wouldn't let mediocrity ruin the relief every bite brought. He started to think they'd be okay. No matter what.

Teresa fondly watched him as he gobbled the parsley and fan of kale that decorated the plate. The level of oatmeal in her bowl had not lowered more than a centimeter. After drinking a quick sip of orange juice, he set his cup down and rotated it with the sides of his fingers. "I've pretended I don't care anymore, but you know how lousy I am at putting up fronts. I think we should do as the doctor recommended and take the next step."

She glanced away, her face falling out of the sunlight. "Martin, goddamnit already...let's not bicker right now. Let's not talk about chemo and radiation or any shit I won't be doing. Can't you get it? We can't go that route. The Messenger doesn't even like us to stay in one town for more than a week. Just forget about my lung and try to focus on what really matters. Take a look, it's all around you."

"Who says we give in? I'll deal with Halloween like I deal with it every year."

"You're getting loud."

He reached across the table and took her hands, tried not to read into why they were so cold in such a stuffy restaurant.

"You were a fighter when we first met. Maybe the next doctor will actually help. It's about time someone helped *us* for a change. Isn't it worth trying?"

She pulled her hand up from under the weight of his. "I'm just slowing down after running so long. It's natural to slow down."

"You're as old as you feel."

Teresa made a patronizing *how cute* sound and pinched his cheek. He rolled his eyes and she shifted in her seat, undefeated. "Look, I'm not trying to piss you off, but I'm gonna go outside and have a smoke while you pay."

"Go ahead then."

She leveled her dark blue eyes at him. "I've cheated death for thirty Octobers, Martin. I don't have the energy to fight something else. Let me be."

Teresa scooted down the seat and stopped.

"Excuse me, folks." Their waitress stood there in her rose uniform and dangling grape earrings. She set the check on the table. "You folks are all set—I'll take that up whenever you're ready."

"Thanks." Martin slid the black folder his way.

"There's also this." The waitress placed an orange envelope on the table. "The manager just told me or I would've brought it sooner. I guess one of your friends left this off earlier today."

"Our friend?" asked Martin. "What did the person look like?"

The woman blinked back at him, speechless. She pursed her lips and shrugged, and then shuffled off.

After they paid and were outside, walking back to the van, Teresa laughed a little. "You asked her what the Messenger looks like. You still do that?"

"So?"

"Nothing, you're just a broken record."

"It doesn't hurt asking," he stated. "Maybe one of them will remember. I just want to know."

"It doesn't mean you ever will, Martin."

He decided to let it go. They got into the van and drove down the blacktop road to a bleached out gas station. As they pulled up, he noticed a pair of stout biker women trading a muffled conversation the next pump over. He wondered what they could be talking about. Tattoo sleeves? Harleys? Tailgate parties at the football game? Leather chaps? Pabst Blue Ribbon? Mullets? None of those stereotypes probably, but at least it all sounded somewhat normal—safe. He liked that notion.

He took a deep breath of desert air and gazed at the road that stretched beyond them, a bitter gray line of cigarette ash flattened by time. He felt the heaviness of the drive before them, even though it might only be a few hours. His entire adult life had been spent on freeways and highways and tollways and side streets and thoroughfares and parkways and boulevards and lanes and avenues. How many red lights had they seen? How many road construction sites had they passed? How many oil changes? New places even looked familiar now when they arrived.

Teresa grunted as she fell into the seat. "All gassed up. Open the thing up for chrissakes, so we can get going already."

He tore through the top of the intense orange envelope. The single page of vellum unsheathed like a paper blade. Teresa leaned in with him and they read the deep typewriter font burned into the pale beige surface.

TAKE NO MORE DETOURS AND HURRY WEST TO COLTON, CALIFORNIA. ROOM AT THE HAPPY MOON TRAVEL LODGE ON MOUNT VERNON AVE. STAY PUT IN THE ROOM AND KEEP UNDER THE COVER OF STORM CLOUDS.
REST WELL. NEXT LETTER SOON.

—Messenger

"The letters have never mentioned *resting* before," said Teresa.

"Or storm clouds," Martin added, tapping the touchscreen of their portable GPS. The multicolored map pivoted under a gauzy film of leftover fingerprints. "Says Colton's six hours off."

"What do you think it means about resting?" she asked.

"I'm just going to assume we were supposed to be there earlier."

"Don't bring up the trip to my mother's."

"I'm not, let's just get to Colton." He continued stabbing the GPS.

Teresa took the envelope and pulled free a banded stack of hundred-dollar bills. An ATM card was tucked under the yellow band, which had a pin number scrawled across it. She peeled the fresh bills over and counted. "Looks like ten grand here. If that's on top of our usual fifty deposited in the account, we're doing nice."

He turned the ignition. "We got a raise this year. Sweet!"

She took out a clove and dabbed it on her lower lip. He stared at her and Teresa chuckled. She shook the near-empty lighter and coaxed a flame out. Through a racing plume, she traced the foggy landscape outside, ignoring the severity of his gaze. He gave up and moved his eyes in the direction hers had gone. The desert rolled on, a dry echo caught between the earth and sky; it was endless, like them. They were always moving, all year long, some of the Messenger's jobs small and some large, but only at the last thrashings of October did they see their real purpose. No year had ever gone by without him doubting its worth though, and with age the doubts haunted every crack in the road.

The clove cigarette crackled.

"What kind of person do you think the Heart of the Harvest will be this year?" Martin was only half-interested in his own question.

Teresa shrugged, in the moment incapable of caring either. When they met a Heart there was little choice in the matter. "Can you put on Sam Cooke?" she asked. "Please."

He located the album on the CD changer and soon they were drifting on the sad-hopeful sound of *A Change is Gonna Come*. Martin knew the song was about civil rights but he pretended it meant something unique to only them. He pretended all the way to California.

Fifteen

PAUL WATCHED THE FLEET OF LIMOUSINES SLITHER DOWN the desert hill. Melissa drove, silently dismissing his presence. Paul didn't give a fuck. *Let the bookworm mope.* He sunk deeper into thought as he traced the caravan of limousines. Intermittently the sun struck bumpers and projected faint orange dazzles between the black exteriors. After surviving last night and this morning, this wasn't an image Paul wanted to endure. He bent his head down and shuddered. The marrow seeds spread their dry-ice roots and every time a blossom opened cold napalm filled his bones. He couldn't believe his old pal Justin had gone through this. It made Paul slightly regret dismissing him as feeble.

A day later and Paul was watching people lose their heads just from a touch, and worse, he was beginning to understand what it took to accomplish something like that. Before sunlight had even painted the Mojave, Cole took him out into the rolling dark morning and taught him two mental exercises. Both were meant to control the blossoms' growth. The first was a color game. Concentrate on the spectrum, separate the colors, one at a time, and then two and three at a time, and then put *all* colors together. Darkness formed a wall against the barrage of information flooding into their minds from the Old Domain.

Once the wall was established it seemed natural to reopen a shutter of sorts and control what flowed in. Paul'd happily learned this ability. He didn't need to hear anymore songs from Cloth's children. Paul had his shutter closed tight right now and it felt damn good to see the world as he remembered it. There were still worries however. Cole cautioned about closing the shutter too long with the seeds in bloom — this would cause some sort of imbalance in the garden cropping up in his lungs. You didn't want too many black blossoms; you didn't want too many orange.

Opening and closing had come so easy Paul didn't even recognize it as a *skill* when Cole had shown him. The big man almost kicked his heels he was so happy with this instant progress. Paul didn't get it though. It was like receiving a gold medal for taking a leak.

Now the second exercise, that was the one that got Paul's mind all loop-de-loop. Essentially, he had to touch an object — this morning, a rock fragment — and then *push* it with his thoughts. Only he wasn't pushing the rock from one point to another. He was pushing particles into the Old Domain... and if he had the shutter open the process was a great deal easier, as he learned with that *chola* back in the ghetto chapel. Everything in Paul's head lurched forward when he pushed, veins wanted to disconnect from their beds and rip out of his face. All of those bits of matter that flaked off the rock's surface tugged on particles in his face as though they were long lost couples reuniting. He could feel his skin wanting to join the departing rock molecules. But he wouldn't let them; he concentrated on pushing *only* the stone. It took some sweat, but he figured it out in a few minutes. This last part had left the well-scarred Cole dumbstruck. Probably a bit scared too.

Something about that fear had gotten Paul's wheels turning about Bishop Cole Szerszen. Paul's role had been far too static in Szerszen's scheme. After watching the man in action with that Hector fellow, a new plan had come together. Paul Quintana's plan.

Melissa stole a glance at the decaying quartz in his palm. Her hair was in a neat bun stabbed with chopsticks and her spectacles had slid down her nose. Paul thought that on a pretty Asian chick the look might have worked. It might have worked on *any* pretty chick. But he'd had his way with Melissa; Paul couldn't pretend otherwise, couldn't erase that more than embarrassing night. In fact, he didn't want to erase what happened. It was going to set him free.

"Long day ahead," sighed Melissa. "Why do you keep looking at that thing?"

Paul put the quartz in his suit pocket. He didn't feel like talking much, not to her anyway, but there was an angry hive of questions buzzing in his head. *This isn't really the time or place, but what the fuck?*

Reflections of the other limos crossed the sparkling lenses of her glasses. "Cole said conclave is tonight in Ontario."

"Aren't we headed the wrong way?"

"Ontario, California," she explained.

She has no idea the things that could be done to her and her man, thought Paul. "How is my fellow Bishop, anyway?" he asked. "He didn't seem too well. With that bandage over his head people are going to think the villagers finally got him."

"You're hilarious."

Paul gave her a once-over. "You thought I was funny that one night though, didn't you? In the archives…have you ever been with Cole there, I wonder?"

She didn't say anything, too stunned that'd he brought it up.

"Do you ever still think about that night? Was I your favorite in the lot?"

Sideways revulsion, "Absolutely not."

Paul glanced up wistfully. "I wonder what would have happened if everybody wasn't so sloppy drunk."

"I'd be a whole lot happier."

"I think a lot more would have happened, more coordinated at least. That's what I think."

"Cole's sleeping in the back. Remember? You're fuckin' playing with fire here Quintana."

"He's out like a light." Paul turned, his seatbelt restricting him at the throat. He pulled it loose. Despite his bravado, he lowered his voice, "Something I've been meaning to talk to you about. I don't care much for this power play you two made on me. I didn't want a thing to do with either of you. I needed to ascend— "

"To meet the Priestess of Morning," Melissa pointed out. "There's a real need."

"—And now Cole's trapped me into performing some ritual he's probably better suited for, while he goes out to play insurrectionist and assassin. We're doing this behind *Cloth's* back on top of everything else?"

"Cloth will be told."

Paul ignored this as misdirection. "I know Cole thinks I'm taking to all this jazz easily, but how do I know this Heralding ritual won't kill me? I never asked to have a hand in killing the

Archbishop. I could give a fly's fuck if Sandeus stays seated for fifty more years."

"You killed Margrave. Don't twist this up," she spat.

"Once the Archbishop is dead, won't I be next? Tell me Melissa."

"Sandeus Pager will never secede— "

"And he's leading us to ruin," Paul finished mockingly. "Somehow I don't feel any safer with Cole as Archbishop. Come on, I might not even live to see those days. The Heralding may cash me out."

"Cole's survived every year he's been through it."

"Yay Cole! I hope his survival doesn't have anything to do with that pit-bull head on top of his neck."

"Stop that!"

"Anyway, I would leave you guys alone if I could. Really I would. Zilch is what you two mean to me. *Zilch.* But there are issues here—I have to take precautions, you see. I won't be used and thrown away. I have plans to live a nice long, happy life giving the Priestess of Morning her fair share of Quintana."

"Just quit speaking to me. I don't want to hear your voice anymore."

"What? You think I'm disgusting?" *Wait for it you ass! Stop smiling!* Paul took out his cell phone, flipped it open and navigated to the video folder. Selected one of his favorites. He'd almost forgotten he had this one and then this morning he watched it again. Magical. It'd helped him remember he was still human.

The sounds of slurping, suction and moaning came from the little phone speaker. Melissa's eyes twisted over and widened at the small image of her head going up and down between Paul's legs. The view changed. From the waist down another man thrust into her from behind, his black slacks and boxer shorts bunched around his ankles. A grinning blonde woman, who Paul would have later that night, dipped underneath Melissa and began suckling a nipple. The file was too short for Paul's tastes. He did admire the end shot, as Melissa pulled back from his penis, a long white strand bending from her lower lip.

Melissa's face looked prepared to split in half. "Paul! What—?"

"You looked right into the phone, precious. You *saw* me taking it."

The dismay in her eyes told the story clearly. The camera phone memory had been lost in the mistake of that drunken night.

Paul folded up the phone and rested it on his lap. He tilted his head, playing a mock, sensitive version of himself. He could play that role when he needed to. Most people bought it. Melissa's fists clenched the wheel now and blanched her knuckles white. Most people.

"I need a few things to make this video and its twins go away."

Her soul paled underneath her skin. "You made copies?"

"Hell yes I made copies. I always do. That's not the point now. Point is, I know how Bishop Cole would feel about seeing this. The chatter around my people is that you've got Cole thinking you were a nun before you met him. Poor fool has to be delusional with how much we all stretched you out that night—"

"Lower your fucking voice!"

Paul did, though hers was too loud for comfort. He needed to ease back on the teasing. "First, I want some peace of mind, some security. I can't wiggle out of performing the Heralding, but now or later, if there are any plans on my life—"

"There aren't!"

"If Cole plans to send some numbnuts to cut my throat when I'm sleeping, I'd be thrilled to know that piece of information ahead of time." Paul paused, on the verge of laughing but holding it together. "And if I don't hear from you and I'm sent down the drink, a few of my own numbnuts will act on my behalf."

"Meaning?"

"This morning, when you were patching up Cole, I sent my acolytes instructions, along with a copy of this wonderful short film. In Technicolor! They know now who to email should I disappear. Filthy perverts are making a DVD as well and might even uploaded it to an Internet porn community. Are my guys brilliant? No way. Are they tech-savvy though? Yes way."

"You think you're smart now?"

"Quiet down," he cautioned. "And don't be so mean. I haven't shown anyone else the video yet, on my honor. Just do something for me and everything will be good."

"What the hell do you want?"

"Swipe Sandeus's box of marrow seeds from his vault. You're the head of logistics and supply, if anybody—"

"I'm not risking my life, you fucking idiot."

"Oh. That sure sucks. Because what will Cole do when he sees this?" Paul twisted the phone in the air. "I won't be Cole's favorite person, but he's loyal enough to the Church to understand losing another Bishop would be a waste. You though? You're just some slut who took one for the team and fucked him. He can take his pick of the church women once he's Archbishop."

"Why do you want the seeds?" Checked violence shimmered in her eyes. "Are you going to use them all? Go right ahead. See what happens."

"Of course not," said Paul hastily. "I don't think I'll even touch those things again. But keeping them close means that a new Bishop will never come around and put one over on me. With no others empowered I'll only have to worry about Cole, and with your assistance, I do believe I've covered that angle."

"How do you think of this shit?"

"I had plenty of time last night."

"Shit," she muttered and closed her eyes. They opened slowly, looking brand new, to the road slipping past.

"One more, minor thing."

Her posture showed she knew exactly what he was going to say next, even though he hadn't really planned this part. Maybe it was some wild scent in the air.

Paul unzipped his pants and whistled the *Greatest American Hero* theme. His erection sprung from the divide in his black-gray plaid boxer shorts. He could see Melissa sway uneasily. He found this was too exciting, having her trapped up here and Cole only feet away, too stupefied to know better. Paul gently shut the privacy window. "I promise just this one time," he whispered.

"I'll get you the seeds. Just stop this. It isn't fair."

"You're right; it isn't. But I need something to signify your intent. I want you to keep going until I runneth over. It's no big deal. If you're fast, I'll be fast. I'm tense right now, you see. It'll free my mind. Cole's not waking up anytime soon."

The look of her folding made Paul's body quiver with joy and his mind almost lost control—the shutter to the Old Domain cracked open in his mind like a lazy eyelid. He slammed it shut and focused instead on the strangling heat below. A gasp came to the top of his throat at the painful anticipation. They seemed to be the only two people in the universe at that moment.

With the stony eyes of a fallen soldier, Melissa took her right hand off the steering wheel and reached over.

EVEN IN A DEEP SLEEP, COLE HATED THE IDEA OF MELISSA being alone with Paul Quintana. It was a risky choice, and he didn't make those anymore—reminded him of his days unloading freight in the church's warehouse in Seattle. Every time he tossed a volatile package up the dock he wondered if he was taking his own life. Back then Cole would have never dreamed of becoming Inner Circle and would have laughed at the notion of becoming a Bishop.

Now, even Archbishop was plausible.

He'd earned this position and losing ground wasn't an option any longer. This, Cole had to keep. That meant he needed Paul well trained and close. The Tomes of Eternal Harvest said: *"Misery, like a trembling lipped sow with gouged eyes, had run its course in both worlds. Now there was only pride."*

Cole wanted only a glimpse of Melissa's face. He dug his elbow in the seat, tried to twist his bulk over and face the window. His biceps clenched and body moved. A muscle hitched in his abdomen and he fell back, sucking pain. The cold dry wound in his jaw burned. The marrow seeds in his body had long ago unfurled and spread. He no longer distinguished them as alien, except for times like this. They pounded in accordance with the pulse under his bandages. Still, this was nothing compared to a Heralding.

The black leather smell turned Cole's stomach in two different directions. He swung his other leg off the seat and grabbed the opposite bench seat for support. Bile soaked his throat. Pulling a breath through his lips, he dragged himself up and looked out the privacy window.

Through the rearview Melissa stared back. A flimsy smile came to her lips as she tucked her nondriving hand under her thigh. She was always cold, even on hot days. He couldn't believe someone like her had saved herself for so long to finally give it all away to someone like him. Cole was blessed. He was really blessed. Rumors would not sway his devotion for her. Paul Quintana would be his sword and Melissa would be his Priestess of Midnight. Both of them would mold his paradise. Cole just needed to hold on. He needed to believe he could rise above the petty hatemongering of the Inner Circle.

Paul looked through the driver's window. His joy was heaven-high, had no bounds, was glowing.

"Hungry?" A silly grin came to Paul's face. "I'm starving after all these brain *exercises*. Should we stop?"

"No," Cole replied hoarsely. "Keep going. We have to get settled in Ontario as soon as we can."

"You make the rules, Bishop." Paul smiled wider and smoothed his slacks as though trying to wipe something away.

Friends with Paul Quintana thought Cole. They had to be. It was the only chance for the new Church of Midnight to exist with any power after the gateway finally opened for all time. Friends…

Cole Szerszen wasn't worthy if he could not sacrifice something so small as pride.

Sixteen

RAMON CASTILLO HAD TRAVELED A LONG WAY AS TWO people. The burden of carrying his companion had finally taken its toll and it was he who would be carried now. His companion petted his mind with frozen bone digits, coaxing him onward. In spite of the agony there wasn't a spot of blood, or a bruise, or a welt. In the window of the Greyhound bus, a changing man fiercely looked back at him. Ramon's skin had once been dark-dark (some of the acolytes had made jokes about him being black, or a ranchero Mexican-Indian), although now his pigment had drained away. His face had tightened into a white beyond snow and milk and frost. This was brighter, more intense, a starlight white. The color lived while it worked. With its glow it twisted the structure of his cheekbones, jaw, eye sockets.

And those eyes that reflected back were not Ramon's eyes anymore. He could already tell they saw differently than his old eyes, which had been pushed back into his mind with the rest of his fragile soul.

He wasn't possessed. Ramon firmly believed this. This was what his dream had told him. In the dream he read a page from the Tomes of Eternal Harvest. He'd never seen the page before, which wasn't saying much because like everyone else in his chapel, he'd only really thumbed through the old book once. But when the words were spoken, the dream lifted, he shouted himself awake and something inside him overflowed. Filled with *the man with those crazy eyes*. Anything left of Ramon's resolve had been sinking ever since.

This experience wasn't about sharing the space of one vessel. This invasion of Ramon's body was leading to complete absorption of his soul. He could feel the tenuous filaments of his remaining memories snapping with every beat this body's new heart made. Particles of his life: his brother Roberto in prison for tax evasion, his sister Alicia pregnant again, his pinscher Rascal wiped out on the freeway last month. They lost all value. Now that he understood the universe better, he realized they'd never meant much. Not really. Chaos was larger than love.

"Beautiful, sunny Colton," the bus driver hollered back. The bus pulled off on a busy street that chased the rolling foothills of Reche Canyon.

Ramon stood; Chaplain Cloth stood.

United by one body, they walked to the front of the empty bus. The driver was a portly man in his late fifties with a closely shaved head. He smelled like Swisher Sweet cigars, which Ramon loved, and in which Cloth remained uninterested.

Their standing there, thinking, attracted the driver's attention.

"Woh, creepy contact lenses, mister. You're going to win whatever contest you're headed for."

Chaplain Cloth smiled; Ramon frowned. They stepped off the bus.

A grain silo probed the stormy sky from a cluster of eucalyptus trees. Ramon staggered through the knuckly root systems, using the trees to brace Chaplain Cloth's body—his body. The silo imprinted on Ramon's memories and dreams. He had seen this silo his entire life, written stories and drawn pictures of it as a kid. He'd memorized its every red blemish and leaking rivet. In those dreams he walked up the dirt slope, holding a clammy hand, always too afraid to see whose hand it was, but now, drudging toward the silo it could not have been any clearer. He was still being led, one body and two beings.

He had a feeling that soon there'd only be one being. Ramon Castillo would be gone.

Ramon approached the granary and wrapped his hand around a cool ladder rung. This is where the dream details ended. He'd always been approaching the silo and never quite arrived there. He took himself up a few rungs. He wondered what this Cloth person could achieve through climbing this old tower. Ramon scoured the bottom depths of his occupied brain but only found Cloth's insistence, tunnel vision toward one goal—*Two worlds, two churches. Midnight and Morning. Black & Orange. The Heart of the Harvest must be reaped, then praise be given! The path will be overfed on the fruit, the gateway unhinged for all time and the ancient way, the ONLY way, restored.*

"Thanksgiving to the blood feast," Ramon murmured and took several more rungs.

Santa Ana winds shoved him to the side. His sweaty T-shirt and baggy jeans clung to Ramon as though fearful of falling. In the Old Domain the silo's location was sacred, a massive temple built from bone bricks and blood blessed mortar. Men, women, children and newborns gave to the structure. The concept didn't disturb Ramon, even though his sister Alicia had a baby girl on the way. The image of him sinking his teeth into a chubby arm and ripping the flesh from the bone only made curiosity spike. The raw meat Ramon could taste in Cloth's mouth, in his mouth, would be bittersweet to those who recalled their sad moralities, or would be delicious to others who never swam those shallow waters. Ramon could do nothing but continue upward, licking Cloth's lips, wondering which kind of person he would be. *Person?*

Will I be a ghost when you're through with me, Cloth?

"To those who would mourn you, yes. To the universe, you are restored, a fundamental correction." Chaplain Cloth took two more rungs and heaved himself onto the roof. The person inside this human frame became an echo of an echo and then a buzzing insect sound in the underworld of consciousness. Ramon Castillo rippled away into the ether.

Cloth stared into the scrolling shadows in the silo's opening below. It was welcoming. A warmth lifted with a smell of rotten soil and grain. Cloth inhaled it blissfully. That he had come into this world so early, days before the Time of Opening, gave him a sense of security that made him almost capricious. He'd never had a head start like this and it was all due to last year's spoils. *Tony Nguyen*, so delicious. The fruit yielded had been more powerful than many other Hearts in the past and the gateway to the Old Domain pushed open wide enough to allow two church members through. Cloth could still feel that Heart's power eating away the path, letting more Old Domain influence drift over to this world. Perhaps this year it would allow for an army? Or perhaps the other church could fit the pillars into place?

They were wonderful fantasies, but the job had to get done first.

Staring down, one eye black, one eye orange, Cloth put his legs into the silo's mouth and shimmied in. *Nothing better than swimming on the seam between two worlds.* Now it was a matter of storing strength until the Day of Opening. Cloth edged in farther. Something itched in his mind. It sounded like a gnat buzzing in another galaxy, but Cloth could touch the insignificant speck of dust with his thoughts.

Goodnight, Ramon.

Cloth dropped into the silo. Never in all of his wandering had he ever been this prepared. He shivered in the abyss and felt his temporal body slam to the bottom of the empty silo, bones cracking and breaking and splintering and fluids shooting from his mouth and ears and nose across the filthy darkness. Then those pieces lovingly stitched together in a new form. His form. His black suit sewn from the dark smoothed over him like another skin. His orange handkerchief plumed from his breast pocket. Once more beautiful. Strong. Hungry. Invincible.

Thanksgiving to the Eternal Feast.

Seventeen

ALL THESE YEARS HAD BEEN ABOUT PRESERVATION FOR Archbishop Sandeus Pager. This wasn't as simple as a bright yellow stripe down his back. There was a reason he didn't perform the Heralding or go out on the hunt for the Heart. For one, he was too important to be bothered with all that sweating and grunting, and for two, he wanted to live to see the Old Domain. People like Cole Szerszen wouldn't last long in a unified world. Szerszen had too much invested in the Church of Midnight and his scale would tip, heavily. Call him forgetful, scatterbrained maybe, but Sandeus knew how to prepare.

While the others chased after the Heart of the Harvest, he tackled a bigger question. On October 31st just where did Chaplain Cloth draw his power from? It took research, meditation and intense practice every year to even begin to understand the answer to such a question. When the worlds opened to one another, Sandeus would spend his time searching. And he had learned more than he'd ever thought possible. But he still felt he'd fallen behind. When the final union of worlds occurred, and he believed it could be this year or next, he'd possess the ability to harness both worlds, just as Cloth does. There was a special test Sandeus had planned for just this occasion, and waiting until then would be difficult.

His limousine and sentinels rolled into the gas-station town. Sandeus now trailed the exodus by a significant margin. His driver lowered the window. "Archbishop, she approaches."

"Thank you, Lex." Sandeus opened the door and made sure his lace was tucked into his suit. Four sentries slid out of their ebony Vipers and touched their side arms. He glanced to them and shook his head. They stood at ease then but kept ready. A year wasn't enough to build trust between the two churches. A shame.

The young woman stepped lightly through the rising dust. She wore a wonderful tangerine dress and ambrosia hair spilled down both shoulders. Her servant, an aberration in an otherwise pleasant sight, resembled the Brawny Man. The two didn't exactly look like they were from another world, but they had been here for a year now. Perhaps Earthliness was an unavoidable sickness.

They stopped before Sandeus and he grinned. "So what name did you choose?"

"Mabel—I heard it on the television." She gestured to her bearded companion. "And this is my faithful father."

"Of course he is." Sandeus hoped he hadn't overdone it with the perfume this morning. It put some people off. "Please, let's have a sit. I have refreshments. After you."

The servant helped the Priestess of Morning inside the limo.

She was a striking woman. No question. A striking woman with a wonderful figure. But really, more than anything else, Sandeus wanted a face as flawless as hers. She wasn't even wearing makeup. In a better life he would have worn this woman's tender skin. With all her beauty and grace, it was easy for Sandeus to worship her, and he had little doubt now why she'd brought a guard from the other world.

"Addressing our last correspondence, I sent some Flagstaff acolytes over to the old lady's house. She was a bust—no Heart of the Harvest."

The Priestess's pretty amber eyes went to slits. "I told you not to bother Celeste's mother. I have the Nomads in my sight. They left the old woman's house empty-handed. I thought I was specific about that."

"It never hurts to be certain, Priestess." Sandeus took up a wine glass from the bar. The syrah slopped a bit on his sleeve. He pressed the drops to his lips, prospecting for a little color. "So tell me how it went. I never had the chance to ask you, and I am fascinated. It sounds like the beginning of a bad joke: two Nomads walked into the bar— "

"They were somewhat early. But we were ready." The Priestess sunk her full lips into the bloody looking juice in her own glass. "Destiny often takes other routes. Archbishop Kennen had seen many different versions of the outcome."

Sandeus swallowed a larger gulp than intended and breathed in; the wine burnt his nostrils.

"They came into the bar wearing the same clothing and talking about the same things Kennen described. The woman even asked for clove cigarettes." The Priestess brought one leg over the other. Her peach stockings had the loveliest floral lace Sandeus'd ever seen.

He grounded his thoughts in a hurry. "I understand Kennen paid dearly for this prediction. His wife of many years offered herself to the feast. Dear me. *To build the foundation of the future, you must tear down something permanent from your past.* So the Tomes read."

Eggert and the Priestess bowed their heads a moment to acknowledge the words. It was a gesture too few in Sandeus's own church observed.

"Archbishop Kennen should be praised. To have given over his beloved only proves how anxious he is to cross over. Do you know any of his plans for the unification? How he envisions the Church structure?"

"I don't spread rumors," said the Priestess, "especially not about the Archbishop of Morning."

Sandeus's patience ran dry with these outworlders' constant reverence of her Archbishop, as though he were not an equal. He took his wine, sipped and chuckled a bit. "So what are you willing to spread, Priestess?"

The bodyguard's eyes flared.

The Priestess of Morning, not as affected, set down her glass and folded her slender hands on her lap. Sandeus found his eyes sliding over the deep crevasse between her breasts. The Priestess eyed his interest coolly. He could see the soft tip of her tongue just behind her teeth. "It's hardly fair—the woman's flesh in this world is devoured constantly with the eye and yet the male's flesh is always obscured. Has your kind purposely tried to starve us?"

Sandeus touched his makeup accidentally and cringed. "I'm afraid my fascination can't be helped, Priestess. After all, you know midnight always seeks the morning." The bodyguard Eggert's gaze cut through him. Sandeus cleared his throat. "So you put the Nomads in your sight then, Priestess? You can see them in your mind. Well then, where are they now?"

"Driving their big horseless wagon—*van*."

"You can see everything happening to them. Clearly? How does your sight work? It has been a constant fascination of mine."

The Priestess bit into a chocolate cherry. After a moment, she dabbed her lips with a bar napkin. "I share the same ability as the Interloper, although not as developed. It is said that I share bloodlines with the Messenger, the Interloper, or whatever you may call him, or her."

"Interesting. So how many people are in your sight?"

"I see the Nomads now, but I can also see my own church, out there. I put them in my sight before I left last year. There." She pointed to the passing waves of brown desert and Joshua trees. "The Church of Morning gathers on Ekki fields, singing for the gateway to open, sharpening their staves, offering the feast. Anything I put into my sight fills my mind, until I look away."

"Sounds overwhelming, Priestess."

"I like taking more than I can handle. It exposes my limits."

Sandeus finished his wine and set it on the wet bar. He crossed his legs almost as well as she had and he felt childishly proud about it. "I let your Church operate in its own fashion, but I must ask this. I still don't understand why we couldn't just kill the Nomads at the bar."

"Cloth needs them to lead us to the Heart. There can be no delay."

"Cloth and his children track down the Heart of the Harvest, every year."

"Perhaps," she remarked, "but Cloth wishes to go at this new Heart with speed and precision, not an extra breath of effort spent. The opening will be taxing on him once it comes."

"Cloth speaks to you?"

"Through Archbishop Kennen's offerings."

Sandeus suddenly felt empty; he'd hoped to put all the worrying aside this year, but to learn Chaplain Cloth wanted to go cautious made him fear the worst. These Nomads worked well together. It was a miracle how well. Most Nomads lasted one October, maybe two. Not Martin and Teresa. It had been two decades now. They won some, lost some, and always came back for another go. Sandeus heard that the woman, Teresa, had been protecting Hearts for thirty years. That was longer than his tenure as Archbishop.

This conversation started to depress him, so Sandeus wheeled around the subject yet again. "Anyhow, I want to speak of a new Bishop, Paul Quintana. I believe you met briefly at the Celebration last year."

A satisfied expression crossed the Priestess's face. "He is the winner of the gauntlet? He wasn't allowed in the celebration ballroom with the envoys and other Bishops. The blond, who looks like a film actor?"

"Very good looking, yes."

"I would like to meet him, formally of course, now that he has ascended. He might be of use to me."

"Forgive me, but wasn't there just a new Bishop recently?" Eggert the bodyguard asked, beard bouncing with worry. "Jason? Or somebody?"

"Justin Margrave. Yes, he's no longer with the Church."

"Something happened?"

Sandeus shrugged. "*Some of us fight against the wind, and some of us are taken with the dust. We are too strong to embrace the departed.*"

They bowed their heads again. The Priestess finished her wine but held onto the empty glass as her eyes roamed the desert. Those eyes saw everything great and small, everything near and far. Those eyes saw their destination ahead, for better or worse. There were equal parts pain and pleasure languishing in their brilliance.

Sandeus Pager gazed at her in breathless admiration, despite Eggert's stare. The Priestess of Morning was too lovely to ignore. So unbelievably *superb*. If only Sandeus could steal such perfection and make it his own.

Eighteen

Teresa startled up in her seat as Martin punched the horn. A convertible Mustang rocketed around them and a chubby finger sprang into the air, the nail polish a stop-sign red.

Teresa smacked her sleep-gummy lips. "Welcome to Southern California."

Martin still hadn't recovered. He was strangling the steering wheel, muttering, and probably fantasizing about pushing each sleek silver car into a shallow ditch. When he finally got over it, he leaned back in the seat and shook his head. "They're bad in Arizona, but out here there are just so damn *many*."

"Makes you wonder why we bother to save the world." She snapped open her box of cloves. Only three left. Better conserve, she thought.

Driving weariness had branded into the contours of Martin's face. A creature of the road. "If you could dress up for a party this year, what would you be?" he asked.

"Adults don't dress up."

"Sure they do, Teresa. They go to parties and dress up. You can buy one of those pirate outfits, a rock chick, a *tiger* woman, maybe a refrigerator or one of those fat lady suits—I dressed until I was twenty, up until when I met you."

"Sorry."

"So answer the question," he prodded.

"I'd be one of those ghosts with the holes cut in a sheet."

Martin shook his head. "That's the lamest costume ever."

"So what would you be?"

He shrugged. "I'd show up as anything if it meant going to a party on that night rather than...you know."

"Yeah, that's something we gave up. Halloween parties."

"Hey, you want to play?" he asked.

Their eyes met for a moment and she tilted her head. "Haven't done that in a while. A few years?"

"I've got more things to add to the list. It'll be hard to top me this time around."

She folded her arms. "You go ahead and start. Tell me your first thing. *Martin, what has the Messenger taken from you?*"

Martin sat up, excited to play. "Aquariums."

"Say what?"

"I've always wanted an aquarium, but I think it'd be difficult to maintain one on the road. Not with how you make those jackrabbit starts and sharp lefts."

"Oh, you're going to have to do better than that," said Teresa. "*Cruises.*"

"Oh, but we've been on ships before."

"They weren't vacation ships. Can you imagine us going to Jamaica? Being trapped on a boat for weeks? Then on the island, walled in by the Jamaican chapels? The Church would be all over us."

"Point taken. *Mowing the lawn.*"

"Oh now you're just being silly."

"Give me a dark Heineken, some sunglasses and the early morning allergies—ah! We'd need a house though first. I'm not mowin' other people's damned lawns."

She gave him a sidelong glance. "*Weddings.*"

"Are you proposing?"

"A friend's wedding or, God forbid, a family wedding. The ceremony, the reception, the dancing, the bouquet— "

"The garter belt. What about pets?"

"Now hold on, we've not been deprived there. We picked up at least half a dozen strays this year alone."

"And then gave them to a shelter. It's not the same."

Teresa looked out the window, disconnecting from the conversation. "Pets just die too early anyway. Guess we're better off."

Martin kept driving. Dealing with the tailgaters and excessive lane-changers almost became a therapeutic diversion, even as they hit rush hour.

The Messenger never led them to five star hotels. They were lucky if they even got a hotel instead of a motel. The Happy Moon Lodge was the prototype for this manner of dwelling. A two story building with a barren, sun-scratched roof and lazy air vents spinning. The place slumped in the bottom of a depression just off Mount Vernon Avenue. The second floor overlooked a swimming pool filled with some kind of limeade and dappled with mosquito larvae.

"A hospitable resort," Teresa read from a travel book.

"Oh so they got massages here?"

"Yeah, but you have to go up the street and meet the leper with the shopping cart."

"Is it far?"

Teresa smirked before slipping outside. Martin checked that his door was locked. "I wonder. What about the God thing? Like this is our test? Just think about it this time. It makes more sense than anything else."

"I thought this conversation died about a thousand times ago."

"No conclusion was ever drawn," he replied.

"If the Messenger was God that would make us guardian angels and you're no angel. I've known you too long."

He grinned and leaned in to put her in a guillotine choke-hold. A nervous laugh died in his throat as he stopped and withdrew. *What the hell am I thinking?*

Teresa cocked an eyebrow. "I better not be that brittle yet."

"I know but—"

He missed a beat and she fell sideways, swung around and grappled him. Though he knew how to break a blood choke, he couldn't believe her speed, this woman who'd been barfing a lung for the last hundred miles. Teresa applied gentle pressure to a carotid artery, just to show him she'd found it. Martin didn't need reassurance. She could have given him a case of cerebral ischemia right then, and he didn't have to speculate long about that. He raised an arm buzzing from blood restriction, aimed a pulsing finger to the motel office. "After you, wonderful, brilliant, beautiful lady."

She gave him a cool kiss on the neck and released the hold. "There's a good boy."

There was no front door, just a wobbly screen. The office had two cubicle-sized rooms. A man sat on a stool, his plump tropical shorts running down the sides. An Asian soap opera played on a nine-inch television sitting on top of several torn maintenance manuals. The air in the room hung with the odor of cheap cigarettes and Martin could tell that in the summer this place would be the worst kind of hell imaginable—he could almost foresee the sweat waiting behind the man's broad forehead.

"We'd like a room through the first of November."

The manager tweaked his chin. Martin and Teresa waited a moment, while the man completely ignored them. After politely reading the subtitles for a spell, Martin opened his mouth to repeat their request, this time with a spicier conclusion, but the man cut him off. "Cash or Card?"

"Cash," they chorused.

He turned one eye to them. "Five hundred, seventy-five. Credit card for deposit please?"

"We don't have a credit card." Martin glared at Teresa.

"Two hundred cash for deposit."

Martin knuckled his way into his pocket. There was plenty of money, but he wished it spent elsewhere, not given for this rundown pusbucket of a motel. They dropped by a credit union in San Bernardino and deposited most of the money in the Messenger's secure checking account. After the credit union they went to a fantastic Mexican restaurant called El Sombrero. Martin could still feel the onset of a carbohydrate crash; the beans, rice and tortillas anchored around his waist. It was not doing anything to improve his mood. Besides which, this motel manager looked like he could have been Tony Nguyen's father. It made last year sharply return. Did they *have to* stay here?

They did. Teresa had taught Martin to never question the Messenger's instructions, no matter how unreasonable. It was a code to live by, he guessed.

After the manager put the cash in his safe, he handed over a torn copy of the receipt. He took down a pair of keys. "Second floor. Room 218. You come here for pool key. No loud TV. And this is for you." He brought up a black envelope from under the counter.

Martin felt dizzy. The second letter? This soon? Teresa looked differentially at him. "Did you see who it was?" she asked the manager.

"Watching TV—I didn't look up. Nice voice. They had a good voice."

Teresa gently took the envelope.

"Tall or short?" Martin asked. "Man or woman?"

Something lit in the manager's eyes and then instantly failed. He shrugged as though in response to a more trivial question.

Outside rain sprinkled and every color looked crippled with black. They took up their necessaries and waited to get settled in their shabby little room before opening the second letter. Everybody had a vague story about who left the letters that controlled their destiny each year. Each story contradicted the next. And as always, the Messenger remained unknown.

Nineteen

For the last twenty minutes, images of the Nomads decayed in the Priestess's mind. Once they reached Colton, Martin and Teresa guttered like torchlight, and then they dimmed to translucence, which made the Priestess labor so hard that she had to abandon all other visions, including her homeland. The Nomads were ghosts now. They were concepts. And once they had reached some locus in the city, they evaporated.

This was the Messenger's doing.

She looked for the answer outside the tinted window. Storm clouds could muddle her sight but not dissect it into a million pieces. The clouds over Colton were not weather. They rested across her eyes like a sleep shade. The Archbishop of Morning had fermented and drank of his own wife. All for this failure! Now his sacrifice had been spoiled. He would blame the Priestess. It would be painful, but not sweet.

There had to be a way to get them back. The Priestess had the Nomads. If she focused, maybe she could reassemble all of those drifting solids in space. Just dissipate those clouds! Through lesser storms she had restored her sight. Patience. The

Messenger did not have unlimited power. He could not hold those clouds forever. Could he? She?

The Priestess's inner eye twisted and strained and searched and groped and aborted...

She *should* have killed the Nomads back in that abandoned bar. Caution. *Calm.* No, she had played it the only way she knew, and now it had all gone to salted dirt. She no longer felt worthy. The Church of Morning should have sent someone else to this world.

Her eyes pushed open to their mental limit and saw only falling raindrops, fast as steel darts from the skies. Her servant Eggert and Archbishop Pager sat there in the limo, both scrutinizing her, both sharing a painful restraint.

Her voice trembled. "I've lost them."

"Well, get them back!" Sandeus's painted eyes sharpened to daggers.

"I can't yet."

"You must!"

"I've tried! The storm over the city—those clouds shouldn't be there."

"Where did you last see the Nomads?" Eggert calmly asked, though his beard had flattened from nervous stroking.

"Just outside the city."

"Fuck!" Sandeus leaned back against the leather seat and clasped his arms together. "What good does that do us? We already know what city they're going to! Come on, damn you. I'm not waiting another year."

"She's trying." Eggert's eyes turned. The Priestess had seen those eyes spin into rage before. Never an amusing prospect from an Ekkian barbarian. But, to give Eggert credit, in the past she'd usually been the one to put that rage there.

"Cloth will rip out our spines for this." Sandeus grasped his bald dome to work out the stress there. "I trusted you Priestess. I trusted Kennen."

Eggert's lips trembled more than hers now.

"Don't be foolish." Sandeus looked up at him. "I'm not ruining this suit over the likes of you."

"I have pledged nothing to the Church of Midnight." Eggert patted his knife under his coat. "Are you quick enough?"

Sandeus leaned in, startling the big man. The odd she-male face hardened in the muted light. "I know a quick and easy way to send you back to the Old Domain, big guy. So stop fucking around."

The Priestess sensed a bluff, but she didn't intend to prove anything. "Eggert, be calm."

Eggert deflated a bit. But only a bit.

Sandeus was scarlet with annoyance. "Just keep trying."

The Priestess of Morning shut her eyes and opened her other, keener pair to the burning boundaries of her mind.

Twenty

THE LAST NEEDLES OF LIGHT RETRACTED AS THE SUN WAS dragged under the foothills. Teresa stood at the window of the room and fought another coughing fit. Keeping her lungs calm reminded her of building mantles in a way; concentration could not be broken or there was inevitable collapse. She swallowed the itchiness and focused outside. The raining world looked so different at dusk; vibrancy had left tint, clarity had become murkiness, people had slowed down, night beasts had awoken.

"So evil looking out there."

Martin sat on the bed, rereading the Messenger's latest letter. The black envelope lay in fragments at his side like a shattered crow. "What I don't understand," he said, scratching his jaw, "is why *four* this time? Don't we have enough on our hands protecting one Heart of the Harvest? What the hell are they trying to prove?"

"Who?"

"Whoever's behind this sick game."

"I told you already. The Hearts on the list all have the same last name. They're related."

"But only one person grows the fruit—just one—that's how it's always been. What the hell? We go out to Flagstaff, so we get less time for planning and, and, and," Martin stammered, "and more people to look after now. Why doesn't the Messenger step in and help? Doesn't he know you're sick?"

Teresa wanted to slap Martin. She wondered if she did, if he'd stop bringing up the obvious. It was driving her nuts. She'd bitten her fingernails down to sorry nubs. One of them actually throbbed because the nail had been shorn down too far.

"Why are you looking at me like that?" he demanded.

"Sometimes I can really appreciate your age Martin. I can."

"I'm nearly forty years old. I'm no damned child and—"

"No!" she snapped. "If the messenger needs us to protect four, ten, or a thousand Hearts, so be it! If one billion of Cloth's children hatch this year, we have to deal with them and Cloth and the rest of the Church! Like grinning, grateful idiots we have to endure. As always Martin! Stop asking useless questions!"

Teresa fell on the bed beside him and stared up at the moldy ceiling. Martin said nothing and after a moment she felt bad and playfully slapped his thigh. He didn't respond to this though and she stopped. "When I was in fourth grade I used to help the lunch ladies in the cafeteria."

His head did not turn to her. "Yeah?"

A coughing fit sneak-attacked. It sounded awful, like bones roiling in snot. She grabbed a tissue from the nightstand and wiped her mouth, steadied, tried to will away the next series. It worked after a minute.

Martin turned now. "You okay?"

She began to mindlessly fold the wet tissue into halves. "So I worked at the cafeteria in fifth grade and one of the lunch ladies had cancer. Lucky her. She came to school missing a breast. I didn't even really have boobs yet, so I couldn't image how it would feel to lose one, but I remember the woman's face. It looked so distant, like she was missing more than just her breast—I never thought I'd understand that face. It was too old, too miserable and hopeless. But I understand now. You can be surrounded by a million people and still be absolutely lonely." She paused. "Which is to say, I don't want to go yet. I don't want to leave you. But things happen."

Teresa wasn't crying, but she could feel tears dropping inside her mind. Martin took her hand and clutched it. He didn't seem to care if it hurt her. Maybe the hurt would heal her, maintain her life force. "I'll keep you safe. If I can protect a Heart, I can protect you."

"You can't do both."

"Don't put a challenge out there, girlie."

"Chaplain Cloth is already in this world, Martin. That can only explain why we need to hide in this room. You were right. We shouldn't have gone to my mother's. Somehow, I think the Church got a bead on us somewhere."

Martin was silent for a minute and softened his grip on her hand. "So what are we going to do?"

"Follow the letter, go out tomorrow to see the Heart Bearer and then get back here, just like it says. We follow our orders, like always."

"In the meantime, we practice building?"

"I'm as good at that as I'll ever get," she answered, then drew up her pant leg to a knotty scar from knee to ankle. It was puckered pink and red and looked like second-degree burns had melted the perimeter. "Don't want to get another of these to match last year's. I would better use the time exercising these old legs. You can practice building mantles though. If you want."

"Maybe they have a workout room here." His hopeful smile spread and it made her feel bad for ever losing her temper with him. "I should get my knee ready for the big day too."

She bit her lower lip and threw a soft play punch to his jaw. Martin brushed his fingertips over her cheek and to her lips. "I won't let them through again. I promise. I won't let anything happen to you."

"Our purpose is the Heart of the Harvest."

"Remember it's plural this time," he corrected. "Heart*s*. I'd like to say double trouble, but it's really more like double-double trouble."

The next logical question about Cloth having the opportunity to harvest four this year, made them mute. Teresa just hoped these four Hearts were faster than poor Tony Nguyen.

Martin reached past his semiauto and tapped on the power from the TV remote mounted on the nightstand. Teresa twisted off the lamp and the lightbulb flickered and burnt out for good. The dingy room sunk into shadows, became blue-washed in the TV's glow.

She could tell in how Martin sidled up to her that he wanted to make love, but he never asked anymore, possibly because of the malignant third party involved. Instead, she held him tight and they watched the news. The world wasn't doing so well. Teresa wanted to care about the war and the hunger and the environment and the power-playing politicians, but she knew these were largely symptoms of a sickness trickling into the world every October. And they'd never be able to cure it completely.

Twenty-one

PAUL FELT LIKE HE WAS GOING TO THROW UP. HE HADN'T had time to settle down with the rest of the church at the hotel. No shower. No lunch. With the marrow seeds sprouting through Paul's lungs to other internals, with the panic of sitting next to a three hundred pound cuckold (Paul's cock still filmy from Melissa's hand-jive), and with the dizzy impression of meeting the Priestess of Morning tonight, he found no room left in his heart for a boogeyman.

Chaplain Cloth had always been just a symbol to Paul, not an actuality. He knew that every big organization had its symbols, whether they were religious in nature or just emotive. Any story told about an October hunt featured Chaplain Cloth and Paul always took him as a metaphor for the Eternal Church, a united Church—these were romantic, sentimental stories that anchored the weak-minded and helped grow the Church of Midnight through fear.

But—Paul's rationalizations were beginning to stretch too thin. As much as he wanted to continue to disbelieve the precepts of his affiliation, the matter remained. The seeds had changed him. Even the world moved differently. Paul saw things on another scale, his analog eyes switched digital. And not just his eyes...his *soul* felt high definition and this change would be ongoing. He would continue past high definition and into something better, and then a breath later even his memories would be obsolete and he would charge forward into an unending state of improvement, and his mind would brim over—he would feel safe, for a moment—but then everything would splash down into a newer, better, larger mind, which was already conceiving another replacement that would outdo the rest.

"You look like you're about to shit a roll of barbwire," Cole remarked. "You did well this morning with that girl. Are you still practicing those exercises?"

"Trying," Paul replied. The shutter to the Old Domain was still sealed in his mind. He felt the quartz in his pocket but let it go, too nauseated.

Cole swung the limo around a strangely configured intersection, half fork and half roundabout, and let a pickup truck go ahead of them. "You're afraid of meeting Cloth, I take it?"

I shouldn't have made Melissa do that. It was overkill, thought Paul. *But her crestfallen expression had been so priceless when I came through her fist.*

"I'm not so afraid, just filthy, famished and worn-out."

"Good," Cole put simply. His bandage had been removed and left behind a sour red crater in his jaw. It no longer bled. Now it just looked like someone had taken out a flesh divot with a miniature golf club. "There's really no need to be frightened of Chaplain Cloth. He's here for the Heart of the Harvest, not anything else."

"So he's real. Is the Heart of the Harvest real?"

Cole made a right down a residential street crowded with delineators and cones. He squinted at every street sign, trying to find his way.

"So you don't know either?" Paul prodded.

Headlights glanced off the face busy with scars. The Bishop adjusted the tight band of his black tie and smoothed it down his worn Armani. He turned down several more streets. "The Heart of the Harvest nourishes Cloth's children, who are pieces of the gateway born into this world. They are the only creatures able to interact and open the gateway, but they must gorge themselves on the Heart before expelling such power. The Heart grows inside a different vessel each year and it matures on the Day of Opening."

"Yeah I know all that, but what happens when a Heart survives? I wasn't in the Inner Circle yet, so I only know how success looks."

"After the 31st the fruit dies, the vessel's body becomes just like any other mortal."

The words came out before Paul could stop himself. "What a load of shit."

"You may get to see it all happen, if you survive the Heralding."

That did not set Paul at ease. He told Cole to pull over and once the car came to a stop he popped open the door and proceeded to vomit into a rushing storm drain.

Light pollution from Colton, San Bernardino, Rialto, and assorted neighboring cities cast a gross hue over the stars. It reminded Paul of when he mixed coke with milk as a kid. Out here in Reche Canyon though, one could probably see more stars than anywhere else, except the mountains maybe. *Fuck the stars*, thought Paul. *Fuck this place. Fuck the idea behind all of this.* It was for one woman? He questioned what had brought him to such lengths.

The headlights cut through a cloud of dirt. The brown particles looked electrified for a moment, turned to silver silt, like they were under a lake. Paul just wanted to leave. His nerves couldn't take this a second longer—

Someone in black moved through the cloud and Paul shot up in alarm. His newly attuned awareness lighted from the marrow blossoms and suddenly his mind pushed forward.

"How—? Don't!" Cole barked. "Cloth will kill us, you asshole!"

There was no stopping it now. Paul had sent something vicious outside of his mind to push Chaplain Cloth back into the Old Domain. Frantically Paul clawed at his seat belt. Couldn't waste a moment, had to run—

"Quintana!"

Cole's voice was a water molecule in a tsunami. Paul's fingers dug at the buckle; his seatbelt came free and slapped the interior frame. Cole reached for his sleeve, but Paul already had the door open. He threw himself outside and felt the cold, dirty air squeeze his body. A vile taste gagged him. There was no way he was going to participate in this shit—there was no way. Run away. Run far. Get those heels kicking. Never look back. Forget the Priestess. She was just another whore like mother...

Paul slid downhill into tumbleweeds, fighting and ripping up his hands unlatching the skeletal plants. The limo headlights lessened and now Cole ambled across a dismal watercolor painting of browns and yellows and grays.

Gravel crunched to his left. Paul automatically sent out another push. This time he had no chance to feel anything cross over. Instead, the impulse returned, a two thousand pound fist that nudged him back. That was all it took. Paul lost footing and dropped.

Sounds of Cole's searching through the dust grew louder on the hill above. Paul wiggled around and found his feet. With nothing left he charged into the hazy white light. Cole reached out with disembodied arms and tried to grab him. Paul slipped away. He heard new shoes pounding the gravel. He almost pushed out with his mind again but wasn't able to control it, and kept running.

He darted out of the dust into the blue desert night. An arm stretched out, then a pearl white finger. Paul had seen this ahead, wanted to stop, to turn, escape. But he sent himself right into that finger and before it even had a chance to touch him, Paul went rigid and his nervous system exploded. A hiccup of stomach acid blasted into his mouth, his heart seized and guts twisted.

Cole ran up. Apologies were already forming through the big man's heavy breaths.

"The new Bishop?" a silky voice asked.

Cole took a second to answer, either from lack of breath or confusion. "Yes, but he didn't— "

"Very well," answered Chaplain Cloth.

Paul managed to open his eyes. Cloth had melted into the surroundings, but his eyes floated in the night, one burning bright orange like a small sun and the other so black it sucked in the darkness around it, making the night seem gray.

"Come this way, brothers. I mustn't leave the gateway unattended."

Cole tucked a hand under Paul's underarm and hefted him to his feet.

"What the hell is the matter with you?" Cole grumbled in his ear. Louder, "What the fuck?"

"He startled me," Paul said. It sounded just as stupid to him as he imagined it did to Cole, but it was the truth.

The men and the monster walked up the black hill to a looming grain silo. A giant mouth swelled in the silo's side like a meaty abrasion. This was the first time Paul hadn't felt the marrow blossoms since they were implanted. He had no doubt it was Cloth who had put them into hibernation. Now the blossoms were hiding. Paul would have hidden also, had he the chance.

Something, a lot of things, lived inside that silo. Gears turning; the calls of bats; tangled voices; songs of hounds. The smell from inside came and went on the breeze, maggots and Malto Meal. Chaplain Cloth had retreated inside the silo, into the mouth of the gateway. All they could really see now was a single smoldering orange eye.

"I'm glad you came to visit. I have high hopes this year for the bounty."

Cole sat on a hay bail, his curly gray hair looking like a Spartan helmet in the drizzling moonlight. He lowered his head, and despite feeling silly, Paul followed.

The Malto-maggot scent peaked again and Paul's empty stomach fluttered. He had to do something. He couldn't just sit there after nearly attacking this thing. Paul tried to speak clearly, but it still came out as mumbles, "Can I ask something?"

"Can you?"

Paul was afraid this was a test but carefully went on. "What will happen after the worlds come together?"

Lips smacked in the shadows. "Normalcy. Most of this world has already been populated with broken spirits, tenderized for us—blindfolded, gagged, bound and dropped into ethereal quicksand without much corralling. Its defenses have been lowered, especially in this land. Walking contradictions. The human animal has a dead heart but celebrates love and brotherhood. Funny." Chaplain Cloth purred at the last. The bat songs, the howling hounds, the muttering insanity from inside the silo calmed suddenly. "The Eternal Church will begin its rule on them soon."

"I've decided to have my own say in that rule, as it pertains to the Church of Midnight," Cole said carefully.

"Would you now?" The orange eye flared and its color outlined its black twin. Chaplain Cloth was quiet for some time. The rain's force lessened to mist.

"I just thought you'd like to know."

"Really?" The eyes twinkled merrily. "And why?"

"When you learn what happened to Sandeus Pager, I want you to know it was me. I am more worthy than he. I will prove the Church's greatness by sacrificing him for ineptitude and lack of passion to the call. And I—I'd like your blessing."

"I'm a Chaplain in the Eternal Church," Cloth explained. "There is no need to ask a blessing from one beneath your station. Besides which, I don't involve myself in mortal pettiness, you understand."

Cole looked away, embarrassed. "Certainly, Chaplain."

"Now, I would think it wise to go build your strength for the Heralding. And take Bishop Quintana there. He smells like he needs a shower."

The black and orange eyes watched them leave. There was a smile in the darkness somewhere. Paul was sure of it.

Cole slammed the car door and dropped his heavy body into the seat. A minute passed, with him searching around like a man on the verge of a breakdown. He drove a big fist into the radio and Paul shrunk back. “Motherfucking shit!”

Cole pulled back his big arm again and let another punch smash into the sagging plastic components. One of his knuckles burst and he ripped his hand away. He made like he was about to punch the console again, but threw his head back against the headrest and took a deep breath.

Paul found himself pressed against the passenger door. “Something the matter?”

Cole palmed his jaw wound absently and then sucked at his bloody knuckles. “He knows Sandeus should not hold the position. That twisted fuck knows that!”

“He doesn’t have a problem with it. Does having a blessing change anything?” asked Paul, warily.

“It does for me. After performing the Heralding year after year, being invaluable in tracking the Nomads, lasting all this time, gaining so many scars, I imagined Cloth would find me worthy.”

Paul relaxed a little. “Maybe Cloth knows you’ll be worthy only if you pull it off. That’s all that matters, Bishop.”

Cole turned over the ignition. “Forget it. This was a waste coming here. We need to get back to the hotel. Conclave will begin soon.”

Paul fell back, heart still reeling. The limo shrugged left and right as they went onto the paved road. The lights from the city brightened the night. In the back of his mind, Paul heard Cloth’s children scratching at the shutter.

He turned to find Cole looking at him. “What?” he asked.

“I hear them too. They’re anxious this year Quintana,” Cole told him as shadows slashed over his distorted face. “And you’re going to open the door wider than ever. You will let them in.”

THE CHURCH OF MIDNIGHT OCCUPIED FOUR FLOORS OF THE Doubletree hotel in Ontario. The drive from Colton took around twenty minutes and that gave Paul plenty of time to splash around in his dread. He was fairly convinced Cole needed him for the Heralding and there weren't any plans to get rid of him, at least not right now, and he was also slightly sure Melissa would have her acolytes watching the situation steadfast, just in case. She couldn't afford to have that video go public domain. If Cole didn't break her neck, he'd find a way to throw her out of her job in supply and logistics, maybe even toss her out of the Inner Circle. Paul couldn't worry about it tonight though. Now that he'd lived through his meeting with Chaplain Cloth, tonight was all about the Priestess. He refused to not enjoy himself.

Cole checked them in at the front counter. The hotel was nicer than most places Paul'd been to: red carpets, sitting areas, wide-open and airy spaces. He sat in a daze by a potted fern across from the counter and looked around to see if anybody cared enough to watch. *Nope*, just a few sweeping bodies carrying luggage, waiting to put it down somewhere. Paul took out his quartz and practiced. The blossoms had unfurled again and he'd rather have his mind on this rock than on the memory of those freaky eyes. Everything *could* be fine.

"Put the rock away," Cole said, making him jump. "You do that in private. We don't advertise."

Paul slipped the stone in his pocket. Cole handed him a little envelope with the key card to his room. "Are your acolytes bringing up your luggage?"

Paul nodded a white lie. He still had to give the lobotomites a call. They were probably drunk by this hour. Hopefully they were only a little stoned.

"I'll see you at conclave."

Paul nodded, then he flipped open his phone and put it to his ear. Cole Szerszen stood there looking at him for an uncomfortable moment while the phone rang.

"Our bargain in the desert will always stand," said Cole. "I want you to know that, no matter what, you have my word on that as a Bishop of Midnight."

Paul didn't know what to say. It was almost embarrassing. Cole clapped him hard on the shoulder and headed for the elevators. An exasperated sigh burst from Paul's mouth. *That is one odd duck there, boys and girls,* he thought.

The ringing ended in a lazy sounding message, "This is Vince, um, I'm not here to take...your, um, message, but if you leave me, uh, your number I'll return your call. Thank you. Buh-bye."

Paul hated *buh-bye.*

"Hey fuckhead!" he started. Two passing elderly women toting carpet suitcases gave Paul sidelong looks. "Get your ass to the Doubletree in Ontario. Bring ten acolytes, strapped. The hotel is booked, so tell the rest they're sleeping in the parking structure. Call me when you get this, which better be fucking soon."

Paul smacked the phone shut and then rubbed at the anxiety locked in his face. It was okay. In a couple hours, conclave would begin and he would be in the same room with the Priestess. The thought of that practically floated him to the elevators.

Before a second knock could hit the door, Paul was off the bed. His bath towel fell off his hips and he almost tripped through its terry-cloth layers. He cursed the towel and ripped it off the ground and stationed it over his crotch with one hand. What the hell had taken Vince so long? Paul took a breath and got his game face on. He'd stood toe to toe with Chaplain Cloth and renewed confidence flowed through his body like an electrical current.

The door came open and he said, "Where the—?"

Melissa stood outside. She was dressed in a black evening dress. Had she lost those silly horn rimmed glasses she may have passed the minor league test for Paul, but as it stood she still reminded him of a boarding school teacher on her perpetual period. A parcel was tucked under her arm.

He grinned at the box, then at her. "Why are you here? Come back for seconds?"

She shoved him into the room and closed the door. "I need to get back to Cole. He really doesn't need to know I'm here."

"No shit." Paul wrapped the towel around his waist. It began to sag and he readjusted. "So you brought them?"

She handed the box over. "I'm going to report them as stolen when we return to Mojave. You need to know that."

"Do what you have to." Paul went over to the small gray safe in the closet and put the box inside. Twisted the dial. "I'll test the seeds on someone sooner or later, so if you fucked me—"

"I know you don't care and you don't even have a shred of decency, but all I have is Cole. Without him I would be nowhere."

"The Melissa Patterson story," he said. "Next Tuesday at seven."

"Destroy that video. Cole doesn't deserve to be hurt like this."

"I agree."

"I'll offer my two best acolytes," she said reluctantly. "If that's what you require for this to be over. If there were plans made, you'll be the first to know when they pledge to you. This just has to end already."

"More acolytes sounds good, but I don't want anyone wittier than me. I just want them to be able to tie their shoelaces without the double loop trick."

Melissa put her hand on the bony ridge of her hip. The words were hard-formed, as though she planed over them. "You really don't have to be suspicious. I think you know that if Cole found out, he'd only hate me."

"Yes," Paul replied, "Cole's not so bad. Ugly as a mutt on a butt-hunt, but I have no real problems with him. He wants to be the Archbishop, which after what I saw tonight makes Cole either delusional or suicidal. I wouldn't refuse an ally on that level. I certainly never want to slide into that position. Hell, I don't plan to be in this church forever."

"Sacrilege."

An obnoxious knock came at the door. *Shave and a haircut*. Paul shook his head, sickened by the sound. Melissa hurried to the peephole and squinted through it. "One of yours, I think."

"Please, I take no ownership." Paul ripped open the door. A lanky, longhaired guy in a *Slayer* T-shirt swaggered over the threshold with Paul's suitcases. He jangled as he walked, earrings, wallet chain, bracelets all announcing his arrival. "Awesome room, Quintana! Woh, put some clothes on, man."

Melissa stepped around Vince Stogin and ventured into the hall. Paul thumbed over his shoulder. "Do you see why I need new people? I'm not just being a dick."

"Yes you are," she returned. "That's all that you are."

"I hope you haven't washed your hands since."

"The video?" she whispered firmly.

Paul leaned back into the room and swiped his phone off the little round table. Melissa watched as he scrolled down to the video and selected delete.

"And the copies? How do I know you'll erase those?"

"I'm not getting rid of them right away."

Skin bunched in her brow. "So why did I do all this? How do I know you won't keep screwing me over— "

"Because my dear, it's very simple. I'm sick of looking at you."

Melissa's mouth dropped as the door shut in her face.

Twenty-two

Cole waited in the hallway for Melissa for more than forty minutes and his patience had thinned to transparency. He'd tried his best to clean up his jaw and busted knuckle, and comb back his donkey gray hair so that he looked as presentable as someone like him could possibly look. He wore the dress shoes she'd bought him even though they were too narrow and gave him blisters on his ankles. He also had sprayed his neck with that awful cologne she'd purchased for his birthday.

His tuxedo felt like an anchor that grew heavier with every breath. He'd never grown fond of suits and dreaded the night of conclave when he had to put on the suit of all suits. It just felt phony. People should not wear clothing that suggested achievement when they had none. He wasn't worthy of a tux yet. He still felt like an old demolitions toady from the Monterey chapel, happy to do what was expected of him.

Cole stood by a sign from one of the earlier church seminars. *Inner City Recruitment: Dealing with gang factions, reversal of loyalty and incentives.* He thought that might have been a good one to take before going out this morning.

The rest of the Church of Midnight lingered outside the ballroom, chatting and chortling and chugging cocktails from the bar. Many of the faces hadn't changed. Some had grown older. The entire Inner Circle wasn't present, of course, and this left all the international factions to send the most politically palatable members. They were ad hoc Bishops now, for sure, but Cole would see they received the titles someday. That there should be two bishops and an Archbishop, and that they be American was something that some scholars interpreted from the Tomes. But it wasn't there. It was projection. And it wasn't fair. These men and women had done their time. They *were* worthy. As Archbishop, Cole wouldn't kneel to tradition and hoard the marrow seeds. He would give the others what they deserved and they would love him.

Where in the hell was Melissa? This was really beginning to worry him. He looked through the walls of tuxedos and evening gowns. Paul Quintana had come down moments ago and already had taken to a few women. Cole was somewhat impressed. Last year Paul hadn't gotten past the hallway. Sure, a few ordained clergy had congratulated him on the gauntlet, but otherwise he'd been a glorified drink-fetcher and never even got to see conclave. At least Cole knew Melissa wasn't with him.

A hand clasped his shoulder, tight as talons, and he jerked around and caught the powdery fingers by reflex.

Archbishop Pager stared back, startled for a moment. Sandeus's face was not made up and it looked more male, sadder. With the plan at hand, Cole got a sick feeling seeing him in this light.

"Bishop Szerszen, relax friend." Sandeus undid his grip.

"I'm sorry, Archbishop, forgive me."

"Don't kiss my ass, Cole." Sandeus folded his arms. "What's the matter? Your visit with Cloth did not go well I take it?"

"It went fine."

"I'm sorry I couldn't accompany you. Perhaps next October, provided there is a next October. So how was the new one?"

Cole's eyes flitted to Paul again. He was feeding a maraschino cherry to the tall blonde envoy from Sweden. Instead of putting it on her tongue, he dropped it into her cleavage. She smirked, amused but not impressed by him, and fished the cherry out. "Quintana has some issues to work though, but he's coming along nicely. I foresee the Children being numerous this year."

"I still can't believe Quintana isn't out cold, what with the seeds so recently planted. It took you two weeks I think."

"Three," Cole corrected.

"Archbishop!"

Sandeus stumbled forward as he was slapped hard on the back. The Scottish envoy had an elegant black beard tied in ebon bows.

"Camden." Sandeus took his gnarled hand and tried a hearty, manly shake. "I'll be with you in a moment, brother."

Camden showed an imperfect row of teeth. "Good, good. Nice to see you too, Bishop Szerszen."

Cole nodded. He'd always liked Camden Amherst. The Scot wasn't catty or marrow seed-jealous like the others. He was probably the best liked of the European contingency, bar none.

When they were somewhat alone again, Cole resumed, "Quintana got spooked and tried to vacate Chaplain Cloth."

Sandeus's face glowed with laughter that never came. "Are you messing with me?"

"No," replied Cole. "Cloth didn't do anything to him. I thought we were done though."

"You should have been. Sometimes I don't even know why we bother giving the seeds to the new Bishops. I should have stopped with you. Really. What's the point? We only need one person, strong enough to herald the children. Backward tradition, nothing more. We should lose it altogether."

Cole ignored this, now feeling at ease again with his plans for this man. He didn't try to respond because he would have screamed out loud for all the Doubletree to hear. They would be stronger against the Nomads with more Bishops. It wasn't a difficult concept to digest for someone less of a power hoarder.

More tuxedos plowed past, ushering the Priestess of Morning in their core. Sandeus and Cole shared a glance that said—*We'll take this up later.* The caterers pushed carts with silver chafing dishes past. The aromas had Cole's mouth watering. The meals at Conclave were always delicious, and always interesting.

At the far end of the hall a woman turned the corner. She had mousy brown hair and glasses, so at a distance, Cole was relieved, but then as the woman got closer, it became more obvious she wasn't Melissa. If conclave started Cole had to be in there. He couldn't just duck out to find his girlfriend. Every laugh from every stranger started to hurt, to feel wrong. He should be looking for her, searching the crowd. Black, and black, and black, and then his eyes found the Priestess of Morning in a honey colored ballroom dress—she was lovely, like an x-rated Disney heroine, but not prettier than Melissa.

The double doors to the Empire Ballroom swung open and hungry church members rushed in like a dam rupture. *Melissa*, his desperate heart called.

And then, Cole's own priestess was there. Melissa was flush in the face, coming down the hallway in the evening gown he'd bought her. He didn't want to ask where she had been, because if her answer sounded suspicious, even in the least, he wasn't quite sure how he'd feel for the rest of the night.

She wrapped her arms around him and gave him a weak squeeze. "I got held up with some slow acolytes."

"Everything all right?"

"Sure, sure. I had to free a couple from their pledges."

Breaking the pledge of an acolyte was a *big thing*. He had to suspect a lie. If Cole didn't he knew she'd take him for a fool. "We'll talk about this later." His words hardened her countenance, so he added, "Let's just go in. I'm really hungry."

He offered an arm and she took it. *Christ!* thought Cole. That feeling of her little arm around his never got old. They walked side by side and as they approached the door, she leaned into his chest and said, "How was Chaplain Cloth?"

Like many in the Church, Melissa had never met Cloth before, so when she asked about him it was like she was asking about a normal person.

"He was ready," Cole replied and they entered the ballroom.

Paul tried. He tried in the hallway, he tried walking into the ballroom, he tried with the Priestess standing two feet from him in that golden gown. He tried to do what he'd been doing for almost an hour, which was to appear that he wasn't completely controlled. He knew enough about women to understand that they didn't want some sappy, slobbering guy that did everything they asked just to get a whiff. Women wanted men that they could *change into that*, but there was no fun in the game if they got a castrated bull from the start. Such a thing would leave them standing there with a pair of scissors but nowhere to snip.

So Paul tried. He continued to try even as he could sense the Priestess standing nearby and felt electricity arcing between them. He smelled her and thought of a breeze over a meadow in heaven. His mother always had different flowers arriving from her various lovers, and Paul knew their names and their scents. The Priestess contained them all: shrub roses, pineapple and trumpets and regals and oriental lilies, snowdrops, foamflowers—Paul shook his head suddenly. The Priestess had the scents of her own world baked into her flesh and he'd opened himself to the Old Domain to breathe them in. He didn't even remember pulling the shutter open...

Thanksgiving to the black feast! Children's voices called from the backyard of his mind. He'd been ignoring them, keeping the shutter closed, but it was open now like it had been open for centuries. Cloth's children picked up on his disquiet and the voices cheered at the attention.

Let us in!

Blood bread! Bile stew! Blister-meat pie!

Let us in!

The shutter wasn't moving. *Let us in!*

"Fuck!" he blurted.

The Inner Circle envoy from France coiled his lip. "Pardon, Bishop Quintana?"

Paul grabbed his head. "Sorry—I've, uh, got headaches everywhere today."

"Shall I call an acolyte for some painkillers?"

"No thank you, you're kind though."

Just then Cole Szerszen walked up. He had taken Melissa to her seat like a perfect gentleman. It was apparent that Cole too was trying. Cole's tux didn't look half bad on him either. Paul surmised that Cole and Melissa were quite the pair: *Booky and the Beast.* He had to at that moment admit, however, that he was happy to see Cole. The big man had come to his rescue.

"Brother Cornett." Cole took the man's limp hand, cranked it hard and tugged. "How are things in Rennes?"

Cole knew as much French pronunciation as Paul, and that was saying little since Paul only had *Pepe Le Pew* as a primary source. So, the Frenchman winced at *Cornit* and *Renz.*

While Cole chitchatted, sweat continued to pelt down Paul's back. Twice he scrubbed away salt at his hairline. The shutter closed abruptly and the children's voices left angry echoes. Paul looked for the Priestess. There were several strapping young men circling her at the head table, like Makos in dark suits. Her bristly bodyguard—Eggert, Paul believed his name was—keenly watched these men but kept a certain distance for the Priestess's sake. *That's right, big man,* thought Paul. *Protect the honey pot.*

Cole and Cornett exchanged some spirited banter now and Paul's attention slowly fell back on their exchange. The Frenchman's eyes widened with shock. He'd clearly expected an argument from his last statement, which Paul hadn't heard.

"You agree with me, Bishop?" Cornett asked suspiciously.

"Of course," Cole replied. "I have a different outlook than Archbishop Pager. We need an adopted organizational structure for every chapel, worldwide, not just in the States. Everyone here, I feel, should be granted the title of Bishop in their own countries."

Cornett was pleased with this but clearly not sold. "Titles are a start, Bishop Szerszen, but we're not equals until we join bodies with the Old Domain, through the blessed seeds of Marrow Forest."

A man with a thick handlebar mustache bullied his way between them. "Brother Cornett has more objections than suggestions."

Cornett rolled his eyes. "This was not your discussion, Brauer."

"I've made it my discussion, Pierre. Go practice your English elsewhere."

Both men looked at Cole fiercely, who calmly answered them, "We're working for some big changes this year. I administered several hundred grand in the church curriculum to all Great chapels and several that have applied for great status in the past two years. That's only the start of bringing the Church together internationally. So patience, brothers."

"You are a trailblazer Bishop Szerszen. The sessions here have been extremely informative," said Brauer. "I meant to compliment you on the Tomes study groups, very enlightening. Though coordination was better this year, placing us closer to the Heart, I wish my plane had arrived earlier."

"I'm glad you benefited. This is a good year to be at conclave. It may be *the* year."

Brauer's deep brown eyes told that he didn't completely agree with that and they moved over to Paul. "So what made you wish to take up the onus of this title, Bishop Quintana?"

"Huh?" Paul answered.

The ringing of a fork on glass disbanded every conversation, including their own. Cole guided Paul by the elbow. He probably looked as though he needed guiding, so Paul made no comment. He was going to be sitting to the right of the Priestess. She would be so close he would feel the warmth of her body.

Just as he stepped before his seat and she to hers, the shutter in his mind flew up again. *Let us in!*

Opening and closing, closing and opening. The blossoms in his stomach began to drip astringent. Paul uneasily stared at the black and orange bone china before him. He was getting practice right now, whether he liked it or fucking hated it, and all the while she was sitting just to his right, an angel from the Old Domain. He hoped he wouldn't blow vomit all over that dress of hers—he'd already puked once today and that should have relieved his quota. Yet, something inky churned, rising up in his throat. *Let us in. Maggots in a dead sow's ass. Taste the treat. Spoon it up!*

Paul swallowed, but the acrid spit sat in his esophagus, halfway to his mouth. Sandeus Pager stood before a black lectern and spoke to the hundred-plus audience. He had been speaking for a while now, doling out *Thank Yous* and pleasantries like they were attending an award ceremony. He looked odd without his makeup. Paul had seen him last year in the hallway, only briefly, and had thought the same. He looked powerless, almost brittle, like a bald Samson.

"And my friend, the Archbishop of Morning, told me once," he said, "Archbishop Pager, years will go by, on and on, but so will we. Time cannot divide us forever." Sandeus's eyes had moistened with emotion. The audience began cheering and clapping.

Milk a bloody tit, swim the bowels, rip the treasure from the scrotum—

Paul put a fist to his mouth for a moment and then cautiously took it away to clap with the others. When the revelry died down, Sandeus stood there a moment, beaming. "I would like to welcome the Priestess of Morning to speak briefly on her own church's behalf. She and her servant Eggert are the only members of the Church of Morning here tonight, and they honor us with their presence."

Clapping again. Sandeus tried to speak over the frantic hands. "Doesn't she look beautiful?"

The Priestess stood and grazed Paul with her scent. *So stupid!* he thought. He hadn't even introduced himself. At this point she probably figured him to be some creepy pervert, which he figured he really was.

The Priestess stepped up the stairs to the small stage, helped by her faithful bearded guardian in a tuxedo. Sandeus kissed her hand and let her in behind the lectern. She leaned toward the microphone and took everybody in with a sweeping glance.

"Our thanks go to you all. We're indebted for your hospitality and kindness, not to mention helping us adjust to a new home." She retreated a little from the microphone's boom. The audience shifted in their seats. "The Church of Midnight and Morning's only true separation is the gateway—we have the same hope. Let us pray for the endurance of that spirit. Let us be strong together when we unite. Let no pride or self-pity tear us apart. Let the Eternal Church thrive through our love!"

The standing ovation that followed almost killed Paul. He stood, trying to make eye contact and trying to clap louder than anyone else, but it wasn't happening. Too many crazy, disgusting things bounced inside his head and forced him to take action. He braced himself against the table and slammed his entire mind shut. A burning hot spike splintered the nerves in his skull. He ate it, gritting his teeth. After a moment, the pain went.

He lowered into his seat and realized the Priestess had already returned and was seated. Making a god-awful mistake, he looked into her satin eyes. She was looking straight at him.

"Great speech," he mumbled.

She leaned over and a stray ringlet of hair tickled his cheek. Her engorged lips were in kissing distance and he felt close to losing control. "I don't like to drone on and on. The problem there is that I keep things shorter than some prefer. Nobody here seems to like when you get right to the point."

"I liked what you said, very much in fact." He stared at those lips and their every movement.

"It's almost the same speech I made last year at the harvest celebration," she told him placidly. "It sounds more like a lie this year, but the applause was louder."

"Maybe they know it's a lie," Paul told her. His confidence felt partially restored with the voices gone. "I've never believed the unification would go smoothly."

The Priestess's eyebrow rose. "So why do they clap at all?"

"They aren't clapping for your words." He winked and turned away, hoping she liked him, wishing she would talk to him some more, and praying she wouldn't.

Either way. He was still trying.

A bell chimed as the caterers started pushing their carts around. Dinnertime. Two men, separate from the others, came toward the head table carrying platters with orange cloths draped over the food.

"Special treatment?" he asked the Priestess, going out on a thin, thin limb.

She only smiled and folded her hands in her lap. Sandeus Pager picked up his knife and fork, ready to fill his stomach. Cole did the same and straightened in his chair.

Thanksgiving to the eternal feast, thought Paul. After a second he realized the thought had not come from him.

Paul couldn't look away from his plate. The rest of the ballroom dined on prime rib, creamed spinach, potatoes, French rolls: normal food. What had been set before him was an atrocity. There was a strange looking bird that had been roasted. A thin layer of crackling scales sheathed the gamy flesh and the bird's neck coiled to the side with a head that became a startling reminder of Sandeus's snake Alexander. An ice-cream scoop of something rust colored had also been plopped on his plate. The Priestess pointed out this treat was crushed fireroot, and then there was a dessert dish of tiny white beads that she explained were frosted windcherries. The smashed root and the cherries appeared edible and even smelled pleasant, but the rest of the platter had no place in this world. A cob of opalescent corn was cradled under one of the bird's leathery wings. Paul slid the cob out with his fork and nearly shrieked. The kernels all looked like tiny staring fish eyes.

The Priestess peeled off the scales of her bird and ran her knife into the bruise colored flesh. He looked over and saw Sandeus spooning great helpings of fireroot in his mouth. Cole had also begun work on his bird.

The fireroot and cherries, thought Paul. But he wouldn't touch the bird or corn. He could say he wasn't that hungry.

"Be sure to try everything," the Priestess whispered. "This is part of the yield that came with us through the gateway last year. It's preserved all year for conclave. Our people used to assemble feasts much like this one and offer them to the gateway—they believed this would suffice in lieu of the Heart of Harvest."

Paul lifted the limp bird with the far end of his fork. "Did it work?"

She smiled brilliantly. "That was superstition, something both worlds share in common, wouldn't you say?"

"Sure," he admitted.

"You haven't introduced yourself to me, Bishop."

"Where are my manners?" He fell into business mode, ignoring her hair, her scent, her face. It made Paul proud to the bone he could accomplish this with his mind in knots and libido spinning like a windmill in a hurricane. "Paul Quintana."

They shook hands. "I chose a name for this world. Mabel Milton," she said.

"Priestess suits you better."

Her eyes sparkled. "Very well."

Paul scooped up some fireroot and shoveled it into his mouth. Needed salt and pepper. It was baby-food bland and he could only sense a gritty texture on his tongue. Next, he went for the windcherries and was surprised that they tasted like sugared grapes, yet their flesh had a pulpy citrus quality. *Not so bad*, he thought.

The Priestess bit into the corn. Her teeth burst the little eyeballs and a milky substance ran down her chin.

The bird next, Paul decided. He went about the process the same way she had, removing the fine layer of scales and then cutting away chunks of tender purple-blue-yellow meat. It would have been great to say it tasted like chicken, but he wasn't that lucky. Astride of the fishy-birdie flavor, there was an extremely spicy aftertaste. Paul had no stomach for even mild spices. At once he felt his eardrums burning. He chugged his ice water, glad it wasn't some kind of tar-soda from the Old Domain. Then he refilled the glass from a pitcher and drank more, trying to calm the inferno.

"Hot?" The Priestess laughed.

"Just temperature-hot," he joked. He went for another bite, but his willpower collapsed. His fork clattered on his plate. "No, it's damn spicy. I don't think I'll be going there again."

The Priestess chewed her bird daintily. A mischievous light came on in her eyes. "There's something about you, Bishop Quintana. I feel like we've known each other for a long time. It's calming in a way."

"We saw each other briefly last year. Never spoke though."

"I hope you don't mind me saying so, but you have a way of taking my mind off the obvious."

"I suppose that's a good and bad thing."

"I lost something important today, so it's a good thing."

He took up the corncob. The sick little ocean eyes gazed into him. She put her hand on his arm. "Don't eat that. It's horrible. I only took a bite to honor the ancestors. One show of respect should suffice."

"But I thought you said to try everything."

"That was before I decided I liked you." Her smile melted Paul again and he dropped the hideous corn on his plate.

"Everything okay, Priestess?" Eggert leaned over them suddenly, his beard cordoning them off.

"Completely," she answered and then glanced Paul's way. "In fact, Bishop Quintana will be joining me in my room after our event, to discuss church matters. Please arrange refreshment."

The bearded man cocked his head. "Priestess?"

Her gaze leveled on her servant. "Was what I asked for complicated?"

"No, but— "

"You understand then. Go right now and make preparations, *please*."

Eggert nodded, dumbstruck, and left the head table, visibly disconsolate.

"Oh, but I'm presumptuous. We don't often have single mates in the Old Domain. You don't have anyone, do you Paul?" the Priestess asked him.

"I—no, no. Nobody. Not anyone. Nothing."

She laughed softly and rubbed the side of his foot with hers. "I had several in my land special to me. There hasn't been time since I arrived here. There still isn't now, but..."

"Yeah?" he squeaked.

"I like how you make me forget, Bishop Quintana. I haven't thought about today at all since I saw you in the hallway. You have a spell over me, I think."

He trembled now. *Trembled!* "It's over us both."

Paul knew this was it. He should have been happy it all came together this easy. He felt like this had to be a dream. He'd waited for this moment for over a year. He'd even killed Justin, blew his best friend's head into vulture kibble, just to sit in this chair, just to say hello to her.

"You're sure about this?" he asked.

The Priestess didn't answer him and instead delved into a discussion with Archbishop Pager.

Soon everybody got up and mingled. Cole left with Melissa shortly after and Sandeus went out to hobnob with the envoys.

"After conclave, Room 8128," the Priestess whispered, tickling his ear. Paul wanted to say something in return, but she was already submerged in tuxedos.

Twenty-three

THE PRIESTESS OF MORNING ACQUIRED A PRESIDENTIAL suite down the hall from Sandeus Pager. There was more security on the top floor, more hallway, more exquisite paintings, more intricate tile work, more of more. Sitting there on a velvet divan, looking through a rain-pelted window twenty feet wide, Paul could positively say he'd never been surrounded by such ostentatious furnishings. He'd never even *dreamed* of being in such a place and in such a position. Most of the décor belonged to the Priestess, donated from the church and its legion of admirers, and he could smell her scent on everything.

Paul stood and took off his tuxedo coat and draped it across the back of the divan. The Priestess had been in her bedroom changing for about fifteen minutes and the waiting caused him to drain three flutes of champagne and attack a bowl of strawberries and a pyramid of white cheeses. He was relaxed, if not approaching a stomachache. *At least the food isn't alien*, he thought. Remove the nosey bodyguard from the hallway and Paul would consider this a happy ending to another day of lunacy.

After another flute of champagne, he began to feel his bearings tilt a little. It was a pleasant buzz, nothing harsh. As he tipped the bottle, his eyes burned. It reminded him of the smell of his mother's gin and tonics and the sex-sweat-funk of her bedroom. So long ago and yet well remembered.

The Priestess's bedroom door opened. Paul's heart trembled and in his mind the children roared. She had on a soft peach teddy that showcased every weapon she possessed, and they were formidable: peaks and valleys, hellfire and angel-rain.

"Incredible," he said.

"I'm offering myself to you. I think you can do better than that." Her eyes were sinfully bright.

"Wow."

She approached and all Paul's inner foundations crumbled. He felt uprooted, for the first time since storming out of his mother's house. *Christ, just one time I'd like to have those memories die*, he thought with more self-loathing.

The Priestess slid up to the divan and took hold of the empty champagne bottle, wiggled it from side to side before dropping it back in the ice. "Wicked of you."

"Do I need to get more?" Paul was practically gibbering now, unable to speak like a human being. This was happening. This wasn't a dream. This was real.

"I'll call." She pressed her ass into his stomach and straddled Paul while she picked up a phone on the end table. As she dialed, Paul remained stock still, not breathing. He could hear tinny ringing in the phone's headset. The Priestess took up his left hand and popped his index finger into her mouth. His will crumbled, but he focused to retain some control. Paul had never been the weakling and as devastating as her beauty was, the Priestess was just another woman, like any other, and he'd have her eating out of his palm soon enough.

She tucked his moist finger between her legs. A sharp sound came from Paul's throat as his finger went inside and her warm interior bloomed to his knuckle. The Priestess's phone voice didn't hint anything scandalous. "I have some requests Eggert. Get in here at once." She dropped the phone on the charger with a pleasured exhale, "Oh..."

The door to the suite opened and Paul went to move his hand. The Priestess caught it and rammed the finger deeper. He tried to pull it away again, but her eyes brightened with a challenge and Paul let it be. Once he caught a glimpse of the scene before him, the bodyguard Eggert shuffled over to the divan, sideways, averting his eyes. Even his beard looked embarrassed.

"More champagne and two buckets of ice."

"Of course, Priestess." He tried to duck away.

"I didn't call you in here just to make an order. *Look at me,*" she commanded.

Eggert's sullen eyes flowed to hers. Paul could tell Eggert had been put through this before, perhaps many times before.

"No, no, no. I want you to look here." The Priestess spread her legs wider.

The big man suddenly dwarfed and his eyes went down and popped back up. His gaze was impressively stoic. "Is there anything else you require?" Eggert asked with a sigh.

With a lazy hand, she pumped Paul's finger gently in and out of her. Paul circled his finger around, to show his participation still mattered. This small act caused the Priestess to shiver and her eyes retreated to the rain streaked windows. "I don't know, Eggert. Can you make the clouds outside leave?"

"Priestess—?"

Her gaze came back, clear and hateful. "If the clouds leave, I will see the Nomads again. Understand? Tell me that I won't lose them again. That's all I want you big fool."

Eggert's lips pursed, out of anger or confusion, Paul could not tell.

The Priestess's legs spread wider yet. "Just because Archbishop Kennen put you on me, doesn't mean you can resume where he left off. I have Paul now. I'm free."

Eggert's eyes were cast down again. "Very good, Priestess. I'll be back as soon as possible."

When she said nothing else, Eggert strode out of the room. The Priestess slid off Paul's finger and sunk her hand into his shirt, clawing it open, sending black buttons ringing on the tile. Her hands ran down his abdomen and she cooed in approval. Next she took down his slacks and boxer shorts, peeled off his loafers.

"I don't have any condoms," said Paul, but it sounded like a joke.

With rabid passion, the Priestess climbed onto him, but Paul caught her by the neck and twisted her body around so she was on her back. She laughed and grabbed greedily between his legs. Paul pulled away, teasing. The Priestess brought up a hand and struck him across the face. His head cracked sideways and lower lip numbed suddenly. Something wet slid from his left nostril. Dazed, he glanced down and found daggers looking up. "You're a breath from leaving this room, Paul Quintana."

Before he could say a word, she thrust him down inside her. They rocked back and forth like a diabolical machine. Just then Paul cried out for help. This wouldn't last long and he pulled out—she leaned into his chest with a shoulder, knocking him back. He extended one leg, but the other remained folded. She climbed onto him and took him inside again. Paul was closer now than before. "No!" he cried.

Her weight trapped him. He squeezed his eyes shut.

"Oh my," she sang, going back and forth. "So deep. I've missed this. How I've missed this feeling. Like the orgies in the Wexxan glades, night after night."

She went faster and Paul panicked. "Not so quick, goddamn you."

Her penduluming lessened as she heeded his warning, but a wry smile twisted her lips. She grabbed his hand and rubbed circles into his wrist. "I'm putting you in my sight," she told him. Her eyes were startling to Paul, but he couldn't speak. "I will have a single mate just like the other women in this realm. You'll never lay with anyone else, unless I tell you to."

"To hell with that," Paul said, but whimpered. Her insides clenched around him fiercely and he mumbled softly. "Fuck, I love you."

"Of course you do." She got off him. He thought he might start bawling then at the loss. Something severe settled in the Priestess's eyes. He hadn't noticed in the fray, but Eggert had reentered the room with a tray containing two bottles of champagne on ice. The Priestess rushed over, rainy moonlight painting her body. She pulled the champagne bottles from each bucket and let them drop to the carpet. Something awful, like a hiss followed by cackling, came from her throat. Eggert stared at her, obviously comprehending some communication from the sounds, and he didn't seem to like what he heard.

The big man placed the tray down on the coffee table and then headed swiftly for Paul. Paul staggered to his feet, knees watery and weak, and tripped over his loafers. Eggert caught him with two powerful hands and shoved him face first into the sofa. Paul pushed forward to the Old Domain—Eggert yelped and drew his hand away. "Shit, stupid," he self admonished.

A savage hiss escaped the Priestess again.

Paul felt something soft press into his back. Eggert put a hip into it and held Paul there, buffered by the couch cushion. Paul mentally pushed at the cushion, attempting to send it over so he could reach Eggert. But he couldn't concentrate anymore. He pushed with all his mind had, but he could hardly breathe—then he felt the Priestess's soft hands spread his ass open. Paul bucked, but Eggert's weight and his delirium proved too much.

The Priestess spoke from somewhere nearby. "There is no true sacrifice in lust. We must first calm your loins with frost before we set them to flame. This is the way."

The ice cube mostly melted as it was pressed into him, but a sharp frozen peg lodged inside and Paul howled. Adrenaline shot through him and Eggert really had to hold on now. "Hush hush," the Priestess told him and inserted another. This ice cube's sides melted only a little and shot freezing cold all the way into Paul's abdomen. He couldn't help it—she'd won, damn her anyway—he trembled and began silently crying.

An immense pressure left his shoulders. Eggert had released him.

"Get out of here!" the Priestess commanded, as though her servant had never been invited in the first place.

She took Paul's hair in a fist and yanked his head up. "I want you on top of me! Hurry!"

He twisted around and icy pain shot through his bowels. The raindrops outside struck the massive window like little bullets from a dark heaven. His eyes hardened to stone. "Why did you do that?" he demanded.

"No questions, earthborn!" she roared. "On me, do it now!"

Without thinking he struck her with an open palm. It wasn't full force, but a tart redness went up into her cheek.

"Is that all?" she shouted, tears in her eyes.

With a fist he came twice across her face, understanding this might well be her thing, but it served two purposes simultaneously. His next strike sent the Priestess reeling for a minute, drunk on sadism. A thin stripe of blood slid from her nose. Her mouth opened in awe of him, so relieved he was everything she'd hoped him to be, and she embraced him.

Tremors went through his body as icy water drained out of him and down his leg. "Why?" he asked her again.

She stroked his hair, as though to say *poor baby*. More stroking, more *poor babying*. "I will restore your warmth. Go inside me."

Paul did.

"This is the way!" she cried. He started pumping and she slammed his head into her breast. "Bleed it! Bleed it my lord!"

He bit her nipple until liquid iron tickled his tongue. She viciously came, grabbing hold of a table lamp and ripping it from its power cord. When she hurled it into a wall and the lightbulb exploded, Paul felt her power overtake his emotions once more. This woman was a divine creature, a challenge he hadn't been ready for. She orgasmed two more times, each outdoing the last.

"Plant your seeds in my mouth," she chanted.

Paul withdrew and inserted himself. She sucked everything out of him until he yelped from the sensitivity. She then shoved him away, her demeanor made cruel from satiation.

After coming down, Paul lay wasted on the divan, chest heaving. The shutter to the Old Domain cracked open for a moment and he threw it closed. *No way in fuck I'm dealing with that right now.*

When he finally got his breath, he lifted his head. His skull felt encased in lead. The Priestess sat on the other side of the divan, knees up to her breasts and not looking affected, one way or another, not anymore.

He wanted to put a warm cloth to his raw rectum, but he lay there, doped up on joy. "You were amazing," he breathed.

She nodded. "I'm done for now. Leave me."

"What?"

"I have meditating to do. I need to stay up tonight—try to find the rats that slipped out of my cage."

Paul's entire soul ached as he sounded so pitiful and small. "What about me?"

"Oh yes," she said and tapped her pouty lips. "You."

"Your nose is bleeding."

"Yours is too," she added.

Neither made a move to wipe it away.

"Go out on the balcony," she said softly. "Bishop Quintana."

He sat up. "What for?"

Her face became concrete, her eyes shadowed with impatience. "Get out there."

"I don't understand."

Her butterscotch fingernail pointed to the balcony. "I want you to go out there. Beg the Messenger's clouds to leave. Pray for his rain to stop so that I might find the Nomads again. Ask this of the Eternal Harvest."

"Are you serious? That's crazy."

"Get out there or I'll never speak to you again."

He could tell from her look that she meant every word. Paul couldn't lose her, not after all he'd been through—but he would find the upper hand again. She'd not have him following her every whim forever. He could pull strings of his own. Sometimes though, you had to make an investment.

He picked up his clothes and the Priestess whistled. "Let's not bother with those. Just go out."

A shiver went through him and his teeth chattered at the thought. "It's raining!"

The Priestess stood and coldly faced him. At the moment, she reminded Paul of his mother, and all he wanted to do was hit her again, maybe give her another pounding as well. "You don't like me right now. Do you Paul? Will you disobey?" She charged up to him, breasts bouncing. Paul flew into the wall just to escape. "Will you disobey, you fool—?"

"You fuckin' whore!" His fist smashed her face down and his knuckles rang. The marrow blossoms in his chest took up charges in their petals. Paul was so frightened he forgot to breathe. Never had he been this out of control. What if he had dislocated the Priestess's jaw? He hadn't wanted to hurt her.

The woman from another world held her chin thoughtfully and ran her tongue over reddened teeth. "You are a rare beauty, Paul. I knew I was right to choose you. But this must pass now. Go, go outside, my lover. Do as I say, before this goes too far. I have to see them again. I have to find them. Move the clouds for me, Paul. For me."

He stood there, out of sorts, naked, drunk, on the verge of losing his wits, and there on the ground was his prize. Their coupling had been something brilliant. At that point there was nothing left to do.

Except to go outside and stand on the dark balcony, cold to the core, and plead his case to the clouds. The night would be nasty and long. The rain already stung Paul's flesh.

And the clouds would decidedly ignore him.

October 28th

Twenty-four

I HAD BUT LITTLE TIME TO WRITE THE SECOND LETTER. MY Nomads were not behaving predictably. That interference from the Priestess of Morning was only part of the cause. After all, Teresa herself decided to detour them to her mother—I had to spend precious time trying to locate them again. This wasn't how any of this was supposed to happen.

Traipsing between two worlds, following the movements of both the Church of Midnight and Church of Morning, I was forced to hasten preparations with the Heart bearer. The cloud cover would hold out as long as I did. Unfortunately, all of my power waned the closer October 31st approached. My strength lessened; Chaplain Cloth's grew. With luck the clouds would continue to blind the Priestess to the Nomads' whereabouts.

On top of a dumpster lid, just around the block from the Happy Moon Travel Lodge, my pen had flown across the parchment:

Martin & Teresa,

Go under the cover of rain to the city's north side. Find a neighborhood adjoining an industrial park. Your meet-

ing place is 108 Wenlock Way. Pick a mushroom from the lawn. The Heart of the Harvest has grown within these four: Jesse Jordon, Nancy Jordon, Steven Jordon, & Rebecca Jordon. Make your visit with the Bearer brief and follow his instructions to the word. It is vital you do so.

—Messenger

I delivered the letter then to the hotel manager and as I left, prayed silently for my two champions. If they didn't protect the Hearts, that gateway would be compromised. The Old Domain would flow into this world like a poisonous ocean and chaos would return. They were faced with this every year, yes, but never had it been this certain.

OUT OF EVERYTHING IN THE LETTER, MARTIN KEPT CONCENTRATING on the mushroom. *Why the shroom?* he thought again, shaking his head. Teresa was taking a shower, trying to hurry while the rain still came down in buckets. Getting her up had been a chore to beat all others. Coughing throughout the night, she'd probably not gotten a wink of sleep, and the same went for him.

Her pack of cloves sat on the nightstand by his piece. Nothing ever got through to Teresa, not even saying he'd likely kill himself if he lost her. *Sure—you'd probably just go out and find some redhead with big titties,* she always joked. It wasn't funny to Martin. Because he knew whom she really spoke of, even if it didn't register with Teresa—that waitress she'd caught him with had red hair.

Back then, young and dumb, Martin didn't know if he'd live from one October to the next. Back then, he never thought

Teresa was for real. She was so strong, independent, unbreakable in so many ways. In a sense, the screwing around had been a test, just to see if Teresa could be hurt. Martin had much success and in his moment of shame her psychological walls fell in. Since then he hoped he'd picked most of those walls back up. Bizarre, but Teresa Celeste was all he'd ever wanted anyway. He'd told her as much. A decade later, she probably still didn't believe him about that.

He slid over the cloves and took out one of the slender black sticks. He considered lighting it up, so when she came out she'd see him smoking and then...what would she say? Would she get pissed? He should do it. His stomach revolved at the wild smell though. Carefully he plugged it back inside the pack. Even if they did successfully protect these four Hearts this year, he had to wonder if he'd be sitting in the van one day real soon, playing the game *What did the Messenger take from you?* Replying, "Teresa, my partner, my friend, my life."

Martin scanned the parking lot. The green swimming pool dappled with raindrops glistened like an enchanted lake. It seemed out-of-place with the beat down Chevy pickup and oil stains outside its gate.

He knocked and moseyed into the stuffy pea soup bathroom. Teresa was blow-drying. She clicked off the blow-dryer and her eyes widened. "Did it stop?"

"Still going like a hundred year flood. I'm going to take a shower too."

"I thought you were going to wait until we got back."

"Nah."

He stripped off his boxers. As he went past she grabbed his penis and squeezed.

"You're a tease."

She smiled and released. "Never gets old."

The hot water felt great and the complementary Happy Moon shampoo, though smelling like lice therapy, left his scalp tingling. He scrubbed his flesh with his bath brush in meaningful circles, slowly transforming himself into a soapsuds creature.

Teresa came back through the steam with her hair in a ponytail. It had only been dried enough to keep from leaving her shirt wet—this was sensible Teresa at her best, for it was raining outside, after all. She stopped at the threshold and entered a brutal but swift, coughing fit. Martin counted them. Six, and then a final seventh one that made her gag and reddened her eyes. She cupped some water to her mouth from the sink and dabbed her face with a piece of toilet paper. The soap on Martin's body lost its invigorating quality and began to feel sticky, unnecessary. He started washing off.

"How's Colton water taste?"

"Rusty." She blinked to refocus. "I'm going to run up to that burger place. What do you want?"

"I doubt they have organic meat. I'll have a garden salad, extra croutons. Hold the pesticides."

"A salad! Oh you're going to grow yourself an inner tube fatso!"

He rinsed the rest of the soap away from his neck. It was just nice that she was hungry for a change. "Get me *double* whatever meatwich you're getting, and make sure the animal suffered awhile before they hacked off its head."

Teresa's smile was lackluster. "I was joking. I'll get you what you want."

He became aware of how loud the water from the showerhead was. "Better be quick while we have the rain. Messenger's orders."

Teresa barked another short cough into her fist and closed the bathroom door.

"Be careful," he added.

After breakfast, the Nomads set out into the city of Colton to meet the Hearts of the Harvest. Martin had been to cities in unsalvageable disrepair, but Colton wore a miserable charm around its neck. The city had the smell of time perking from its splintering foundations. Flyer-covered thrift stores, dislocated railroad tracks, blackened radiator shops, intersections that came together in weird arachnidan angles, one bedroom shanties that crowded flaking white Victorians. Everything was clutched in a dearth of American concern, which was a complicated, less honest scarcity than other places in the world. As they drove past a quaint little Catholic Church, Martin saw the grinning masks of the congregating people. They used the masks to hide their irrelevance. Destitution had helped forge a droopy-eyed apathy for anything beyond the liquor stores and strip clubs. Maybe it was Martin's own jaded view projected on them. He could accept that.

But if it wasn't just him, then what a shame for Colton, and other cities like it. This great railroad hub had meant something to someone once. It no longer counted now, but one couldn't deny a notable energy had once run through Colton's veins. No wonder the Hearts had ended up here.

Teresa was taking a catnap. It wasn't a long drive to the Bearer, and Martin had told her as much, but she snapped at him to quit his grousing. The morning had been somewhat peaceful and he didn't want the bickering to evolve. Teresa had been eerily pleasant, even purchased him a silly toy from the burger restaurant.

"You said you always wanted an aquarium, remember?"

It was actually a little fish bowl with a fake cartoon goldfish staring back with bright white eyes. It looked frozen in the plastic sphere; dormant, benign, safe from the outside world.

"Thanks." He kissed her then.

His mind returned to the moment and he enjoyed slowly gliding through the rain in their fortress on wheels. A new vehicle awaited them at the Bearer's. Every October. There always was. Seeing this Quadravan go would be bittersweet. It wasn't the most expensive, the most fuel efficient (not close), and it was not the newest vehicle the Messenger had ever pushed on them. But it felt reliable and felt comfortable.

Bye-bye, beautiful, he thought as he caressed the dashboard. *You've done your job.* Time to rest.

"Tony!"

Something exploded in her ear. Teresa threw her hands over her head and ducked. The passenger door rocketed across the street on a sled of sparks and hit the curb with a clang that made her teeth set together.

Martin twisted her face to his and pressed his fingers into her skull to focus her. "You're safe. You're safe." When Teresa nodded, he gently let his hands fall away and added, "Don't build anything else, quick-draw. You might have sent the mantle my way."

"I had a dream about last year. Tony, we lost him Martin—we lost him! He was with us. Then—how did he get away? What happened—where?" She sounded so stupid, but the blubbering words came out uncontrolled.

"Cloth is playing with you. Tony's not the first one we've ever lost, Teresa. It's okay. We're okay." His words cut through her dream hysteria and made her sober. "It won't happen again. Just don't worry, okay?" he said. "Just pull it together."

Teresa considered a moment if she'd come fully awake or not. She leaned over, held Martin, and her shoulders trembled and guts began twisting. Tears wouldn't come, but she was closer to shedding them now than she'd ever been. She couldn't even remember crying after she found Martin with that waitress of his.

He studied her expression. "Must have been one hell of a dream. You weren't even asleep for ten minutes."

She sat back. Only now did she realize what she'd done. The passenger side door rested across the street, half-propped up on the curb. "We should get going," she suggested in embarrassment. "Where are we?"

"The GPS says about half a mile away from the Hearts. Are you sure you're okay now?"

She went to strip off her seat belt.

"Let me get it." He jumped out of the van before she could argue.

Teresa watched as he trotted across the street and lifted the door up. "Heavy, but the window didn't even break," he commented. "I told you we have a tank."

"Put it in the back of the tank then, General Larson."

Teresa waited for him to get back in and start up the van. As they rolled on the wind blowing through the van's open wound felt wonderful. Houses began to look less rundown, their simple architecture suddenly fascinating. The rain cloudy sky even seemed to grow metallic through its gloom. When they arrived at the location on the Messenger's letter they both had to take a moment to process their new surroundings.

The grass blinded them with green, the house's sandy paint came alive with snapping gold flake, and the Spanish tiles ran down in a perfect formation like a rich strawberry waterfall. Teresa knew this wasn't reality. Without the Hearts nearby, the grass was likely burnt from dog piss, the house's paint faded like said urine, the strawberry Spanish tiles most likely crumbled and dusty looking.

Teresa scanned the area. She spotted a mallard duck on the mailbox. The painting might possess little actual artistic acumen in reality, but here and now, through the Hearts' influence, each of the duck's feathers had fine slices of iridescence running through them. The bird appeared tangible, touchable. So much, in fact, that it might take off and leave the plain black mailbox behind.

She stretched her eyes down the street and found other houses glowing with a hint of the same immaculacy. She wondered if those people sensed even a little of what lived next door. Being that the blood of the Old Domain ran through both her and Martin's veins, supposedly they were the only ones who could notice—and even they couldn't notice the Hearts' influence forever. They became accustomed to the luster, eventually. Last year the Heart had been exceptionally powerful. Tony Nguyen had made his studio apartment shine like El Dorado. But that sight was meager compared to this.

The overwhelming power contained in that house made Teresa's breakfast twist in her stomach. If she was feeling this reeled by the Hearts, imagine what kind of sacrifice they would make for Chaplain Cloth.

Outside the rain had thinned. It wasn't torrential anymore and the hoary old clouds appeared happy with the prospect of death. A large vehicle sat in the driveway under a tarp. Martin gestured with some enthusiasm. Under that tarp would be their new vehicle. Teresa acknowledged his little-boy-excitement but was still entranced from her dream.

She never let Martin take all the blame for Tony, although most of the responsibility had been his. In her case it had been over ambition—pride. Pure and simple. With Martin, he'd gotten fancy with the mantles and that made him sloppy and eventually exhausted. It was bound to happen over so many years, getting cocky after saving five or six Hearts in a row. Over the years Martin had developed a displacement mantle with a trigger point that blasted through the ghost-matter, creating a type of invisible landmine. Teresa had never found these types of mantles as reliable as Martin. She'd rather they set real mines and C4 charges. Mantles were delicate at times, and the long lasting mantles could be debilitating. It wasn't in their best interest to experiment on Halloween. She knew that before last year, but she got comfortable. They both got way too comfortable.

A finch flew into the influence and went from a dull liver color to chocolate. The finch sang and looped around before lighting on a eucalyptus next door. *If only it could stay this way forever and we could put up some strong mantles, seal this place off until November.* It would be like living in Candyland or the southern Californian version of the North Pole.

But there were no mantles strong enough to keep Chaplain Cloth away. If one was set in his way, he'd tear it down. In the end, the barriers she and Martin created only bought them time. That was it. If they slowed down Cloth until the first of November, then that was a good year.

"The rain," Martin said uneasily, looking up. "Time to stop thinking and go in there."

"What if one has a wheelchair, like in Duluth? We almost lost her."

"Yep, but does it matter? We didn't lose her. Of course the next year we lost that track and field guy—"

"And Cloth nearly took your head off," she added.

"Well that wasn't something I wanted to remember."

She stared at the house. "So what do you think?"

"The Jordons are probably a family," he said. "Mama bear, Papa, Gilligan and Beavis."

She didn't find his humor appropriate and sighed.

Martin sighed too. "Well, you know we can't drive away."

"The Messenger should have found someone else, someone *in good health*. I didn't even think I'd make it here—not this time last year. Look, this is too much responsibility. Four? *Four?* We couldn't even save one Heart last year."

Martin slammed the door so hard the hinges shrieked. Teresa watched him for a moment. He turned to look at her. Then, slowly she slid out of her seat and grabbed where her door used to be, pretended to slam it.

He stared in disbelief. "You're too much."

"Oh I know."

They locked hands and crossed the street. She plucked a chilly white mushroom from the lawn. "Good one," Martin complimented.

He looked up just in time to see the drapes in the front window fall away. The Bearer knew they were here.

When they got up to the porch the front door opened and a hand came through. The skin was a rich bronze, the fingers male but delicate, the wrist forked with veins. Teresa placed the mushroom in the palm and the fingers folded over like a Venus flytrap. A sigh came through the door. Teresa couldn't tell if the sigh was of relief, exhaustion, or disgust. She was aware only of splendor ebbing through the doorjamb. Sugar fumes. Vanilla hope. Life-giving dreams of pine and clean skies.

The hand dropped the mushroom on the porch. A finger jutted at Martin. When words came, the very sound of them was a stinging annoyance through golden bliss. "Pick that up please."

Martin gave Teresa a sidelong look. "Anything you say, chief."

He stooped down.

"Not with your hands," the voice said quickly.

Martin's brow lifted.

"Draw from the Old Domain."

"Yeah," answered Martin and he looked at her. "I get it now. This is our proof of ID."

A cool shadow crept over Martin's face for a minute. There was no sound in the neighborhood. Nothing. Stillness. The process seemed to stretch on forever. Teresa felt a small, paper-thin mantle come into being. With his mind Martin slipped it under the mushroom. The mushroom rolled a little, but he rooted underneath it with a mental shove. The mushroom lifted to eye level. It floated there, as if supported on nothing, and wobbled as his concentration fluxed for a moment.

The Bearer's finger swung to Teresa. "You, crush the mushroom, please."

Teresa dipped into the freezing pond in her own brain. Her mantle came into existence immediately, yet did not have the style or grace of Martin's. His was a slip of royal parchment; hers was a paper ball destined for the trashcan. Stylish or not, when she brought it down on the mushroom, Martin forced up and the mushroom flattened.

They released and a mushroom pancake dropped down onto the porch.

"Anything else?" asked Martin.

The hand pulled inside and the door shut. A chain unlatched and clattered against the doorframe. The door opened, steady with deliberate caution.

The Bearer was not short in the conventional sense; he was in that four-foot category that didn't midgetize or dwarf him but had the stature of a taller man. Or so Teresa thought anyway. He was a handsome man. His deep, romantic black eyes stared from within graphite caves. Not as romantic however, was his wife beater and boxer shorts with a school of extraordinarily happy fish. Teresa caught the subtle addition of sombreros on each smiling mackerel.

"So you are the Nomads." His voice had a Bearer's usual dislocated accent, like textbook English language. The Messenger had Bearers moving constantly and they never had time to absorb culture, let alone dialect. In a way, they were the same creature as the Nomads, except that their job eventually had a terminus. Usually.

The Bearer extended his hand and his lips peeled slightly for a smile. "I am Enrique Gonzalez. I am sorry I am not dressed yet. I expected you to arrive here at this house yesterday."

Teresa drove two sharp coughs into her fist to get them out of her system.

Concern touched Enrique's eyes. "We must get you on your way before the rain stops falling."

Martin held out a hand to catch raindrops. The sky was white overhead. All gray had fled. They began to step over the threshold and Enrique held out a hand. "I should mention that the Hearts' potency is harsh at first."

Teresa gestured to the brilliant cast of the neighborhood. "We couldn't help but notice. Don't worry, we've done this for a while now."

Enrique's dark face pinched. "Yes, I am certain. But as you come inside, things will intensify. I will walk you through and we can take breaks along the way to make it easier."

"Breaks?" she asked. *Did this kid think they were rookies?*

"Try to hang on to each other or something stable, so that you do not fall and hit your head. It may take a while to acclimatize. But you will."

"We know how it goes, Mr. Gonzalez."

Enrique waved them inward. Teresa went in first, steeling herself. When they both stepped completely inside the house, the atmosphere roared into a symphony of terrifying beauty. The living room was only the first movement of that symphony.

I KNOW THE FEELING OF DEDICATED WORSHIP. IT GRABS ME completely against my will and subjugates my initial detachment from an otherwise complete stranger. Though I follow these special people all of my life, meeting a Heart of the Harvest always creates a lightning strike of loyalty—there is boundless pride just sharing the same oxygen with them. After only a moment I feel I've known them for a thousand lifetimes with not the slightest spark of a secret having ever fallen between us.

And this experience was no different for my Martin and Teresa.

Crossing the threshold took Martin to a completely new, painful location in the territories of love. It would be natural to assume the feeling would be four times greater with four Hearts, but that wasn't the case—calling it just exponential would be vapid. The experience transformed everything into a cerebral circumlocution of both the fascinating and abhorrent. Martin cared about Teresa more than anything else; his soul was patterned around their bond. Yet at that given moment he'd have ripped apart the ties to that bond and done something awful just to service this new love.

Teresa pitched over and he winged an arm under her chest to keep her from falling. The discharge of her wheezing lungs made Martin sweat and taste blood. His empathy had pulled him into a different zone. He felt as Teresa felt: a burning piece of murder in his chest, a quaking need to soothe it in smoke. All this and he still didn't *care* about her problems; he cared about whether the Hearts were safe and if his head would keep spinning on three separate axes.

"Here if you please," offered Enrique. "You will sit on the couch and you will try to regain yourselves from the influence."

Martin didn't remember the man. If he and Teresa passed out, how would they know the Hearts were safe? What would they do if they woke up and found them gone? It would induce suicidal heartbreak.

"You okay?" Martin must have been staring at Teresa for some time now, and she him, but neither processed the other. Teresa had just pawed her way out of a grave, her pretty brown hair coarse like decaying plants in a riverbank, her skin bloodless and true white, her eyes two simple stones with the intelligence amputated from their shine.

"Teresa?"

She turned away, stoned on the Hearts. "It doesn't matter."

"I will fetch you both some water." Enrique was talking to different people, *coherent* people.

Martin rubbed his temples and concentrated on the wrinkly contours of the gray carpet. His head was sore from worrying. An endless song emanated off everything like heat waves. Being inside the house wasn't getting easier—the love was getting worse.

Just then the living room sang at the top of its lungs,

Oh Hearts, come unto me and give over your fear.
Rest your heads in my company, rest your heads for old time's sake,
Rest your heads in my cool gray wrinkled flesh. Love me, love me.
Sink into my couch and live inside my excellence.
Don't forsake my love, and Hearts, never fret.
Oh-oh-oh, Hearts, you can never, ever, never fret!

"I don't think I can stay here anymore," said Teresa with a wild animal look in her eyes.

Martin hated her for even suggesting such a thing. "You want to leave?"

"I can't stay in *here*, knowing they're so close." Her knees popped as she sprung up and rounded the couch.

"Wait!" The world went flat and tipped. Martin's shoulder crunched against the corner of two walls. He laughed as the bone relocated into its socket. Why he laughed was beyond him, like everything else.

In the kitchen Teresa grappled the stove. Enrique filled two glasses of water from a pitcher. The ice water and lemon wedges cast silver and gold shadows across the mauve tile countertops. Enrique nervously giggled, softly for a moment—or had it been loud, had it been a lot? "Couldn't wait, huh?" he said. "Okay, but you will need a longer break than that I fear, if you both do not want to pass out on the floor."

Martin stumbled to the adjoining dining room and sat at a card table with peeling avocado vinyl. Teresa joined him. On his tiptoes Enrique rummaged through a cupboard. Martin wanted to help him, for the first time feeling taller than someone else, but he was glued to the avocado table. To the left of Enrique the refrigerator sang an angry song with its compressor:

Hummmmmm, Hummmmmm—My waiting's so atrocious!
Hummmmmm, Hummmmmm—Precocious but so hating!
Hummmmmm, Hummmmmm—To be cold without your love!
Hummmmmm, Hummmmmm—My waiting's so atrocious!

"Do you hear the song?" Martin whispered.

Teresa leaned to his ear. "You mean the whales mating?"

Enrique set down the glasses and pulled a box of Saltine crackers out from under his arm. "This is the best food that I have to offer. I cannot go out much, as you might have guessed. I am about sick to death of cheese pizza."

Teresa took a long drink of her water and then her head moved side to side like a junkie. "How can you live like this?" Then, what seemed like an eon later. "Mr. Gonzalez."

Enrique's smile shone like a pearl boomerang. Martin was afraid it would come after him. "In about an hour you will both feel normal again. That is why the Messenger wanted you to meet them before the Hunt. It is just something our kind goes through from this kind of exposure."

"Our kind," Martin mused. "Tied in blood to the Old Domain."

Teresa's voice boomed over the appliance caroling. "This is so much different than the Hearts of the past. I have a question." The last sounded really boisterous, so obnoxious that Martin wanted to run screaming from the room, but he shook his head violently to regain control. "The Bishops are tied to the Old Domain, aren't they? This is more intense than anything...anything...we've ever seen. What if the Bishops can sense this?"

"As you know, the Bishops are not tied through blood. They're corrupted earthborn. We're safe from them, at least for now."

"Cloth?"

"He belongs to neither world, but you know not to underestimate him."

"Yes, we do know that much."

Martin writhed against the need again and had to thrash a little. The sensation had stacked up. He needed to be free of it. "Can I ask something?"

"You don't need permission," said Enrique.

"Aren't we fooling ourselves going through all of this? One way or another, the gateway will open. The churches will unite."

"If we fail, you mean."

"*If* is damned generous. If the churches are this close then it's only a matter of time. Maybe not this year, but what about next year, or the year after? It'll happen. It almost happened last year. We've lucked out that the Bishops haven't posed a problem, but we know they've made major trouble for Nomads in the past—the Church in this world only grows stronger. We're only two. Why won't the messenger get the hint that we need more help?"

"He asks the Bearers this every year," Teresa said, abjectly.

Enrique's eyes warmed like simmering peanut oil. Martin suddenly wished he hadn't embarked on this subject. "We trust in the Messenger."

"That's *all*? And what does that mean? Plain craziness, if you ask me."

The Heart Bearer leaned toward him. "Every day is crazy. What can you do about it? Nothing. The Hearts must not be sacrificed because we get down on our lot."

Martin couldn't tell if he disliked Enrique now, or just had no room in his heart for anything else. Absently he toyed with his puka shell necklace in an attempt to forget the Hearts. The cool ridges of the shells calmed him sometimes. Not now. They were rough. They were wrong. He suddenly stood from his chair, thinking it would help. The world didn't agree. He couldn't pretend any longer. He needed the Hearts.

"Oh, sit down," said Teresa.

Martin dampened the urge to wail and pull his eyes out. The kitchen and dining room were still alive, the refrigerator still singing, but he was learning how to live with the racket.

"I know you are tired." Enrique looked him up and down. Martin pictured him as a little boy, not because of his shortness, but because of the clean clarity in his eyes. Innocence lived there. "But I cannot protect them the way you two can."

Martin laughed silently for a moment and they stared at him. Finally, he straightened. "You can't protect them, so what good are you people anyway?"

Teresa shot him a nasty look.

Enrique entwined his hair-cuffed hands. A few moments passed. Nobody human said anything, but the refrigerator wanted to embark on an adventure.

At last Enrique said, "You will be more at ease when we go down to meet them."

"Down?" asked Martin.

"The basement. They're waiting for us."

"I don't hear them."

Enrique's smile looked like that of the mackerels on his boxer shorts. "The Hearts are resting."

Teresa wobbled as she got to her feet. Martin thought about helping her but decided he was still angry at her reprimand.

They followed Enrique down a bare hallway to a sepia door. He flipped a light switch. The stairwell flickered several times. Underfoot the wooden stairs belted out an ode. With every step the words became more incomprehensible. Martin's hands moistened as he gripped the rotting banister. Teresa descended behind him and her footsteps added a chorus section.

How long?
Soon.
Where?
You should know.
I don't. Where?
Where? Ha! Where and where and there and here; love lives, love dies, who knows, can we, into the where,

there and here, there to hear fear; dying to die, living to lie, now we're inside, wiggles in, wiggles sin, to fear and mirror and tear and here.

Andwhere? Waiting. Andthere? So atrocious. Andlovelives? Never. Anddieloves?

Ever. Livesdies? Fret. Wholivesdies? They? No. Onelivesdies? Theyareone.

Fourareone. They-are-the-way-way-the-are-they. LOVE LIVES. Thehearts.

Thehearts. Thearts. Who?

Love lives within.

Not long. So soon.

Enrique swung a newspaper back and forth. The image was a little disturbing at first and Teresa flinched. The Bearer only smiled and tossed the paper away. "I had a feeling you both needed more...decompression time."

Martin was at her side, his arm pillowing his head against the bottom of the stairs. Out cold.

"It's a good thing you guys did not faint at the top. I do not think I could have guided you to the ground the same way." Enrique shook his head.

Teresa poked Martin in the ribs. His eyes flew open wide, hand going for his handgun. She grabbed his hand and didn't let go until relief poured over him. He looked around suspiciously. "The stairs were talking."

Teresa snorted. "Really?" she said. "And what did they say?"

"You're laughing at me."

"Yes we are," Enrique slapped his thigh. When Martin glared at him, he said, "Please come this way. The Jordons are waiting to meet you."

The basement buzzed with fluorescent light. The room itself was a shallow brick box. They were all weary bricks down here; the grout had struggled for years to hold an illusion of support and now there was no illusion left to give. Cracks, spider holes, running fissure tangents leaking from corroded pipes. The light painted contours in the gray stones.

Teresa wondered what would happen when the Hearts left this place—would the bricks give in and collapse? She could feel the stinging heat from the light fixtures above and yet she was drowning in icy shock. She had seen many Hearts on the road, and in many shapes; the Hearts came in all varieties: moms, dads, grandfathers and mothers. Some were lovely, others lunatics, and some were teenagers. As Nomads they had no say. They just had to protect them no matter what. She and Martin loved them every year, without a choice in the matter, and at least for the short time they knew them, through and through.

So why's this so hard to accept? she thought.

Martin stretched his neck at the twisting pink forms in their basinets, his jaw hanging. "What in the hell?"

"Wait a minute," Teresa reproached.

"You feel them, do you not? They're stronger than the others." A proud smile spread on Enrique's face. "The blood fruit grows within all four."

Martin pointed at the babies, apparently too in the moment to voice any concern.

"I don't understand," stammered Teresa. "They can't all have it?"

"They are quadruplets. As potent as Tony Nguyen was, last year's fruit was only a glimmer on the sun. They are enough to blow the gateway wide open many times over."

Martin stepped toward the basinets, overcautious.

"Babies? We don't know how to take care of them," said Teresa.

"Never changed one diaper, not one," Martin said to himself, sounding slightly crazed.

"They are marvelous babies. You will easily learn."

They studied the Jordons for a moment. The four didn't look vastly different from one another. All had that soft, reddened look of new life. All had thin downy pates, too frail for full color. They indeed looked to be healthy babies. Teresa tried not to make eye contact; it would be difficult to concentrate on anything but them if she did. Martin averted his eyes as well. He would probably act out against it, try and cheat the obvious—that was Martin, the silent revolutionary.

"As you might have guessed, I have not been a Bearer for long. You might say that I have had an intense cultivation period, very short, but challenging. This is an uncommon situation, without doubt. Nguyen's Bearer worked with him all the way into his college years—I've only had four months with the Jordons."

Martin grasped the back of his head to keep from pitching backward. Here came that acting out part. "Wait, wait. Nah, I've got issues with this. What happens on the Day of Opening? Carry a baby in each arm like grocery bags? With the whole church coming down on our heads? This is fucked, really, Enrique. Who made this shit up? We've never had babies before. There's too many. We're only two people."

"Knock it off," Teresa told him. "A Heart is a Heart."

"Oh please," replied Martin. "At this age these kids have the brains of a jellyfish."

"You could only be so lucky—"

"I have papooses for twins," Enrique interjected. "They are quite comfortable and secure for running. I'll be bringing them along when I drop the Hearts off."

The Nomads turned together like mirror images. "We're not taking them right now?" asked Teresa, "Why wouldn't we? We can be out of California before nightfall."

"Things are different now. You are being watched. The Messenger has sheltered you from the Church, but only here. And he cannot keep the entire city of Colton covered forever. Away from the motel, the sky coverage will fluctuate."

"Outrunning the church is smarter than hanging around."

"They will go after you. Cloth knows the importance of the Hearts this year. He'll make sure his mortals follow you. There can be no adjustments," said Enrique. "The Messenger was unambiguous in the directions. I will deliver the children around six o'clock pm the night prior to the Day of Opening. Take enough supplies up and stay in your room until I arrive. I put a duffel bag in the Wrangler out front. I'll contact you at the motel if the plan changes."

"We can't keep the babies with us?" asked Martin.

"They're watching *you*, not me. Do you understand?"

One of the babies whimpered and cocked its head to the right. Teresa examined the miraculous foursome. So wrinkled, so easily in distress, so terribly young. Her affection forced itself inside and warmed her blood.

Martin deflated completely. He'd been through too much now to ask a lot of questions, and as always, he knew that he had no say in what happened as far as Halloween went. "Once you bring them to our room, what then?"

"What has it always been?" Enrique watched them, a somber oil painting. "You run like the devil. *From* the devil."

Twenty-five

The Priestess of Morning watched the goldfish awhile longer. A tiny man in an archaic diver's suit squatted behind a treasure chest that opened and shut with the aquarium's pump. One fish darted away from the school and went to hide behind a waving a mass of plastic seaweed. The Priestess did not move her eyes off this one and brought up her double Bloody Mary. Vodka and tomatoes. They were her favorite discoveries in this world, aside from the tractable males. In her birthplace men would have spit on easy manipulation, thought it tactless and insulting. She learned their game there long ago. They could be bought through the gift of sacrifice, through power. In this world she took what she wanted and men gave themselves to her will, as though her attention was prize enough. So silly. She wagered men were idiots in both places, though on completely different grounds for idiocy. But they kept her spirits up.

Speaking of spirits, she thought, and picked up the half empty bottle of vodka. The Mary had become a trifle thin on the bite. A *Bloody Mabel* perchance? She took out the celery stalk and dropped it into the aquarium. Goldfish scattered like orange shrapnel. The outsider fish remained hidden in the plastic weeds. The Priestess's reflection shook with disgust. *Like a Nomad...* They could hide from her sight and have their delusions of safety, but she would find them again. She'd see through the rain. It could flood the streets of this dirty land and create rivers and lakes and seas—back home, this pompous hotel would be sitting at the bottom of their largest ocean, *Olathu*. The krill were so thick it made the water soft and red like...

She tipped back another healthy swallow.

Ringing. The annoying chirp came from the Bishop's slacks on the divan. She shuffled across the bitterly cold tile floor. She retrieved the slim phone from a pocket containing a small stone, whatever that was for...

"Hello?" She hadn't lost interest in telephones yet. *An act of power without sacrifice was magnificent magic.* Or perhaps she hadn't learned what sacrifices in this world actually were.

The man on the other end sounded nonplussed, and inebriated. "Bishop Quintana?"

"He stepped out for some air."

She went to the sliding glass door. Her face reflected. It looked starker than it had in the aquarium, but there were no bruises, no cuts. Maybe a slight swelling of her lower lip. Amazing. Paul's strikes had felt like they'd caused permanent damage. He thought himself so powerful. Now the blond man huddled next to a few potted lilies. Crouching there, he looked like a newborn ape, body bald and goose-dimpled. What a great hind end he had—skin wasn't too pasty or browned either. His staff wasn't too small, or big, or warped. She would share more bedtime with him, without doubt. The urge for children with him drove her mad.

As soon as she slid open the door, Paul bolted upright. His face was flushed from anger and agony, and his blond hair had parted down the center in the downpour.

"Priestess," he squeaked, shivering, "it's not raining that hard anymore."

It wasn't. Just misting. The clouds were clearing as well. *Soon.* She offered the phone. "We'll take a warm shower together."

Paul Quintana followed inside. He stood there, staring at her with boyish fear and hatred. She smiled and ran her fingertips over his cold lips. "Aren't you going to answer that?"

He pressed the phone to his ear and tried to sound controlled. "Yeah?"

She went to the aquarium again and remembered her drink. It was weaker than she liked. She wasn't much for making drinks or cooking; she always under did the spirits, always enjoyed burning food rather than making it taste divine. The half-finished drinks and blackened chicken eggs in the kitchen were proof of that.

"Never better." Paul nodded a couple of times. It was odd to see him fall into formality when he stood there so cold and shriveled. "No, no. Set them up with a room. Yeah...I know, yeah...okay. Yes, call me tonight. Don't forget." He pursed his chalky blue lips. "You remember? Yeah? Good. Little insurance never spoiled the race. Okay. Good, good." The phone snapped shut and he tossed it on his slacks. His reddened eyes dragged over to her. "About that shower?"

The Priestess poured the rest of her Bloody Mary into the aquarium and the red spread through the watery atmosphere like a quick toxin. Now she had a small *Olathu* Ocean of her own. *Home*, she savored. Paul watched her do this, but not with much surprise. He now saw beyond thc ceremonial orange dresses and titles. That was nice. Paul was different than the others. From both sides.

She took his large hand and pulled him toward the bathroom. Her entire body cried out to live and die at the same time. By the time they got into the bathroom, Paul's body had outgrown the night on the balcony, and he was ready for use.

"Stop!"

Paul smelled blood. It may have started from biting his lip or the side of his tongue. *Hell*, he thought, *it might have been from the children's voices sawing back and forth through my fucking cerebral cortex*. It could have been a lot of things. The marrow seeds were exploding in his veins like microscopic kernels. Every flower produced more seeds and implantation, and therefore less balance in the dark and light garden. It hurt his chest. The pressure. The love. This needed to end. This needed to begin. Couldn't go on any longer. Can't stop the endless hunger.

Cloth's children claimed the lonesome space behind his eyes. *Thanksgiving!*

"Stop!"

Paul smelled blood again. Blood matted his public hair. "Shit," he cried and began to pull out.

The Priestess swiveled around. "What are you doing?"

"You said to stop...*twice!*"

"My insolence, my weakness, my shame—don't you *ever* stop!" She forced his hand between her legs. "Don't ever STOP!"

"But you're blee—"

Her dark look made his mind up for him. Once she came, he tried to reach his own peak again but found he'd reached too many. Besides orgasmic exhaustion, the chill from a night on the balcony had come back into his bones and there was a rash up his ass.

"You're cold?" the Priestess asked flatly.

"Getting there."

"Eggert built a fire in the sitting room." She offered a delicate hand to him like a sophisticate. He pulled her up with him off the bathroom floor.

The thrill of heat caught him. The fire wasn't exactly roaring, but it was enough to warm his bones. He watched the firelight play on her perfect skin. The shutter to the Old Domain was open. *So* open. Despite the keening of the children and his promise to Cole Szerszen, right then nothing mattered besides his Priestess. He was already too wrapped up though. *Have to watch myself or I'm gonna be her next automaton.*

"I can't keep you all day," she said. "I'm sure you have your duties."

"No," he said, more loudly than intended. *Great job playing the game, idiot.* "I don't want to leave."

"And I don't want you to go—but the Hunt is closer. That means the Heralding is at our feet."

"I find it difficult to care," he said.

"What?"

"I've never known anybody like you."

The Priestess raised a soft, bladed eyebrow. "But I care, of course. Bishop Szerszen said Chaplain Cloth needs his soldiers. The Heart will be consumed and the path will clear, for all time. Then I can show you my world."

"You already have."

She took a poker down from the rack and stuck it into the fireplace. A golden train of hair cascaded off her shoulder down to a russet nipple. After a couple of jabs under some blistering, glowing logs, she seemed to grow bored and left it there. A loud crack rent a log in two and Paul jumped. "I might have been rasher with myself," she said, "had I not met you. I don't like failing myself, you see, but failing others I find more deplorable. A great man gave up his first wife to foresee the Nomads' location. I thought once I had them in my sight, they'd lead us straight to the Heart and our troubles would be gone. Such foolish dreaming. I should have known better." She gazed out the window and Paul could almost see the raindrop reflections falling down her face, backlit by the fire.

He said, cautiously, "This man who foresaw the Nomads—you mean the Archbishop of Morning?"

She didn't meet his eyes.

"What kind of a man is he?" he asked.

"He likes his playthings," she said. "We had that in common for a time, until he saddled me as church concubine. A Priestess should never be controlled in such a doggish manner, but it didn't surprise me, not with Archbishop Kennen. He does things the way it fits his vision and none else. He will choose to lead the unified Church on his own when the time comes. He and Sandeus will be at odds. Wait and see. I can't imagine Kennen taking second to anyone. He's given everything for the chance."

Paul extended his palms toward the fire. "Cole and this guy won't be the best of buddies either."

"Perhaps not." She went back to ramming the fire some more.

"Enough with this talk of power games. We're bigger than that. Don't you think? Tell me something you want," he said. "Anything. I want to give you something special."

The Priestess pulled the poker from the fire. The end was not red-hot yet, but smoke waved off the gray dust at the point. "Kiss my stomach with this. Even if I tell you to stop, even if it burns down to my vitals—this is your gift to me."

Paul shook his head. "I was thinking a necklace or something..."

"It's not the pain," she answered quickly, reading his thoughts. "It's the absence. Agony clears the mind. It's a sacrifice that can almost outmatch death itself."

"I'd rather not."

"Coat the burn in your seed." Her mouth pulled back into a shark's smile. "Soothe and cleanse me. Maybe my sight will strengthen from the offer of torment."

Paul didn't care much for it termed as *seed* anymore, not with the tangled jungle cultivating in his chest. He laughed her concept away, but she placed the poker's handle in his palm and aimed the point at her abdomen. "I don't really—"

Her stomach drew closer. Paul could imagine the poker first creating a red blister that popped and blackened and then the iron sinking through soft muscle tissue. He was too selfish; there could be no ugly terrain in his wonderland.

The Priestess jumped to her feet and Paul thankfully dropped the poker on the tile before the fireplace. At first he thought he'd made her upset and that she'd press the issue, as she had with the balcony, but that wasn't it. There was something else.

"Priestess?"

She ran out of the retreat area, a naked blur through the living room. Paul vaulted after her but remained distant once he saw her near the balcony; he'd had enough of that location. She put her hands on the glass and began heaving. Sunlight sliced through the sky and the living room filled with color and dissolving shadows. Her amazing lips parted for something sweet.

"Are you okay?"

Something was discovered in those wild amber eyes. She was breathless. "Oh I'm splendid!"

Twenty-six

IT FELT EASIER ON HIS SOUL TO BE RELEASED FROM THE Hearts. Not that Martin wouldn't miss them. Uncontrolled love and devotion for the little ones would be dialed up until November. There was no getting around that, like it or not.

He shut the Quadravan for the last time. "Bye old girl."

The only thing left inside was the passenger door. He'd miss the crackling speakers and the faint mildew and clove scent: they were the van's signs of life. Maybe he was getting softer as he approached his middle years, but he couldn't see the point in switching for a newer vehicle.

Teresa and Enrique were loading the shiny black JK Wrangler Unlimited with supplies. All in all, this new vehicle would be a faster, more streamlined transport with less room than the Quadravan. Had to be dealt with. The wooden crates of dry goods and bottled water had to be cut down to a week's supply. The assorted ammunition, concussion and incendiary grenades had to be reduced to a fourth. They only retained their M16 rifles and their personal handguns. The Messenger had freshened their plastics and detonator kits—couldn't have enough of that stuff in Martin's opinion.

The leftover freight would remain with Enrique. Teresa hefted one last crate on top of another and a cough echoed through his dusty garage. After the coughing passed, her shot, watering eyes found Martin. "Everything out?"

He lifted up his toy aquarium and shook it before reaching through the passenger window and sticking it on the Wrangler's dash. "The important stuff, yeah."

There was no real amusement in her smile; all of her energy had been spent and left her despondent. Resting at the motel would be good for her. She looked like she needed some uninterrupted sleep.

Enrique jimmied a case of flares inside to fit. Several packages of formula and baby food had been set in plain sight among the crates of weapons. They were pretty much set, except for the two twin rear facing car seats. Bases for the seats had been tied in the back of the Wrangler for an easier transition when he dropped the babies off at the motel. Martin shook his head at the thought. *Babies—we don't know a damn thing about them.* They were so fragile. The idea terrified him.

Enrique ducked out from the back and closed the hatch wearily. His head craned to the sky. The Bearer put his palm up. Martin noticed his hand was shaking. Wide bands of light cut through the clouds and crept over the distant homes, slowly at first, and then began to build momentum like a radiant fungus spreading down the hill.

"In the car!" Enrique shouted. "They're trying to see you again. Stay under the clouds! Go to the motel. Go now!"

The Nomads yanked open the doors and jumped into their seats. Martin fumbled with the keys and the new configuration.

"Hurry!" Enrique's yell was dull outside the jeep. As fast as his stumpy legs could take him, the Bearer made for the house.

Yes, get to the babies, thought Martin frantically.

The Wrangler rolled into the street, bottoming out with a metallic crunch. Martin threw it in first gear and they lurched forward. He had to get used to this new clutch. Teresa held her breath. Warmth from the sunlight touched his neck and the rearview mirror dazzled with golden beams. It felt like someone with burning eyes stared through his back.

Martin crammed the accelerator against the floor.

The Wrangler's wheels squealed as he brought the jeep around to the main thoroughfare. Industrial buildings flew past. The stone giants leered as they plunged through withdrawing shadows.

"There," Teresa said.

He saw. Fifty feet ahead the sunlight swept out between two steel plants. The light dripped over the buildings' surfaces and colored every drab square-foot. The light was searching, stretching, licking the world for a taste of them. Martin cranked the wheel left and sent them into another sparkling pool. Teresa cried out in surprise as the jeep squealed the opposite way.

"We're all right," he said through teeth.

A T-intersection; a stoplight. Martin's heart machine-gunned. A veritable parade drove past: truck, 4-door, truck, truck, 2-door, truck, truck. Everything that crossed was painfully long and lumbering, and the drivers oblivious. The signal was clearly on a sensor system.

"Where do they all come from?" he asked. "Doesn't anybody work anymore?"

Sunlight filled the east and seemed to catch sight of them and charged forward.

"Martin—we have to go!"

"It's a red light."

"Go!"

"Hang on!" He took off, switching from first to third in only moments.

A Buick swerved with a snarl of its horn. In rearview a bald man stuck his head out and cried something that sounded like, "You shit-ass!"

Their tires hummed up a handicap ramp into a park and took them onto the grass. Martin went diagonal across the field. A Frisbee flew surreally over the hood. Teresa turned, her eyes hard. "Where are you going?"

"Like I know!"

Two boys walking a gray terrier were suddenly in front of the hood. They'd come out of nowhere. They didn't see the jeep. *And why would they be looking for one driving across the park?* thought Martin in terror. Two boys. One dog. He was going to slam right through them. He aimed left and closed his eyes.

A mantle flung out and Teresa gasped. The boys and dog were sent sideways. Martin watched them twist like paper dolls down the grassy slope. The dog started barking and the boys picked themselves up, hollering.

"Get us on the road!" Teresa pointed.

He went off the curb into the street again. In the rearview he could see two rotund men in baseball jerseys and a few other adults leading a futile chase after them.

The light closed around the jeep in bursting honeycombs. Every time they built speed, he had to slow down to turn away from it. *Stay under the clouds*, he reminded himself.

Right.

Left.

Engine purring and shifting.

Another right. He turned down an alley behind a strip mall. Sunbeams macheteed through the side alleys. Burnt rubber lifted through the vents. He went sharp into another alley. Another orange ray clawed its way out.

Right-Left.

They hit another wave of traffic with a stoplight. He jammed on the brakes and their bodies punched forward, he against the wheel and Teresa against the dash. Not speaking, they both pulled on their seatbelts now.

"Martin?"

He watched for an opening. Down the street, light filtered through the gloom. *Just after a few more cars.* Then he would take the red light. He counted and at the same time looked sideways at the brilliant wash headed their way. An opening formed and they rolled out.

Teresa put her hand out. "Don't go."

"Are you crazy?"

On the other side a train rumbled across the street.

The streetlight lingered red. Lazy eastern clouds moved. The train slowed. A rail change? Martin edged the Wrangler out. From the right, the sunlight gained a striking distance of twenty feet, and from the left, maybe ten. The train rolled on, no end of the boxcars in sight. Sweat boiled down his ears. Teresa watched like an eagle ready to take wing. Light jabbed from both sides, five feet away. And three.

A big rig pulled up with a hiss and pushed a looming shadow over them. The streetlight blinked green and they pulled out with the truck. The train had made its way through. They bounced over the tracks, keeping with the bar of cloud cover narrowing on the street. Once they were around the corner on Mount Vernon, he drove the accelerator down again and shifted up to fifth. They were only a couple blocks from the Happy Moon Travel Lodge.

Teresa's eyes stretched above. "The rain's starting up again."

The covered sky glowed from the light beyond. They pulled into the motel parking lot and rain began drumming noisily overhead. Thunderheads hugged the sky again.

Maybe the Messenger had taken back control.

After he killed the engine and pulled the parking brake, Martin leaned over to Teresa. She was trembling, but he could not muster a single consolation. He'd never seen her frightened in a chase. Her trembling worsened. She never liked being doted over. She wanted to be stronger than steel most times. *But still I should hold her, or at least ask if she's all right.* But before he could open his mouth, she took out her cloves and patted her pocket for a lighter.

THE PRIESTESS PRESSED HER HEAD AGAINST THE SLIDER. SHE was still naked, still beautiful, didn't even leave a greasy forehead print on the glass, but the sound of disgust that came from her throat was ugly. Paul cringed and stepped away.

"You saw them though. Didn't you?" he asked.

"Not long enough." Her eyes smoldered with tears, her face was filled with self-betrayal. An image came to Paul's mind: his mother, when she turned on the bedroom light and found him beside her in bed; not her boyfriend, but her son. He smiled in that time of triumph, but Paul couldn't smile about it now. It was a hideous memory, yet strangely a perfect moment.

Paul had dressed once the Priestess began having visions. The warmth of his suit felt nice after a night of stinging goose-flesh. He had a mission now. The Priestess wasn't happy and that had to be remedied right away. He felt he'd bitched-out on the balcony and almost with that poker—but he would not bitch-out again. She could only have what he decided to give, even if he decided to give everything.

He took out his cell phone and dialed. The practice stone still rested in his pocket. In a way he looked forward to getting back to work. The shutter to the Old Domain had been closed too long and once the Priestess started using her sight again, Cloth's children had writhed with energy, a dark hum from beyond the surface.

The other side picked up suddenly. Cole's voice was flaked in ice. "Where have you been? You were supposed to call."

"And just what am I doing right now?"

"It's already noon, jackass. I wanted to go over your exercises. The Heralding is tonight."

"Tonight?"

That must have been why the children were pulsing like they were. Paul sucked in through his nostrils and blew out through his mouth. This made him feel slightly less soul-fucked. "You could have called me too, you know."

"I did. More than once."

"Stop being grumpy," Paul said. "I have good news."

"Can't wait," mumbled Cole.

"The Priestess regained the Nomads."

"*What?*"

"It was real quick," said Paul, "but she saw them again."

"Where were they? Where did they go?"

"She has an idea of where they *were*." Paul picked up the old champagne bottle from last night. He casually sniffed its interior and winced, unsure why he'd done so.

"Are you going to tell me?" Cole almost shouted.

"At the Bearer's house."

"How could she tell it was the Bearer?"

"She's from the Old Domain. The Priestess felt the Hearts' influence, said the whole area in her vision was nearly on fire with their energy."

"Their?"

"Yeah Cole, she tells me there are four Hearts this time."

"You're shitting me."

"They're babies, Cole. No more than five months old." Paul sat on the cushy divan and regarded the Priestess's rump. Raindrop shadows rolled down the milky slopes like dark static. He smiled a little at the dried streak of brown blood on her thigh. He'd done that. Wasn't proud of it at the time, but he was proud now. Would he have put the poker on her? *Hell no* was what he wanted to believe.

Cole's giddiness was too apparent. "Are you sure the Priestess knew what she was seeing?"

"It's what she says. I don't know, damn."

"Have you told anyone else?"

"You're the first, papa bear."

"Well don't drop this on anyone else, understand? Not even trusted acolytes. I'd prefer to relay the information to the Archbishop, if you take my meaning."

"I might have shit for brains," Paul replied, "but I know how a politician's filter works."

"Is the Priestess ready to talk details?"

"Priestess," Paul called. "Bishop Szerszen wants to talk about what you saw."

She nodded but held at the darkening window. Lightning made a brief radioactive glow around her figure. Paul's gaze went top to bottom, bottom to top, and made for another trip when Cole Szerszen grumbled, "Paul?"

"She just needs to powder up a bit, but she'll be ready by the time you get up here."

Paul dropped the phone back in his pocket and jumped up. He cupped his hands around the Priestess's warm breasts.

"Why don't you want Archbishop Pager to know?" she asked.

He thought she'd ignored his conversation. "You uh— "

"So why don't you?"

He cleared his throat and took his hands off her. "I think that's a private matter...for the Church of Midnight."

She twisted around and a bleak smile cut her pretty face. "I don't care for how Sandeus Pager looks at me."

"How does he look at you?"

"As if he wants to jump inside my skin."

"Can't blame him there." Paul slid his finger down her belly and through the coiled butterscotch hair below. "You better get ready. Cole will be here soon. He's anxious to know what you saw."

"I saw little. I am not worthy."

"You are." Paul nodded. "The worlds can come together, stay apart, or end altogether and it doesn't matter, just as long as I'm yours."

Her arms locked around his neck and she kissed him, until his mouth bled.

On the way to the restaurant Cole struggled to recall the exact words of the passage about the folly of personal pursuits. It wasn't even found in the main body of the Tomes of

Eternal Harvest—the *Mizon's Fall* appendix (section Q&z:II or R&a:i). All of this vainglorious running around in the past year had taken Cole from his studies. He was to blame. There was no excuse. *Never put off time for enlightenment.*

This was the first lesson he'd learned in prison. His cellmate Rufus had pulled out a Tome from under his mattress one day and changed everything. Had Cole never been caught and sentenced, he might have never joined the Church of Midnight. He supposed he owed much to *Vehicular Manslaughter without drugs or alcohol but with gross negligence,* and he owed much to Rufus, his first real teacher, who unfortunately had his skull split with a Nomad's mantle the October after his prison release.

Cole jaywalked across an empty intersection toward the restaurant, Rufus's craggy voice still clear as a bell in his mind, "Every October Szerszen, you put your ugly head down and fuck the consequences. You show 'em you're worthy and you'll last forever in this outfit. You buddy up with a Bishop or get on the Archbishop's good side—secure a spot in the Inner Circle. Fuck, if you got worth, you got it made. And how's that done? Easy. Stay clear of the man with one black and one orange eye—don't even talk with that one if you don't have to. Just put your soul into nabbing just one sonuvabitch a year and the rest is cake. Prove your worth, shit, it's good then."

According to the Priestess there were four sonuvabitches now. Her clues were more confounding than anything else. *North side of Colton. A duck painted on the mailbox, the street name had something to do with a lock...?* What the hell could it mean?

Cole's best people had already set out to scout and Paul had donated twelve of his own acolytes, two of whom Cole recognized from Melissa's stead—that was something he'd like to know a lot more about. Something was off there. *Instruction*, thought Cole, rubbing the raw patch on his jaw. He had to pry Paul away from the Priestess and continue a crash course in marrow blossoming. The Heralding had to go off without a hitch. He certainly couldn't assassinate the Archbishop if Cole himself had to participate in the Heralding; it had to be Paul, all the way.

Deep in thought, Cole hadn't realized he'd walked into Marcos's Italian restaurant, and joined Melissa at a booth. He picked up the red leather menu and opened it.

"Well hello to you," she said. It had been her idea to forego the hotel bistro and come here, for a change. It was her idea of being romantic and Cole had obviously punched a hole through it.

He shook his head free of the mental cobwebs. "Sorry, too much going on."

"I know." She skimmed her slim hand over the table.

"You okay?"

She pushed up her glasses. He loved her glasses. "Remember when I told you I had a nightmare last night?"

Cole hadn't. This morning he was too concerned with Paul Quintana to process anything. "Sure," he replied and put his hand on hers. "But I don't think you said much about it. Did you?"

Her face said she hadn't, but also that she didn't believe he cared.

"Tell me."

She dragged her hand out from under his and her fingers rapped the checkerboard tablecloth. He thought she'd just tell him right then. Instead, she picked up her menu.

"What—?"

"Good afternoon," said a bald waiter with horrible beard stubble. The waiter wore slacks and a chambray shirt, had a cell phone on his hip. *Must own the place*, thought Cole. Some kid probably hadn't shown up to work. Youth, what a wasted lot.

"Can I start you with some drinks?" asked the waiter.

"Water," Melissa told him.

Cole looked at the man, who smiled patiently and masked his degradation. "Do you have any white port here?"

"Certainly sir, we have *Trentadue Viognier*. It's a dessert wine."

"I'll buy a bottle."

"Very good. I'll get that and be right back."

The waiter disappeared into the region of unoccupied tables in the back.

"What's the occasion?" Melissa sunk back into the booth, maybe to look at him better. He didn't like people looking at his face too much, especially her, but it was what it was.

"Your dream is the occasion."

Melissa sat there, silent and uncomfortable.

"I didn't listen the first time," said Cole. "I'll listen now."

"It's okay."

He looked over the lunch menu and the veal parmigiana called to him. When he was finished with perusal, he set the menu down. She was staring at him. "What is it now?"

"I don't like keeping things from you. But what if I knew that telling you would upset you?"

He stopped breathing. "This is about Quintana?"

When she nodded, everything rent inside and Cole just wanted to reach across the table, grab her hair and slam her mousy head into the table. He dry-swallowed instead and waited for the blow.

"We do have somewhat of a past together."

Cole's skin burned. The marrow blossoms in his chest clenched to fists and filled. "Past? What's that mean? You told me you'd never— "

"Calm down. It's nothing big. You are my first."

He mumbled a hateful chuckle from the corner of his mouth. The waiter returned and presented the wine bottle label. Cole nodded fiercely, then watched the man uncork the bottle and pour a sip. He picked up the glass and tasted the syrupy yellow wine, looking at Melissa the entire time. "It's not quite what I expected."

"Does it taste okay, sir?"

"For now," Cole coldly stated. "I want to see how it plays out."

Both glasses were filled. Their orders were taken. The waiter left again. Mercifully. Cole looked down. His hands grasped the sides of the table. Muscles quaked through his chest and thighs. The blossoms inside were provoking a heart attack. He opened himself and heard the distant call of the Children.

Melissa glanced away. This time, Cole could not help himself. He clutched her face, yanked it to his, *made* her face him. "You don't deserve to be the *Priestess of Midnight* if you can't be honest with me. What did you do?"

She wedged her hands between his and shucked them off. "I kissed him once—when I was drunk. And you know what? I even liked it. So shoot me already for kissing someone before we were even together!"

Burning air escaped his nostrils. "*Kissed?*"

She picked up her port, turned away from him and drained it. She made a face from the alcohol and said, "I told you it was nothing. Just calm down."

"A kiss? So you gave him something in return to keep quiet for a fucking kiss? Two acolytes and what else?"

"Nothing."

"Sure."

Cole hammered the table. His fist caught the edge of his wine glass and toppled it. He didn't bother to wipe up the mess and instead reached for the bottle to pour another. "I'm not jealous," he hissed.

"I said to calm down."

"Why?" he spat. "We're the only ones in here."

Her spectacled eyes implored him for a moment before another long drink. She set the glass gently down. "It wasn't easy to tell you, you know."

Cole dabbed at the spilled port with his napkin. The mess had gotten to him. He exhaled slowly. "No, it probably wasn't easy."

"I wish I hadn't kissed him. I wish you could have been the first, and I— "

"Why did you do that with *him*?" he whispered. "He's a sleaze."

A handsome sleaze, he thought bitterly.

"Cole, I— "

He raked his fingernails over the scabrous plains of his face. He'd have given anything to leave, to not have to look at her. He felt lost. He felt small. It took him a while to find words. Slowly he tapped his chest. "Don't you understand why I'm like this? Can't you see? I—I could never be like Quintana. Don't you see why that would bother me?"

Melissa's eyes misted, but she tried to remain strong, unashamed. "I should have told you everything in the beginning. But I was too scared to hurt you."

"I'm not hurt," he returned.

"Oh can't we just forget this? Can't we move on, please? I just wanted you to know. I don't like keeping things from you. This is something small, really. Nothing has changed. We had good news today, and we should act like it."

Cole's back went straight as a board and he ignored his boiling insides. He knew it would return once his mind began to think endlessly over this again, but he canned it, for both their sakes. "Sure," he breathed out in fake relief. "Let's enjoy lunch. This is wasting time anyhow. I have to get going soon. So…" He tried to find a new thought, new words, something, "… Did you call your people out yet?"

Melissa nodded and tipped back her port to taste the golden drop at the bottom of her glass.

Their food arrived. The veal parmigiana was not as juicy as Cole would have liked. Melissa played with her pasta, doing pirouettes with the noodles around her fork and then letting them fall, unattended. It was a nice distraction for about ten minutes.

"Tell me your dream." Cole was determined to forget everything that had happened from the moment he walked in until two seconds ago. It wasn't working but he was damn sure trying.

She simpered. "Did you hear me shout?"

"I think the shower was too loud. I couldn't hear anything. Was it a long dream? One of those weird ones with different parts?"

"No," she replied. "I think it started on a cliff overhanging the shore of some ocean."

"Sounds all right."

"This ocean looked like blood, in a way."

He put his fork down. Cloth's children clamored at the back of his mind to hear her words. Cole had long ago learned to keep them contained, but sometimes they were tenacious buggers.

"You were there with me—I slipped off the side of the cliff. You tried to reach for me, but it was too late. I fell off and went deep into the blood."

The waiter sauntered up. "Well, well, are we doing okay—?"

Cole snapped, "Yes goddamnit!"

"Super." The waiter bounced back through the tables.

Melissa laughed and Cole reached over and adjusted her spectacles. "So what came next?"

"I don't remember. I think I drowned when I tried to scream."

There was his Melissa. He'd made her terrified of him. She couldn't even tell him something trivial about her past without him losing it. "Just a dream, sweetie," he told her.

Her lips tried a smile but then fell. Cole didn't want to think about those lips pressed into Quintana's. "I'll never let you slip, Melissa," he said. "Just be honest with me from now on. I'll always be there. I'll never let go. I promise."

Cole finished his lunch and the rest of the port. By the time they left he felt a powerful buzz from the wine, but he'd have rather thought the feeling activated from love. He didn't want to think otherwise. It would kill him to have this love taken away. It was love. Wasn't it?

Cole would be Archbishop soon and that would change a legion of things for the better. When Melissa became the first Priestess of Midnight, that kiss with Paul would fade forever from her mind. And with any luck, his as well.

Twenty-seven

MARTIN SAT DOWN ON THE BED, HIS NERVES FINALLY starting to calm. Teresa had marked the Colton map with black X's. Sunlight tried to burn through the crimped Venetian blinds. The weather had cleared and reverted to rain four or more times since returning, but the clouds always held firm around the Happy Moon Lodge. Now the Nomads were confined to this room with only canned food, bottled water and the occasional string of great programming: *Beavis and Butthead* reruns, *Survivor: Alaska*, and even the latter half of a *Hawaii 5-0*.

"These are the freeway entrances." Teresa touched the X's with the capped marker. "We've got one up Mount Vernon—that's closest. There's also one here and there." She tapped two others.

"So Enrique brings the Hearts in, and we shoot off, probably for the exit up the street?"

"Makes the most sense."

"What about the Voids?"

They would need the Voids if they got cornered. *With Cloth that was the more likely reality.* Trying to outrun him forever was a rookie mistake. Teresa grabbed for a poster tube sitting near the nightstand. The white top popped as it came off and she slid out a transparency with a general outline of San Bernardino County. Shaded areas were random across the glassy sheet. She set it over the road map. The shadowed areas covered portions of the city of Colton like an illustration of organ locations in a cadaver. These were the sacred places Cloth's children could never tread. *Voids*. Martin loved them. The world would be a better place with more of them. If only the voids kept Cloth out too, Martin might have built a home in one.

"The Messenger left this?"

Teresa shrugged. "Enrique gave the transparency to me. Saves us some homework since we're cooped up here."

"Saves more than that. We should fill in those areas on the paper map."

"And input void destinations in the GPS."

"Absolutely." Martin blew out in relief. "It's easier than locating them that night. When did Enrique hand this over?"

"You were busy goo-gooing inside with the Jordons."

"They're kind of cute," he admitted.

"You miss them?"

Martin had been trying not to think about the Hearts since they got back to their room. It hurt too much to consider being apart for two and half more days.

Teresa smiled thinly. "I miss them too. Did you see the big eyes on that one baby girl—I don't remember their names yet."

"I think that was Rebecca—or was it Nancy?" Martin went to a canister of organic dried vegetable sticks on the dresser. "I don't know. I can't tell the boys from the girls when they're all dressed in the same lime green onesies."

Teresa watched with a long yawn. "You know those kids and the dog you tried to run over today?"

"Screw you," he joked and took out some dehydrated carrots.

She pushed the map and transparency aside so she could sit on the bed. "Building that quick mantle took a lot more out of me than usual. I should probably use our time here to rest. All this damn coughing, all this weakness...I can't imagine how I'll hold up on the 31st if I tire so easily."

Martin sealed the canister. It popped solemnly in the silent room. "It wouldn't be ideal."

"We cannot lose even one child," she answered his thoughts. "I think the other three would die if that happened."

"I wouldn't want that option anyway."

"Me neither," she replied.

"And I don't think I could leave them like how we left the others, how we left Tony. Even if Cloth had them—I don't think I could run the other away."

"No," she agreed. "Living to fight another day, no, that's out. This changes things."

He sensed the somber edge to her voice. "Take it easy. I'll mark up the map and go through the first round of checking the artillery. Then I'll probably make some foot pedal detonators."

"You're programming the circuit boards for remote activation?"

"Yes."

Teresa tugged up the covers. "You're calibrating the pressure between two and three hundred?"

He rolled his eyes and crumpled up a flyer from the TV stand. It bounced against the headboard behind her. "You just rest, okay?" he laughed. "I got this."

Her head dented the flat pillow. A hundred mile stare came into her deep blue eyes. "When will the Messenger decide we're too old for this sort of thing?"

"You've asked that before. And speak for yourself, I'm young at heart."

She reeled back to cough, face tensing up, but she conquered it. Martin was glad. He was sick of hearing the assault; all that retching made his optimism fizzle away. But he knew it wasn't fair to judge her anymore, everything she was going through and him so critical. An hour ago she'd called her father in Texas with the business card from earlier. He'd hung up on her once she told him who she was. Martin was all she had.

Martin studied the oily black gun parts with a bored sigh. Teresa soon began to snore. A much better sound than coughing, indeed.

Teresa's dream bled into the quiet motel room. There were hundreds of babies and Cloth wanted them all—the fragile little bundles, lined up around the room's flaky walls, weakened by underdevelopment, sick, coughing up birthday gifts for her: retches wrapped in ribbons of blood and bows of green sputum. Cloth's own children fell into the room and tore through the soft nursling flesh with spiny teeth. Red freeze-frame-flashes lifted on the air in staggering parabolas. The gurgling blared in layers, as though each begging wet mouth was at her ears. The wailing. Louder and deafening. Thriving with intensity, until she opened her eyes to superheated darkness. Was she tanning on a beach somewhere? Was Martin out body-boarding? This was summer. Isn't that right? She was supposed to be relaxing...but they were crying! The babies were.

Her real eyes flew open to the motel room. She watched the woman in bed as an outsider, hacking and coughing against her own will, jerking the bed right and left. Martin brought his hand away from the long oval of blood on her pillow. This was no dream. She'd woken up. And all the blood had come from her throat. She could taste it. Her hand found the lukewarm spot on the pillow too, coming away cherry red and panic constricted her chest. Her sleeve—the white cotton blushed with violet dots and whips.

Martin was buttoning his jeans. Without zipping them, he began shoving his feet into his tennis shoes. From the nightstand he grabbed his wallet and the Messenger's false ID packages. She watched in numbed awe. Metal salts corded through her gums and dripped down the back of her throat. Martin jammed his gun into the back of his pants.

Her eyes wandered. Such a depressing little room...

The Wrangler's keys jangled somewhere in oblivion.

Fight. Teresa wasn't weak. She could fight. She could sit up. She forced a hand to her chest. It felt good to press there. She wheezed; blood sprayed up from her lungs into her throat.

Martin yelled, "Let's go. Now."

She hadn't noticed its intensity before, but his short-cropped brown hair ran silver at the temples. His hazel eyes were sunken, intense, unrelenting, abused, terrified. *Desperate.* Martin crossed the bed and grabbed her arm. "I'm not fucking around anymore. This is bullshit. You have to see a doctor. Whatever kind of surgery, radiation, chemotherapy or pill you have to take, you're taking it."

"Stop being stupid," she rasped. "It's impossible for us to go—you'll get the Hearts killed."

His eyes suggested she had a point, but he wasn't giving up. "I can handle this on my own. But you need to go."

She pulled her arm away from him. "It's just some blood. It looks like more because of all the spit. I'll be fine tomorrow. Just calm down. We're not going anywhere until it's time. They'll find us."

"Let them come then. I'll kill everyone in a black suit. I don't care. Let's just fucking go, Teresa. Come on!"

"Quit it. Please? Just stop talking. Stop *this*."

Martin began to frantically search for something to demolish. When he found nothing he slumped down on the bed and snatched an escaping sob through his lips. "Fucking hell!" he shouted through clawing fingers. "*Fucking hell*," he whispered now, shaking his head. "I won't let it end like this. I promise you."

Teresa wanted badly—needed—to force out the snag in her lungs, but she wouldn't allow it. She willed the fit away and clutched his shoulder to brace for the interval. The room dimmed. Her hand looked so spotty, an old lady's hand, decaying flesh over rickety bone. She wanted to chop it off rather than see some ancient sickness pooling up. Softly to him, she said, "Imagine the world with every day another October 31st. That's what you'd do. There's *four* of them, Martin. That's too much power to play around with. That gateway will slip open wide enough for the columns to hold it in place—that'll be that. The Eternal Church will destroy everything we know."

He turned, looking crazy with fatigue. "Stop—I don't care about that shit anymore. Just so you know: you're not going to leave me alone."

Teresa's eyelids drooped. She was about to say something else and suddenly, without warning, she began to cough. This time the fit would not be controlled; this time the pressure in her lungs wasn't going to linger but live on forever. She wouldn't even be able to die because she'd be too busy coughing, like a machine built by cancer, caught in an endless logic loop.

Then something slammed into the side of her head and that loop stopped. Martin said something that trailed away with consciousness. "I'm sorry...*not gonna happen*."

She couldn't be sure, it might have been a dream, but somehow, somewhere, Teresa could feel rain sliding down her face. Martin had lifted her body into the air. She heard the jeep's doors shut. Heard an engine turn over. The tentative raindrops pitter-patted on the Wrangler's windshield. Her thoughts ended before they fully formed.

Martin, no...

Twenty-eight

NOT LONG AGO THE GRAIN SILO HAD SAT IN OBSCURITY on a bald hill, but now from the gateway's mouth an overgrowth of poison-green vines laced the ground in a myriad confusion. While most vines stretched so far into the distance they were lost, a few journeyed downhill and coiled around a cell phone tower. Others explored a dismantled tractor all but vanished in a coiffure of weeds. Some vines were as thick as bridge cable, and others thin as spider web. The disparity in size extended to the pumpkins as well. Cloth's pumpkin was a definitive monster in size, a Great Dane of gourds, but all the pumpkins shared the same cruel appearance, a horde of orange pit bulls. Cloth sat on his pumpkin, casting down his black and orange gaze, making for an odd looking king atop his spherical throne. "How are you and the Priestess of Morning getting on?"

Cole hadn't heard Paul speak the entire way here. The man probably hadn't been in a hurry to return here. *Poor baby*, thought Cole with an inward sneer.

"Splendid," replied Paul, though his voice had no flavor for the word. "We're getting along just fine." He pushed a shock of blond of out of his eyes.

Chaplain Cloth's ghostly lips spread with perfect pearl rows. He leaned back on the massive pumpkin and his voice sprang with mockery. "Did her royalness have any luck locating the Heart?"

Paul's jaw muscle twitched, but he remained quiet. The kid at least had some smarts. This would be tricky, delivering news like this. Was it disrespectful to know more than Cloth?

"She acquired them only for a moment, Chaplain," Cole answered, filling the silence. "The Nomads left too quickly for her to take in the area thoroughly—but we have learned that there are four Hearts of the Harvest this year. Infants, Chaplain."

The black eye cooked with oily lust; the orange eye fermented tangerine. "*Four?* How did she discover that?"

"A break in weather earlier. The Nomads...they were visiting the Bearer."

As he sat up, Cloth's black suit *shhhhh*ed like fingertips running over an obituary. The sound made Cole grimace. "So the Nomads have them?" asked Cloth curiously. He adjusted his black necktie, though it looked perfectly straight.

"The priestess said the Nomads were alone in their vehicle."

"It makes sense. The Messenger knows we've sighted the Nomads. This was a foolish way to track them." Chaplain Cloth let go of his tie and nodded, processing something else.

Paul spoke up, "The Priestess gave some clues to the Bearer's location. It's not much, but we have acolytes on the streets."

"We'll find them," Cole put in.

Cloth's dark form slid off the pumpkin. Cole was a foot taller than the Chaplain, yet felt as though he could sink between the grains of sand beneath his shoes. After all these years he'd never gotten used to the monster, and he was glad to not be scrutinized. Instead Chaplain Cloth ran his eyes up and down Quintana. He stepped closer to them. The black licorice breath floated on the air. "Are you scared, Bishop Quintana?"

"Yes."

"Why? I need someone in this world to bring my children to me." He studied Paul closely and decided. "No, you don't look honored."

"I'm sorry, it's just that this isn't what I'd planned for."

"Well, most good plans are malleable."

Cloth pressed his fingertips into Paul's chest and closed his eyes. Paul looked to Cole, who nodded, and tried to communicate through his expression—*just let this be, for both our sakes.* The corpselike hand twisted. Cole knew what the burning touch felt like and he even pitied Paul its silent torment.

"The marrow garden inside you *is* interesting," Cloth observed. "Unbalanced, but interesting. Curious."

"Unbalanced?"

"If you draw too much, the blossoms wither and die. If you don't draw enough, the blossoms overtake the vessel. A balanced garden distributes power equally like a fork in an efficient waterway."

"How do I bring balance back to them?"

"Sow more seeds from the healthy blossoms until you find balance. Takes time and patience, and depends on the fertility of your soul." Cloth chuckled, as though he found the idea deplorable in regards to Paul. His hand dropped away. "You can only learn the power boundaries and stay within them."

"How do I discover my boundaries?"

The chaplain twisted around, his bone white face twisted and disturbing. "I believe Bishop Szerszen will show you those boundaries right now."

Paul's face shot over.

"A Heralding can be deadly Quintana," said Cole. "You must know when to hold back and when to surge forward, just as we practiced earlier. Keep yourself open to the Old Domain, no matter the pain that comes. You will know when to close again."

"And what will you do to help me along?" asked Paul.

Cole leaned forward and whispered, "Oh you're doing this alone. All my energy goes to the Archbishop. That will not be easy."

Paul's eyes flared.

"You *owe* me," added Cole.

"It only takes one to bring them," said the Chaplain. "Whether you die or not makes no difference to me, Quintana. My children are calling and they deserve a guide that will light their way here."

"Your Priestess wanted this," Cole reminded him. "Make her proud." He guided a dejected Paul Quintana then, led him to an open area in the vines. Now he really felt sorry for him. Cole told Paul to lie down in the dirt and get comfortable.

PAUL KNEW NOW. IT HAD ALWAYS BEEN STRANGE THAT COLE would sell out Justin Margrave so easily. *This* was the pay off. Justin wasn't stupid enough to agree to do this alone. Lying there, amongst the cold vines and gravel, Paul Quintana thought of ten thousand different excuses why he couldn't do this alone—but all excuses were out. Cole's hideous square face drifted in the night shadows above, a grim reminder of what may be in store for Paul. He could not see Chaplain Cloth, but Paul certainly felt the freaky son of a bitch.

"Open the shutter in your mind and let them through," Cole said quietly. "Simple as that."

The vines became cold underneath Paul. They started to freeze to his skin to the point of burning. At first it reminded him of getting snow in your shirt. But here the flesh peeled at the touch. Icy parchment.

"Something's wrong." He began to sit up.

Cole's loafer forced him down. "Stay calm. Let them through. It'll hurt more if you don't."

Paul swallowed, concentrated. The shutter had been closed tightly for most of the day. Since the training he'd cracked it open only slightly to keep the children at bay, but now they pushed with the knowledge of what was happening.

The vines burned colder—Paul's undershirt split and jagged hooks on coarse vines pulled his skin closer—when the hooks sunk in he sensed every pumpkin on every vine—a series of nerve centers in a colossal being.

Thanksgiving to the Blood Feast!

First a trickle, then a deluge. The children's souls flooded through and scoured the tender planes of Paul's body. The marrow seeds went up like torches. Darkness cut through. Paul was screaming, had been screaming, would keep screaming, even though it had taken time to realize the pain. His every cell felt about to give birth to something a hundredfold in size. Trillions of nether-babies. Down into his groin, his testicles were pulled forward with talons. Intestines went too. They slithered down into his colon. Every nerve was raw plasma. Pleasure and pain existed in the same place; relief became agony and torment became soothing. Everything pulled at him now. His face stretched into infinite boundaries, his chest and arms flowed out onto the universe in an energy ripple, and his legs pierced unimagined dimensions between space and time. *A human body can't be meant for this,* Paul kept thinking. *This is playing with godhood—this will kill me if I don't fight it. I can't lose her now that I have her—cannot let go and give up.* He readily brought the marrow blossoms to attention. Both flowers—black and orange—readied to fill with incredible power, but the strain sent him grasping for one set and not the other. It was easier, quicker to invoke one color and not both. The black blossoms shed their power and exploded within, making him remember a grand finale fireworks display, but he knew the Heralding wasn't over yet.

Blood feast. Blood feast. Blood feast. Thanks to you. Thanksgiving to you.

He fought to contain his energy and drew from the boundless pool beyond the gateway. This was where Cloth lived, where he grew powerful. The pumpkins drew those nether-babies out with a single tug on a billion points. *Keep the shutter open. The Children were almost through...*

And with one final rush, like passing a bowling ball, the pain clapped like thunder and fragmented into departing pieces. Paul blinked at the drizzling sky above with a relief he'd never known possible, gratefully sucking up mouthfuls of air. His soul felt scarred forever and the world would never be the same—a part of his humanity had been maimed for this genesis, but Paul had power greater than before.

He closed the shutter and almost fainted. Another breath of fresh air revitalized him and he felt good, better than ever in fact. Dizzy and sweating, he leaned up on one arm, feeling satisfied after performing something he'd been born to do. Something inside him was...*stronger* for it. Paul understood the force of chaos that Chaplain Cloth was, although he'd never be able to describe it completely.

The chaplain turned to Cole. "You did well by this one. He didn't succumb or even so much as pass out. I daresay we can use him on the Hunt."

"He has acute control," Cole whispered.

The chaplain regarded Paul like a successful science project. "Fine," he said. "That's fine."

All of the pumpkins, even the giant Cloth had sat upon, had grown. Their skin had sharpened to a glowing orange, like orbs of cooling magma. Paul staggered to his feet and turned in circles, dumbfounded. "Where are the children?" he asked.

"Incubating," Cloth said, returning up to the silo.

Something cool ran down Paul's back and he checked through his ripped shirt. His hand came back with rich, glistening blood. He wondered what scarring had been left behind on his back. His nose caught a whiff and he flinched. The blood smelled like pumpkin guts.

Twenty-nine

A ghost blew through Melissa's bones as she stepped into Archbishop Pager's suite. She didn't know why he'd called or what he wanted, but it had to be about the missing marrow seeds—if Pager knew who stole them, she was dead. It was easy. That reality had crept up as the sentinels allowed her entrance. One of the meatheads actually gave her an impatient shove.

Sandeus Pager had taken the liberty of decorating, as was his way. The hotel suite, though expansive, was crowded with antique furniture and the gilded excess of a man with too many resources and too much time to ponder creative uses for them. Strawberry incense burned; she couldn't see the smoke, but the choking sweetness powered through the air.

Standing in this room, in the presence of the Archbishop, put her in danger just to save Cole's ego, and made her silently hate him. It couldn't be helped. Melissa began to wonder if she'd ever loved him as much as she once thought.

"Come into the bedroom, sweetie," Sandeus called. He laughed and said to somebody else, "No not you, Archbishop Kennen. Of course, if you have a bedroom handy, by all means." Another chortle.

Melissa edged by a bronze replica of Medusa, into the spacious bedroom. Melissa's shoes shifted through coils of black and orange potpourri layering the carpet like a forest bed. The Archbishop stretched out under the canopy bed next to someone. Somebody naked and female. Somebody naked and female and with a cavernous red mouth of gore smiling in her throat. Wires connected to the organic circuitry led to a phonograph that had been placed on the bloody pillow beside her. Sandeus lay on his side in an evening dress almost identical to the orange getup the Priestess of Morning had worn at conclave.

"You're not lying to me, are you Sandeus?" the voice on the phonograph implored. "The Priestess hasn't lost sight of the Nomads, has she?"

"I don't know what else to say, Kennen, other than we have them."

"But the Hearts?"

Sandeus looked at Melissa and winked, then patted the side of the bed. She treaded over. The body of the dead woman came into full view. The corpse was arranged as though she were doing snow angels. Melissa recognized the woman. She worked janitorial. Such a pretty thing. *Lupita,* she remembered the name plaque had read. Before Melissa left for the restaurant that day, she'd given this dead woman a ten dollar gratuity. A shy smile in return. Now Lupita's body served as an audio conduit to another world. Sandeus had festively adorned her breasts and pubic hair with black and orange glitter.

"Don't worry so much, Kennen. The Heralding has begun."

Lupita's lips frothed with words from the other side. "I sacrificed my wife to smelt visions of the Nomads' future. I had to choose the time. *I* changed reality so that the Priestess could find them. So why are we learning information about the Hearts in fragments—this diminishes everything my church has suffered for. This was to be the year, Sandeus."

Sandeus shared a smile with Melissa. "They haven't gone to retrieve the Hearts yet," he lied and tapped Lupita's cold purple lips. "But I look forward to giving you the good news." He lightly lifted the needle off the phonograph plate. His eyes moved over Melissa's clothes for a while, beaming under his peach eye shadow. "Why we keep our women in those hideous suits, I'll never understand."

Melissa felt her cheeks warm. "Yeah."

Sandeus reached forward. "I like your glasses. So cute." He pulled them off with a coil of his finger and her world turned into a blurry wasteland of black, orange, and red. She could tell the man had put on the glasses but couldn't really see.

"They hurt my eyes," he told her, handing them back. "Can't you wear contact lenses, honey?"

"They hurt my eyes when they dry out." She put the glasses back on and found Sandeus's smile had vanished. He sat cross-legged now in his evening gown, his hands folded in his lap.

"I asked you up to talk about Bishop Szerszen," he stated. "Point is, I value Cole. Hell, he's a better politician than a face like his would usually permit. But the sad thing is, lately I don't think he values me in return. Actually, truly, honestly, I don't think he cares whether I live or die."

"That's not true."

"Cole's no dummy. He sees things are changing and wants to be able to change with them. Plans have a funny way of flipping and only the smart roll with them. You're in on his insurrection, aren't you, Melissa sweetie?"

"He wants what's best for the Church. What would cause you to believe anything besides that?"

Sandeus leaned forward. His spicy perfume made her eyes water. "I don't mean to scare you, even though I know I am."

"Not scared," she mumbled.

"Yes, yes you are. But you don't have to be. I need Cole on my side. You two are lovers, and that makes you a perfect go-between. If he's planning something, I want you to try and convince him otherwise."

"He would never—"

"Let me be clear. This is between you and I. Okay?"

She nodded.

This didn't satisfy him. "Say, 'Yes I understand'."

"Yes, I understand."

"Every October 31st I take a vigorous dose of marrow seeds. I experiment with the new power they bring to my garden while our worlds have connection. And Melissa, this process brings me more power than Cole could abide. I tell you this, not as your Archbishop, but as your and Cole's friend. If he tried something this Halloween, he wouldn't survive."

"What makes you—?"

"Melissa," he said. "Just stop. Okay? Now if you love him, encourage Cole away from the idea. I saw how the envoys were clinging onto him and giving me the stink eye. I didn't get to this position by being foolish. You just have to know that I will recultivate my garden again and Cole doesn't want to swim in these waters, believe me."

She shuddered. *He still didn't know the seeds were gone! He hadn't checked? But for how long?* Taking the seeds might actually work out for the best in the end—

"He hasn't mentioned any plan, Archbishop. It's silly to think of him in that way, but I will ask him and honestly report anything out of the ordinary."

"Fabulous. I'm just a paranoid person, I guess." Sandeus petted Lupita's brown tresses and gave her cheek a few reassuring smacks.

PAUL WATCHED THE RAIN WHILE HE WAITED FOR THE ELEVATOR. The light gradually went down the floor buttons, taking its time. He leaned against the wall and tried to collect himself for another night with the Priestess. Everything was slow. The atmosphere of the Doubletree felt like a big vat of syrup. The Heralding had left his body charged but his mind tarred and feathered.

The elevator opened and he nearly collapsed inside. The marrow blossoms clenched and unclenched. Paul should have felt better now the Children's voices had left his mind. He despaired though. He wanted to understand their absence. It was easy to feel betrayed by the loss. He'd mentioned this to Cole in the lobby just before parting ways. The Bishop's cracked face had looked grave. "Don't worry Quintana. They're never gone forever."

Wonderful.

Eggert waited outside the Priestess's room, as he was obliged to do. Paul sidled up and stuck out his hand. Some human contact would be good for a mood change, even if the human was Eggert.

The bushy beard lifted with a dry smile. "Having a pleasant evening? I thought you looked sad after all that ice I filled you with. What? Did a twenty horse carriage run over your balls?"

Paul's hand fell. "But I feel stupendous."

A prickly moment passed. The barbarian's eyes were all business. Eggert's usual smell of Aqua Velva had soured from many trips out into the rain, probably at the Priestess's whims.

"Are you going to call her, or should I?" asked Paul.

Eggert stepped closer to insist upon the fundamental size difference between them. "I think she could do better than you by randomly picking a warm body out of a crowd."

"Good thing nobody cares what you think."

"You're an imbecile, Quintana. You and the Priestess, you both want two very different things out of this."

"What does that matter?"

Eggert backed away. "Because this won't end well."

Paul was too exhausted to toy with the man, although the prospect of making him squirm did have a lingering appeal. At first he had been revolted by the Priestess's suggestion of Eggert watching them. Friends in the bed were one thing to Paul, but Eggert was no friend. Now however, he found the idea had potential. It might knock the big oaf down a notch or two.

Eggert rapped on the door with a brace of gnarled knuckles. "Bishop Quintana to see you, Priestess."

After a few seconds, he nodded, as though the Priestess could actually see this. *She could.* The door popped open and Eggert lethargically gestured inside. Paul slipped by the man's stench and it brought to mind that Paul, himself, hadn't showered since the Heralding. Eggert reached to shut the door and he turned. "Maybe I'll see you later, Egg." He winked.

The door slammed.

Paul explored the massive suite for a moment, happy to be through with the Heralding. He already contemplated extended bathtub debauchery. Hot and cold water. And lips. And ass. And tits. He thickened at the fantasy.

The Priestess of Morning stood at the balcony window. She wore only panties, something from her world that looked like the briefest of skirts made of black scales. The hanging material barely covered her ass. Her nipples had stiffened in the cold room and her areolas lightly bubbled. As devastating as she was, the worry cut into her face spoiled Paul's glee.

"It's letting up a bit," he told her, taking off his coat and tossing it over the end of the divan as he had the night before.

She bit her lip and came away from the window. When he embraced her, he felt her body tremble. "I saw the Nomads again, only for a second," she told him. "The woman wasn't well."

He stroked her hair. "That's good."

"The Heralding?" A smile flickered to her apricot lips. "Did it hurt much?"

"I don't want to talk about it, if it's all the same."

She tapped his nose gently, her mood lightening. "You're so thin-skinned, Bishop."

Paul shrugged. Her hand slid between his legs, found his penis and clenched it through his slacks. "You want me then?"

"Actually," his voice squeaked. "I wanted to unwind first. Everything's still crazy inside my body."

"You don't make the rules." She gripped him harder and her serpentine eyes threaded into his. "You'll have me, *hard*, and you're not allowed to release. If you release any seed—you're on the balcony again."

He pushed her away. "No fucking chance."

Her head cocked to the side and she pointed to the door. "You'll do as I say, Paul, because if you don't, I'll send for Eggert."

"The bastard's not touching me again."

"We'll see about that."

He grabbed his coat. "I'm too tired for this tonight, dear."

Exhaustion and terror cinched in a perfect knot at the base of his throat. He locked onto her breasts and the smooth slopes of her abdomen. This was going to be impossible. She slipped the otherworldly undergarment down to the floor and kicked it aside. Then strode toward him, smile growing.

"He's not touching me and I'm not sleeping out there again." A whimper crawled up Paul's throat. "Not again. I've been through too much tonight—I won't do it. You can't make me."

"I can."

"No—you don't want me to show you what I've learned tonight."

"That's where you're wrong, Paul," she said softly. "I want you to give me everything inside you. Give it to me."

"I'll give you what I want to give."

Her fingers brought down his zipper. "Stop my agony."

Paul had an answer for that.

THE PRIESTESS HAD NEVER FOUND COUPLING AS POWERFUL AS this. Now the insanity began. And the cramping muscles. With the clenching, gnashing teeth, and the nails disinterring curls of hot flesh, tears creased her face from all the disappointment. Losing the Nomads. Paul took her away from the failure that towered over every moment. She could sense power from the spiritual chambers deep inside him. It was a vast, new power, chilling in its scope. Billions of tentacles suckered onto her perception and then—then—

She saw him.

The night sky must have cleared outside. She saw the man at once. She saw the Nomad named Martin. He was in a brightly lit room, playing with his necklace made of seashells. She tried to have a look around the room, to see something that would give away the location. Just a name...

But she couldn't concentrate with Paul drilling into her.

"Stop!" she yelled. "Stop now!"

Paul's hands clamped around her shoulders and pinned her down. His hips swung fiercely and a mania of hateful delight rained down. She loved him for it. Hated him also.

"Stop!"

But Paul wouldn't. Beyond the flags of damp blond hair his eyes burned with the challenge she'd put there.

"You don't understand!" The Priestess kicked through the foggy images. She was losing sight again. "Please!"

His hips came at her faster, and his hold numbed her and *pushed* consciousness elsewhere, forcing her to become some kind of ghost flushed from one world into another. *Wait!* He was sending her somewhere—yet, her body remained beneath him. She could feel the movement of ideas, the slipping sanity. Moving. Again, not her brain; her being. She screamed one horrified name at the top of her lungs before her soul left this world for the Old Domain.

Eggert!

Paul hovered over the Priestess, swatting at her face, trying to loosen those fixed, lifeless eyes. He felt her neck for a pulse. There was a strong thumping there. Snapping his fingers in front of her eyes got him no response. He began mumbling prayers to a nothing-god of his own determination.

"Wake up Priestess—wake up! What happened? What happened?" But Paul knew. He had felt the newly awakened creature inside him, working under the influence of the intoxicating blossoms raining more seeds from under their petals, and he knew that the Priestess's soul had been stripped from this world, this flesh, and transported on the ethereal winds that blew through the valleys of the Old Domain. He should have never fought the power during the Heralding. Paul should have let it draw from his life, not rob it in the way he had. He'd cheated and now the Priestess had paid for it.

Paul bent forward, hoping he could draw her soul back—but it didn't work that way. He wasn't like the Nomads. They were powerful enough to pull things from the Old Domain into this world, but as Cole told him, they could never do the same. That meant that Paul had to find them and force them to bring her back. If that was easy, the idea might be reassuring. *If you do find them, they'll just fuckin' kill you,* he thought.

Getting up from the floor, Paul staggered deliriously, trying to remember where his slacks had ended up. He nearly ripped them open to retrieve the phone. His fingers dialed Vince's number and he pressed the send button. Before an answer came, red darkness sliced through his vision. Paul's head bumped a wall and he fell, naked body crumpling. Hot copper dripped over his lip. Everything went in and out. *How had Eggert snuck in?* A gallows laugh struck through his core—*The man was built like a bear and moved like a tiger? How did I not hear him?*

Eggert tied Paul's hands behind his back with what felt like a zip tie. Paul tried to flex his fingers and get a hold on the big man, but Eggert kept a safe distance. Paul's cell phone pulsed with green light. A boot crushed the sound out of it. Its cry faded.

Paul started blacking out from the throbbing head wound. He heard Eggert begging the Priestess to wake, over and over. Each time the man's voice became more panicked and more sickened with loathing. Consciousness washed away at that point, but somewhere, maybe somewhere not that far away, a man was being beaten. Pummeled. Paul realized he was that man but could do nothing about this. He knew he'd awaken to suffering, or perhaps wouldn't awaken at all. Reaching out for the Priestess did no good here. There was only dark.

Thirty

For Martin the hours at Arrowhead Regional Medical Center had been a quicksilver streak of plastic waiting room chairs, bad TV, bitter coffee and his unbridled anxiety for the inevitable white-coat meeting. The Messenger had secured a new PPO insurance, which turned out to be just outside of incredible—he or she had already paid the deductible and Teresa had X-rays and lab results ready that same evening. *So there's no dicking with incompetence, laziness or any bureaucratic matters,* thought Martin. There was just dicking with emotional ones.

After all the waiting and knuckle grasping, a dumpy, ashen doctor finally shuffled out to meet Teresa's alleged husband. The doctor talked and Martin absorbed every word, pause and facial expression as though he'd need them later for all-out war. Many things were iterated and reiterated and Martin dwelled on those more than anything else. Aside from the head trauma from her fall, which Martin was assured Teresa would recover from, he also had these beauties to chew on: *Localized squamous cell lung carcinoma. Stage 2b. Maybe video assisted thoracic surgery? Lobectomy.* And in the recent hour he had a new line of items to add: *A pulmonary embolism. She's sedated, oxygenated and drugged on a blood thinner called* enoxaparin.

Martin double-checked everything in memory from the library of med books he'd read. He drew a blank and cursed himself for not asking more questions. Now questions prevailed, but only in his mind. What had the doctor meant by her *doing well*? Was she doing well with the embolism? With the head wound? Or with the cancer? Or was she doing well with everything? And cancer in stage 2b, was that all that bad? There were more numbers and letters, so was she even half way there? She still had more stages to go. It might be possible to skip a stage. What if her stage 2b wasn't like a full-blown stage 2b? Were there such distinctions? Who the hell rated these things? Who determined the level of tragedy associated with an alphanumeric?

"We need to get her ready for some hard work ahead. Tests, possible surgery. Undoubtedly she'll need a course of radiation."

"She won't do that. We can't—it would keep us here too long."

"Pardon?"

"I guess I'll speak to her when she comes around."

The hospital wouldn't let Martin in yet. They'd said he could visit in half an hour, which really meant an hour and a half in hospital time. That meant he had time to meditate a little more. This could be a good thing. Martin felt that in times of panic, Mother Nature was his only refuge of solace. He wondered sometimes if this affinity for the outdoors had been inherited through blood—through the Old Domain. It didn't matter right now. All he knew was that he'd seen a lake up the street from the hospital on the way in, and that's where he headed. Teresa's medical folders were snuggled inside his jacket under his arm, to shelter them.

He found a cold stone bench and sat in the rain. For a time he just moved his eyes across the rippling surface of the lake. In the outlying shadows he saw indistinct humps: a golf course. The nets of a nearby driving range shuddered in the wind. He'd studied everything in Teresa's file so carefully there was no need to even look at the past results of sputum tests or needle biopsies. The chest X-ray preformed today was foremost in his memory, like a map to a buried treasure chest filled with radioactive gold. Leaning back and pinching between his eyes, he could see the white hacky sack lump floating in her lung's outline. The lymph nodes hadn't started metastasizing yet, and the tumor's growth was slower than other types of cancerous masses. But did any of that sit well with him?

Hell no, he thought. *I'm losing her.*

Thinking about the Hearts crushed him with guilt, so he tried to push away any thoughts associated with the babies. It didn't work. The idea of abandoning them to schedule an appointment with a thoracic surgeon left a bitter taste on his lips. Teresa was right: it couldn't be done. The passion they had for the Hearts would not let them run from duty. Martin would go to the Hearts, as though under a spell, just like he had every year. And yet that doctor had no idea when Teresa would be coherent—it could be a couple days. Maybe if she woke up tomorrow they could see about that surgeon—

"You're fooling yourself," he said to the night.

Teresa would hate him for bringing her to the hospital in the first place. *She's going to wake up pissed.*

The need to be absolutely alone overtook him. Not just alone from people but from this world. He glanced up and down the street. Nobody was coming. The cold zone in his mind fluxed and that strange feeling of lost virginity sluiced down his spine. A mantle shaped around his body like a balloon. There wasn't much ghost matter, only a thin layer with the capability of fifteen minutes or so of residence. Martin rolled forward inside it, the rain running at crazy angles around him from the bending contours. He coughed a bit, having sacrificed some oxygen.

The mantle bubble rolled into the lake with a subtle splash. Dull gray-brown fluid hugged the mantle and drank him in. The lake dipped to about ten feet deep in the center. He dropped under the surface completely and sat down inside the stuffy bubble. Snaky silver movements in the dark indicated fish, but he couldn't see them through the darkness and silt. Regulating his breathing in short gasps, Martin reached into his coat and pulled out the medical file folder. The chest X-ray was on top. He couldn't see the image, but he knew the white blob sat there on the cold paper, displaced from its environment, just as he was right now. More than anything, he just wanted to bring Teresa here, or somewhere deep in the ocean, and wall them in with a mantle that would last forever. Doing something like that would be worth the agony of creation—to be away from the world. They'd be like his little fish in its plastic bubble aquarium.

And you'd both suffocate, dumb ass. The thought came with a sharp gasp. *Inside a permanent mantle they would wither and die. Would they decompose? Or would their bodies remain preserved at the bottom of the ocean?* That was an interesting thought. He tucked the file into his coat, stood up and began rolling his way back to shore. He felt done with his communion with nature and his mind raced with new ideas.

His eyes broke the water's surface. A sedan sped down the road. When its headlights vanished, Martin crept forth. The weak fibers of his mantle crackled. He pressed his fingers one more time into the wall. No matter how they were shaped, weak mantles tended to feel like warm sandpaper. He'd never enjoyed touching them. Once he was firmly on land he let the mantle go, grateful for fresh air.

The half formed plan stuck in his mind like an arrowhead. His steps back to the hospital quickened. This time he wouldn't balk. He would make it work. All he had to do was setup some kind of fallback for Teresa if something happened to him. A safe zone like none they'd ever built. Safe for her and the Hearts, not for the Church. But the safe zone was the easy part. If Teresa didn't regain consciousness tonight, he could go out tomorrow morning. Then he had to use what little time they had remaining. That would be where all his energy would go…

The automatic doors of the hospital lobby parted with a sigh. Martin's blood felt enriched with hope. It was a new feeling, knowing exactly what to do and why. He almost wanted to sing out for the first time in this unending chase. He understood the near future, despite the underpinnings of his decision. Something harsh and irrational howled inside him, promising that with a slight misstep this plan could destroy them both.

Well, he guessed it might. But that was love.

October 29th

Thirty-one

COLE TRIED NOT TO GO FOR HIS GUN RIGHT THEN. HE could tell the acolyte had just pulled himself out of bed. From the look of it, the grungy man had probably been awake earlier, grabbed a bong and smoked himself back to sleep. He smelled as though this was the case. Lennon's *Instant Karma* played somewhere in the background haze.

"What's up dude? I mean, *shit*, how may I help you, Bishop?" A drowsy terror constricted the man's gaze. "I'm not ready for the Hunt. Bishop Quintana said I didn't have to— "

"Calm down." Cole shifted his weight. Sandeus often sent out acolytes to trip the Nomad's minefields. This guy had probably heard as much, but the Hunt was the least of this one's problems. "I'm inquiring about Bishop Quintana," said Cole. "This is where his acolytes are staying, correct?"

"Yes, Bishop. Well, just me and Vince." The man scrubbed his hand through his greasy hair and ran it down the side of his zit-riddled jaw. "The others found a motel in Rialto."

"And his new acolytes acquired from Melissa Patterson?"

"Same place I think. So can I ask, Bishop, sir, what's this about?"

"I can't get a hold of Quintana. I wondered how he was holding up. He performed that Heralding last night, as you might know."

"Yes, I know," he said softly.

"Has he called in from upstairs?"

The acolyte shrugged. Several oblong holes opened the stitching of his T-shirt. Cole saw a pimple on his shoulder peering up through the cut like an angry eye. These people did not belong under a Bishop of Midnight. It showed how little Quintana cared for the title. It made Cole's hand itch for his gun again, but he ate the pain of it.

"We knocked on the Priestess's door last night," said the acolyte. "Vince went this morning. We didn't get an answer. Her bodyguard wasn't outside neither." Realization brought down the sky-high gaze. "You think it was the Heralding?"

"No," Cole put simply. The man blinked. By his demeanor, it was obvious he and the others figured something fatal and nasty had happened to Paul—it didn't break them up too much, but that wasn't a surprise.

"Vince has been taking care of everything. But Bishop Quintana gave him instructions if we couldn't get in touch. We're pretty worried."

"I can see that."

"Bishop?"

Cole turned to walk back down the hall and sensed the door start to close. Now it all came down. He wheeled around and the man blinked again, askance. "Oh, yes," Cole said. "I forgot. If I want to call back later and check in with you guys, is your cell number 5612?"

The guy rubbed his crusted eye with his shoulder. "Yeah, that's Vince's."

Cole's .45 swung out. The first silenced slug collapsed the man's right cheek, a surprisingly dry cave-in; the second darted through his gaping mouth and smacked the door behind him, sending it flying against the stopper. A tooth fragment split the skin near Cole's left eye socket. He waited a moment in the hallway, to listen for any sudden movements in any other room, or any doors flying open. A minute went by. He fanned the air, disipating the gunsmoke smell.

Cole stepped over the acolyte's body. With his foot he pushed the mushy head to the side and shut the door. The layout of the room was similar to his, except there were only two bedrooms and the kitchenette was half as large. The door to the corpse's room was ajar. Pungent marijuana smoke drifted over the threshold. Cole went farther into the living room, knowing the flow of murder had only just trickled in the mighty river to come.

The other bedroom door came open. Vince Stogin padded out with a bowl of cereal held close to his crunching jaws. His long hair was up in a ballerina bun with a florescent orange hair clip biting into it. Through slurps and crunches, "Hey fool, wanna see that thing with the Bishop one more time—?"

When their eyes met, the bowl dropped. Soggy golden squares scattered over Vince's flip-flops. His hands went up so high his knuckles smacked the doorframe. "I just did as Bishop Quintana told me. Please don't kill me. Oh fuck! I'm so sorry. Please. It's Paul's fault. He made the fucking thing!"

Cole lowered the barrel a hair. Red thoughts still burned in the forefront. His ears drowned in hysteria.

Vince laughed nervously. "It's no big deal—right? You weren't with her then—a lot of people do this kinky shit. Don't get carried away."

The next moment Vince's brains strafed over the ceiling in a stunning red-gray detonation.

MELISSA WATCHED THE PIXILATED PENIS SLOP OUT. NAKED male bodies thronged around her. Her mouth ran with syrupy white strands. Paul's puppet strings. Astonished wasn't the word for how she felt. *After I stole those damned seeds too!*

The video played ten times before she deleted the file. The video had also been forwarded to Cole. That aspect hadn't really settled yet. Cole had left their room early, in good spirits, to track down Paul. That had been about fifteen minutes before this thing infected her phone. Maybe someone killed Paul last night and that's why his acolytes sent this—one last fuck-you.

She hoped the bastard was dead, or at least suffering somewhere. Wishful thinking. This shouldn't have happened. Melissa should have been more firm with Paul. In some way she didn't think he'd really follow through. There could be some hope though. It was possible Cole wouldn't check the phone. He hated technology most times and refused to learn anything new about cell phones other than how to send and receive a call. He even remembered most phone numbers rather than build a contact list.

Oh Cole! This is so fucked. She couldn't take this back, not after lying. All she could do was try to make him understand that she hadn't wanted to lie. The truth was too much. Maybe if he overlooked the message, she could delete the video. As Cole often liked to quote from the Tomes: *"You will set yourself free, no one but you."*

Melissa gripped the comforter until her knuckles cracked. The room had become frigid. The rain was hissing outside. She had to entertain a bitter prospect: Cole knew. Avoiding that as a possible outcome could prove fatal. Could he really do that? He loved her so goddamn much. Too much, yes? He wouldn't do anything. Would he? Wouldn't lay a hand on her. Don't be naïve, she told herself. She was going to die if she didn't champion through this.

I do love him. I do. I do love him. I do.

It wasn't a reassuring mantra. Her breathing matched her heartbeat. She wanted to bawl, but the fear of clouding her vision burned the tears away. *He forgave me the kiss. He can forgive me this. It'll be difficult, but he'll come around in time. He needs you.*

What if he doesn't?

She deserved it then. Was that it?

Several solutions existed, even though they were painted in pessimism.

Her phone's alert went off and she shrieked. *Main Menu. Text messages. In-Box.*

NEW MESSAGE – Cole

The sweaty pad of her thumb touched the select button and held there. She could use what Sandeus had told her to get his mind back on Halloween. It was time she told him about that anyway. But—no, it wouldn't be as easy as changing the subject. She could beg forgiveness and try to reassure him that one encounter wasn't important to her. Because that's what this was really about—she was ruined when they met. This was a male thing, a pissing on a hydrant thing. If reassuring Cole wasn't appealing, she could always drive far away and never return. But Cole wasn't some estranged ex-boyfriend. He had those seeds growing inside, making him a surrogate denizen of the Old Domain. What if they guided him to her? What then?

Her thumb descended on the button and she read Cole's text message.

VIDEO SENDER IS DEAD.
JUST LIKE US.

He'd learned his phone after all.

Outside the raindrops fell quicker, a countdown to zero.

Thirty-two

PAUL WATCHED EGGERT GRINNING LIKE A FERAL CAT, gnashing his teeth, moaning in husky *ohs* and *ahs*, rolling his eyes to the whites. The coitus was preformed not two feet away, which Paul figured was intentional. The barrel-chested grizzly propped his bulk up with one planted arm, and pulled up his pants. He whistled a sigh of relief and his eyes lowered to Paul's. "Excellent," he said and cleared his throat. "I was hoping you'd wake soon. You missed everything that went on before. I'll have to go again to show you how it's done."

Paul stared away. He couldn't assemble his thoughts into anything meaningful. The only fully realized concept took little deconstruction: this was a *bad* situation and this man would probably kill him soon. Paul's body twisted at the notion. Threads of fire stringed into every nerve and his wrists throbbed where the zip tie cut into them. Sweat stung his flesh.

The Priestess lay there, eyes up and *out*, a pool of honey hair around her precious, empty face. He saw her breasts rise and fall, lifting gently with the expanse of her lungs. Paul wanted to weep. Her body was keeping alive somehow—maybe a part of her still lived deep inside? After he quit the throes of self-admonishment, Paul cupped through the muck layering his own consciousness. The room cleared and images redefined. *Had to get rid of Eggert. Had to bring her back. Had to.*

Eggert set a pillow from the divan on the floor.

Paul refused to show emotion. When Eggert sat on the pillow, he saw two other things he'd brought over: a full bottle of Everclear grain alcohol, and a hunting knife that could have once belonged to a Mongol warrior. The big man watched him with crocodile eyes. Paul tried to will himself into passing out again. Eggert's voice crept through the darkness of his mind. "You don't understand a thing about us."

Through the hum of his swollen lips, Paul said, "Is this where you give me a lesson?"

His head cranked to the side and a million starbeams snapped in half and collided. Eggert had struck him with something short and blunt. The impact had broken a piece of tooth and driven it into Paul's gum line. He felt the blood dam up behind his bottom lip and rush over the side.

"I won't waste my time educating you," Eggert replied a moment later, with not so much as a deep breath. He was holding the butt of his knife up and tapping his chin with it. "But you do need to know what you took from me, what you took from our land, from the Ekki fields."

"What did I take?"

Eggert's lower lip trembled as though he'd been the one popped in the face. "We've sent many of our own through the gateway. The Archbishops use Ekkians for *personal guards*—" The word didn't fit well on Eggert's lips. "Mere sentries guarding the vanity of power stricken fools? We do not complain. Though our blades lust for the Hunt, we are made to govern hallways."

"What the fuck does this have to do with— "

Paul flinched as the knife rose in the air. Eggert thought a moment and lowered it. "You've taken my only reason for coming here."

Paul opened his eyes slow, like movie curtains. "If you would just— "

Eggert's laugh was a hound's cry. It made Paul wince. Eggert twisted the jagged blade in the air. Dull, rainy light from the windows patterned the silver surface. His nostrils flared. "Only the Nomads could undo what you've done."

"Let's find them, now, tonight. Untie me— "

"Stop talking! Stop your foolish throat!"

"You don't want to save her?" Paul demanded.

Eggert pointed at the Priestess's inert body. "She's already *dead.* All that remains, I will enjoy."

"Her heart still beats. We have a chance."

Silence filled the space between and sucked the oxygen from the room. Paul glanced to the Priestess, then at the shattered cell phone near the wall. His acolytes would be looking for him. Where the hell were Melissa's people? They were supposed to be keeping an ear to the ground too. *Oh, but wait,* thought Paul. *Oh shit—there was more to this now.* He hoped those assholes hadn't finally followed through with one of his orders.

Eggert ripped through Paul's right pectoral. The incision didn't hurt at first. He was still partially numb. But the cut flared in the seconds following. It flared and then *raged.* Paul screeched. A trickling flow from the chest wound went down his stomach and into his thicket of pubic hair. He spit at Eggert, but the bloody wad did not find its intended home. "The hotel will come, you know. You can't cut me to pieces without them sending someone up here."

Another wildcat grin. "They've grown accustomed to screaming in this room. They've been paid to ignore it, in fact, and the other adjoining rooms are inhabited by church members who know the Priestess's tastes. So you tell me, will the magistrate really send soldiers here?"

Paul just wanted to fold into himself and die. The cut didn't hurt as much now, but it bled steadily. Not gushing though; Eggert would torture wisely.

Then Paul's voice hit a note he'd no idea he was capable of hitting. The grain alcohol boiled in his wound. Through his tears he saw Eggert take a swig of the pure alcohol as though soda pop. He brushed some droplets away from his beard and breathed out through his teeth. "The only libation here that comes close to Ekkian mead. It will empower me for all the pleasure to come." Then he raised the knife.

THERE WERE SEVEN CUTS PAUL REMEMBERED. DESPITE THE lyrics of that popular song, the first, then the *third* and then the *sixth* were the deepest (in that order) and consequently these cuts were also the most brutal coupled with the Everclear. Piss-ass drunk, Eggert became sloppy with the knife around the sixth cut, although the seventh, not deep, was a nasty drag from armpit to hip. It marked the skin like a red highway. Eggert took a minute-long swig and his eyes bloomed with the taste. He'd already thrown up on Paul two times. Laughed about it the first time. Laughed *through* it the second. Then went on cutting. Eggert's eyes had become pasty and self-aware of his drunkenness. Through the careless torment, Paul's eyes roamed to the Priestess, just to see, to be sure he hadn't lost her. She still breathed.

The big man pulled his pillow closer. The smell of the alcohol had the intense quality of nail-polish remover, and the leftover vomit hit Paul's nostrils with a caustic tang. Eggert scooted a bit more, careful not to get within touching distance—he may be drunk, but he knew the power Paul possessed and wouldn't risk a fate worse than the Priestess's. Paul couldn't have done anything though. His pain muddled everything. He'd tried to dissolve the zip ties several times but couldn't break through the anguish. In the beginning he might have had a chance if Eggert hadn't beat him unconscious. Since then the voice of the marrow blossoms had gone mute.

"You not blee-ding," Eggert slurred, "enough. Enough. Enough." His bushy head rolled to the Priestess as though it might fall off his shoulders. He whimpered at the sight of her and his swollen, blood flecked fist clenched the knife so tight it looked like a speckled dinosaur egg. "Sho beautiful. Wanted her sho badly, sho long. Followed her to this land. Now shuy's gone home. Lef-me. I want t'feel the knives o' her voice…just one mores time."

Eggert's crying eyes turned. His arm went up. The knifepoint sailed high with a perfect trajectory for Paul's throat.

This was the end. Paul's eyes clamped shut. And for three terrifying seconds nothing happened. He waited there, wondered, Eggert's dried vomit sticking to his lap. Paul'd looked down at it only once before. Half-digested flies and cockroaches and bones of unusual shape and sharpness matted the sludge. It had made him dry heave before, but now, carefully, his eyelids peeled back and focused on the mess. It might be the last thing he saw...his head lifted slightly, carefully—*fuck, you need to be slower*—and finally he got another view of his torturer.

Eggert leaned sideways now, knife across his lap. His strength had waned; his skin had turned the color of pus. He swiped up the alcohol and fumbled. Both paws battled the bottle for a moment before he found balance. When he did, his lips flickered with a stillborn smile. The bottle flew up. Clear, burning fluid splashed through the brown beard. The last ounce disappeared and the bottle fell hollow on the carpet. Eggert put his wide hands over his face and raked up and down, side to side, giggling silently. Paul swallowed. Waited some more. The hands came away, crimson fingernails. Eggert's blighted eyes stared back through the crosshatches he'd created. The eyes were more determined than ever. So Paul knew how this would all end.

Eggert fit the knife in the crook of Paul's neck and shoulder. The blade stung as it sawed the soft flesh away and took a downward course. Paul tried to savor his last bit of blood-free air, right before the final slash. Something loud and visceral was spilling down. His ears picked up on it: the noise was his body being unfastened in such a way that he could actually hear the division.

But that was terror-induced hallucination. Paul's body wasn't the one coming apart. Eggert was vomiting again, although this time hearty blasts of orange bile fell out of the beard. He was on all fours, knife still in hand but pinned to the carpet. His body rocked side to side and the beard swayed like soggy brown moss. Paul watched in some bleary-eyed satisfaction as the man rolled into the fetal position and convulsed.

After a few minutes Paul rose up, baby-naked, bloody, covered in puke. He hopped for the kitchen. His penis bounced as he went and even in the moment this seemed really funny. Laughter wasn't really possible though; each hop created an impact that sent shocks of raw pain through the zip ties on his ankles.

Eggert shot up behind him. More vomit exploded over his face and choked him. He circled around and pressed his forehead against the carpet to contain the release. The big man concentrated on his body's slow death again.

"Motherfucker." Paul spat, but nothing came out.

When he got to the phone in the adjoining room Paul felt near to blacking out. He knocked the phone off the cradle. Blood sprayed over the tile counter in bright wisps. He dialed Vince's number from behind his back, leaned over and pressed his ear onto the headset. The phone rang several times before picking up. It wasn't Vince.

"Who's this?"

The voice went high pitched. "Susan McDonald. It's great to hear from you, Bishop Quintana! Some of us thought something bad had happened."

"*Who* are you?"

"I used to be pledged to Melissa Patterson. She sent our pledges to you— "

"Where's Vince?"

She paused. "Dead, Bishop."

"The Nomads?" he asked, almost hopefully.

"This morning Bishop Szerszen shot him through the eye—we believe the Bishop responsible because of the phone... message that went out."

"How do you know about that?"

"Vince forwarded me."

"Asshole," said Paul, shaking his head. He did have to wonder what this girl thought about the video. Paul decided to ask her sometime.

"We came to clean up the room," she went on. "We've been holed up here for some time, actually. Nobody seems to know what to do and we were just about to send word to Archbishop Pager. We were hoping you would call and let us know how to proceed."

He was glad he'd acquired some of Melissa's people. They were already paying off. "Good girl. Let's not bring Sandeus into this."

"But the Archbishop— "

"Trust me."

"Yes, Bishop Quintana. But do you think Bishop Szerszen will come after any of us like he did Vince?"

Paul thought for a moment.

"Hello?"

"Don't worry about it. Listen, I need you to come up to the Priestess of Morning's suite. Arm yourselves and watch your fucking tail."

"I think the hotel security has been paid— "

"I'm not talking about the Doubletree staff. Just bring me a change of clothes and a first aid kit, along with someone who can suture without leaving Frankenstein scars. And I'm going to be hungry once I get all this up chuck off me."

"Bishop?"

"Bring food," he clarified. "Something quick."

"Absolutely."

"And most importantly—what was your name again?"

"Susan."

The marrow seeds needed to be close at hand with Cole ready to cut his throat. *Or send my head into the Old Domain.* "Most importantly, Susan, I need you to bring the black box in the safe in my closet. It's the only thing in there, so it should be easy to spot."

"Yes, but the combination?"

"1031."

"Um, may I ask one more thing?"

"You need to hurry."

"Will Melissa be okay?" she asked.

Paul licked his chapped lips. "She's fucked, Susan. Now get your ass in gear."

THE CLUMSY SUTURES WERE A LITTLE WIDE, SCARRING INEVITable. Paul wanted to take it out on Eggert: drag him into the bathroom and send his brains down the bathtub drain. But according to his acolytes that wouldn't be necessary. The Priestess's manservant had either poisoned his body with all that 190 proof lighter fluid or filled his lungs with vomit. Either way, nobody here would have sent him to a hospital.

Paul carried the Priestess over to the bed, his sewn flesh contracting. Cool semen dribbled out of her vagina and over his arm. The warmth of her body and her breathing made him sense the hope he'd thought long gone. The thought of her slipping away made Paul want to breakdown, so he went to the bathroom for a quick shower. Hardly dry, he returned to the bedside at once. His acolytes chatted in the living room. It was a pleasant white noise and it made him somehow miss the children. *You're a sick bastard, Quintana. If your mother could see you now.*

Just a few weeks ago he and Justin Margrave had had T&Ts in his loft in L.A. and discussed their plans for this holiday. Paul smiled sadly. Justin didn't have a clue then what would happen weeks later. Neither had Paul really. It had all come together perfectly in some ways. Now Paul was here and it was time to become something greater than they could have ever imagined. Life happened quickly.

Paul opened the glossy pine box and glanced inside the charred interior. There were a few rolled cigarettes and a sandwich bag of glittering gray seeds. Someone could easily mistake this as a teenager's stash. There were differences however. The thin pods were about two inches long and half an inch wide. They appeared sharp enough to cut, like the chrome trimmings from some industrial machine. Paul's face reflected in every marrow seed and he was reminded of staring through the eyes of a housefly. Next to the box, near a lamp, sat the tall bottle of water he'd half drunk to wash down his medium pineapple pizza. God bless that Susan McDonald.

If it came down to it, drinking the seeds would probably be quickest. Besides, Paul couldn't imagine another onslaught to his lungs—not now. The marrow garden in his chest was too dominant and fast-rooted to allow newcomers. Better to put them in his stomach and grow them in a new area. Then the thought assaulted him, *what if swallowing them was worse?* There was no time to go through a steeper magnitude of all of that hallucinatory shit again.

How could it be any worse?

There was no time to play with the idea. Shouting in the other room pulled him from his thoughts. Paul crept over, sutures burning with every step. "Hey!" he shouted, yanking the door open. His group of acolytes turned to him in surprise. "Do I have to ask what the fuck all the noise is about?"

Johnny Allen stepped forward. His baby-face looked stricken. "Sorry, some of us thought you should rest—"

"And?"

"Word just came in from one of Patterson's acolytes. They've found the Heart Bearer." Johnny held up his cell. "We have the address."

The news hit Paul hard. He felt dizzy from the blood loss already and this almost made him faint.

"They were afraid to go because Bishop Szerszen will be there," Johnny added with accusation in his tone. The other four people started talking angrily all at once.

"Knock it off," Paul barked and his acolytes quieted. "We need to get the Priestess down to a car. I'll need strong arms. I can't carry her down there right now."

"A limo?" Johnny asked.

"Something faster."

"I have a Honda Civic," said Susan McDonald. Her dark eyes fluxed from person to person. "But we all won't fit."

"You're not going." Paul went back into the bedroom, put the box of marrow seeds under his arm and came back out.

"Bishop, we don't have to go?" Johnny asked.

"Just help me get her to the car," Paul said with a besieged sigh. "We have to hurry. None of this is mentioned to the Inner Circle either. Pledge it."

"This we pledge," they mumbled in sync.

"Good," said Paul.

Priestess, you'll be back to see the Day of Opening.

COLE CHECKED HIS GUN FOR A THIRD TIME AND CONSIDERED taking it apart and examining the pieces in greater detail. It was a quiet, coy little game, ignoring the five hundred pound gorilla in the room, or, to be more precise, the five hundred pound videophone message. And he wasn't even in a room. He was at a park, on a bench. The rain had broken half an hour ago and neither the Priestess nor Paul had contacted him.

Kids were getting off a bus near a picnic area. They were dressed in dark costumes, laughing, screaming; for them, there was no misunderstandings about their age. The kids knew this was the time to scream and to really be human. Cole had never been that way. As a kid he'd wandered the playgrounds, stoic and impatient, awaiting a batch of foster parents that would remember just one thing about him. Nevertheless, he had made the same mistake every kid made. He believed adulthood an impossibility.

Hurriedly he put his gun away. Other than the school gathering, there wasn't much going on at the park. Some idiot had driven across the lawn recently though. Deep tire tracks cut diagonally across the baked grass. *Teenagers*, thought Cole. Even worse than little kids.

Melissa had joked once that they should have a child.

Cole's body quaked at her memory. He'd killed church acolytes over this. Over *her*. He was almost past the fact that Melissa had done what she had. She'd lied to save his feelings—but she could have told him in the beginning, before they were serious. Now, of all times of the year, he had to deal with this.

All those faceless men were something Cole might get over, but seeing Quintana, seeing him inside her mouth…

Cole shuddered. A child dressed in a Dracula costume yelled at another kid from across the field. His tinny, aluminum voice found its way over the distance, "That's not fair!"

No shit, thought Cole.

Why had Quintana's people sent the message? To be cruel? No—it wasn't in Paul's best interests—unless it was a form of revenge. Quintana could be dead.

Cole's cell phone vibrated in his pocket. Checked it. Not Melissa. Not Paul.

"Yeah," he answered.

His acolyte, Frank Ruben, sounded like a manic sportscaster, "Bishop Szerszen. We found the house! We found the house!"

"House?"

"Wenlock Way. The Hearts! We found the mailbox. There's a duck!"

Cole would have never believed that phrase would make his heart thump a new rhythm. "You haven't gone there have you? You haven't been seen I hope?"

"We doubled back. Just like you ordered. Bishop Quintana has been contacted as well. He's already on his way."

Oh. So you are still alive, Paul. Cole put that out of his mind for the moment. "Consider yourself invited to the Inner Circle, Ruben. Call Chambers, Lance, Phillips and Miles. Tell them to take separate cars. No limousines! What's the major cross street?"

"Busch Boulevard."

"East-west, north-south?"

"North-south."

"They'll meet half a mile north on Busch. Tell them to stagger cars. I'll be going in alone at first."

"Alone, Bishop?" The concern was deep. Frank probably thought his opportunity for Inner Circle would be compromised. "What if the Nomads are there?"

"I'll chance that."

"How can you be sure, Bishop?"

"Are you going to question me all day?"

Frank's voice sharpened. "Of course not, Bishop. I'll make the calls. They can be there in half an hour."

"Get them there quicker," snapped Cole. "I want to seal off all routes. Got it?"

"Yes Bishop."

Cole hung up.

He *wanted* to forgive Melissa. It was the right thing to do. He wanted to find something to elevate him to that likelihood. Maybe this stroke of good fortune would work out. Or maybe he'd die without ever speaking to her again.

The kids squealed happily, running around through the park in masks and capes. Cole did not envy them.

Thirty-three

Enrique cautiously added the next playing card to his little castle and his hand trembled as he retreated, warily, tenderly—then the cards blasted in every direction like escaping hovercraft. He pressed his lips together as he stared at the ruins. His wife, Samantha, had enjoyed building castles on the more mundane, rainy days at their flat. She never helped him sort through one that had collapsed though, said that fifty-two card pickup was a game for one soul. How right she was.

He stared down at the Queen of Hearts that had almost slid under the refrigerator.

When he left their home she'd been out buying groceries. The Messenger was not ambiguous in his wishes. Everything would be kept from her. Enrique didn't know if that was the Messenger being thoughtful for his wife's well-being or for the mission's, but he had an idea where the truth lay.

So Enrique didn't get to say goodbye. So he didn't get to hug Samantha, kiss her. So he didn't get to say he had no choice. Since birth he knew his time for duty would come. And to make matters worse, that entire hell-week beforehand,

Samantha thought he'd been screwing around. Couldn't blame her: he disappeared sometimes without notice. Now he had been away for the longest time ever, going on two years. He knew he ought to start thinking about his departure as a little more permanent than an afternoon out, but Enrique couldn't. It felt like an extended errand, like he would return to Bristol and find her waiting.

He'd spent a year wandering South Holland and then a year in Heerjansdam with the Jordons. Quiet people; nice people. *Strong.* The mother, Cybil, never shed a tear when he carried the babies away. Boy, Samantha wouldn't have been able to stop screaming for her babies. They'd tried to have children for years, but nothing ever came of it.

In a way he felt relieved Samantha knew nothing about his fate. She should have predicted the outcome; Enrique had warned her in the beginning he wasn't like everybody else. Maybe then she'd thought he had delusions of grandeur. But it was the only warning he was permitted to give within the Messenger's boundaries.

The Queen of Hearts stared back at him with a squashed, dead face.

Sometimes he hoped his wife had found someone else and other times he just hoped she couldn't find it in herself. That wasn't fair to expect though.

Enrique turned his eyes to the backyard door in the kitchen. He saw that the deadbolt was set, but he got up anyway and felt it, turned it, made sure his eyes weren't fooling him. Locked. Good.

A rapid knock at the front door made him start. The pizza man had arrived in less than twenty minutes. Enrique patted his pants for his wallet. Another knock came, this one heartier.

He hoped this racket wouldn't wake the Jordons. They'd fallen back asleep after a long night of catnaps and he prayed this sleep would last long enough to invigorate him.

He didn't see anybody out the peephole. The empty porch, bent under the lens' concavity, was stale in the drizzly gloom. Enrique waited a few seconds and thought about going for his pistol in the silverware drawer.

Another knock came and he jumped.

In the view of the peephole lens he could see the pizza kid's warped body. He recognized the pocked face, ears hanging with silver flesh tunnels and spiked butterscotch hair. "There's my man," he mumbled and pulled out his wallet.

As the door came open, the pizza man raised his hand to knock again and then smiled a bracey smile. "I remembered the 'no doorbell' rule." He started to slide the boxes out of the warming sleeve.

"Yes, yes, let sleeping babies lie." Enrique took out three twenties, his customary payment and tip for having the same pizza delivery guy. The less people that saw him, the happier the Messenger.

"And no pineapple," Chris assured. "You and your company are safe."

Company, yeah right.

"Thanks. We all know pineapple on pizza is only for ravenous mad men."

"I like it," Chris said and grinned. He accepted the money without counting it and put it in his back pocket. "I won't be working tomorrow. Night school."

Tomorrow would be too frantic a day to send the kid out for groceries anyway. "No problem. I'll have leftovers."

"Yeah, thanks again for the extra cash. This is a lot more

than I usually get."

"Worth every penny. Don't mention it."

"I won't. My boss would fire me." The braces shone in the dull October afternoon.

"Thanks again, Chris. Study hard."

"Sure thing!"

The door closed and the salty scent of pepperoni floated up. A while back this might have made Enrique's mouth water, but now eating had become a dreary chore. All the canned food had been used up long ago. So there was stale pizza, baby food jars, rows of premixed formula cans, a carton of expired milk and a box with a spoonful of cracker dust, and lots and lots of tap water.

Enrique set the pizza on the table and flipped open the box. After eating a slice like a starved bear, he knelt down to pick up the cards. One of the babies stirred in the basement. *Oh great, now it begins.* All over again. He loved them, but his body couldn't keep up with their need. Well, they would have to wait. Seeing the spilled cards later on would just piss him off and make him feel less in control of his environment. Not that he didn't have damn good control, checking all the doors like a manic compulsive.

Thinking on that, he glanced at the backyard door. It was slightly ajar. His body seized. Several cards twisted out of his grip. Enrique rose to his feet and threw open the silverware drawer and snapped up his pistol. A few forks clattered to the sides and spilled out.

Hurrying to the back door, he hunkered down like he'd seen soldiers in movies do. His brain turned to a pile of sand. The doorknob was deformed, melted somehow. From the aperture in the side the deadbolt stuck out like a gnarled spike.

Both bronze knobs had deflated like rotten peaches; the entire assembly was brittle, yellowish red, drained of density, as though most of the metal's molecular makeup had been replaced with air.

Enrique pulled back the pistol's hammer.

Downstairs the babies began to cry.

He knelt at the top of the basement stairs, pistol at ear-level. His bowels quivered and he cursed the sound. Someone had come into the house, walked past him while he chatted with Chris the pizza guy.

The babies needed help and he was up here, miles away from soothing them. Shadows moved in the swinging light below. A bass voice shushed them.

Real good, Messenger. Keep the Hearts here and the Nomads over there. Real good planning. Enrique knew this would happen. He'd just known it! How did someone get inside the house so quietly?

You and your company are safe.

Chris the pizza guy had seen someone walk past...right behind him!

Enrique's stomach ulcers actively bled. He trained the gun downstairs. The gun sight swayed out of control. Once the perpetrator rounded the corner, he'd nest a bullet right in the forehead. He would try anyway.

Two cars roared up outside, *suddenly*, so close Enrique could hear their parking brakes chirping. Doors slammed. Footfalls were quick and intense on the sidewalk.

"Shit," he breathed. The gun slipped through his fingers.

From the basement came a rustling. What was going on? Enrique edged closer, stomach roiling. Another pale shadow against the lower stairs darkened as the figure sloshed into the sick yellow light. One baby screamed relentlessly over a throaty voice, "Hush, hush now. Quiet."

Sounded like Rebecca. She was such a fusser.

The front door shuddered and the hinges flexed. Enrique's brain went through options with the frantic, incoherent pace of an auctioneer. I-can-shoot-through-the-front-door. Come-on-lets-go-can-I-hear-two-need-to-hear-two-come-on-two-do-I-hear-yes! I have two-but-then-leave-myself-open-to-the-basement-door-could-go-downstairs-three-hope-to-drop-babynapper-four!

Downstairs the shadow lumbered over the brick wall and a gun snicked, ready. Enrique thought Samantha-thoughts. He remembered how she washed her face every morning and looked like a squirrel drinking at a stream. It'd been so long ago and he wanted to remember something more meaningful, but that was it; that was all... He'd never see her do that again, no matter what happened. But those Hearts, his babies, they had to be safe. *Fuck it all—they still had a whole life to mess up*. It couldn't end here.

But how will you save them? he read the Messenger's query written across the parchment of his cerebellum. *You can't protect them. Not here. You won't survive what's downstairs.*

True. The Church of Midnight would kill him. And the Nomads would never know where the Hearts had gone. The gateway would open forever and life here would end, because of Enrique Gonzalez. Because of a stupid man who couldn't think straight through his fear.

From behind, sunlight burst into the living room as the front door flew open, chain busting. Enrique heard footsteps on the basement stairs. He shot out the backdoor. The house thundered with commotion. Shouts moved with the aimless ferocity of unspent adrenalin—Enrique shared this ferocity; it propelled him over the rotting wood fence and made him tolerate the splinters in his palms.

As soon as he hit his feet the same miraculous surge pushed him down the street like a maniac. Every breath felt like a tragedy stabbing his gut. After three blocks he stopped to catch his breath. Tears hung in his eyes and his ulcers stirred. He knew he had to form some kind of plan, although he had no clue what that would be. The Hearts, the baby Jordons, were going to be taken to Chaplain Cloth. To his hideous Children. And not only would the babies die, they would be the food to strengthen the pathway between worlds—the sacrifice of their precious flesh would be the undoing of the world.

Reaching into his pants pocket, Enrique took out his cell and dialed the motel. That would do as a start. But by the time they got here—

It kept ringing.

A black Honda civic was just up the street. Some blonde woman slept in the back seat. Enrique never thought the day would come, but he'd have to do his first carjacking. There was no other choice.

Enrique would call again. He hung up and stuck the phone in his pocket.

He approached. An arm came from nowhere and hooked around his throat. The cold barrel of a gun pressed to his head. When he went still, the man said, "The Bearer, I presume. Drop the piece."

Enrique wanted to fight this but couldn't think of a way out. His gun clanked on the pavement. "Bearer? What are you talking about?"

The man released him. "Get in the car."

Enrique slowly moved toward the Civic and the man stopped him. "Driver's seat."

Once they were seated in the stuffy car, Enrique got a better look at the church member. He looked to be suffering from some injuries, though he was doing well at ignoring them for the moment.

"What do you want from me?" asked Enrique.

"Take me to the Nomads."

"No." Enrique shook his head. "No, I won't."

The blond man sighed. He lowered his gun a little. "I don't want to hurt them shithead—"

"You're Church of Midnight! I won't take you anywhere."

"I don't want to hurt them," the man repeated. "My friend in the back needs their help."

"So what?"

The man's eyes heated and his voice was deadly steady. "Just listen to me you little fuck."

Enrique swallowed, but there was no saliva in his mouth. "Why would they help you?"

The man nodded as though this was a fair thing to ask. "I'll make a deal with the Nomads. If they help me, if they help her, I'll take them to the Hearts. My name's Paul. I'm a Bishop in the Church—I'll know their location, trust me."

"Bullshit," whispered Enrique. "Why would we trust you?"

"Because you don't have a choice. Not now. We have the Hearts. You're just lucky that this woman here means more to me than they ever could. I'm giving you people a chance. There is no time for stand offs. We have to do this, and now."

Yes, thought Enrique. *He's right. There is no time. I have to take him.*

He turned the ignition key.

Melissa looked down at her phone.

> **NEW MESSAGE - Cole**
> THE HEARTS ARE IN CUSTODY. I'M NOT COMING BACK TO THE ROOM. I NEED TIME. CALL TOMORROW MORNING.
> MAYBE I'LL ANSWER.

October 30th

Thirty-four

THE NOMADS OFTEN WONDERED WHY I HANDPICKED them, and only them, to protect the Hearts. Was it because they'd mastered their power? Surely there were others out there who had. Out there in the big blue-green world...

Was it fate? Lottery? Did I draw names from a hat? And why didn't I protect the Hearts instead? Controlling the weather wasn't the feat of the average man; to them it bespoke God status—and yet, October 31st was always left up to them to handle alone.

I would have loved to tell them it was my choice and that I always selected the best of their kind to protect the Hearts of the Harvest. But the real reason, the truth, was more fatalistic than what they'd have cared to listen to.

MARTIN CONSIDERED A DIFFERENT ANSWER. THE MESSENGER was waiting, rolling the dice, hoping this year wouldn't be the time to step in. The Nomads had to hold out in the meantime. And that honor should have made Martin feel important. It didn't. Sitting in Arrowhead Regional for all these hours, wearing body odor like a desperate cologne, drinking pungent cups of cafeteria coffee and considering eating everything in the vending machine from AA to ZZ, he realized how vagabond he was; *the only home I want to go back to is an old van that we don't even own anymore.*

The next days would strike and disappear like lightning. It always did. Victory or failure, before Martin and Teresa knew it, they'd be driving again and the Wrangler would be singing along some highway. Many diners, many gas stations. What kind of carbon footprint had they left from all those years?

The Nomads would follow the two week rule: don't linger for more than that waiting for the next letter to show. If you followed instructions, the Messenger found you, one way or another. Months could go by with nothing, but there were usually minor objectives during the regular year—last summer, not so minor, they had to incinerate a cache of church documents in a crypt in Düsseldorf. He and Teresa had no clue what they were, just a bunch of numbers and equations that littered the pages of several large bound books. But it didn't matter what they were. The Messenger didn't want that information to exist and so they obliged their master.

There had been about twenty Church of Midnight guarding the vault. Well, they'd more likely guarded the gold ballion also present in the crypt. The Nomads had been there for the documents, but a third party had been tipped off about the gold. Bullets were exchanged. A few mantles popped in and out. Martin and Teresa achieved their objective, and left the church to deal with the vault robbers, got the hell out.

And yet, they were tailed for weeks afterward. Teresa's coughing had started to become a real in-your-face kind of problem, Martin's knee was bothering him, and their pursuers fearlessly assaulted them whenever they closed their eyes to rest. *Finally ran the bastards off a bridge in Amsterdam*, thought Martin, his bitterness renewed. Such was the lesson they'd learned: the church could kill you just as dead any time of year, not just on Halloween.

Martin had been thinking about that lesson quite intently, since the rain in Colton had let up.

"You smell cheesy," said Teresa.

He bolted up in his plastic chair and his spine stung at the movement.

Teresa scooted a few inches up in bed and her deep blue eyes went east to west in a drowsy sweep. The rest had helped. She almost looked as she had five years ago. Now that she had somewhat grounded herself, she appraised him. He'd never seen her eyes so cold and far-off. "How could you do this? To them? To us?"

It was difficult to put an edge on his voice after all the hours he'd been awake. "You had an embolism and blacked out, smashed your head on the nightstand—what did you want me to do? Sit around and hope you regained consciousness on your own?"

Wincing, she touched the rough scab on her temple and inspected the ridges. "I woke up earlier and you weren't here. I spoke to the doctor. You told them I want some procedure?"

"It's noninvasive."

"I don't give a goddamn what they call it. There's no time for that sort of thing and you damn well know that."

He grabbed his head and wanted to crush the thoughts out of it. All the hard work and his veins felt empty, his heart's chambers chafing together, his outlook fuzzy. He just needed a full day's rest, not much really, when he considered everything he'd accomplished yesterday. Still, he needed every minute of today to get his mental and emotional strength back for Halloween.

"Well let's not talk about this. Just get us back to the motel. Is it still raining?"

"Not anymore," he said.

Panic spread over her like palsy. Her mouth hung askew for a second. "When did it stop?"

"I'm not sure."

"Nobody's shown yet." He flinched. "Knock on wood."

She noticed the chest X-ray he'd set on her chest during his latest studies. Several of his medical books had been stacked on another visitor chair. She squinted at the monochrome image. "That's it, huh? The tumor."

"Yeah."

"You thought I wanted to see this shit?" She tossed the X-ray at him. It spun to the floor and glided across the linoleum. "I can't believe I'm here. I just, I can't believe you did this."

He ignored her and stood. The world bowed and he almost tipped over. Lack of sleep, too much work, gifts of the past two days.

"What have you done?" Teresa's brow rose.

He shook his head. "I've been working."

"I'm too tired for cryptic-Martin."

"So get dressed and stop scowling. I'll tell you about it later." He hoped that would be enough, but her scowl deepened. He met it with a grin. "I regret nothing."

"Of course not, you're a concrete-head. Have you heard anything from Enrique?"

He shrugged one shoulder. "I checked the messages at the room."

Her words tripped over each other, "How—how long ago?"

"Yesterday morning. We'll check as soon as we get back."

"He could have called."

"He didn't," he insisted.

She slid her legs off the bed and sucked a short breath. "What did you do when I was out? Sit there and stare?"

"I set up a boom field at an abandoned train yard a few miles from here. There's a Void there and it's a great place to hole up. There's vehicle access through one barbwired gate, which I've already padlocked. I'm just about through with the plastics. There's this really sturdy train car too. Planted a shitload around it. With all the weeds and restricted escape routes—once you study the layout, you'll love this area, really."

"Thanks for asking my opinion."

"Don't sweat it. I'm serious. This place is perfect. Anyhow, when I wasn't there, I was here with you. I practiced the mantles a little."

She sighed. "Well that explains your face. You practiced too much; you look like two-week-old road kill."

Martin smiled. "Handsome two-week-old road kill." He was exhausted down to his soul. He'd hoped she wouldn't notice *how* exhausted, because he was sure to hear more of it later.

"Wait—did you say you planted almost all of our plastics? I didn't sleep through the next day, did I? Martin?" she demanded. "How *long* was it?"

"Let's get you out of here," he replied.

Platinum sunlight diffused through the cloud ceiling. Teresa thought it a sullen excuse for a morning. Her body felt better and mind worse. She'd really been out for more than a day? Hard memories stopped at the motel when she found the blood on her pillow, and then there was this vague realization she'd been admitted to a hospital. She did remember some conversations with doctors throughout, but they were dreamlike. Several ghostly, stoic, sterile visages had hovered above; their mouths moved, but nothing substantial had issued forth. Martin had been there too, drifting in the fog, telling the medical administration the Messenger's lies. Their existence was lies.

Her chest pounded with worry so long it had left her heart numb—or had the cancer made it feel like that? The white lump in the X-ray burned bright in her mind, like a hunk of phosphorus. Under her ribs she felt its impassable boundaries. It was growing fast. Something else was wrong though. Something more important than her disease. Martin had to feel it also, even if he pretended not to.

The Hearts were in trouble.

The Wrangler sped over the cracked streets of Colton. They drifted into another lane a few times, Martin always returning them with a deliberate jerk. He looked like hell, like he was about to keel over—snowdrifts of exhaustion in his eyes, skin oily and tallow, a gap formed between upper and lower lip, breathing shallow. How could he be so foolish? They always set up the safe haven together. Building long-standing mantles could send the body into fits, make you puke and faint and ache. He'd done it all on his own, just to let her sleep off a head bump. The dummy...always trying to make up for the past. This heroic bullshit had to stop.

The rain had come again, but there was less and less of anything close to a downpour. Every dry intersection registered a warning in her nerves and every person in black sent thrills spiraling into her core. She hunched down several times without thinking, flinching with embarrassment. So exposed now.

"Do you think we're being tailed?" she asked.

Martin's eyelids sagged. "I haven't seen anything. We'll get a hold of Enrique, let him know the situation, meet somewhere different tonight."

"Yes," she agreed. "We don't want to be wedged in."

Suddenly he pulled over in front of a yellow fire hydrant. The emergency brake trilled so loud it made her jump. He stripped off his seat belt.

"What's...going on?"

"Can you drive?" This wasn't a request. "I'm too tired to go on. Don't want to wreck us."

"Sure Martin, sure."

They changed places. She adjusted all the mirrors and felt the warm reassurance of the accelerator under her sneaker. Before she had even gone a block, Martin was already snoring.

MARTIN JERKED AWAKE. HIS STOMACH WAS SOUR AND HIS LIPS were fat, ready to weir bile out. Sleep deprivation. This happened every time. His nap had only been fifteen minutes, if that. He'd hoped for a few hours back at the room, but there would be no more resting; the screams had pulled him out of the darkness and back into the bright world.

Across the parking lot, the motel manager flew toward them, wholly out of control. He wore an open bathrobe with floral patterns, the pale bulb of a stomach lounging over bright-white boxers. His cool demeanor had sunken so far below the surface, he looked like a different person. Panic cut lines in his face and a shredded, smoldering cigar leaned out of his mouth.

Martin rolled down the window.

"Men up there bothering other guests—I call police. You stay down here with me."

"Who are they?"

"In your room, beating the walls. One have blood on him."

"Did he have children with him? Babies?"

The man frowned in puzzlement and the cigar dipped. "Police never come. They *never* come." He then said something incomprehensible through the cigar.

Martin sensed Teresa had already formed a mantle, but he didn't dare try for one. "We'll take care of it. He won't bother anybody else."

"No, don't go up. Come inside." The manager wrung his hands and made for the little office, bathrobe flapping behind. Teresa pulled up poolside. Martin scanned the upstairs and couldn't make out any snipers. He jumped out of the jeep, not shutting the door and went to the hatch of the Wrangler. He'd cleaned and oiled their handguns yesterday but gave them a cursory check anyway before popping the magazines in. He stuffed the ice-cold weapon under his T-shirt at the hip. Teresa pushed hers up the wide sleeve of her raincoat.

They moved swiftly alongside a dark Honda Civic and ducked into the stairwell. The upper floor swam with looming, beastly shadows from sunlight cresting the foothills. Martin could feel several rogue mantles shifting into this world from Teresa. She regulated them well though, considering her condition. The air in his lungs felt too hot. His head spun. There was no way he could make a mantle after all he'd done the last two days. His gun would have to be enough for here and now.

Teresa took point and tucked her hand into her sleeve. He

flanked, palm resting on the grip of his own piece. After so many times in similar circumstances, his heartbeat kept time, his mind became a tunnel. Adrenaline still surged though and made him more alert than he deserved to be.

They passed the thrumming ice machine and Teresa peered around the corner. The door to their room had been left partially open. Shuffling noises from inside. They stood there, waiting a moment, before impatience got the better of his judgment. He cleared his throat. Loud.

Teresa glared back at him.

The door banged open and out came a blond man in black, holding a huge handgun. A resounding *fuck* echoed over the parking lot. Teresa struck his wrist with a sharp jab. The magnum fell like an anvil and twisted once. Martin lunged for it and out of the corner of his eye saw Teresa put the man into a full nelson. She shrieked, pulling her arm off him as though his skin had scalded her.

"He's a Bishop," she told Martin and backed up. A mantle heated instantly.

"Wait!" cried a voice in the doorway. Enrique stood there between them. "Wait!"

The Bishop had his hands raised. Martin just now noticed how badly injured the man looked. Several hasty stitches had been worked into his jaw and above his brow, and from his sloping posture Martin guessed there were many more injuries to accompany them.

Several doors to other rooms cracked open at the commotion.

"What is this Enrique?" Teresa demanded, not taking her eyes off the Bishop.

"Come inside the room," he said. "All of you. Quickly."

Martin wagged the man's gun toward the room. "Church

of Midnight first."

The Bishop sighed through his nose and slowly made his way into the room, hands still up. He went into the room as though it were his own and sat down next to the body of a woman. Martin instantly recognized her. Mabel from the hole-in-the-wall bar. The déjà vu that belonged to someone else—

As she slammed the door, Teresa noticed the woman too. "What the fuck is that?"

"The Church found the Hearts," Enrique said, more calmly than his face should have allowed for. "I tried to reach you." He picked up their phone on the nightstand.

"I— " Martin started.

"Just stop! I don't even care." Enrique closed his eyes a moment. "We don't have time. Just listen to this man's offer before it's too late."

The Bishop glanced at both of them. The handsome man didn't seem to be used to being on the other side of power and it took him a moment to consider his words. "I know where they're taking the Hearts. I've been there twice now to visit Cloth," he told them steadily. "But I'm not telling you— "

Martin cocked the gun. The man didn't flinch. "—I'm not telling you anything, until you bring her back."

Teresa's eyes narrowed at the passed out woman. "Back?"

The Bishop turned and put his hand on the sleeping woman's leg, poking out from under the thin comforter. "Part of her consciousness has gone into the other world."

"Bullshit," spat Martin.

The Bishop shook his head. "I can't pull her mind back from the Old Domain without your help." His face trembled on the border of stark emotion. Martin could tell this was something new for the man, because it didn't fit his face well.

"You do that for me, I'll take you straight to the Hearts."

"And fall into a trap? No, you'll bring the Hearts to us," said Teresa.

"There'll be too many church members and another Bishop."

"How do we know you'll keep your end?" Martin asked.

The blond man nodded as though he'd thought of this. "I'll take you there. Once you feel I've lived up on my end, we'll go our separates."

"You wouldn't do that to your church," said Martin.

"Just watch me, mister."

"This is a trick," Teresa said. She was rubbing several bright-red finger print burns on her arm that the Bishop had left behind.

"Sorry, reflex," the Bishop muttered, looking at the burns.

Martin lifted the gun for effect. "How about you just take us there now?"

The Bishop glanced down at the gun, clearly not intimidated. "You can hold that on me until your arm goes numb, but I'm not telling you a damn thing until she's back. Don't think I'll cave just to save my own life—if the Church finds out I'm doing this, I'll be dead before long anyway."

Enrique rubbed his eyes. He looked like Martin felt. "I don't see that we have time to discuss this. It's the only chance we have now. The Church took them—they took the babies."

Teresa glanced over at Martin and after they shared looks of doubt, she shrugged. "I can't do what he's asking. There's too much relative placement and displacement of the ghost matter—the shaping is beyond me. What do you think?"

The Bishop's face filled with panic as he waited for Martin's answer. Truth be told, Martin understood the concept behind connected locations of ghost energies. It was entirely different than pulling ghost matter and more taxing. He wasn't sure he had the strength left after the hospital. But this might be a chance to save the babies. He put the cold gun into his waistband. "I could give it a shot."

The Bishop stood. His eyes grew sharp, resolute. "You won't hurt her though— "

"Do you want me to try this or what?" He didn't wait for an answer and looked at Teresa. "Keep your eye on him. If I manage this, we need to be sure he'll still play."

She turned a hawk like pair of eyes on the Bishop.

Sidling up to the bed, a cold wash fell over Martin. He at once felt the displacement in the young woman. It stuck out in the ether, a ladder with missing rungs. He knelt beside the bed. His body quivered. The permanent mantle he'd created had caused him to pass out a few times through the night. Martin had emptied everything he had into it. But it had to be done. Now, with his energy just rebuilding, he would donate a mighty portion again. But this had to be done also.

For the Hearts. With shaking hands, Martin pressed his thumbs into the woman's clammy temples. The energy scattered as he groped mentally at the other end of her connection and sensed the raw, misappropriated neurological power. He concentrated on tugging it across the divide. It started to move quickly and Martin relented—he didn't want to bring it over as a mantle. This had to be done with deft mental hands. Slowly, the rungs to the ladder started to fit into place and Martin's body hollowed with every fix. His abdominals twisted.

"Is it working?" he heard the Bishop ask.

"Just wait," Teresa said quietly. "*Something* is happening."

Pain tethered around Martin as all the pieces fell in at once.

He clenched his teeth and they creaked under the stress. Then, without warning, the connection restored itself and Martin's body flung back as though struck by a god-fist. The Bishop awkwardly caught him and hauled him to his feet.

"Thanks," Martin muttered. The Bishop at once fell to the bedside.

"Oh shit! You're bleeding!" Teresa grabbed three half-used tissues from the nightstand. Something warm ran from Martin's ears and down his nostrils. He took the tissues and wiped away the bright red. Teresa hovered over him. "I'm fine," he said. But he wasn't fine. His mind went in and out in rapid-fire succession.

The Bishop stroked the woman's damp face. "Her eyes opened a little—I think she's going to be all right."

Martin pulled the magnum out of his waistband. "Now," he breathed. "Your end."

The Bishop regained composure. "Let me just get her into my car—you can follow me there."

"Not hardly," Teresa answered. "You're coming with us in the Jeep. Enrique will follow in your car, with your girl."

Something dark settled over the man's face. "Whatever you say, Nomad."

Thirty-five

THE AIR SMELLED OLD. HALF-FASCINATED AND HALF-worried sick, Cole leaned against a damp beam, watching an acolyte administer droppers of cough syrup to the Hearts. Cole wanted the babies to shut up too but questioned the method. There wasn't time for much else though. None of his men knew anything about babies, and no women members were present yet, and even if they were, most of them hadn't started families.

The medicine dosage wasn't the only thing that worried Cole. This place was no nursery; with ragged holes in the ceiling and drafty tunnels of light through the walls, the musty barn could hardly be called shelter anymore. The whole structure was getting ready to take a shit. Carefully he removed his weight off the beam and stood back.

Jake Weins twisted the cap on the Robitussin and rubbed the stickiness away from between thumb and middle finger. The babies, seemingly content in their mother goose patterned pajamas, wriggled in the makeshift bassinets of spoiled grain. Aside from medicine, the babies were nice and full of formula, but Cole's thoughts were still wild with anxiety. Was he missing anything? *Three had taken a dump and been changed: asses wiped, diapers replaced. What more was there?* He tried to make the babies as comfortable as possible, like giving veal calves extra slop before slaughter. They were so damned fragile. What if he did something wrong? What if one of the men dropped one during their bottle feeding? Would the fruit die in all of their little chests?

Black suits chatted in cliques inside the barn. They were all acting a little too easygoing for Cole's liking. The Nomads had not shown yet, but he couldn't bank on them staying out of the picture forever. He cupped his jaw and squeezed his wound under its shell of scab. It had been a while since he'd spent an October 31st out of bed. Around this time Cole was usually dead to the world from the effects of the Heralding.

Jake Weins looked at him, askance.

"Call the two Ekkians inside," he said to Jake. "I don't want anything less than twenty guns in here at a time. More would be better if there were actually room."

"Do you wish to pull acolyte support from the freeway posts?"

"Keep them in position. Get another limo down here from the Hotel. Sandeus can part with some more Inner Circle—hey, and ask him for five of his sentinels."

"I believe he only has the five Ekkians, Bishop."

"Well he won't need them tonight," Cole pointed out. "So hurry up. Tell the Archbishop to talk to me if he refuses."

"Understood." Jake went off quickly, dusty black suit swishing.

Melissa had arrived a few minutes ago and Cole knew she was waiting down the hill. The whole affair had been expertly extracted from his mind today. Finding the Hearts had given Cole the escape, but the illusion of solace vanished.

"Bishop? One last thing." Weins stood in the bar of light, a dark, manicured hand lifted. His Inner Circle garb fit his slender form well. It reminded Cole that he needed to get a new suit coat. Archbishops had to look the part.

"Yes Weins?"

"Out of curiosity, will the Chaplain be dropping by? I heard someone mention he's in the grain silo, not far from here."

Cole couldn't help but grin at the man's greenness. Weins had only just made Inner Circle at the end of July. "Why do you ask?"

"Just out of curiosity, Bishop."

"Cloth can't leave the gateway," Cole said, "not until tonight."

Relief flowered in Jake Weins' eyes.

"If you like, I can introduce you to the Chaplain." Cole grinned.

Weins swallowed. "No Bishop...I'm sure he's busy. Thank you though."

As the man strayed outside Cole wanted to laugh, but his sense of humor had no body today. Melissa had wiggled back into his head and power-spiked all senses. His gun dug into his armpit, nudging. The greater part of him could never hurt her and the lesser, well... Just looking at her might be enough to set him up for what needed to be done.

Or looking at that video again...he wished he hadn't deleted it, but it had been the right thing to do, for both of them.

Cole went out the back of the barn. Half a mile down the hill, Melissa stood by her Audi. She looked fantastic. Her makeup had not been overdone. The burgundy lipstick and dark eyeshadow had been applied with careful consideration. Her smallish chest was reshaped with a wonderbra, an item which she had once joked about, *yeah, a guy takes it off and WONDERS where they went.* Melissa knew she didn't have to do those silly things for him. But she had.

Cole unbuttoned his coat for better access to his holster. *What the hell are you doing? She's scared shitless. What more do you want?* As long as they'd been together he'd never really listened to her, never tried to abide by her wishes. Didn't he owe her something for that? She hadn't cheated on him. Not really. She'd just gypped him out of some barbaric notion. Did it matter that he'd found another flag on this piece of territory? No, it shouldn't. He'd already ripped the other out and planted his own flag. So who cares?

Right?

The space between them lessened. He stopped and searched for words. She'd brought the black satin handbag he'd given her for her birthday. She was clutching it like a life preserver—maybe she thought this emotional relic would put his mind at ease. Cole had seen her deal with a few dangerous situations in the past and she'd always taken the most reasonable, logical escape route. Standing there, horrified in heart and soul, she must really love him—because being here was downright unwise. Facing him took guts.

Where would he go without her?

The weight of his gun lightened until its presence vanished under his arm. His brow unraveled, his face softened, and Cole actually wanted to kiss her slighted lips. "I don't want to hate you. I can forgive anything...but there can be no more lies."

"I never wanted to lie," she said gently. Her hand dipped into her purse. "I have this for you."

Her words became lightning fast pain. Two metal slugs cut through the side of her purse and into Cole's stomach at different angles. One moment he'd been whole and the next the bullets hissed through the back of his coat. Misery crossed Melissa's face before he even realized what happened. Cole questioned why she could look this miserable, even with all things considered. The gunsmoke smell was his realization, and then burnt meat on the air.

His only word, "What?"

She spun off the silencer, took a quick look around and tossed it in some weeds.

"What?" he asked again, stupidly.

Her lips, hands, arms, *everything* quivered, even the eyes staring behind the horn-rimmed spectacles. "I loved you, but I'm not dying for this, Cole. You may forgive me now, but it won't last. I'm horrible."

The pain quickened in the two cavities in his stomach. He'd fallen on his knees and had become very cold, but he couldn't recall when exactly, though it must have been seconds before.

"I did love you, Cole."

His lungs groped to feed him more oxygen. The marrow blossoms screamed. Her slim hands fiddled inside his jacket and retrieved his gun. At first Cole thought this was the end. She would take him out with his own goddamn bullets. Put one right in the brain-box. But instead, she walked up the hill to the barn.

She was leaving? She was going back to join the others? Like nothing happened? His astonishment was only paralleled with the awful genuineness of her actions: she wouldn't do him the honor of ending this humiliation.

Go then. The Church will find out you assassinated a Bishop and you'll suffer worse things than I could have ever thought of—

His body went into shock. All Cole's dreams were set afire and love ate its way out from his heart to the surface, to the truth.

Melissa found a place around back where the others couldn't hear her. Questions and answers were for later. Right now she could only sit on an old, blackened tree stump and rock back and forth. As many times as she'd rehearsed the scene in her head, it felt more heartbreaking. Cole was suffering down there—she should have finished him. That possibility still existed, although she couldn't bring herself to really go back down there and *end* him; being the cause and being the terminus were different somehow; she could always tell herself that Cole died from blood loss, but if she blew his brains out then she would be the one fully responsible.

Her teeth clashed with her lower lip to stop the trembling. She took off her glasses and wiped her eyes. Some of the make-up came off in a streak across her wrist. It looked like a row of squashed ants. What had she done? *Fool, you killed him. Don't make silly rationalizations. He was forgiving you and you shot him. Twice.*

She put her glasses back on and held her sides. Rocked faster. Thoughts of home, a warm bed, a warm hug from her mother. The hate for her old life had vanished this morning. There was no point staying in the Church of Midnight anymore. Even if they didn't connect her with Cole's death, she'd always be ostracized. Sandeus would find a more tractable Bishop, which was sadly ironic because aside from this foolish assassination plan, Cole had been every bit of that and more.

Then he fell in love with you, she thought cynically. Things changed. He'd set all this up for her.

Tears wobbled in her eyes, hot and fresh, and fell down her cheeks. One hooked between her lips and she tasted the saltiness. The memory of her deed lingered and the cold smell of blood saturated the air. She'd only fired shots at the Nomads in the past but had never killed anybody. So this was what it was like? The odor of death followed you wherever you went, was that it? How could the smell of blood still be so fresh in her nose?

This is what Melissa thought at first. Then she realized someone had come up without making a sound. Her victim had more grace than she'd ever given him credit for. Cole caught her around the waist and slammed a hand over her mouth. Hot breath rattled in her eardrum. He grunted for something meaningful. Nothing sensible rose to his lips. Her body tightened. The atmosphere coiled in helix strands. She could feel Cole's mountainous form clasping tighter; pain flared in her feet and legs and midsection and chest, into her foundations. Flesh went brittle. Sound hissed out in venomous static. The cool breeze outside curdled in her nose, fat and meat-laden waste that thickened to a liquid.

Salty red liquid.

But not blood.

Before her body slipped over to the Old Domain, Cole cried out orgasmically. The world went rusty and dim, and suddenly the surface of a mighty ocean hung above Melissa. It was real. She was drowning. The atmospheric pressure collapsed her ribcage into a trodden tumbleweed. Black-eyed things with razor fins and serrated overbites sought her from a distance. Silky maneuvers through the water brought them to her in seconds.

Swish. Swish. Briny water engulfed her mouth. She slammed her hands down at her sides, kicked her feet furiously for the surface.

She made little progress before the first set of teeth pierced her flank. Other creatures joined in and pulled on her in different directions. Bones disconnected in a succession of underwater pops. Right before the demonfish shredded her into meal-sized divisions, Melissa thought of Cole.

I NEVER CEASE TO BE FASCINATED WITH THE LIVES ACROSS THE divide of Worlds. I turn my eyes there and always find a piece of truth, no matter how odd or disturbing.

I am aware that not long before the Day of Opening a group of slave children combing the shores of Olathu Ocean discovered an item entwined in onyx kelp. This was all very exciting to the slaves, for their lives were comprised of only two realities: servitude and castigation. They were there to collect *pina-trego* shells for the new palace of the Archbishop of Morning, which was close to completion now. These slave children, holding fast to their delicate lives, couldn't help themselves when they found this wrapped up gift.

The spectacles were foreign, like nothing they'd ever seen anyone wear. The tips were bent like fangs and the smooth black material was like hardened ice, yet with a temperate surface. The young slaves already knew their limitations for idle distraction set by their masters, and quickly returned the item to the red tides. Some still wondered, however, what had been seen through such spectacles. They would never know for sure, but they could always imagine. Some told stories about it in the dungeons, hypothesizing that the wearer had witnessed a great many extraordinary things, and unlike the life of a lowly slave, the wearer had probably loved deeply and had also been loved deeply, in return.

Cole stared. The human imprint in the dead grass could still be seen, but Melissa was completely gone. From the messy transaction, the chaos done to his body started to catch up to him. Blood striped his face from empty craters. The plugs of flesh had departed with his beloved murderer. Despite the burning holes in his face, the bullet wounds in his stomach still hurt the most. Taking his coat off, rolling it into a ball, he shoved it into the boiling stain in his undershirt. He would be finished if he didn't get these wounds under control. At least both bullets had exited his body.

Now that Cole decided he wanted to live, something spun inside him like a clock's hands. Whatever this apparatus was, it spoke loud and clear. His work was not yet done. He could go around and get help from the others, but they would probably slow him down, tell him to wait for medical.

That wouldn't do. There was one death that needed attending. If Melissa was gone and Cole was near to checking out himself, Sandeus Pager was coming with them. If Cole couldn't have the whole fucking thing, then that joke of a leader couldn't either, and he would prove to Cloth who the worthy one had been. Plans get twisted sometimes, and this one had corkscrewed pretty badly, but Cole could still go out his own way. He had a last chance to smile before he rolled over and died.

He shuddered ferociously as he limped downhill to the Audi. With much effort, he got inside, adjusted the seat and turned on the vents to blow away Melissa's lingering perfume.

He started down the bumpy dirt road, still holding the coat firmly into his side. The face in the rearview mirror belonged to a casualty of war. Maybe. Maybe Cole was. And there was one more battle yet.

Thirty-six

PAUL GLANCED IN THE REARVIEW MIRROR. THE MAN known as the Heart Bearer was one car behind. The Priestess was in that car...maybe even awake now.

"Make a right onto Washington," Paul instructed the Nomad woman. She said nothing, waited for traffic and pulled out onto the busy street. The guy Nomad was in the back seat with Paul's gun in hand and pointed in his general direction.

"I suppose I should thank you," said Paul. "Martin, isn't it?"

Martin's eyes rolled back into his head for a moment. Whatever the Nomad had done back there to bring back the Priestess had really fucked him up. Martin blinked his eyes to stay conscious and swallowed several times, pretended to be more alert. "We don't have to be friends, just get us there."

These motherfuckers aren't going to let me and the Priestess live. Once they have what they want—It was a great thing Paul'd stuffed the marrow seeds down his boxers.

"That might be," Paul replied, "but you don't have to point my gun at me. You have those Mantle things that come from the Old Domain."

Martin rolled his shoulders and blinked again. "Let's just be clear— "

"Turn left up at the freeway," Paul told the woman.

"Let's be clear," Martin repeated. "We can't let you go until the babies are back in our hands."

"That wasn't the deal. I said I'd take you there." Paul straightened. His heart thumped in his throat.

"And let you return to your buddies and give away our position?"

"I told you— "

"We know what you said, but that's not what we're going to assume will happen."

Paul glanced again in the rear view mirror. The Bearer had caught up to them and he could see him and the Priestess. Slumped on the passenger's seat, she still looked out for the count, but Paul knew she was back—there was a color to her that put a smile on his face. "I don't want to go back to the Church. It's her I'm after."

"That's sweet," said Martin wryly, "but the risk we've taken here is too large."

His voice sounded dopey then, as though he were about to pass out. With a jerk of his neck, Martin readjusted his position in the back seat. Still, his eyes were sliding.

"How are you?" Teresa asked him.

"Fine," Martin said, "I'm fine."

"Take Reche Canyon, up here on the left," Paul mumbled. *This has to be, by far, the most retarded thing you've ever done,* he thought. With a glance back he noticed Martin's eyes had closed. Paul crept his fingers along his waistline and tried to scissor the bag of marrow seeds. They'd made him wear the Bearer's driving gloves for some kind of a weak deterrent. Paul knew he could probably send over the gloves to the Old Domain no problem, but that would be too clear of a signal. Through the obnoxious leather gloves he felt the bag of seeds and gave a tug. "Turn left over here, take the dirt road."

The woman, Teresa, pulled up next to the curb. Paul noticed Martin was attentive again. Paul's fingers froze. The Bearer wheeled the Civic alongside them and rolled down his window. "Stay down here Enrique," said Teresa. "If you see something, just head back for the motel."

Enrique parked down a short side street along an orange grove.

"Can you feel them?" Martin asked Teresa.

She started up the dirt road. Blinking fiercely, her eyes searched. Paul considered her for a moment. He didn't feel anything unusual, but clearly the Nomads were hooked into the Hearts. "Yes," she said finally, her voice filled with relief. Her face contorted as though to cry, but she stayed it. "Yes, they're up the hill."

Paul tugged on the bag of seeds a little more and it began to peek through his pants. Martin had lulled off again. Paul had the bag palmed, but it would not be long before one of them noticed. "Park up there, under those trees," he told Teresa. "I think we should probably go on foot the rest of the way."

Teresa glanced at him, but Paul felt the jeep slowing down under the shadows. Now came the time to convince himself this wasn't another big mistake. The marrow seeds were the only things he knew of to keep him safe from these powerful people. He just had to hold on.

As the doors popped open, Paul Quintana opened the baggie and dumped all the seeds into his mouth. Swallowed.

Teresa warily watched the Bishop as they slid through the trees. The man shook a few times, as though he'd acquired an intense case of the chills. Martin watched him too, from the right. "What's with you?" he asked the Bishop.

"Nothing," the man mumbled. He gestured to a dense clutch of trees. "Look, let's stop there for a second."

"Why?" Teresa asked. *We should have just killed him when we got out of the car.*

Martin glanced over to her and she could tell he was thinking the same thing. They already had a sense of where the Hearts would be located. The Bishop was only a liability at this point. She hated making decisions like these, but there was no way around it.

She trained her gun at the back of the Bishop's head and Martin followed her lead.

The Bishop didn't turn to them. Instead he put an arm up against an elm tree and leaned his head against it. He sputtered for a moment, smacked his lips and twisted his head miserably. "Has love ever made you do foolish things?" he asked them.

The question was meant to distract them, and it had. Teresa sensed Martin stiffen at her side. "I'm ill with it, I think. Diseased." The Bishop laughed. Suddenly his body gyrated with another violent spell.

Teresa exchanged one last glance with Martin before they fired their pieces. The silenced rounds struck the tree trunk as the Bishop rolled away. Beyond swinging blond hair his eyes were dilated and face distorted with frenzy. He clawed past the Nomads. They sidestepped and took aim again. The man collapsed against the ground with a scream. Teresa thought one bullet had struck home, but the Bishop's fall had been caused by another strange fit—and now the man was up again, charging down the road. Martin took careful aim and fired a round into the back of the man's head.

But the bullet absorbed into the space around the Bishop's head as though shot through water. The man tripped over a root but kept running.

"What the—?" Martin whispered.

Teresa brought a mantle and launched it with full force. The mantle immediately recoiled and bounded back to her. She let it dissolve the moment it did. Down the hill the Bishop disappeared in a mad streak of black.

"What?" Martin asked. Teresa sensed him trying to build, but it was a thin attempt.

"There's too much resistance—like with Cloth."

Martin moved forward, but she caught him. "How did he manage that?"

Shaking, Teresa took out the radio and thumbed the button. "Enrique, come in. It's an emergency, come in."

They waited a few moments. "Enrique? Come in? Enrique—"

Martin shook his head and stared down the hill.

She gave it another try. "Enrique. Get out of there. He's coming. Go back to the motel. Enrique?"

Voices came from the other side of the trees and they hurried for cover.

Paul hardly felt the seeds go down when a supernova of dread exploded inside him. The taste still flexed in his mouth: cantaloupe and brown sugar and blood. It hadn't been this way last time. He'd expected more control after the effects of the Heralding—but this was too much. His abilities would flourish. *Just had to hold on.* Twisting nightmares already paraded across the hillside. Murder was in the air. Black hearted fiends groped every atom in the cold sky. Something rotted nearby... in his stomach. Branches poked through the thick wall and wound around his ribcage like razor wire. Then he heard something rising up. *Pipe organ music.* Soft (evil); harsh (kind). The notes haunted the passages of his heart with a song that offered an irrevocable promise and a ruthless truth; it would play forever. He would die someday, still listening to the dirge's hungry melody.

The pipe organs played on as the orange grove came bouncing into his view. He grasped his face for control and a dagger of bloody snot fell from his nostril. He wiped it on his sleeve without much care. The body didn't matter. Not right now. His new ability had lifted his emotions to the screaming skyscrapers of his soul. The marrows bloomed through his entire body now and power was easy. Control was difficult. Every now and then he encountered a lump of ice in his mind and when he touched it, he touched the Old Domain like a groping blind man. *Am I becoming like the Nomads?* The lump grew frost tumors, hot-cold and freezer-burning. The pipe organs strayed from a rhythm into a high-pitched solo.

He saw the Civic parked along the road. One door was open. The Priestess was struggling, half in and half out of the car. As Paul approached he saw that she and Bearer were wrestling for a gun. They'd dressed her in jeans and a man's white T-shirt, but her beauty was still agonizing. *My Priestess...* The words were lyrics to the forever-song blasting inside. The pipe organ played as a biological organ, a fixture of his anatomy. Paul continued his search for control across the staffs of flowing notes. And the dissonance would eat him alive.

Paul went to the other side of the car and grabbed the handle. The steel turned malleable in his hand. He pulled and twisted out a metallic chunk, leaving behind a hole. The car door had come open with the force. Paul took up the gun from the seat. Enrique and the Priestess both froze from the sight of him. He wanted to blow a hole though the little man's head, but reality was so disjointed Paul feared he might shoot the Priestess at this range. Instead, layers of growling, snarling voices in his throat rolled forth, "Get out!"

The Priestess let go and Enrique scrambled past him, falling into the grove with a shout of pain. Paul went around. The Priestess climbed over to the passenger seat as he fell into the driver's seat. He twisted the key and as he pushed the gas pedal to the floor, the car pulled away with a screech. Trees flew by fast. The world flowed around them, dangerous.

"I thought I was lost." The Priestess leaned over and kissed his neck. "You brought me back!"

Paul couldn't feel the kisses, although he surely knew they were there. He could only drive. The road slithered. The cracks in the asphalt became shining black and orange scales. After two miles down the country road, he couldn't take it anymore and pulled off to the side.

"Why have we stopped?" the Priestess asked. "Paul? Where are we going?"

Paul looked into the serpent eyes of a human-sized black and orange snake and he screamed.

Teresa considered the church members. There were only two acolytes and a suit. The men descended in height. If you drew a boundary line from apex to nethermost point of their heads you would have a long triangle. The height probably represented a scale and counter scale: the tallest man was most dangerous and less significant socially, the middle average in both ways, and the scrawniest garbed as Inner Circle. They stood in a row, all studying the grain silo up the hill, exchanging chunks of unintelligible conversation.

"One of those wide mantles," she whispered to Martin and demonstrated with a subtle karate chop to the back of her own skull. "Should give them a few hours rest."

"Go for it."

"I can't manipulate them like that," she insisted.

"We'll go old school," said Martin.

She cocked her head. He wasn't serious, was he?

Martin stood.

Guess so.

She grabbed his wrist and pulled him down. "What in the fuck are you doing?"

"Come on," he said. "I'm ready."

"Let's think through this."

His hazel eyes baked in the sunlight. In the intensity they were almost the color of the grass swaying between them. "You want to take them out? Then we have to go—"

In a flash they flattened against the cool grass, packs held underarm. The tallest acolyte turned to check the safety on the Browning tucked into the puffy side of his paisley boxer shorts. This was the guy to look out for. Sure, his sweat-yellow wife beater and oversized jeans gave a few handholds, but the craggy knuckles told enough about the man to make hand-to-hand a less desirable idea.

Mr. Middle had no visible weapons. But Teresa suspected he had several in the massive folds of that gray USC sweatshirt.

The Inner Circle man had no notable weapons in sight either.

"Such a nasty place up there," the Inner Circle man's pinched voice contrasted the bass rumblings of his two companions. "Probably a bunch of rats and spiders up there. Fuck all that. I'm glad we're put down here."

"Yeah, right," the others agreed, a little ceremoniously.

Martin was suddenly up again. This time Teresa couldn't grab him. As though trapped in a dream, she watched as he casually approached them. Her knees felt watery when she stood. A mantle readied on the cusp of her mind...

From the man's boxer shorts, the Browning came free in Martin's hand. In a blink the muzzle met his skull. Martin seized the opportunity and latched around the middle guy's head and put him in a rear collar choke. The suit twisted around in surprise, in terror, in shock, in wide-eyed holy shit, only to get the heel of Martin's hiking boot in the orbit of his right eye. Dirt blasted up from the grass as the man's body punched the earth. He rolled sideways, crying, and pressed his injured face into the ground before blacking out and relaxing.

Martin huffed. The wind left his lungs. His captive pulled back and rammed an elbow, again, deep into his side. The man sneered and had the face of a venomous toad, a backstabber. His red mouth parted wide to make a call for help.

Teresa pitched a mantle. It stuffed into his mouth like a glassine gag. The sides of the man's mouth folded from the force and made him look deformed.

Martin swung into his face—but struck the mantle instead. His arm halted with an unnerving crack. "Fuck!" he reeled.

The suffocating acolyte tried to bowl him over. Martin

struck with his other fist. He hammered the soft disc of skin over the man's temple. The off button.

Eyes flickered back and the body dropped. Teresa let go of the mantle.

Martin bounced back, already kneading the pain in his hand. For a moment they surveyed the fallen, both breathing the dusty air in heavy draughts. It seemed that someone else would show up then. No one did.

Teresa dipped into her pack for the rolls of duct tape. Martin bound each of the church members, one ankle back to one wrist, and then a couple circuits around the head to gag them.

Teresa began taking the rifle pieces out of her pack, one at a time. When Martin finished, he sat by her, building his weapon too.

Teresa tucked into the grass in attack position, *goddamn ready*, just as she had been so many Octobers before. From their location the wood structure resembled the silhouette of a dark head with a sloping, brimmed hat. It leaned to the chalky foothill, clearly off its foundation, if ever there had been one. Tangles of weeds and farm equipment. Under the overhang were three limousines, dreary with new dust. Martin tried to smooth the blurry view through his rifle scope. He wrung out his hand a few times. Teresa watched. *He better not insinuate it's my fault he'd punched that mantle.*

He glided the sight across the earth. "They're all pretty calm inside. We haven't made a scary enough name for ourselves, I guess."

Teresa rotated her rifle in the snaps of sunlight. The smell of cinnamon and nutmeg came fist over fist. *The Hearts.* She pushed her sunglasses up her nose. Martin's eyes began to flutter shut.

"You haven't recovered yet from the motel. That took something out of you."

He winced at the mention of it

"I need your aim." She leveled her sight and inspected the barn within a cold, bobbing sphere. "Have to flush them out somehow. We'll have to take the barn down."

"The Hearts are in there," he reminded.

"If we go slowly—"

"Wait," he said, "How will we take the barn down *slowly*?"

"Cut the support beams." She pointed.

"Mantles again. We don't need to whip ourselves yet. The gateway hasn't opened. What if the whole place collapses? You're just out of the hospital—"

"Shut up with the whining. I'll do it." The locus in her mind, that special zip code, that vagueness never explained, *turned.* Her eyes told the mantle where to move—another distant mechanism described the width and height. She extended the structure. The fibers of old, mealy wood projected onto the screen in her mind. Every thread of wood could be examined, every contour, every exit, every entrance, every pocket, every cul-de-sac, and she worked the mantle through the compounds and sensed the weakened bonds.

Sawdust bloomed through the openings. The barn lurched. Shouts lifted.

"Wait it out," Martin breathed. "Let them all come first." His finger steadied on his rifle's trigger. His aiming eye narrowed to a cut.

Misty forms emerged as the barn's walls leaned. Then, through the pouring black suits, two came, babies squeezed under each arm.

Teresa inched her pointer finger around the trigger.

"Now."

Four suits hit the earth. A woman careened sideways, taken in the chest. It was like watching a mannequin fall off its stand. Inhuman. Until pale fingers touched past her chest and fear flashed in her green eyes. That lustrous hair flopped through the dirt and the gaze clenched tight and immediate. Martin moved his sight to another.

"Find cover for fuck sake!" yelled one man who struggled to hold a baby under each arm. A brawny man kept nearby, handling two Hearts of his own. He stuck the babies out between them for a bullet buffer.

With three separate jerks of the rifle, Teresa took another group hurrying around the barn—*twinge!*—another limped twice toward a tree and collapsed.

To the east, random fire came from a mound of corrosion that used to be a tractor. Several shots went by and ruffled Teresa's hair. A bullet ricocheted off a rock somewhere behind.

"Martin, we need cover."

"I—"

"Hurry!"

No mantle came.

"What's the matter with you?" she demanded.

The men holding the Hearts ran for the tractor; covering fire accompanied their clumsy strides. Up until now shots had been sloppy and adrenaline-dumb, so it wasn't shocking to see one holder twist around, a whip of blood lash from his stubbly brown neck. His knees knocked the ground and the papoose slipped into the dirt. His comrade dipped down to hurry him, but it was too late. His eyes turned up into his head.

"Cloth!" Shouts from behind the tractor. "*Chaplain Cloth!*"

A grain silo burned on the hillside. Martin and Teresa ignored the intimidating roar. Cloth could do nothing for his followers.

The Nomads waited for a head shot. The remaining holder reached for the discarded papoose.

"Give it up, buddy," Martin whispered.

The man glanced to the tractor for assistance, but his answer came in a horrifying groan. The barn shuddered to the side, finally unable to endure the internal damage Teresa had caused. Inner Circle scrambled from their hiding spots like plague rats—Martin brought one crashing down and Teresa had another in her sight when the barn finished the job. A mountainous dust cloud eclipsed any evidence of the fleeing group.

The lone man stumbled through the grit and pulled the four babies over his lap like a blanket. He had a strangely triangular face and blue-black hair, both on his head and jaw. Teresa spotted a train of vehicles coming up the dirt road to the north. "Come on, let's get this over with."

"Keep an eye out."

Martin followed her, rifle leveled as they crossed the field to the last one standing from this spent platoon. The man yanked out a .38 special and fired through the haze. Teresa instantly met the shots with two flash mantles. Both bullets plinked off the invisible resistance and exploded into whizzing red-hot scrap. The man dropped his gun hand to his thigh. His fevered eyes went back and forth for any trace of support. There was none.

The scent of the Hearts warmed the Nomads from the inside out. "Hand over your gun," ordered Teresa.

With a flavorless laugh the man put the .38 to a baby's temple. She turned to the barrel for assurance with soaked eyes.

"There are legions," said the man. "They'll be here any moment with Bishop Szerszen. You will not win."

"Think you'll live that long?" Martin fingered his trigger. His hands were slick with sweat.

Another bland laugh and the man pulled back the hammer. The smell of love clung to the dirt and rotting wood. He regarded Martin and Teresa, hardboiled sorrow in his eyes. His wide lips twisted into a smile, just before the gun stuck in his mouth.

The shot buckled Martin's knees. Teresa called out a late warning. The man keeled over, face first in a clump of bone white weeds. The shot rang in Teresa's numb eardrums.

Tension pulled above and below. Teresa could feel Chaplain Cloth trying to escape, enraged for his absence and the failure of his miserable humans. Martin took a knee and began adjusting a papoose. The other Teresa picked up. She wanted to cry. The pink faces peered back in wide-eyed wonder. They looked really tired. It wasn't the right moment, but she'd always daydreamed about a little girl of her own. Fertility was not a power Nomads had been granted. Not for this life. This was more difficult than she could have ever imagined.

The hiss of acceleration on dirt grew louder. A few distant shots rang out. *Stupid to try firing at such a distance.* Teresa could feel Cloth's anger as he withdrew back into his hellish pit.

It took little time to reach the Wrangler. The Nomads did their best to adjust the restraints to fit each child. While Martin rechecked the babies, Teresa went back to change out the rifles. She turned the corner into a sharp sounding *thwack*. Her body lurched. She heard her head strike the bumper with the ringing pitch of a tuning fork.

Martin retched. Putrescence billowed off the man in the suit. He had a vermillion tear from ear to throat. Some of the wound had clotted and gummed, and some had split open as he turned his head. The black suit was a mélange of multicolored stains and rancid fragments. Toilet paper hung from his mangy hair like ornaments. The man let the broken plank fall to the dirt and drew a knife from his pocket. *He must have been in the outhouse when the barn collapsed,* thought Martin. He wanted to go for his gun, but it hadn't been reloaded.

The man stepped forward and slashed. Martin parried and raised his palm to the bastard's nose—but the guy caught him one-handed and flung him into the Wrangler. Martin couldn't take a breath before he was pinned under a thick forearm that smelled of sulfides.

Martin touched the cold spot, still lukewarm from exhaustion—there was nothing to draw. A merlot pebble tumbled down his neck. He breathed faster, hoping his muscles would compensate. The knife sunk deeper. An inch more and a stream pumped from the wound. He became lightheaded. Darkness boiled in his peripheral vision and terror pulled through his guts with freezing claws; the sensation cooled his mind; the tiny drop of power he found drifting on adrenaline drew forth a sandstorm of ghost matter—

In one hot instant, a mantle jumped between Martin's skin and the blade. White sparks zipped away as the knife tore from the man's fingers. The mantle flew forward and wrapped around the man like quick-drying cement. The man's body encountered the trunk of an elm with a suddenness that made Martin wince, then smile. The mantle closed in, a perfectly contoured cocoon and pressed into his body. Gripped like a god fist. Bones crackled like dry twigs. Martin let the mantle recede. The indistinguishable mass slipped straight down to the ground in a bony mush.

Martin went to Teresa. The sweet sound of her breathing filled his ears and he saw her eyes stirring behind the lids. It wasn't like her to pass out so easily, but she'd had head trauma already this week. She wouldn't be out another two days, thank goodness. The cut on her head, just below the one from the nightstand, was wreathed in splinters and dirt crumbles. Two concussions in the last two days, her headache was going to be large. But he hadn't lost her.

Martin checked the babies. They were thrashing around and fussing but otherwise looked unharmed. He gave them pacifiers and they took them into their wet little mouths, almost with gratitude. Their faces blurred. Murkiness tumbled over anything Martin's eyes took in. He slipped his arms under Teresa and stumbled left and right. *Oh shit, you've gone and overdone it again.*

He buckled Teresa into the passenger's side, shut the door and bumped into the Wrangler on his way around. Building the mantle had not been a mistake; *it had to be done*, he reminded himself. Just in case this loopiness really set in, he put the train yard destination in the GPS before driving down the foothill and losing his bearings completely.

They hit a paved road that curved around the canyon in an S shape. He glanced in the rearview. Nobody was following. His eyelids scissored. He blinked to keep them from closing again. Teresa turned in her seat.

The road narrowed and the canyon's wall jutted perilously close. He avoided a few clusters of fallen rock. A horn blared. He pulled off into another, denser copse of elms, and killed the engine. *This wouldn't work.* He held his breath, waiting for a limo to drive past. Maybe the horn hadn't even come from this road.

Rest felt nice.

His eyes popped open. They had closed on their own. They fell shut again.

Thirty-seven

PAUL IMMEDIATELY CONVINCED HIMSELF IT WAS A DREAM. He put his hands on the Priestess again and she shook her head. "Where'd I go?"

The notes of his whimpers complemented the epic pipe organ music. The Priestess stretched out to touch him. A sheen of sweat glistened over her brow and dark circles had hammered into her eyes. Her fingertips touched his lower lip and the contact sent his body into a sudden panic. Huddled in the passenger seat, he sought to roll into the tightest ball possible.

"What have you done?" she whispered.

Paul couldn't answer. Her hair moved off her shoulder and it sounded like a flood of sugar notes trailing into a minor scale. Her skin fluxed between bass drumbeats. The question did process though, even if his lips were unable to shape an answer. But he heard his words, "The seeds. All of the seeds."

Everything the Priestess did now seemed hyperactive. Reality sucked in all at once. Next she took the plastic bag he'd handed her and she smelled inside. Her eyes swelled into planets and the pipe organs transitioned to a different melody.

"All of them?"

He could only quiver as an answer. The harmonies chilled him.

"Paul, you've got to slow down. You've got to balance your garden, somehow."

He didn't want to understand what she meant. The atmosphere itched and he felt the world spin faster with each new blossom popping open inside his body. The strength of the universe flexed inside the feebleness of an atom. Paul drank in the seconds like golden wine.

"Slow yourself," she repeated. "Then we can find more seeds."

More?

She read his eyes. "You must obtain another source to cull the dark blossoms, that which controls the strides of the universe—but first you must recover command of them. You *must* prevent more dark blossoms from opening."

His teeth grinded at the impossible prospect.

"Hurry," she said. "Try Paul! Try!"

He did. He tried. He was always trying. But there was something else bubbling to the surface. Through all of the madness since the Heralding, Paul had forgotten the children. They'd been the furthest things in his thoughts. They sang angrily along with the cacophony. The choir announced premature arrival into the world—he had to slow things down or they wouldn't have time to thrive!

Pumpkin flesh flew into the air: birth! The children escaped from the broken pumpkins with slavering jaws. Verdant claws raked the dirt as they turned inky eyes up to the slipstream of clouds: life! Paul's connection with them sent his mind into a backspin and he fell a thousand leagues into the deepest of all possible darknesses.

THANKSGIVING TO THE BLEEDING BLACK FEAST!

THE BABIES' SCREAMS RIPPED MARTIN INTO CONSCIOUSNESS. There had been moments when he heard their needy calls, but he'd been too out of it to wake up. His body shot straight and he clutched the steering wheel with clammy fingers. He accidentally set off one blast of the horn and let go. Another baby *waahed*, and three hollered, squirming in their seats.

Teresa's hands went to her forehead and she looked around dizzily.

"Hi," said Martin. "You really need to cut that out. I have enough brain damage for the both of us."

He squeezed his watch in the quickly dying light. An indigo window floated on his wrist. "I can't believe we weren't found. We were out here for a while— "

"Déjà vu all over again," Teresa muttered. The babies' shrieks jerked her alert. "They're hungry, I think."

Martin shrugged. He wasn't really listening. They had to think of somewhere to go. Quickly. He started. The minutes on the display clock flipped away. Shadows began spearing through the car.

THE PRIESTESS GRIPPED PAUL'S HAIR AND HER EYES OPENED wider with every word. "Paul, please. Do this for me...control it, Paul. Control it."

Paul wanted to die. Everything he ever wanted to do had already been done. The Priestess was safe. Living like this was not living. All of the dark blossoms killed the other golden flowers inside of him—a black colony that had consumed all.

Time wailed from the disparity.

"Please!" she yelled.

He lingered above his field of fresh, radiant power and threw a shadow over them for a moment. The action made Paul's bowels run. Veins engorged in his face. Something hateful traveled up his spine and caught at the base of his neck. The Priestess yelled again, miles above him, and Cloth's children continued to sing, miles below.

Paul Quintana knew then. Controlling this was not going to happen. If anything, time would start to go even faster.

"Do you feel that?" Teresa asked.

Martin swallowed. "It's like standing still with the world— "

"—racing past?"

"Yeah," he agreed.

"Can you hand me my watch? It's in the cup holder."

Martin fished the cold, snaky titanium out and—

—handed it to Teresa. The face flashed indigo. 8:04 pm.

"What's happening?" she asked.

"I—We're getting closer to the Opening."

Teresa jerked the key for him. He stomped the pedal and they cut out on the road without headlights. Nothing moved in the night; everything had a vacant, frozen look, from the hanging branches to the feathers of light through the trees from nearby track homes.

"You think the Messenger is doing this?"

Teresa shook her head.

9:43 pm.

"I've got the train yard in the GPS," said Martin. The bright glowing map showed them as a green arrow traveling over an uncharted road. "As soon as we're on a real road I'll— "

The Wrangler stopped. The blue and red lights of a police cruiser rose up from the canyon. The jeep was obscured behind a ranch home but had only one way to go.

Martin slapped the steering wheel. "Should I just go?" A dozen more minutes had passed and now his heart thumped in time.

"I think he's going. Then we'll gun it."

Blue and red blades swept through the trees and out of sight. Martin edged the Wrangler down the road. The tail end of the patrol car could be seen just down the two-lane road. A flashlight aimed from the driver's window into the trees.

11:54 PM.

THE FLOWERS PETRIFIED TO STONE INSIDE PAUL AND THE GARden calmed to a deadly silence. The Priestess kissed him so hard their teeth gnashed.

Something still wasn't right. Time had gone from silk to marble. A numb feeling prickled Paul's stomach. He spoke his first words in what felt like centuries. "Time's stuck, Priestess. The flow has stopped! I can't move it—it weighs too much!"

WITH TREMBLING FINGERS TERESA REACHED FOR A CLOVE. THE box had been crushed when she fell. *And hello, the babies? They matter, only them.* Her headache rolled to the front of her head and her pulse fed the pain.

The patrol car finally vanished into blue midnight. *No running around now*, she thought. They had to get to that train yard fast. The front tires bumped onto the road and Martin turned on the headlights to see better in the falling night.

In the next moment, she wished he hadn't turned them on.

October 31st

Thirty-eight

A MAN IN A SUIT, A MAN WITH TWO DISPARATE COLORED eyes. Black and Orange. A man and not a man. "Happy holiday!" Chaplain Cloth greeted.

In the burning white beams, Cloth stood just off the road between a pair of flinching Eucalyptuses. In the night his kerchief flared like the head of a raw flame. Directly behind, clumps of earth slipped away and the gateway opened. Bat songs and screeching winds lifted from below, an Armageddon sigh. The ravenous grave edged closer to Cloth as he took a few surefooted steps closer. "Will you make this one last?" he asked simply. The headlights glinted off the black eye and heated the orange. "I daresay it hasn't started well for you."

Martin revved the engine. The jeep was so quiet he could hear the babies' milk gurgles.

"Make this hunt count, Nomads. It'll be the last this world ever sees."

Liquid eyes filled the night around Cloth and the gateway. The Children's rolling snarls came from all around, but especially behind the Wrangler. Teresa glanced back and tried to see through the red brake-light glow. Hundreds of bulbous forms crawled forward, waiting to spring.

Martin stomped the gas.

The Wrangler fishtailed as Cloth slapped them with a mantle. The back tires squealed. Martin cranked the wheel. Children exploded from the night, a hybrid species of gourds and two-legged terrors. Martin watched as they caved the hood in. Thorny arms made of pumpkin stalk thrashed for purchase through the steel. The Children were more vibrant in color, supercharged. One stem-headed child gained distance toward the windshield in two metallic slaps. Headlights from a passing pickup caused Martin to jerk. More children flooded down from the right side of the canyon and swarmed them. The orange mass rolled into a ravine. An explosion flew into the air just behind. Chaplain Cloth's silhouette slanted over the hills in a long black dagger.

"Fuck," Martin said.

Other children clamored forward. He swerved, but the creatures held strong.

"Can you do something?" he shouted.

Teresa had her eyes closed. He hoped she knew what she was doing. It wasn't easy for her to place mantles while moving—she had no sense of building in a changing position. *Give her time, don't panic...* The stemmed child's mouth unhinged, revealing curling orange fangs that stretched back through the syrupy environment of its mouth. It was a call to its brother. A signal for the kill.

Martin's heart fisted. The children leapt into the air, maniacal eyes volcanic with hungry wrath, and then their bodies collided with an invisible hammer and orange rain patterned the windshield.

"Nicely done." Martin hit the wipers. "Here, take the wheel."

Teresa shuddered. "Wait—?"

"Do it!"

He turned in his seat and peered out to the dark road behind, still freckled in light from the explosion. The Hearts thrashed about in their car seats, glistening eyes turning this way and that way. "Hold on kids," he told them.

The air grew hot around him and his mind went numb with ice. He couldn't see the mantles, but he knew where they were as surely as he knew where his heartbeat was located. He knew where to lay the mantles and how to plug instigation points into them. Once set the mantles would be independent from his control. Despite the weariness inside, Martin pushed through it and brought a storm of mantles into this world, one and two and four and eight and sixteen and thirty-two and sixty-four. Ribbons of blood coursed from his nostrils and the corners of his eyes.

"Goddamnit that's too much!" Teresa caught him in the rearview.

Martin staggered his invisible traps across the road and shaped them.

Teresa screamed, "Martin! Brake!"

Cars blasted through the intersection ahead. Martin crushed the brake. A horrid *hurrrrr* came from the brake pads. The babies lurched forward and began blubbering. *One of them shit*, Martin thought absently at the smell. *Sorry little one.*

The Wrangler stopped, ten feet from the stoplight.

"They're coming!"

Martin put them in park. "Take the wheel again."

He crawled over her and switched positions. Teresa turned off the still humming wiper blades.

Slobbering children charged down from the canyon's inky maw. Martin waited for his traps to spring, breathed to calm himself. The psychotic exodus instantly went prone and dozens launched into the air on their backs, impaled on transparent lances.

The light changed and Teresa tore off. One of the babies cooed, enjoying the sensation.

In the rearview, a dark figure raised his arms.

"Mantle!" Martin winced.

Teresa brought her own. It was too late though. The two mantles blitzed and for a moment became visible, a thin slate shell rent into shards. The jeep spun and clipped the side of a VW bus's tailgate. A tire blew out and the VW hobbled across the lane into a much larger bus, the front end slamming into the words *Correctional Facility* painted on the side.

Cloth lashed out again. It was meant for them, but the prisoner transport slid into the brunt of it and bowled over. The wide steel body sealed the intersection between a narrowing of foothills.

Teresa sped into the dimly lit city and quickly turned down several random intersections: Franklin Street, then Tamara Drive, then Live Oaks Lane. She had lost the Church more times than Martin could count; she was good at it. With those children so powerful, Martin hoped it would work out like it had in the past. At least get them to the Void in the train yard.

"Martin," she said.

"Yeah?"

"The clock is stopped at 12:12."

In one swath of darkness, in an insignificant canyon, the California Rehabilitation Center's inmate transport was involved in a collision with a Volkswagen Bus. The driver of the VW died instantly of a massive brain hemorrhage. Only one man was knocked unconscious in the rear of the state bus. The inmates crawled out the emergency exits. Work detail had been scheduled from noon to six thirty in the evening, but then night fell so suddenly they didn't have the chance to finish picking up litter on the I215.

The growling, at first heartbeat, was taken for coyotes, and then with the fangs clashing like scissors there were other notions of bobcats or cougars or mountain lions or rabid jackals—who knew? These were quick considerations.

"Get your asses back in the bus," one of the deputies whispered. But the bus was on its side. It was useless and she saw the creatures too and only took one step back in commitment to the idea.

An inmate's eyes bugged in the moonlight. "Did they bring the night?"

"Yes," said a voice. It was too dark to make the man out. Something large followed him, a giant hole that swallowed even the scarcity of light.

The deputy shined her flashlight on the man's face. Something funny in the eyes. The Maglite reflected a weird spectrum.

The inmates shifted as some livened to the idea of returning to the overturned bus. With the movement, the creatures tightened their circle. A couple bravados bantered with the enclosing predators with the intent of kicking *these fucking wild dogs* right *in the putos*.

Seconds later the canyon floor was slick. Slices of jumpsuits lay all around. A few police uniforms seasoned the gruel.

Readjustment occurred in moments, and then Cloth and his children resumed through the hills toward their goal.

One of the inmates, George Johnson, regained consciousness a few minutes later and climbed outside. The air twitched with an earthy smell—*and squash?* The road was wet, even though it hadn't rained in some time. It appeared everybody had forgotten George, including the deputies. George decided to wait. He wanted to get early release and he wouldn't go wandering around these hills at night with wild animals lurking. *Fuck that.* Life was too short and he'd never been one to be blessed with good luck.

Sandeus Pager reclined on his leopard skin spread and quaffed a pinot noir. Soon the worlds would twist together and he could lay back and enjoy the *change.*

Cloth had taken the Hearts. What else could this sudden buckle in time mean? The anchors on CNN looked like billiard balls smacking together with all the hysteria. Astrophysicists with pointed noses and shallow wells for eyeballs haunted other news channels. Sandeus laughed in his wine. *These buggers hadn't seen nothin' yet. Wait until the populace of the Old Domain start showing up.*

The Archbishop placed a cold pair of fingertips on the pouch of skin between his legs. *This was all that mattered right now.* Now that the Time of Opening had come, the blossoms spread to drink in both powers again. Could he actually do it this year? Make the change? Yes...he had more than enough of the power needed.

His fingers poked the pouch like two viper fangs. He had kneaded the flesh raw already and now the current inside him (her) had begun to build. Something transient flashed through his mind; a question. Both powers radiated there. His finger felt the divide, the flesh pouting and the pubic hair rolling back, a tiny but significant orb swelled into a clitoris behind it; his pelvis reshaped with a painful string of snaps; sweat dappled her (his) brow in giant beads. Nipples lengthened and areolas widened, both rising above layers of enlarging fat cells—Sandeus knocked over her wine and stained the leopard skin. How would she make the Church understand? Someone who is now both Archbishop and Priestess of Midnight?

Sandeus's breasts were growing sensitive. He began damming up the power. Her labia had also engorged and she had to call off the flow there. Stretching out, he ran her hands over his nipples and across her belly to the lovely crevice. The power from the black blossoms ceased, but the orange hadn't calmed their output. *Let's not celebrate yet.* Sandeus, he, she concentrated on the flow. Hundreds shut, thousands opened. The garden had become extremely unbalanced.

Reaching for the hope chest, her breasts swept into her elbows like rubber mallets. She moved forward and realized her ass had also plumped. She opened the chest and sorted through some silken apparel. After a moments search and a curse for being so scatterbrained, she pushed up from the floor and snatched up the phone.

"Don't bother calling. The two Ekkians outside are dead."

The bedroom door had opened and she snatched up the leopard blanket to cover herself (well, just a little). The man who entered was demolished. Top to bottom. A ghastly wound in his stomach made his black suit glisten. Old injuries had caramelized on his skull and popped opened, eager to fester. It took a few seconds to even realize that this man was Cole Szerszen.

"B-b-bishop?" she said. "You're supposed to be out, with the Chaplain."

Cole held himself against the wall. He pushed forward a little, leaving a bloody fan behind on the wallpaper. "I had other issues this year. Looks like you did too."

"What did you mean the guards are dead?"

"As in," Cole tried to find air, "not living any longer."

"I don't have time for jokes, Szerszen. I was in the middle of something important."

Cole shook his head. She noticed now he had one of the Tomes of Eternal Harvest tucked tightly under his arm. "Not important. Only important to you. You never cared about us, about the Church. You've forgotten about leadership and direction."

"I finished with those books before you were even working with wharf rats on our docks! So who the hell are you to judge? You, you novice." She went to the closet and began throwing scarves out of the way to get to some other storage chests. "Why've you come? To help your chances for promotion, I gather."

Cole said nothing. Sandeus felt her deformed labia swinging between her thighs. *This isn't happening! I just saw that damned box. It was here!* How could she have started without checking first for the seeds? *Idiot!* This could be undone though, surely it could. Just had to remain calm and find them. When she turned, Cole looked at her with morbid concern. "What have you done?"

Blood poured down between Sandeus's legs, her menstrual cycle accelerating. Her head spun and back creaked, the weight of her breasts tugging her down. She became entangled in the elephantized flesh and her bones were unable to bear the load.

She collapsed under the weight.

Cole limped up. It seemed he was looking down at her from the top of a mountain. Her breasts rolled to either side of her face and pressed into her skull. She could feel them growing still. Her voice sounded underwater. "Bishop," she gasped, "find the seeds! Help me."

Cole wouldn't though. Sandeus knew before she asked. It was in Cole's eyes, some strange fascination with the outcome, as though a child receiving the exact toy he'd always dreamed of—but with a hint of disappointment. Sandeus made one last attempt to cull the excess in her marrow garden, but it was fighting against the impossible.

The labia flopped backward, spreading her legs into the splits and pressurizing her chest cavity. Blood fled her womanhood by the gallon. Darkness spilled into the room with it. Cracking, splintering sounds came from the peak of her skull. Sandeus fought for air, but it was only flesh that filled her mouth.

Cole knew it was finally over when the smell of feces and Chanel hovered in the room like a besotted ghost. Sandeus had reduced himself into several different wormy piles of pink, purple and white flesh, all abscessed at the collapsed head. Bright blood billowed out to meet the darker.

It was done. *The bitch had done it before I even had the chance to pull my gun.* Cole realized though that his anger remained. Sandeus had deprived him of one last release. *He* was the most deserving, the most worthy. Cole had been robbed of the only thing that would've sent him out with a smile, the only thing that would have got his name written into the catalogue of heroes in the Tomes. He should have been proven as the top of the church's food chain. Now, him dying and with no Archbishop, the Church would go back to the days of disorder. They would look only to Cloth, but he wasn't a guide. He was an antithesis to nature. Cloth didn't need any of them, not really. He wouldn't turn the congregation away, and after the worlds combined, it wouldn't matter if the Church dissolved. And the leftover, apathetic rabble would let Cloth do just that.

Tears bobbed in Cole's eyes. The Tomes would be abandoned without the right prophet. Only words. Only dust.

Melissa...why this?

He slid to the floor in a corner across from the monstrously swollen cadaver. Not an ideal resting place, but it was convenient. He placed his favorite Tome over his belly— *The Tides of Loss and Martyrdom*. The leather felt as though it could heal the disturbance beneath his skin. Of course it couldn't and maybe Cole didn't want it to. Dying seemed comfortable, if heartrending. *Yes. Comfortable.* He stretched, took a deep pull into his lungs and let himself bleed out.

Thirty-nine

A TRIO OF PAINT CANS SPUN OUT FROM UNDER THE BACK of the jeep, clacking on the road. It wasn't the first hidden treasure they'd encountered in the canyon, and it wouldn't be the last.

"You're sure about this shortcut?" Teresa asked.

"Now that's a dumb question."

They'd traded places again since he felt it unlikely he could bring more mantles. Driving was easier and let his senses regroup. Teresa's .357 was trained outside to the colorless grass. It all looked like spun sugar blades out there. In the rearview they could see nothing else. But if something did poke up its head, there was no question Teresa would soundly remove it.

Shapes stood out in relief to the moonlight. They were unmoving, dense shrubs. "Teresa—you see that?"

She did. He leaned closer to the windshield. One of the Hearts squealed in a random fit of unease. The shapes came closer. Was it a cherry orchard of some kind? Or?

He hit the high beams and hundreds of eyes reflected at once.

Teresa yanked her gun back inside.

Out of nowhere, one came straight at them—Martin went left. The Wrangler maneuvered around the startled beast and headed toward an ugly rush of them cresting the hill.

"Stop!"

"I am, I am!"

Wild burros braided around the jeep. Martin waited for a break in the chaos, shaking his head while he looked at them. Above, a stone signpost pointed west. Runic scrollwork ran from the flat body to a giant reptilian claw at the base. The high beams fed a dark purple glaze brushed into each symbol, which made them glow.

"I see it," said Teresa before Martin could ask. "Looks like some things are crossing over from the Old Domain..."

Martin nodded. One of the donkeys turned its barrel-shaped head as it passed. The eyes were the same purple as the runes, mauve tears hanging in them. The mouth tucked back to spiraling black fangs. Martin recoiled and saw the animal trot off with the departing pack.

"Did you see *that*?" he asked. He spotted a building. "Look there."

Her eyes narrowed. "Pump station?"

"Yeah," he agreed. "Sewer lift-station or something. There's a Void there. We can get our bearings."

They drove up to the silent station. The fence surrounded a concrete pad where a small block building sat amongst a large pair of pumps. There was a padlock on the front gate, but it hung unclasped. Teresa lifted it off the bracket and let it fall on the gravel. After backing up, they rolled into a shadow-bank alongside the lift station building.

Martin tapped the GPS. "Yeah, we're inside the void."

He didn't really need to clarify that though. The air had

become more humid and the telltale sweet taste rolled in their mouths. Voids did not protect them from Cloth though and Teresa's grimace, whether for a clove or for this inevitable truth, told him to be quick.

The pumps drummed beneath the surface, pushing Colton sewage. Martin brought out the map and clicked on a flashlight. His finger glided to the northwest side of town. He prodded his largest Sharpie circle. "That's where we're going. The train yard there."

Teresa's face angled out the window. "But they're coming from that direction."

"We have to go to the train yard. It's our best bet."

She glanced dully at the map for a moment, as though it had no real significance. "Can we get there without running right into them?"

"Probably not." He sighed with another glance at the stagnant clock. 12:12 still. "We can go west. It takes longer, but with how things are going it looks like we'll have all the time we need."

"And so will Cloth."

Martin's head hurt so much. A cranial collapse felt imminent. All that time zipping by hadn't given him a chance to rest.

"We'll go west," she said suddenly and then undid her seat belt. "I'm going to kneel on the floor back there with the babies for a while. They didn't look that secure."

Martin nodded. Before she opened the door, he grasped her hand. "I don't know if this matters, but you ought to know before we get going."

"What now?"

He let go at her sudden coldness. "The sign back there was pointing west. That's where those donkey-things came from.

Do you think there are other things out there that have crossed over?"

Teresa gave him a really slow nod. "Let's find out."

For half an hour the drive westward seemed uneventful. Only moments before, the night was plowing along in a steady ebon-blue stream. Suddenly the Wrangler banked a rocky dirt hill—and that was when it happened, when they came down the other side. The jeep crashed into a body of water. Red water. It came first through the doors, soaking the floor mats, smelling of mummified fish. Everything gurgled outside. Raw meat mist was thrown over the windows. Martin shouted, out of his mind, out of sorts. An old dead sky peered through the slashes of red current on the windshield. It was night, but a different moon hung above them, a pale green hole in a dark sheet that stretched over merciless trees across a slash of toneless sand and rock. Just to the right another runic signpost stood proudly in a mound of stones.

"Where are we?" Teresa mumbled.

But they knew. This was the other side.

The Wrangler tilted. The floors grew heavy with red seawater. Teresa stood up. "Try again!"

He pushed the gas. It sounded like a submerged dentist's drill. The tires couldn't grab hold. Martin cursed and attempted another go. They were only off the shoreline by fifty feet, give or take. The tide pushed at them. The jeep sunk deeper. The tires spun in place again.

Teresa turned from the babies and her gun came free from her pants. Martin caught movement in the trees. Figures emerged.

Orange robes, scythes and oily muskets in swaying arms, tallow faces under hoods. Some human. Some ginger hued and reptilian. Eyes glowed with equal parts moonlight and sin. A dark faced human with a pointed mustachio put his musket at eye level. Martin threw a mantle.

It was a strange feeling. The cold spot in his head felt sticky—instead of ghost matter, a sheet of ocean water lifted and surged forward, departing at once into vapor.

Martin stared for a moment.

Teresa said, "How'd you move the water like that?"

"Fuck if I know."

Just then a sheet of sand lifted on the shore and ruptured. The approaching orange throng sidestepped and shouts were exchanged.

"Did you—?"

"I did," she answered. "The mantles aren't the same here. We're not pulling matter over—here, I think we *move* it."

Martin didn't understand at first. Then, light. Four small boulders from the shoreline jumped into the air. They spun around on a stiff axis and shot forward. The hooded crowd folded at the impact and some bodies were ripped backwards into the trees. Undeterred, others kept on. Some had reached the water and their orange robes glided around them in the foul dark red broth. A reptile man had his scythe poised overhead as he trudged deeper.

"Throw more!"

"It's...harder," Teresa said with a grimace.

Martin's ankles were frozen and stinging and the sensation traveled up his body as the level rose. A scaled hand stroked the front right wheel well. Sharp, translucent nails peeled curls of paint.

The Wrangler lunged. Ocean floor assembled behind them and slammed into the tailgate, moving them into shallower water.

"Yeah Teresa!"

The Wrangler's tire caught and they were off, zigzagging through the shallows. The jeep burst onto the beach, kicking sand. Church members struck the front bumper and rolled away. Martin glanced in the rearview. Teresa draped her body over the babies.

And just in time. They hit an embankment. Hard. The Wrangler went airborne—

Martin's teeth lathed against each other. Demented trees flung past. Gravity seemed to work better here than at home. The landing would be jarring.

But no impact came. Everything shifted around them, layers of reality peeling back suddenly. They were on flat land again, as though they'd been on land for hours now. The water in the car turned into pieces of mantle, billions of tiny diamonds in the mind. Martin combined them and formed a barrier around the back of the jeep.

They rocketed down a residential street past a costume party. A couple dressed like Popeye and Olive Oyl necked in the street. Shadowy giants in the background, Martin could see some of the industrial buildings near the house where Enrique had been staying. Their trip through the Old Domain had put them on a completely different side of town.

"Well there's something." He pointed at the dash and Teresa followed with her eyes. "Hope it means something good."

12:15.

Paul leaned forward. Their lips touched.

"The blossoms will not grow any more, but there are too many dark... I think they'll kill me anyway."

The Priestess said, "You need constancy, Paul."

"There aren't any more seeds. I took them all. I thought the Nomads would..." He didn't finish and just tried to eat the torment.

"You *can't* do this to me," she growled.

"I love you."

The Priestess smacked his face hard. "Love!"

Paul twisted. Strange words came to his lips. "Pipe organ. Pipes, pipes, pipes, blowing into the night, me, the night, me. The song's going through me, a red-hot shovel, twisting and tossing guts...I don't think anything will ever make sense. Everything will fail. Soon."

"You fought before. Fight now."

"It's killing me." He couldn't look at her but sensed her anger with him growing.

"I don't have time to baby you, Bishop," she said. "You need to think of how to get more seeds."

"How—?"

The Priestess of Morning's eyes lit up just then. "Shut up! Wait. I see again—there they are. I'm regaining my sight. The Nomads! I see. We need to let Cloth know."

"Why not go to Cloth?" Paul gasped and bit away a shriek. "Maybe he can help me."

"We'll use the telephone device, but we can't go see Cloth, understand? We need to leave right away. With Eggert gone and you like this, I have to watch out for us both. Where can we go? It should be somewhere far away from Cloth. Can you drive? I have not learned."

"I think, for a little while," said Paul. He reached into his pocket and with shaking hands, handed her his phone. "I'll need to rest now and again."

The Priestess's warm sigh struck the cold sweat on his face. "Do you have any clue as to where we will go?"

He nodded, an idea coming to him. "I might know a way to find more seeds."

"Are you raving?"

"I hope not."

Paul leaned forward. Their lips touched.

CHAPLAIN CLOTH SQUEEZED HIS CHIN UNTIL HIS JAW CREAKED. The Nomads had been caught in a spatial fold and were nowhere to be found. The luck these two had was one of the great frustrations of his existence. The Nomads could be in the city or a thousand miles away. He had to find them. The possibility of losing the Hearts was out of the question. Cloth wouldn't entertain that possibility, not so close to the Opening. Things had gone from bad to worse with the spacetime distortion. The feast was so inevitable he could smell the roasted gall bladders and buttered bones and cartilage. He wouldn't lose this year. No.

A smallish, rugged man with an Australian accent and cleft lip approached from the shadows. The smell of lager hung thick on his every word. "Chaplain Cloth, what're your orders? If it pleases you."

Disappointing these humans were, but eager to please they were also. Usually Cloth didn't bother with the aid of flesh beyond the body he adsorbed, but this year had been very different so far.

"Search all Void areas in the city. If they're still here, the Nomads will choose one of these locations to hide. They'll not risk a motorway."

"Should I inform the Archbishop?"

"Pager's done," Cloth replied. "Assemble some teams quickly. Do you have a phone?" The man yanked free a small, glossy black oblong apparatus and Cloth snatched it away from him. "Have someone call me if you find anything. Is that clear?"

"Chaplain?" The man's eyes bulged in disbelief.

"I want a smaller team to find Quintana and his harlot. His power has ramped up considerably, so those who go against him must walk warily. They will only take him with words, not with force."

"I understand."

"Finish Quintana before he causes another problem. They're already fleeing. Bring back the Priestess of Morning if you can. She's still handy."

"Thank you, Chaplain."

The man stepped delicately past a knot of Children. They were devouring one of their own who had been trampled. They tugged out a kinky cord of bright pink brains through the orange skull and erupted into a frenzy for the prize. A warm feeling passed through Cloth and he swelled with nostalgia for the days of thrashing darkness and squealing dementia, the time before light, the time before this appalling society.

Forty

Colton's sunlight held little hope. Martin pumped gas in a station across from the savaged trains. Teresa had objected going outside the Void, but he convinced her they needed gas if it came down to leaving in a hurry. *That was bullshit though.* She knew they couldn't really run once they hunkered down. To her this was probably wishful thinking, but in reality, it was Martin who needed the gasoline. Well, the plan needed gasoline.

As the tank reached t-minus ten gallons, news reports buzzed over the speakers. *In the wake of the strange orbital anomaly, the City of Colton continues to be the epicenter of some of the most peculiar reported stories. Local water districts and San Bernardino County Sheriff's Department are checking the possibility a hallucinogenic compound was distributed through a local water treatment facility. In other related news, a missing bus from California Rehabilitation Center...*

Martin had gotten an hour-long nap in the train but wanted more—this was ridiculous. He was paying for his carelessness, just like last year; being tired all the time was so exhausting!

Watching Teresa feed the babies brightened his mood though, as long as he could forget the stakes. Through the back he saw her tilt the bottle for the blue-eyed girl, Rebecca. Teresa had never looked happier.

Martin took his drink off the hood and sipped his ice tea. He grimaced at the raspberry aftertaste. *Damn.*

ONCE THEY RETURNED TO THE TRAIN YARD, TERESA FOUND herself staring for a long time. Particularly unsettling, in the belly of a gray warhorse of rust and rivets, Martin's look changed from several dimensions of thought. There was a part of this Teresa didn't know and she had the feeling he was about to let her in.

He sensed her unasked question. "We're not going to get lucky again—with slipping away I mean."

"Yeah," she agreed.

"But we have the time to act now, while there's still a chance. We can throw him off. There are plenty of hours left in the day."

"*Throw him off?*" She asked incredulously. "That's not exactly how it works with Cloth. Where's this going, Martin?"

His face softened. "I'm going to lure him and the children away from here."

"Are you nuts?"

"The suits will search every Void in town. They always do. We've taken precautions, but there's still too much time for them to break through. You have enough energy to protect the kids— "

Teresa smiled, but it vanished when she saw his expression unchanged. "I'm *not* doing fine, as you might well see."

Martin edged closer. "Best possible scenario is I can keep them chasing me until midnight. Then we're free."

"What if they show up here right after you leave? Would that be the worst possible scenario?"

"Radio me."

She growled, "I'm not keeping a radio turned on in here. They'll hear it! We shouldn't even be talking right now."

He sighed angrily through his teeth.

Putting her own advice to heart, Teresa whispered now, "Cloth won't fall for cat and mouse, and if he did, you'd be taken sooner than midnight. Don't fool yourself. This is stupid. You'll die."

"If I go to the other Voids, I'm sure I'll run into the Church. If I'm in the Wrangler they'll assume it's both of us. They'll follow me to flush out the Hearts."

Her head shook to the point of dizziness. "That's too big a risk. You're too tired. Besides, we do need the Wrangler if he shows up."

"You think we'll have time to pile into the jeep? You, me, and four babies? You want to talk about risk? Going a hundred and twenty miles down the interstate—here is our last stand. Here. We both know that, but Cloth doesn't have to."

She grasped Martin around the waist, couldn't let go. His shell necklace pressed into her neck and his warm breath tickled her ear. He hummed their Sam Cooke song, *A Change Is Gonna Come.*

"This is fucking stupid," she whispered.

"I'm just too weak to help you here. I'm more help as bait. You know that. You have to know that. This city isn't big. If they get here, just call me. I'll be here in no time and have a better position on them."

"You're an imbecile," she said with a sad shake of her head.

"Well you're the best woman I've ever known. You know that?"

"Yeah," she said with a short laugh. "Among the many."

He buried his face into her neck. She squeezed his shoulders for reassurance. None came. *Just say you're going to forget this nonsense, Martin. Please?*

"For the record, you're not too shabby either," she finally said. "What if you don't come back?"

"I promise— "

"Don't promise, goddamn it. Okay?"

He kissed her again, then bent over the bundles, one by one, caressed each baby's face. "You're some cute little devils. Mama's gonna keep you safe."

Teresa tucked a shock of almond hair behind her ear.

Martin fiddled with a detonator the size of an ink pen. "I'm going to padlock the gate and activate the mines now. Remember to go out the other door. There's probably close to fifty rigged together just on the other side. Deactivation's the same pin as before— "

She shook her head. "No, don't go—this—you're going to die doing this."

"If I strand the Wrangler somewhere, there's a bus stop not a block away. For tomorrow, I mean. Just you all stay alive."

"*Don't* go."

"I won't be able to bring anymore mantles for a long time, Teresa. So this is the only way I can be useful. Let me do this."

A sudden, incalculable rage tore through her chest. "You knew this would happen, didn't you? What did you do when I was asleep Martin? What did you do? I sense mantles all over this train yard."

He shrugged.

"Don't fuck with me!"

"I set a few out there when you were at the hospital. One I built was pretty damned strong. It took more than a day. That's why I couldn't go back to the room. I had to stay put and work on it. They're great deterrents, but you know that Cloth can go through them like cotton candy."

She folded her arms and sat back against the wall. For a moment, silence baked in the stuffy train car. "What were you thinking? Stupid!"

Sighing, he said, "Will those be your last words to me?"

She wanted to say, *Yeah, dumbass, those are the only words you deserve.* Instead, "Yeah just be careful—I'll kill you if you die."

He flashed a grin of relief, chuckled. "Wouldn't want that."

Each baby had subtle confusion surfacing. She knew how they felt. Martin never acted like this—this didn't feel spontaneous. This had been planned when she was in the hospital.

She shouldn't let him go. There was too much at stake. They'd been blessed with escaping earlier, and now he was actually *trying* to get Cloth's attention. It wasn't rational. But Christ, there was something in Martin's eyes she hadn't seen in a long time. How could she take that away when she'd seen nothing but the opposite since diagnosis? And knowing she'd put that terminal moroseness inside a light-hearted man who had once joked at everything...she couldn't say no. He was a prisoner, finally skipping out. To throw him back inside would make her happy but destroy him.

Martin jumped out of the train and moved the squeaky door swirling with bright pink graffiti. The light cut away and left her in the mustiness with the babies. About twenty minutes later, after he'd done setting the mines, the Wrangler started up. She heard the wheels crunch the gravel as he left.

Forty-one

THE MUSICAL SCORE ENTHRALLED PAUL'S MIND. THE blossoms still shifted back and forth, drinking his soul from the roots. He could feel the dead, once fragrant, orange blossoms whither from the stress and he could feel pieces of universe stretching.

The Priestess of Morning sat in the passenger seat. Hands poised over her head, she had been concentrating for some time. He'd kept quiet so as to not disturb her. The silence (with the pipe organs playing on a tinny music box in a mouse hole) could be savored. It was beyond enjoyable—it *tasted* good. So when the Priestess let out a gasp, Paul accidentally spun the wheel and they went into the breakdown lane. "Shit!"

"I see him!" cried the Priestess. "The Nomad—the man. He's driving south."

Paul had to muster some interest. "Just the man? Is the woman there?"

"No—she's somewhere dark. In a vault or something. I can't make out where."

"What about the Hearts?"

"The Hearts aren't with him. They might be with her—"

"Call Szerszen," said Paul.

She glanced at him and shook her head.

"What?" Something clenched inside Paul, not grief, just searing shock. *Cole was gone?*

"I think he killed Sandeus Pager too," she said, "though I'm not sure how."

A husky chuckle. "And just as Pager got his own."

"What matters is Cloth—*he's* the one." She dialed a number on his cell phone, touching each number with fascination.

"Who's that?"

"The Japanese envoy said he would be on the Hunt this year. His business card had his telephone number, which I put in my sight."

Paul felt a twinge of jealousy, but it didn't last through his delirium.

She waited breathlessly before the other end picked up. "No this is the Priestess of Morning. Yes, I don't have time. I need to let Chaplain Cloth know something of great importance. A Nomad is heading south on Mount Vernon Avenue. He's arrived outside a tavern named the *Spyglass Saloon*. Tell Cloth at once. I'll call back if the situation changes. Thank you, fine. Farewell." She sneered at the phone before figuring out how to turn it off. "Something's wrong," she muttered.

"What?"

"The envoy's voice sounded strange. I think Cloth might have told them to get rid of us."

Fuck, just when my nerves had begun to settle. "What does he care?"

"Paul," she stated matter-of-factly, "between the two of us, we've done a great deal of damage."

He grunted, but not in agreement. Cars sped by and their

colors shifted and blended as they went. He shook away the distraction and pressed toward ninety-five miles an hour. Paul's eyelids dipped. He had to make it without taking another rest, at least before leaving the state. No matter what happened, there was one thing left to be certain about. For good or ill, today or tomorrow, when they got there, his life would be transformed forever.

Forty-two

Martin had to run into the Church eventually. The waiting was killing him though. His adrenaline was up, his gut was sour, he was in bad shape. He'd eyeballed the neon sign for almost twenty minutes now. It said *Spyglass Saloon* and there was an oblong seafaring instrument bent in the neon framing the name. His brain registered this, but he didn't think about it much.

Put yourself out there and they'll come...your job is to get them far away. Wait for them.

But the waiting was so atrocious.

If this went on too long he'd have to go back to the train yard. What good would he do? He searched for the cold spot to build a mantle. It was dead there, dried to dust. He wondered if in all his ambition he'd sterilized the part that brought mantles. *Oh well, fuck it.* He didn't need mantles anymore. He just needed to be seen—and keep his wits. After one beer and some pretzels to settle his stomach, that might give him time to decide where to go, or it might give them time to find him. Either way.

Either way...

He kept the Wrangler unlocked with keys in the ignition.

Inside the bar, laughter burst to the corners. Two men, who might have been brothers, sat elbow-to-elbow with a gangly guy with a mess of dreadlocks spilling down his back. There were a few lone drinkers at round tables, deep in the neon shadow and excluded from the conversation, at least speaking roles anyway. A bristly man moved the claw of a toy machine left to right, hoping to add to the growing pile of stuffed kolas and superheroes at his feet. Two turrets of quarters rested on the deck of the machine. His shirt said in bold red letters, *Fuckin' A Right!* and there was a bottle of microimport beer "A" NUMBER ONE pictured underneath.

Martin passed. "Quite a stash of animals there."

"They're for my granddaughter." Skunky beer wafted off his breath.

"Good luck with the rest."

Just off the bar Martin took a seat at a round table. A young fair-haired woman with bulging gray eyes slinked up. Two braided pigtails swung at hip level and she had to move one out of the way to slide over a napkin. "How ya doing?"

"Great. I'll take a dark Heineken."

"Those are really good, but we don't have them." She batted her eyes with a flare that would have suggested cynicism had she something like that left. "Newcastle maybe?"

He went for his island alternate. "Red Stripe?"

"In the bottle?"

"Perfect."

She went to a small refrigerator under the margarita blender and the Jagermeister dispenser. The three compadres down the way began shouting again, one barked like a dog, and the man in dreadlocks waved his hand. "You crazy-ass muthafuck-as, tell ya."

One of the cherubs stopped hooting. "The fuck? Crazy? What's that shit?"

Dreads took a dignified sip of something that looked like soda.

The man's look-alike punched his shoulder. "Shut up Berty, you fuck-knuckle! Go put something on the juke."

Berty laughed it off, for the sake of laughing it off, and Martin watched as he stumbled off to an MP3 jukebox near the unisex pisser. The other two began an all new conversation, muffled under a Jeff Healey song. Martin couldn't hear what was said but it didn't matter. As much of a dive as this place was, it had done the trick. He was ready to go out again and fight. Being around ordinary folks (well...) made everything less real. Plus, the Redstripe had begun to work a little magic of its own.

"Any pretzels?" he asked the barmaid.

She shook her Swiss Miss locks. "Cheese popcorn."

"Bring it on."

The salt and cheese flavor complimented the beer. Martin really wanted to stay and listen to the slobbery jokes and watch the man in the corner win more stuffed animals. It would have been perfect if Teresa were sitting here next to him, the two-person army. It would have been perfect if they could have spent this entire night here, and all the days that lead up to this day, anything to take the edge off their duty.

He smiled and finished his beer. He had to tell her the truth someday, about what happened at the hospital. Teresa deserved that much. *What if I never got the chance?* What if the Church had found the train yard already? Fighting the impulse to order another cold one, he tried for eye contact. The barmaid saw him and he raised a pointer finger. She nodded to give her one second while she poured two tumblers of Hennessey over ice.

The door opened. Sunlight hit the dark wooden floor of the saloon in an orange blade. Martin glanced over his shoulder and tried to swallow a knot of popcorn in his throat.

It seemed his waiting was over.

Chaplain Cloth strolled inside as though he'd been in the saloon a thousand times before. He passed the old man at the toy machine. The man didn't bother looking over, too immersed in fluffy treasure. Cloth pointed a twiggy bone colored finger. "The giraffe in the back."

The man grunted but remained focused. Chaplain Cloth's snowy lips cut in a fierce smile as he walked to Martin's table.

"I don't want any company."

"Sure you do." Cloth sat down. The table was small, so Martin could smell his mealy breath. Cloth laced his fingers together and dropped his hands on the table. "Let's just sit and be the old friends we are, have a drink, maybe two, and then you can take me to the Void where you're hiding them. I know you've come here to draw us away from Teresa. She's ill. You want to protect her. Good for you. You're a good person Martin."

The barmaid swaggered over. "Nice face paint—oh and those contact lenses. Hell, are you in a parade or something?"

"Or something," Cloth answered, not looking at her.

"What will you have?"

"A screwdriver sounds nice."

Martin tried for a mantle. Empty. He looked to the door, to the possibility of running. Cloth would tear him apart though. The timing had to be right. He had to distract him.

"Stop testing my patience." Cloth's orange eye glowed to

magma and his black shimmered like boiling tar.

"You took Tony last year," said Martin. "Do you actually believe we're going to let you get another?"

Cloth took a long, hard, deranged look at him. The barmaid came back surprisingly soon and put the screwdriver down. The sound of it on the table made Martin jump.

"Thank you, dear." Cloth twisted the glass up for a casual sip. He smiled. "Not bad."

"You didn't answer me."

"You know your bullshit," Cloth replied, setting down the drink. "Just jump right into the razor blades and drink the fire."

"Right."

"Do you think I care whether the Old Domain gains admission to this world?"

Martin shrugged his sore, heavy shoulders. He couldn't tell yet if this was working out for the better—if he could lead Cloth off, he might die for it, but he'd also save Teresa and the Hearts.

"That is a scrap humans can fight for. I am the way to balance, where beginnings and endings have no cause."

"We won't let you have them," insisted Martin.

Cloth went on, as though he hadn't heard. "All this inane tongue flicking. Have you ever thought about what human beings really are?"

"Of course I have."

"Your ancestors were furry little reptiles that hid underground and cheated their way out of extinction. Do you even *want* to understand what that means? All nestled together, eating stolen eggs from mightier creatures, fucking each other and reproducing incessantly, there in your burrows... Love was conceived to address your constant fear. Even with limited intelligence, you couldn't imagine returning to the belly of the universe. What a striking legacy of denial! You humans have made the Day of Opening all about your attempts to cope with denial."

"I dressed as a zombie cowboy for three years straight. Don't know what that says about my denial." Martin picked up Cloth's screwdriver and brought it to his lips. He was right. It wasn't bad.

Discord fluxed through the white face. "You know, when this started the gateway was the size of a particle. There was no interference with the yearly sacrifice. Progress was slow. My patience had to last thousands of years. Back in that time the Heart of the Harvest grew everywhere. I need only choose the greatest among the billions. I am the offspring of something natural, Martin. Don't you see? My fingerprints have smudged all the windowpanes of time."

"*Were you ever a living thing?*"

"I recall passion," replied Cloth. "It's always passion in the beginning of creation, isn't it? Flesh, blood, bone and brain have no place in the outer dark."

Martin's hand poised on his gun.

Cloth gazed around in mock wonder. "I think I'll put a song on the jukebox." He hovered over the table a moment. "Don't worry, I'll try not to pick something ironic."

Martin carefully watched him go. Cloth probably wanted him to run. He wouldn't take the bait. One of the lobster-faced men at the bar leaned back with wide arms balanced on a rotund belly. "What are you supposed to be? A demon? You the Devil?"

Cloth turned. "The Devil's just a cover song, friend."

The drunkards laughed as Cloth entered two quarters and

typed in a song. A moment after, the chaplain dropped back into the chair. "Let's not draw this out. I just wish to find the Hearts sooner rather than later. I will find them. That, you know."

Martin straightened. Heat flushed under the cold sweat on his neck.

"I've felt you try to pull from the Old Domain several times now. You've no strength left. Teresa is dying. Other people will soon, as well."

"Let's take a walk outside then," Martin suggested. "And talk about this a little more."

Cloth leaned back. "Nah, it's sort of pleasant in here."

Outside the saloon, the Children chorused—

How wonderful is that blood yolk?
How beautiful is that tendon pie?
How bountiful is that seared polyp?
How fanciful is that flea-bitten old rube?
It's dreadful to wait for feast time.

The three men at the bar turned to the singing and shared looks of confusion.

Martin realized something then.

He wasn't afraid. For the first time in almost twenty years, fear did not come into this. There was sadness. There was also helplessness: he couldn't bring a mantle, he couldn't draw his gun and he couldn't call Teresa. The little bar had become calm, the men not howling anymore, everyone softly tasting their drinks. In better company it might have felt like the day at Fisherman's Wharf with Teresa. Just strolling mindlessly through tranquil oblivion.

"You're not going to help, are you?" Cloth folded his arms. The orange kerchief bent sideways.

"I really don't see the need."

Cloth's eyebrow knifed. "That so?"

Styx came on: *"The Best of Times."*

"Irony was unavoidable, I suppose." Chaplain Cloth laughed. His humor departed quickly and impatience resurfaced. "Tell me where the Hearts are. Tell me right now."

Martin gripped his gun, finger wrapping the trigger. "I've forgotten."

No sooner had the words come out, Martin heard a loud thump and a glass shatter. He dared not turn, but out of the corner of his eye he saw Dreads stand. The thin man spaced his hands evenly and then drove his skull into the bar. The two pudgy fellows pushed out their stools, cursing, not completely shocked; possible regulars at this bar and others, they'd seen some fucked up shit before and they'd seen it on a whim.

Dreadlocks obscured the face. A growing puddle of blood shone on the wood under the blue neon glow.

"John—what the hell?" The barmaid took a step forward and reached out, a golden braid hanging over her thin arm.

John answered by slamming his head down harder. Several teeth lodged into the wood and one went spinning down the bar like a coin.

"Good Jesus! Grab him, he's havin' a seizure!" She put her hands up to her mouth. Several drinkers had pushed up from their seats. The brothers tried to grapple with the flailing body.

Martin's mouth went dry. "Stop this."

"Stop what?" Cloth's black and orange eyes were a dead luster.

John's head went down once, twice, thrice, and then the

fourth let out a crunch that must have sent skull shards into the brain because the body twitched and slid quickly off the stool like a greased worm.

"Let's end this day early. Process of elimination. You just tell me the voids you aren't using," the Chaplain persisted.

Martin couldn't tell Cloth the exact location of the Hearts. No Nomad could. Even if he wanted to, the words would not form on his lips. He didn't know if this was the Messenger's doing or something in his biological makeup, but Cloth was trying to get around this.

"I'll tell you," said Martin. "Okay? But let's leave. These people—"

Cloth drained half of his orange juice drink.

The barmaid went bolt-straight and her huge eyes engorged even wider. Her braids whipped around her neck, crossed and knotted. Her hands shot up and worked at forming the knot. The braid noose yanked, clenched by an invisible hand. Up into the air she went. The ascent ended with a spinal snapping and the corpse dropped behind the bar.

Martin swung up his gun and fired into Cloth's face. A mantle shielded instantly and the bullet caromed off and chewed a diagonal hole through the ceiling. The gun came out of Martin's hand, struck by another force, an anvil on a pendulum.

His hand rung deeply with pain. "They aren't even in Colton!"

"Ever stared down from an airplane to see the moist little chiggers winding around the grid?" The Chaplain looked like an eager wolf pawing for more flesh. "Tell me Martin, would you feel remorse gargling mouthwash and purging the bugs living between your teeth?"

Round tables exploded around people fighting for the exit. Their necks opened in bloody screams as they collided with each other and fell to the floor. The brothers' rosy faces detonated across the other end of the bar, yellow-red jelly scattering in a winding vertigo.

Martin wanted to close his eyes. There was nothing left to do. No way out. No turning back. He reached once again for the cold place. Still empty. The Spyglass Saloon smelled of aftermath. The sole survivor, the old man near the toy machine, hyperventilated against a corner, stacks of toys a rampart around his feet.

Martin shook so hard he had to grasp the edges of the table. "I'll go with you. I'll take you where she's gone. But we need to go."

Cloth pulled something chirping out of his pocket. He placed the cell phone on the table and read the text cut into the hot blue light below. "My, my, technology!" He read the text to Martin. "'New tire tracks have been spotted through an unlocked gate at the train graveyard, and there's a partial void in the area. Tracks indicate a jeep Wrangler.'" Cloth smiled brightly. "We have a winner, I think."

"Search it. You won't find anything. I'm telling you, Teresa and the babies are long gone from this city. The Messenger is protecting them."

The black and orange stare became wet with disbelief.

Something horrible started beneath Martin's heart. Salty fluid poured then, from his nose. Inside he felt his organs burst like water balloons, some squeezing shut under the pressure of murderous fingers, some dividing up with scalpel cuts. His bladder emptied into the front of his jeans and warmth spread through his boxers. The pain ultimately canceled out, replaced by shock and terminal blackness. Cloth said nothing, but Martin could feel his eyes as everything fell away. There was something left to be thought, something about a person, a T word. He couldn't grasp the idea, although he clawed the darkness to find it. It almost came, but his lungs filled and he gagged. The lungs...the lungs...

Teres—

CHAPLAIN CLOTH WATCHED MARTIN STRUGGLE FOR A FEW MOments. When the Nomad died, his mouth opened to say something, like he'd finally acquired last words. The hazel eyes beseeched Cloth. The whites had blossomed into a nice scarlet from all the capillaries rupturing. Cloth reached forward and tore off the man's necklace for a memento. Puka shells. *How very earthy.* He regarded Martin's still, peaceful form for a moment longer. *So much well-meaning meat.* He kicked under the table and sent the corpse flying back in its chair. The table upended, screwdriver spilling sideways in an orange arc. Martin slammed to the floor. Blood pooled out from an opening in a busted upper tooth.

Cloth put the necklace and cell phone in his pants' pocket. He was whistling by the time he got to the door. The old man huddled near the toy machine hadn't moved. Cloth bowed. Narrowing his eyes at the machine, Cloth leaned in and affirmed his suspicions. "Still haven't got that giraffe, I see. He's got the long neck. It should be easy."

The man quaked.

"Just keep at it." Cloth placed his fingers on the tavern's door. "Eventually you'll get the one you're after. You just have to keep at it. Never give up."

Chaplain Cloth pushed the door open to the bright world. The gateway howled inside the building opposite. It was a big empty piece of the future there to behold. And his Children. Bloody orange visages huddled obediently around the building's grounds, Quintana's power flooding their every thew, making them quake for the next chance to slaughter. Cloth took the crisp air inside his provisional lungs.

The Hearts were his now.

Forty-three

It would be dark in a couple hours and then the little gears of light that twisted through the cracks of the train's door would go flat, become shadows. Teresa changed the third baby out of a soiled diaper. She scrubbed the bottom too roughly and the baby started bawling.

"Hush, hush!" Her hand floated above the baby's mouth. *I'm not much of a foster parent, am I?* The baby boy punched himself in the eye as she slid the wipe once more for good measure. The train already smelled of salt and urine and mildew, so the scent of baby powder was welcome. The other babies rolled around on their blankets but were otherwise calm. Perhaps they felt they'd returned to the womb.

She positioned the diaper under the baby and began to stick the tabs down. Every Heart she'd met had been old enough to later carry memories with them of the Halloween that almost did them in. To think these babies would never relive this, one way or another, brought her comfort, strangely enough.

She swaddled each in their blankets and took out her radio. Leaning against an empty drum, she folded her legs inward for warmth. Hours had passed and the possibility of Martin's plan working seemed more tangible with every minute.

Until cars pulled into the yard and the sounds of shoes hit the gravel.

I HAVE TO SAY THIS ISN'T AT ALL WHAT I EXPECTED.

As bewildered as I was that Halloween, the Inner Circle that drove into that train yard arrived to outmatch my befuddlement. Chaplain Cloth would be there shortly, and they could wait for his arrival, but if they waited any longer the Hearts might slip away. What would Cloth do if they let that happen? The first church limo at the scene was abandoned. Cordite already hung on the air. Blood was already speckling the dirt and rocks. It wasn't a promising start. The newly arrived formed into squads.

One squad went around a cylindrical tanker car that had once been used to transport high fructose corn syrup. Fifteen different trip mines had been placed just around the corner, buried in dirt and shrouded in standing weeds—and the mines went off, one and two and three and death, death all around.

The remaining suits retreated between two boxcars. This led to the other squad, who approached their target head on. Another trap sprung. Two mantles raced toward each other: one gathered a mass of church members and the other crashed into them like two silver palms clapping dead a swarm of hornets. Most perished in an instant, crushed into leathery bonebags; functional people one moment turned into husks dribbling colon particulate the next.

Five minutes had passed since they separated and their number had been halved. The consensus, not surprising, was to retreat to the limos. It was a wise decision, better than the original plan. What might have made it even better would have been a different route. Thirty mines had been staggered on the main slope and the adjoining slope near the gate. Swift red wings rose and settled. Suits fell in the dirt. Some rolled. Some dropped right there.

Only four made it back to the limos. A young man recently brought up through the Church called his former boss. The phone rang four times before the automated message came on. He shouted his message, "Bishop Szerszen, this is Jake Weins again. If you didn't get my message before. We need help. The Nomads have gone to the train yard near the treatment plant off Rancho—We've taken casualties. We..." He gave up and his phone came away, shaking in his hand. He pushed END and noted how fitting the button was. Jake Weins tripped a mine a few minutes later.

Now, I've never met Martin Eric Larson. Watched him from a distance, truly, and I've written many letters to him over the years, to him and Teresa both, and I have a clear sense of the man. I've watched him. He wasn't a cold, calculating killer. He just knew what needed doing. That's why I picked him to accompany Teresa. I think I did well. Why, oh why, are our greatest works only appreciated posthumously?

Teresa heard another car pull up not long after the screaming lulled. The hungry sounds of the Children came soon after. They would not enter the Void, but she could hear them smacking their lips at the boundary.

Cloth spoke musically, "Oh TEEREEESAAAA! You in there, somewhere? Coughing up your lungs?"

He was just outside the train car. Teresa shook her head in disbelief. She'd heard the other mines going off, but not the large collection Martin planted just outside. How had Cloth gone around them?

She waited for the grand explosion, but nothing happened. Cloth walked around, crunching gravel, his every step making her edge back toward the Hearts. Even if Cloth knew the mines were there, wouldn't he have set them off with a mantle to get them out of his way? Could he really be stepping around all of them, oblivious?

Or were they duds?

Until then she had no idea what kind of mantle traps her partner had erected. The mines were not working, but obviously the mantles were. Chaplain Cloth toiled to disassemble one. It was really complex. Five, no six feet deep—*Goddamn you Martin!* It would have taken Teresa half a day to create a mantle like that.

Although stymied, Cloth didn't seem impressed.

Teresa began reinforcing other mantles in the interior. Cloth quickly made progress, breaking the outer shell like cracking an egg. She placed her hands on the doors. Martin would return soon. He would figure out his plan had failed. Then they could die together.

Teresa wanted to check her watch. Either she'd be delighted or disheartened, but at this point she was willing to accept anything. Cloth had torn down Martin's mantle around the train. This had taken him a few hours. In that time, she put the Hearts in their papooses and practiced carrying each over her shoulder. The weight was hardly manageable, but when the last of the mantles came down, she would have few options.

Singing songs, talking, formula, changing diapers: none of it worked to keep them quiet anymore. She didn't have much time to donate. She had to concentrate outside; she had to stay put, stay by the door, stay and give birth to new mantles. As she put ten up, Cloth tore twenty more down. The strength of the barriers lessened.

An orange eye stared through the slit in the train car's door. Moonlight outlined Cloth's too-perfect teeth and gray gums.

"I'm awed, Teresa. Truly."

She said nothing and set up another mantle, a floppier one than the rest. Cloth continued to talk but did not pause in deconstruction.

"You're sick honey, and perhaps you already know Martin is dead. He's done well out here, but I do believe his well ran dry with the effort."

She stiffened. He was trying to bring her guard down.

Cloth hummed then, taking down thirty and forty mantles simultaneously, like he'd just been fooling around until now.

She wanted to grunt out in dismay but kept silent. She could hear the gateway behind him, growling for the babies. "If I were lying, wouldn't Martin have returned by now?" he said. "I might have made up a story, told you he was out here with me, but I respect you too much by now." Cloth's voice didn't hint at any sarcasm.

Teresa readied to grab the babies and cloak a tight mantle around them. She could go out the opposite doors—foamy blood coursed out from under her fingertips and the sides of her eyes.

Cloth sounded nonplussed. "You know it's the babies I want, not a dying Nomad. Come now, will you make Martin's noble sacrifice all for naught?"

The look of hunger in the eye seemed from disease rather than need. Something dropped outside the train and Teresa looked through the slit. Moonlight defined the puka shells. They were freckled in dark red spots.

Her breathing came harder as the necklace came into focus. *No! Don't think about that.* Her duty was to the Hearts.

She said, "Come inside and get them, fuckhead."

"This is exhausting, my dear," said Cloth. "How about this deal? Give over the Hearts and I'll tell you who the Messenger is. You've always wanted to know, haven't you? Then you can die without it being a mystery."

"You've mistaken me for an idiot." *Okay*, she thought, *no more talking. He wants that.*

"Hardly! After all these years, I'm sure you'd like to know. Add a little meaning to the end. The end is coming Teresa. It's just a matter of how quickly or painfully you choose."

Darkness swirled. She was still.

The Chaplain sighed. "Very well."

He reached out and melted through the mantles like spider webs set aflame. Teresa sent out a heavy mantle and it felt like her spleen collapsed. Through the train door, Cloth had his slimy eyelids shut, concentrating on breaking through. It would not be more than a minute or two.

She unlocked the back doors and hauled up the papooses on both shoulders. Wobbled at the weight. The babies burbled at the swaying. She toed the door open.

A bolt struck her shoulder from behind. She smashed into the iron wall with a hollow thrum. The door had come off its hinges. Cloth's jaw had gone gruesomely slack with glee. Even at several paces she could smell rotten sugar and cotton soaked in death.

A knot of black suits rounded the tanker trains, rifles raised. Their breathless laughter ratcheted up in the night. Across an alley the Children launched off the ground, eager as can be, moonlight peeling back in their demigod eyes.

Cloth stepped up the side. "You've lost. Again," he added. "But at least it's the last time. Right?"

There were only a few more mantles. None were strong. In Teresa's mind she saw the faces of the Hearts, the hope that Martin had for them, years on the road, Octobers where they put everything out there. She could say what the hell and give up now.

But that was when Teresa decided she had something else left.

Something more.

And her feet hit the ground and the papooses rocked over her back. The quick mantle she'd popped around them quickly went as Cloth attacked it with the shark teeth of his mind. Every step hurt like fire and ice slamming to the bone. Inner Circle followed and the Children vaulted madly as she went toward them. A hoarse shout came from Cloth.

Teresa turned a corner and tripped over a forty ounce beer bottle. She used her knees for the fall and the earth numbed them. Standing up, hard on her feet, babies coughing and gagging, she drove on, outside the boundaries of the Void. At once the Children poured over the trains. Chaplain Cloth was the black eye of their storm.

Teresa ran between two train cars. The path ended at a block wall. Her long journey finished there.

The pathway to the Old Domain sucked open in a sidecar. Arms pulled and pried at the apple sized opening, far down its corridor. Marble pillars stood behind them.

Savage growls turned her. The children swarmed around Cloth's legs and went straight for Teresa. She kicked at them as they crawled up her legs and grappled her hair. She tried to summon another mantle. Her mind failed and the surge increased. Teresa crawled back against the block wall. The children slowed, sizing up an opportunity when to attack.

"Chaplain!" someone shouted through the madness. "Chaplain Cloth!"

The man limped through the crowd, a walking mass of scab and bleeding wounds.

The children dove in at Teresa. Some of their teeth sank in and stripped the papooses off her arms and she collapsed under their increasing weight. There was no strength left to scream.

"This is what has come to be!" she heard the man rumble over the fray. It sounded like his mouth was full of mucus and blood. Teresa throttled the children on her and more eagerly moved forward. In the crowd the big bleeding man elbowed past the others. "She'd still be alive. Melissa might have lived! In the tome *The Tides of Loss and Martyrdom*—it has said 'he hath the worthiness of the Church of Midnight and shall move into power through a blessing from the Knight of the gateway, or through immolation.'"

Cloth moved for Teresa.

"Chaplain! Did you hear me? Melissa might have lived!" The man clutched Cloth's suit and suddenly halted his progress.

The Chaplain whipped around, ready to kill. "Szerszen!"

Caked blood cracked over the man's forehead. "I wanted you to know I'm worthy."

Cloth pushed out violently with his mind. In a split second the big man and two Inner Circle women roared into flames. The big man stumbled once with a drunken grin, his fiery coat blowing open to reveal a jungle of wires. Over his bloody stomach, some of Martin's landmines had been cannibalized. The image was brief in Teresa's sight. A green-red-orange-white light brightened on top of the wiry muddle. A blink.

Then the space between the trains erupted.

Cloth brought a mantle. It flickered inside the explosion, brought about too late. Pieces of the chaplain's wormy flesh tossed into the air and bone fragments rained down with black fabric and fire. A number of the children were taken as well, fulminating pieces like spiced intestines.

Unmoved, the remaining Children that had dragged off the papooses pressed forward to the gateway. Slobber fell over their fangs and they licked the points as the babies drew closer to the opening. The gateway widened inside the train's steel and the arms down its hall quickened to pull the tiny aperture wider. "Come to us! The Archbishop of Morning demands you!" a deep voice sang.

The explosion still rang in Teresa's ears so loud as to make her nauseous but she had enough clarity to rip her gun from her jeans and cap each creature in their orange skulls. Jellied orange blood squirted neatly with each shot. They fell limply off the papooses. With strength that came from somewhere completely foreign, Teresa hauled all four Hearts over a shoulder. Holding her gun out, she tramped through the fleshy debris made of Cloth and the church members. Clear across a collection of ghost trains, there was a mottled green caboose. It was not in the Void area, but something told her that was the place.

She told herself it was Martin, to trust him above everything else. Her feet crushed the broken glass and litter. More fatherless children came sliding out of the shadows. The night air was hot now and burned her lungs.

A blast of pain lanced through her neck. A child forced her to the ground. Teresa snuggled her gun into its eye and fired. It dropped off without a squeal.

She clamored inside the caboose and laid the sobbing babies inside. A rolling orange spate seethed outside. She grasped the heavy door. It was rusted open. She put her entire weight there, but it held in place. The orange jack-o'-lantern faces became more distinct, closer. Putting her legs against the wall of the train, putting her whole body into the work, the caboose door inched close. She could see some of the children flaked in the gore of their father.

The door shut and opened again—a muddy padlock lay on the floor. Her fingers grazed it and the lock spun away. The door pulled wider and a rawboned arm swept inside. Using her foot, she brought the lock within reach and rammed the door shut, snipping off the little orange arm at the elbow. The lock's horseshoe snapped around the bar.

Teresa edged back, almost tripping over the babies. For a long while she examined them for injuries. It was very dark, but she believed they were all right. They were breathing and their hearts were beating. But everything was not fine in the world. No, she wouldn't think of Martin. She wouldn't address that yet.

Disturbed thoughts kept her afloat for sometime, until, finally, the Hearts' power faded. Outside the children simultaneously shattered, one after another, like bursting bladders full of orange poison. She could feel the vitality leave the babies instantly and the bond with it. The Hearts were ordinary again; the god-touch had departed, which meant only one thing.

We did it, Martin.

Teresa fell asleep at once. The Jordons joined her.

And daylight burned off the shadows.

Epilogue

November 1st

THE TRIP ON THE BUS WASN'T LONG, BUT IT WAS. A young Japanese woman with blue hair, fishnets and slightly running mascara sat cattycorner to Teresa, head against the window. It was difficult to tell if she dressed this way all the time. The look fit her insouciance.

Hangover-eyes fresh with morning crimson. "Proud mother?"

"Yeah."

The Jordons had not protested since boarding. All of them were perfect little soldiers. They'd survived something many wouldn't, and would likely never remember any of it. No serious injuries could be found. Only little Rebecca had sustained a yellow, star shaped bruise over her right cheek. Teresa occasionally rubbed her thumb over it, as though a touch could heal.

The walk from the bus stop to the Happy Moon Travel Lodge lasted twenty long minutes. Teresa couldn't get excited when she saw the Wrangler parked out front. In a different frame of mind, being less weary and less baby-burdened, she might have gathered hope. She knew the truth though, even before she spotted the Messenger's white envelope under the windshield wiper.

She didn't bother taking it. Maybe that was a mistake. She guessed she'd find out. *Right now, I don't give a fuck.* She just didn't.

Upstairs Enrique paced outside the room. He looked feverish with worry. Dirt and cuts crusted his face and arms. He grinned and nodded as she approached, all of the pain and anguish vanishing. He took one papoose, not saying a word, maybe thinking he'd jinx the moment if he did.

They went into the motel room, which smelled of cloves and old vinyl, and sat on the bed. The Bearer changed each child and from his knapsack made them bottles. He fed two at a time. Teresa wanted to help, but her pulse was racing. She unearthed a well-deserved clove and opened the door. She popped the spicy Djarum in her mouth and let it hang from her lip as she pulled out a disposable lighter. "What will happen to them? Will they go back to the Jordons?"

"They have different homes waiting for them. Different destinies. I will see each of them to their new parents."

"What will you do then, Enrique?"

The unexpected heartbreak in his face almost compelled her to go put an arm around him. It was one of the most pathetic expressions she'd ever seen. "I will try," he told her, "to pick up where I left off back home. I do not expect I will be so lucky. But I will try. One must carry on, right?"

"Right," she blandly answered.

"What will you do now?"

She shrugged. "I suppose I'll start driving somewhere."

After the clove ran too short, she stubbed it out on the jamb and flicked it off the balcony before shutting the door.

Enrique let her hold the babies, one at a time, for one last time. She whispered a goodbye into each soft, seashell ear.

Little pink digits tugged at her hair and neck. Glistening eyes beheld her. She didn't want to get all weepy, so she handed the last, Rebecca, back to Enrique. The man's small stature rocked under the weight of the loaded papooses. "What have you been feeding them?"

"Only the best."

The haunted, hunted look hadn't left Enrique's features, although he appeared more lucid than last time. "Your friend Martin—?"

"At the market, picking up a few things."

Enrique pursed his lips, plainly not believing her but not pressing it. He trudged over and stopped at the door. His head angled as he peered down at his feet. "Did you know there's a letter here?"

TERESA COULD NOT HELP THINKING OF THE PARENTS SHE LEFT so long ago. She couldn't remember if her mother had cried when David came for her. Did her father get drunk that night? Would they have imagined years later their daughter would be in some seedy motel, exhausted from battling the night, dying slowly from cancer and doing it all, completely alone?

Teresa kicked the Messenger's letter off the balcony. *That felt great.* She needed some smokes for tonight, maybe a beer too. It would be a six-pack kind of day. At the Wrangler, she swept up another envelope and tore it into pieces, which feathered down into a weedy planter nearby.

Up the street she bought a bag of lollipops, a bottle of water and a pack of generic brand cloves. She slammed back down into the Wrangler with her goodies, peeled out without her seatbelt buckled, swerved curbside up the street and parked in front of an inoperative radiator shop. Her eyes wanted to move to the toy aquarium mounted on the dashboard. The fake, trapped fish inside the plastic orb desired attention, but she wouldn't let it get to her. She was going to smoke and be silent, be silent and smoke.

The window hummed down and the cold morning air rolled in with a nip. She tore open the cloves and breathed in their heavy, sweet poison. She tugged one free and stared at it until everything blurred. Except the black cylinder. It was the only thing left in her life. Why had she not been disgusted by that before? She threw it then, and the clove sailed out the window. Next, one by one, she threw the rest, hand moving quicker and more assured. When they were gone she sat there a moment, stunned. Didn't know what to do now. Should she go outside and pick them up?

No.

So she screamed.

She pressed her head against the steering wheel. The wind caringly ruffled her hair and though the morning burned bright, she felt encased in dark ice. Her burning eyes lifted. She hadn't noticed it before, but it had probably been there when she came out of the liquor store. Under the windshield wiper, unsullied, another envelope flagged in the breeze. She reached around and grabbed the damn thing.

This time she opened it.

After more stops and detours than the Priestess of Morning could count, they had finally arrived. Paul could not be helped. He was pulling his somnolent frame through the dirt, making his way to a stained Joshua tree. With Eggert's dagger he resembled an Ekkian hunting a spice viper. A bushel of flies spun up from Justin Margrave and went into a fit around Paul. Justin's black shirt came apart easily to reveal a palate of fishy skin.

Paul worked diligently at opening a gulf in the week old cadaver. The knife drove past bone with a thick reverberation, as through a porcelain dish. Only a few arches of caramelized blood ran from the wound over the stippled ribs. The Priestess wanted to help but had to watch in awe. Justin's remaining eye might have watched as well, had it not gone missing, now a dark purple hole.

"The children are dead. Ease their song," Paul mumbled, again and again, and had mumbled for several hours. Watching him carve Justin Margrave's lumpy muscle away was the most sensual, *real* sacrifice she'd ever witnessed. Hunkered there, Paul nearly glowed with the essence of man, true man. The Priestess's loins flooded at the sight and overwhelmed her.

Black and orange blossoms sprung from the evisceration in Margrave's torso and Paul jumped back in surprise. The soil in which they were planted had gone rotten, but the flowers unfurled brilliant petals still. Paul fell back on his knees and began tearing off the orange blossoms. He stuffed them into his mouth and chewed rabidly. Random marrow seeds fell from under the petals. He gobbled twenty or more, his face bloodier and more alive with every treat. He kept at it awhile longer, until it seemed he could eat no more. A look of horror and relief split his face as he gained his feet. He only got a few feet from the maggoty rot before collapsing. He lay there, so divine!

The Priestess could take no more. Giddy like a child, she ran to him, unbuckled his belt and drew off his shoes. He was ready for her. She unfastened her pants and drew them down.

Then she kicked her smallclothes off. They landed in a wad over Margrave's opened chest where the marrow blossoms had grayed and wilted to thin, translucent straws.

Paul smiled. His body and soul reconfigured. *Oh so long!* Waiting in the car for an entire day and not able to—she climbed onto Paul and put him inside her. Their power coalesced. With every grind, she fell farther inside him, putting her sight on his power, realizing it, coming closer to something true.

Paul groaned as they became one and she told him never to worry. They would rest between the worlds, in the belly of the beast, and never take the burning passion that charged them. They would grow stronger and persevere through the night and day. Suddenly she sensed their skin melting together.

A limo pulled through a cape of dust. Four men piled out, guns drawn. One shouted, "Get up and turn around Quintana!"

Five feet away the ground split open and the gateway beckoned. Bats screeched with the pipe organ symphony. The Priestess thought it profound, lovely, true, something she could listen to forever and enjoy.

Priestess/Paul stood up. Turned around. They were one now. They were destiny.

The suited men all wore the same mask of astonishment as they beheld the figure that stood before them.

"Chaplain Cloth?" The others edged back, uncertain why the trail to Paul Quintana had led them to the very monster that sent them here.

"Chaplain?" the lead man stammered, his bony brown face draining.

Cloth's expression was menacing and they all stood back in terror. "I must rest until the next harvest," he told them.

The Chaplain stepped into the warmth and security of the gateway's throat. For Paul and the Priestess separation was no longer relevant. They were diabolically larger than the two human beings that once retained their souls. The earth sealed overhead and the bewildered human faces were left behind in the desert with the *drip, drip, drip, dripping* of the world.

Chaplain Cloth's black eye soaked up the darkness and his orange eye lit the way in the womb where the lovers could grow stronger. They lay across his design, two devils locked at their poisonous genitals, the beating of their love deafening inside their terrible hearts.

Teresa read in the letter that Patrice Middleton lived just outside East Highland. The whole trip had been a dreamy, autopilot type of experience, a series of wheel-turns, signaling, stepping on the brake, stepping on the gas, stoplights, red and green, black and—

Teresa hadn't cried for hours in that loathsome boxcar, only to get choked up now. Things happened, you moved on. If you stopped for too long, your number might get pulled next. It was stupid coming to this place so soon. She wasn't ready for another partner. She couldn't go on doing this. Somehow she had to let the Messenger know she was through with this duty.

A Nomad only stops moving when she's dead.

Suddenly Teresa was on the porch, knocking at the door; this was her strategy, to just let everything play out while she sat back and came to a conclusion about how she felt.

The water-damaged door jerked open. A family hunched in the doorway: a wet-haired mother in a cherry bathrobe, a balding father in boxers and blue T-shirt, and a young platinum blonde girl in a red nightgown, maybe eighteen years old—just about the same age Teresa had been when David first showed.

"Patrice Middleton?" She offered the white envelope to the parents. The father's face puckered. He showed the Messenger's note to the mother, who only nodded. He handed it back.

"You can't do this," the teenager whispered from behind them.

The father smoothed his glazed dome with a quivering hand. "We talked about this. It's done."

"You can't!"

The mother whirled around. "Just be quiet!"

"We'll never see her again. That doesn't bother you?"

The mother glided under Teresa's elbow. Gently. "Let me show you the way, Ms. Celeste."

"You know my name?"

The father chuckled. "We've known your name since before Patty was born."

"It was in the letters," the mother added. "We've been receiving them for some time now…even before we crossed through the Messenger's gateway."

"Well…I just got mine this morning," said Teresa.

They guided her around the front of the house and through a wooden gate to a wide backyard of burnt custard grass. The mother leaned into Teresa's ear. Her breath smelled of black, black coffee and toast. She raised a finger and aimed some place overhead. "Patty's up there."

"What, in the clouds?" Teresa joked, figuring she was a little slow in understanding.

The father grimaced. Before he could say anything, the teenager cut in, "Just walk over if you don't believe us!"

"Knock it off Susan." The bald man softened then and politely gestured. "Please, Ms. Celeste. Go on up and meet her. She's all packed. I guess Patty wanted to say goodbye to her special place."

Teresa didn't understand what these people were on, but she wouldn't mind taking some herself. Regardless of any misgivings, she shuffled over where the grass had been crushed under something heavy. At first she thought of an old doughboy pool no longer present, but then she saw the doorway. The opening cut a rectangle into the air, which led to a hall, which in turn led to a spiral staircase, all spray painted in blues, greens, and some pink. Mantles made the interior and were painted to look...tangible.

The family stood near the garden hose, as straight as posts.

"What the hell is this?" asked Teresa.

"Up the stairs," said the mother.

Teresa gave her a wary look before stepping inside. The hall's length went three yards up to the staircase. She shook her head and began to ascend. Her feet hit each glittery blue stair with a startling resonance. *These couldn't all be permanent mantles—could they?* She rounded the stairwell twice before reaching the upper floor.

There, sitting on the false ground between two suitcases, was a little sandy haired girl, possibly eleven years old. At most.

"I love you, Patty."

Teresa jumped. She hadn't heard the family come up. The teenager, Susan, ran around her to Patty and embraced her sister. They stood there, hugging, in this strange tree house made of mantles. "Love you too, Susan," Patty replied, blank faced.

When her sister let her go and backed off, whimpering, Patty turned to Teresa and offered a hand. The girl's awkwardness made the gesture seem like a weird salute. Teresa crept over, untrusting of the mantle floor, and took a knee—maybe not of her own will—and accepted Patty's handshake.

Their eyes locked. "Did you make this place?"

Patty nodded swiftly. "I've made lots."

"You painted them?"

"Mom couldn't find me when I came up here. I had to."

"I see," Teresa replied, another glance around her amazing surroundings.

"Did you make that one?" the little girl asked.

Teresa smirked. "I don't know what you mean. Which one?"

Carefully, Patty placed her palm on Teresa's chest.

Over her lung.

"You don't feel it inside, do you? It's sorta shaped like a ball, but it's holding a mushy white lump—like oatmeal. It goes out through the back, but it's super-thin. You'd have to think really hard to make something like it."

Teresa turned to the parents for guidance, her heart racing. "What's she talking about?"

The father shook his head. "She can see the mantles, no matter where they are."

"Nobody can see them!" Teresa fired up to her feet, knees cracking. But she wasn't sure she was correct about that. "And why would she say I have one *inside* me?"

Patty blinked, not showing the slightest bit of disturbance. "Because, ma'am, there *is* one inside you."

THEY SAT IN THE WRANGLER FOR TEN MINUTES WITHOUT SAYing a word. Patty had said her last farewells to the family she'd never see again, but occasionally the living room drapes moved aside. If they didn't take off soon, Teresa had a feeling her family would start creeping out to the front yard again, for another goodbye.

Teresa stared at Martin's toy aquarium. She had hung the puka necklace around it. Martin hadn't been one to be fussed over and he would have complained about a shrine. Well, she'd never listened to him before, so why now? Teresa touched her chest, to feel something different there, but it felt like the rest of her body—on the surface. It was glaringly obvious now that a small mantle had been constructed inside her lung out to the exterior. An orb. A small prison. The damn thing was elaborate, and yet so subtle she hadn't sensed it until Patty pointed it out.

Teresa continued to grope her chest for answers.

"It won't go away." Patty was looking forward, not paying full attention to Teresa. "It's *real* strong. Why did you put it there?"

Teresa steadied herself on the steering wheel. "I think a friend did."

"What's it there for?"

Teresa's eyes glazed. "I'm not sure. We'll see, I suppose..."

She knew what it was for, but whether the containment worked would be a mystery, for a time anyway. All those hours in the hospital, his medical books, the X-ray lying on her chest... How had he been able to set the traps at the train yard afterward? And then to pull that thing off with the Priestess of Morning? It staggered her imagination. Martin was lucky he hadn't died right then.

She pressed play and the Sam Cooke CD came on. Martin used to play it when they saved a Heart, a victory ritual. Somehow, Sam didn't sound as happy as he normally did though.

Teresa reached into her pocket for a clove and pulled out lollipops instead. *Oh yes, right.* Smiling, she offered one to the quiet little girl. Patty lifted her goody bag. A stash of trick-or-treat candy from last night. "Dad said it would be my last time for Trick or Treat."

Teresa tucked a cherry lollipop in her mouth. The Wrangler started up with a purr. Before she could drive off, she glanced over. This poor girl had been handed to the wolves. It wasn't fair. "I'm sorry if I'm looking sad. I hope you— "

"I'll be all right."

Tough kid. Still though. "Are you ready for this Patty? I mean, are you really ready? We have a lot of work to do."

Mint green eyes slid over. "I won't let you down Teresa. He won't win."

Steeling herself, Teresa put the car in drive.

"Are we going to fly somewhere?" Patty asked, a little cheerfully.

Teresa glanced at her. It was the first time Patty had looked even remotely like a child. "Sometimes. But if we can drive a car somewhere, we drive."

"Who says?" asked Patty.

"The Messenger."

"That's our boss?"

"Sort of."

"The Messenger makes all the rules then?"

"Probably."

"Will we ever meet him?"

"Or her."

"Well, will we?"

"I'm not sure."

"Teresa?"

"Yeah."

"Is this trip long? I don't like long car trips."

The Sam Cooke CD played on as the Wrangler tracked through star-shaped leaves scattered across the everlasting road.

A BLOCK AWAY I WATCHED THEM GO. BLACK AND ORANGE PARTY streamers blew in the rafters overhead. Some had crossed the street over the golden star leaves, whipped into random destiny. For most people the year was winding down, but for my Teresa it was only beginning. Planning. Everything would lead up to the next October.

I could see the side of her face as she drove off with Patty. I quickly read Teresa's thoughts. It wasn't common practice, not something I felt privileged to do, but I needed to understand.

Teresa's thoughts were about him. Only him. On the other side of here and there, she imagined him waiting, perhaps along a vast shoreline, the warm sun lifting over the distance, the air vital with new life. He would remain there for a chance to hold her again, and say the things left unsaid.

I've been given many gifts, and I had the privilege of knowing the truth. Martin was indeed standing there on that sandy shore of dreams, waiting impatiently for a chance to meet again. And no power known to the universe could ever move him from that spot.

About the Author

Benjamin Kane Ethridge lives in Southern California with his wife and daughter, both beautiful and both worthy of better. He also lives with two cats that meow more than they breathe. But they'll do. When Benjamin isn't writing, reading, video gaming, he's defending California's waterways and sewers from pollution.

Say hi and drop a line at www.bkethridge.com

Breinigsville, PA USA
20 February 2011
255928BV00001B/1/P